Born in New Zealand, Sarah Quigley is a novelist, poet, and critic. She has a D.Phil. in Literature from the University of Oxford. Her short fiction and poetry have been published widely, and she has won many awards for her writing. *The Conductor* is her fourth novel. Since 2000, she has lived and worked in Berlin.

THE
Conductor
SARAH QUIGLEY

VINTAGE

ARTS COUNCIL OF NEW ZEALAND *TOI AOTEAROA*

The assistance of Creative New Zealand is gratefully
acknowledged by the publisher.

A VINTAGE BOOK published by Random House New Zealand,
18 Poland Road, Glenfield, Auckland, New Zealand

For more information about our titles go to www.randomhouse.co.nz

A catalogue record for this book is available from the National Library of New
Zealand

Random House New Zealand is part of the Random House Group
New York London Sydney Auckland Delhi Johannesburg

First published 2011. Reprinted 2011 (five times), 2012.

Text design: Megan van Staden
Cover illustration: Yolande De Kort / Trevillion Images
Cover design: Alan Deare
Printed in New Zealand by Printlink

FSC
www.fsc.org
MIX
Paper from
responsible sources
FSC® C009448

Author's Note

Although this novel is based on real events, the majority of its characters and incidents are fictional. In some instances (such as Karl Eliasberg and Nina Bronnikova), where little documentation exists, I have retained real names but have largely fictionalised backgrounds and personalities. I have slightly altered a few facts for dramatic purposes.

In recent decades, conflicting views have arisen relating to the programmatic interpretation of Shostakovich's *Seventh Symphony*. I have chosen to depict the work as a direct response to the invasion of Leningrad for purely novelistic reasons.

In most cases I have used Anglicised versions of Russian names and place names. I have also simplified the complicated Russian method of personal address; characters are usually referred to by one name only, regardless of their relationship to the speaker.

For Margie

Prologue

I was born without a heart.

At least, that's what they believe. I hear what they say about me in rehearsals. They have little enough breath to make music — whether I coax and implore, or shout like thunder, it makes no difference. But when they whisper about me, their voices sound through the hall as loudly as pickaxes on ice.

Conductors are supposed to stand apart. It's part of the task, the privilege, the burden. Being separate is only one small step away from being disliked. I don't mind. To be more specific, I can't mind. These days, I have no energy for the luxury of taking offence. They may say what they like about my beaked nose, my thin lips, my unfashionable spectacles. They may joke about my insistence on punctuality. Surely, in all my harshness, I must be related to the great leader of our feared regime! (They've become used to mouthing such lines behind their hands, fearing that Stalin's men are listening at the door.) Or perhaps — and this is said more loudly — my inimical nature is more similar to that of Hitler, our country's greatest enemy. I hear these comparisons, and I find them tedious but unsurprising. Ever since my career began I've been accused of being strict, overly exacting, hostile — and, yes, dictatorial.

What can I not allow my musicians to see? That once, I, Karl Illyyich Eliasberg, was as emotional as any man. That on a long-ago June day, when the bright dust hung in the air like long quivering curtains, and the tall windows stood open, and sunlight filled the marble atrium, I stood for a long time on the curved staircase of the Conservatoire. As I listened, my heart split wide open. With jealousy, with admiration, with love.

My adversary, my friend. Over the years, I've thought of him as both. It's because of him that I stand here today: talked of, despised, assumed to be a heartless man. Had I the strength to do so, I would laugh at the irony of it. Of course I have no heart! Many years ago, in that Leningrad stairwell, I gave my heart to Shostakovich.

PART I
Spring–Summer 1941

The knock
at the door

It seemed he'd been waiting all his life for the knock at the door. He
heard it dimly when he slept, tapping on the surface of his dreams.
He heard it when he was working, in the urgent roll of timpani or the
sharp plucking of pizzicato strings. And he heard it in the sound of his
own footsteps when he walked the streets, so that even when hurrying
he could never escape it.

The dread followed him day and night like a stubborn stray dog.

Shostakovich! Shostakovich! Was someone calling his name? He
struggled to open his eyes. The room was blurred at the edges of his
vision, with a bright glare in the centre where he knew the work table
to be.

'Nina?' he called, but his voice was still clogged with half-remembered
dreams.

He reached blindly for his glasses, patting the mattress and then the
low stool beside the bed. It was an effort to lift his arm; his fingers
felt limp and without their usual strength. He'd worked late and eaten
nothing over the past twenty-four hours, except for some hard rye bread
soaked in tea. The good thing about hunger and extreme tiredness was
that they alleviated fear. The sound that woke him — had it been the
knock? If he were taken now, he would almost be relieved.

His fingers found the steel arms of his glasses, then the reassuring
curve of the rims. He pushed aside the rough grey blanket — supposedly
a privilege. But even privilege could make your skin itch.

With his glasses on, the wavering whiteness shrank to nothing. The shabby walls stood back, the room held its breath. Now he wasn't sure what he'd heard: someone in the street? Or simply the *rap rap* of the loose window in its frame?

'Nina?' he called again. He swung his legs over the edge of the bed, ran his hand through his hair, shuffled to the door.

But when he looked cautiously into the outer room, he found it was empty.

The note

Downstairs, in the communal kitchen, a naked light bulb. He bumped his head on it, as always, and swore. The reek of cleaning fluid, cabbage and cheap cutlets made him nauseous. He clamped his fingers over his nose, and breathed ostentatiously through his mouth as he mixed his porridge, though there was no one there to watch his theatrics. He was thankful for this. He'd never liked talking much before midday, and hated hearing, even from the stairs, the racket of several spirit stoves going at once, and voices drilling into his early-morning head. (However indifferent Nina seemed, however closed off to his suffering, at least she never sounded like a fishwife!)

As he leaned on the table, wiping a smear of dust from his glasses, he heard a noise behind him. Small cat-like feet, snuffling breath. Glancing backwards, he saw a cracked pair of overshoes, a skinny pair of ankles.

He sighed. Whenever he'd let the stove upstairs go out and was forced to venture down here, unless he was as quiet as the spring grass growing, he had to face this ordeal.

'Ahhhh, Mr Shostakovich!' There was, as usual, unholy satisfaction in the greeting. 'I could tell from the footsteps bumbling over my ceiling that it was you.'

'Irina Barinova!' He tried to sound as if he'd been lost in his own world. This was, after all, the behaviour she wanted to see in him: an artistic vagueness rendering him useless as a neighbour and a human being. 'A very good morning to you.'

'Good morning?' repeated Irina Barinova, managing to sound both reflective and sharp. 'Is it still morning?' Her voice rose, and so did her wizened hand, floating up to the front of her frayed green cardigan (it was far more genteel to patch old clothes than to buy garish new ones). She rummaged inside her dress. 'Ahhhh,' she said again, and this time the triumph was unmistakable, cutting a path through the steamy air. 'In *fact*, Mr Shostakovich, it is already afternoon.'

He bit his tongue with irritation and tasted blood. 'Shit,' he muttered. He watched silently as old Irina Barinova displayed, with slightly shaking hands, her father's gold watch, a reminder of better days.

'Goodness!' he said. 'Is it really afternoon! No wonder our stove had gone out by the time I woke up.'

Irina shovelled the heavy watch and chain back into her sprigged cotton dress. The slipping of the links, the slow inexorable disappearing, reminded Shostakovich of a boat casting off its moorings. And again, with a lurch of his stomach, he thought: *Where's Nina?*

'You've been burning the midnight oil, I expect,' said Irina. 'What it must be to have genius.' Now that she'd exposed him as a shameless bohemian, a no-good father and a husband who let the family stove go cold, she became flattering. It was all part of the routine.

Get on with the show, thought Shostakovich. He longed to leave, but his stomach was empty and his porridge had not yet boiled.

Irina looked at him almost coyly from under white eyelashes. 'To think that Dmitri Shostakovich should be living in my house. Leningrad's most famous son, living here, under the roof of my dear deceased father.'

Shostakovich ducked his head. This sort of talk made his stomach twist.

'All this.' She waved a twig-like arm. 'Once, it all belonged to my father — from the attic to the basement.'

'Yes, I know. You've told me that three hundred and sixty-five days of the year, for as many years as a donkey's ears are long.' He stabbed the porridge with the wooden spoon.

'Once we had maids and cooks.' Irina sighed heavily. 'Now it's a house full of strangers.'

Shostakovich stared at the porridge, willing bubbles to appear.

'Speaking of maids,' said Irina, swooping swiftly back to the present, 'where is your Fenya? I haven't seen her for days.'

'Fenya is visiting her parents.' He whipped the pan off the stove. Suddenly undercooked oats seemed immensely appealing. 'Therefore I make my own porridge!'

'Well, what about Nina? How is dear Nina?'

Shostakovich dropped the spoon, and porridge splattered over his shirt-front.

'I saw her going out early this morning,' mused Irina. 'With the children. I believe they were carrying travelling bags. Perhaps they're also visiting relations?'

Shostakovich skirted around the table, knocking his head once more on the light bulb. For a small person, Irina Barinova was remarkably adept at blocking escape routes. 'You really must excuse me.' He gestured, slightly wildly, with his saucepan. 'Nothing worse than cold porridge for breakfast.'

'Breakfast?' Irina raised her wizened hand once more to her breast. 'My father was washed and shaved, and had taken a turn around the park before his breakfast, which was served in the red room at eight o'clock sharp.'

He took the stairs two at a time. The empty apartment was no longer unsettling; it was bliss. Standing by the old wooden table, he shovelled the porridge straight from the pan into his mouth. He poured cold water onto strong cold tea, and threw in half a spoonful of honey that fell like a stone to the bottom of the glass. God, he was starving. He was thirsty. He had to start thinking about work.

Halfway through his second bowl, he saw the note lying on the floor. It was smeared with dust from being pushed under the door, but his name was legible, written in a familiar hand. He walked to the window to read it, continuing to shovel lukewarm mush into his mouth. Put down the bowl, the spoon, with twin clatters. Gulped the last dregs of tea. Pulled on his boots, hat with ear-flaps, a patched coat — and left the house.

The bench

On the bench at the corner of Zamkovaya and Klenovaya streets sat a large shaggy bear. Shostakovich approached, a little warily, from behind.

'You're late,' said the bear. 'Very late.'

'I overslept,' said Shostakovich. 'Then Irina Barinova cornered me in the kitchen. I thought I'd never get away.' He swallowed unhappily and sat down beside Sollertinsky, who was bundled in a shapeless fur coat fit for a tramp. The undercooked porridge had been too salty, and an ulcer was forming on the inside of his cheek. 'Brushing up on Language Number Eighteen?' He looked at the book of Georgian grammar in Sollertinsky's huge hand. 'Your loyalty to our leader puts the rest of us to shame.'

'Language Number Three,' said Sollertinsky, winking. 'I felt a little *malcontent* today, experienced a slight *frisson* at this morning's news.'

Shostakovich peered more closely at the book. A light blue cover concealed a dull grey one; inside there was French text. 'You're a masterful dissembler.'

Sollertinsky shrugged, looked around at the high glinting windows, the screen of trees around the park. 'We both know that dissemblers live longer than dissidents.'

The sun was as hard as nails, and Shostakovich pulled his collar up around his ears. 'You've always known how to avoid attention.' His voice emerged in two layers: admiration on top, a kind of envy below. 'If you've got something to tell me, let's go somewhere less exposed.'

The drinking house was dark after the white glare outside. Sollertinsky headed for the corner table, and Shostakovich followed, stumbling over a chair.

'You look a little under the weather,' said Sollertinsky cheerfully. 'Rough night?'

'A rough three nights. No sleep until dawn.'

'Back to the old regime, then?' Sollertinsky gestured to the boy at the bar. 'My poor tortured friend.'

'I only want tea,' said Shostakovich. 'I ate breakfast under an hour ago.'

'And what of that?'

'Well, all right. Perhaps just one drink.'

It was cosy sitting there with his old friend, feeling his hands thaw and the warmth of vodka in his stomach. Cosy, seemingly like any other day — nonetheless, something wasn't right. 'I haven't had a bowel movement for days,' he reflected. 'Perhaps that's why I'm feeling strange.'

'Wait till you hear the news,' said Sollertinsky. 'That'll make you shit all right.'

'News?' Shostakovich had forgotten, what with the cold, and the blinding sun, and the feeling that, back in the apartment, he'd left something unattended to.

Sollertinsky leaned forward, dwarfing the small round table. Raising his magnificent eyebrows, he took a mouthful of vodka and swished it loudly about in his cheeks. But when he spoke, it was in such a low voice that Shostakovich could hardly hear.

'What? *Who* is leaving?'

Sollertinsky touched the side of his nose in a conspiratorial manner. 'My tailor told me when I went to him this morning. Apparently, last week Herr Lehmann cancelled a large order. The next day, Herr Ziegler did the very same thing.'

Shostakovich shook his head. 'Two Germans cancelled orders for suits. So?'

'Two *German* diplomats,' corrected Sollertinsky. 'Two high-profile Germans cancelled long-standing orders with a Leningrad tailor so highly reputed it's impossible to get an appointment with him this side of the New Year. A tailor so exacting, and so brilliant, he wouldn't hurry a seam if his wife were about to be put in a poorhouse. Two German diplomats cancelled at short notice with Yuri Davydenko, whose waiting list is as long as the River Volga!'

'You're sure of this?' said Shostakovich slowly. 'Absolutely sure?'

'Of course I'm bloody well sure. I checked it out myself. You don't think I'd take Davydenko's word for anything more important than the cut of my trousers, do you?' Sollertinsky sounded weary, as if Shostakovich were one of his more idiotic musicology students. 'After we'd ascertained the measurement of my inside leg, I decided the Lehmanns were in need of some freshly baked bread. Right away.' He paused for a mouthful of vodka. 'When I got there with their complimentary breakfast, I rang their door bell.' He paused again, this time for effect. 'I rang the bell once, twice, three times.'

'And?'

'They'd gone. And I don't just mean for a Sunday stroll. They've upped and left, permanently. The apartment is empty.'

'How do you know?'

'I looked through the keyhole, of course.'

'Ivan Sollertinsky! Someone might have seen you. You should think of your position.'

'I listened first, with my ear to the door,' protested Sollertinsky. 'And I heard a deep silence. Not a chair scraping, not a brat quarrelling. Only after that did I look through the keyhole. Mainly out of fear that I'd have to eat an entire loaf of new bread by myself. Which, over the course of the morning, I've nearly achieved.' He gave a comfortable belch. Being one of the most highly educated men in Leningrad didn't stop him revelling in being one of the least refined.

Shostakovich glanced around. The room was empty, except for the pointy-nosed Mikhail Druskin bent double over his notebook, no doubt slaughtering the Philharmonic's recent performance of Prokofiev's orchestral suite. 'So the Germans are evacuating their own?'

'That's my interpretation. One can only hope that I'm wrong.' Unusually for someone whose most common reaction was a laugh, there was anger on Sollertinsky's face — or was it just the smoke drifting from Druskin's table that made his eyes narrow?

'I need to piss.' Shostakovich pushed back his chair and strode to the dingy bathroom. He stood facing the urinals, staring at the long familiar crack across the porcelain. In the past he'd seen this as a horizon over a wheat field, or the thin grey line from the funnel of a steamer. Now he was so agitated that his glasses steamed up and he saw nothing at all.

Sollertinsky shuffled up beside him and turned the water on full. 'Although this is bad news for us,' he said quietly, 'it's not entirely unexpected. There have been rumours for months. From London, from

Washington — and also from within.'

'Yet *he* has chosen not to hear them. And anyone who forces him to unblock his ears will pay dearly.' Out of the blurry wall, a familiar face emerged, both real and unreal, like the ghost appearing to Hamlet. Almond-shaped grey eyes, white teeth, a strong jaw above a collar emblazoned with Marshal's stars. 'Tukhachevsky!' whispered Shostakovich — but already the image was disintegrating in a red haze, blood running down the wall and into the guttering. The Red Army's best Marshal, one of Shostakovich's best friends, shot by Stalin's henchmen.

'Of course Stalin doesn't want to hear,' agreed Sollertinsky. 'Nor to see. The possibility that he's been taken for a ride by Hitler doesn't sit easily with his view of the world.'

'So he shuts his damn eyes.' Shostakovich closed his own. The water, the early drinking, the apparition: he was beginning to feel queasy. 'And the German rats run from the sinking ship, and we — well, what are we to do?'

Sollertinsky shook his head. 'There's nothing we can do but wait. I came to your home this morning simply to tell you what I'd found out, not to rouse you to action.' He sighed. 'As it turned out, I couldn't rouse you at all. When Dmitri Shostakovich finally sleeps, he might as well be dead. I knocked so hard the door nearly crumbled. I thought your wife would be out chasing me away with a broom.'

'Nina!' Shostakovich started. 'When I woke up, Nina was gone.' It was all starting to come back to him. 'She threatened last night that she'd take the children, go to her parents' for a few days. She was very angry.'

'No wonder she was angry!' Sollertinsky turned off the water. 'How would you like to be married to yourself, day in and day out?' He led the way back into the now half-full drinking house. 'No offence, my friend, but even I, with my nerves of steel, would not take on the task of being your spouse.'

Shostakovich signalled to the barkeeper for more vodka. 'Nina isn't easy herself,' he said mutinously. 'She seems incapable of understanding that sometimes I must be left alone to work.'

'Sometimes?' quoted Sollertinsky. 'Be honest. Have you been working twenty-four-hour or forty-eight-hour stints this week?'

'The latter.' Shostakovich flushed. 'But I can't stop now, not possibly. Not until I get down the outline.' He stared into his empty glass and saw the whole of the previous evening there: raised voices, slammed doors, little Galina crying, and the uncertain, insistent melody in his head.

'The English Poets project? My God, Dmitri! Most men would give their eye-teeth to be married to the beautiful Nina, and you shut her out for Romances of a musical kind — for Raleigh, Burns and Shakespeare?' Nonetheless, Sollertinsky gave him a reassuring slap on the shoulder. 'Nina never stays away long. She'll be back in a couple of days. You know she finds you irresistible.'

'Like a moth to a flame,' said Shostakovich gloomily. 'Only problem is, she's as fiery as I am. But I must keep working. You know how it is when you get up speed. It's dangerous, almost fatal, to stop.'

Sollertinsky raised first his eyebrows and then his brimming glass. 'To music and marital harmony. May they one day co-exist.'

'To thinking slowly and writing fast,' countered Shostakovich, gulping his vodka. 'Well, there's no one waiting for me at home. If I'm to live like a bachelor for the next day or two, I guess I can have another.'

Three vodkas later, and the room was loud with voices and laughter. Even Druskin, who was rarely happy, had the satisfied look of a critic who'd honed a hatchet job to perfection. As they left, Sollertinsky boomed out a greeting to him, while Shostakovich sneaked a quick glance at the open notebook. '*Pretentious*,' he read. '*Angular*. More farce than comedy. Melodies limper than a wet handkerchief.'

Druskin, noticing his interest, slammed the book shut.

'Oh, come on!' said Shostakovich. 'Whatever sins Prokofiev may be accused of, you can't deny he has a rare gift for melody.'

Druskin shrugged. 'Unfortunately for Sergey Prokofiev, you're not the one writing the review.'

Shostakovich stared into his dry grey face. '"Be kind, for everyone you meet is fighting a great battle."'

Druskin looked nonplussed.

'Philo of Alexandria,' said Sollertinsky briskly as he pushed through the door into the chilly bright light. 'God, it's cold as a witch's tit.'

'Spring's certainly late this year,' agreed Shostakovich, hunching into his coat.

Sollertinsky turned up the collar of his suit jacket, bought six months earlier but already looking ten years old, its pockets bulging with keys, threads trailing from its lapels. 'Are you feeling quite well?' He pulled on his overcoat. 'I could have sworn I heard you defending one Mr Prokofiev.'

'Prokofiev has the soul of a goose and the talent of a turkey,' shrugged Shostakovich. 'Nonetheless, he's one of us, and we composers must unite against the enemy.'

'Now you're using the language of war. Go home now.' Sollertinsky clasped his hand, kissed him on both cheeks, and warned him to take great care, not only of his marriage but of himself, because he was the best drinking companion in the city, not to mention a reasonably talented composer.

Shostakovich turned to go, and then turned back. 'Do you know the worst thing about all this German fraternising we've had to put up with?'

'No, what?' Sollertinsky's query floated on a vodka breeze.

'That we've had to endure so many years of strategic Wagner,' said Shostakovich, and he marched away.

Anticipation

Karl Illyich Eliasberg, commonly known as Elias, sat counting the times his mother chewed before swallowing. Ten. *Swallow*. Twelve. *Swallow*. A commendable practice, recommended by doctors to aid the digestion. Nevertheless, they were eating only a kind of purée that he'd cooked out of turnips and swede, boiled for hours, reduced to a tasteless grey gruel in deference to his mother's gapped teeth.

He concentrated on eating his own meal extremely quietly, hoping his mother would follow his example. Even when alone, he ate, drank and moved with as little noise as possible, as if not wanting to disturb the inanimate objects around him. The world ran on one track, he on another. This was the way it had always been.

Fifteen. *Swallow*! How could so few teeth mulching through liquefied root vegetables make so much noise?

'Mother!' he said sharply, involuntarily.

His mother looked up. She hadn't yet done her hair; greyish wisps trailed like lichen over her shoulders. The sight annoyed Elias still further. Whatever the state of the wider world, however quickly Europe might be sliding into chaos, there was no excuse for personal slovenliness, even at eight in the morning.

'Karl?' Her eyes were as faded as the envelopes she carried about day and night.

'It doesn't matter.' Soundlessly, he spooned up the last of his sludge.

'I'd hoped we might have fresh rolls this morning.' His mother prodded at what was left on her plate. 'Didn't we have this stuff yesterday for lunch?'

'Yes, Mother,' he said expressionlessly.

'Not that it isn't nice,' mused Mrs Eliasberg. 'But I did feel like a little bread today.'

Elias placed his spoon beside his plate at a precise right angle to the edge of the table. 'I didn't have time to queue for bread this morning. Nor did I have time last evening to set dough. Please try to remember this is a busy time for me.'

His mother ducked away from the reproach, bending once more to her food. 'How light —' she muttered. 'And how —'

'I beg your pardon, Mother?'

Mrs Eliasberg raised her head. Small shreds of turnip swayed in her hair. 'I didn't mean to offend you, Karl. It was merely that I felt for a little bread today.'

'Yes, yes.' His eyes strayed towards the work desk by the wall, but he forced his gaze back to his mother.

'I was simply saying *How light it is here, and how unfriendly!*' Deliberately, vaguely, his mother looked towards the open window.

Silence fell. Down in the street someone who hadn't been eating liquid vegetables with an aged relative was whistling cheerfully. Elias fiddled with his spoon and, out of habit, sprinkled salt on his empty plate.

'Think of your health, Karl!' His mother clicked her tongue. 'You don't want to die before you're forty like your poor father.'

'Chances are,' said Elias, 'that I'll be killed by something other than an excessive intake of salt.' Death by nagging, for instance. He'd be found slumped at his desk, his head on a pillow of scores, driven to an early grave by a semi-paralysed matriarch whose tongue was the only part of her body in full working order.

'"*My tired body has given way . . . And passersby think vaguely: She probably was widowed yesterday.*"' His mother breathed heavily as she quoted Anna Akhmatova: lines she'd used most days for the past thirty years. 'A wonderful poem. It captures my own situation perfectly. If only you had such a gift yourself.'

'Words have never been my forte.'

'True enough,' agreed his mother. 'You were very slow to speak. Of all the autumn babies born within two miles of Pishev Station, you were the last to utter a sound. But perhaps I've told you that before.'

'Once or twice,' said Elias.

With a great squeaking and scraping, Mrs Eliasberg gathered together the last fibres of her vegetables, sucked the spoon and smacked her lips.

25

'Not that you haven't done well for yourself. If only your poor father had lived to see his son become the best conductor in Leningrad!'

'Please, Mother.' Elias gave a small tight smile. 'I'm not the best, and the whole of Leningrad knows it.'

'Bah! Best and second-best are simply matters of opinion, and opinions are as many as leaves on a tree.'

'Perhaps.' Elias took the plates to the sink, wiped them with a cloth, and rinsed the cloth with boiling water from the large blackened kettle. 'Now, Mother, I really must get to work.' It was imperative to be casual, to slip in his requests sideways. *The trout that opens its mouth widest is most securely hooked* ran through his head.

From years of practice, first with his father and then with himself, his mother had developed selective deafness into an art. 'Terrible thing, this German war, isn't it?'

'Yes,' said Elias, looking down into the empty street.

'Suffering like you wouldn't believe, they say,' she said chattily.

'Yes,' he repeated, raising the sash window, leaning out and feeling the wind on his face. High above the rooftops, the pale sky was streaked with clouds.

'Poles, Jews, anyone they can lay their hands on. If your father were alive, I dread to think what they would —'

'Mother, don't upset yourself so soon after eating. You'll give yourself indigestion.'

'Indigestion, from that dull muck? Now, if I'd had some meat, even a tiny piece of sausage, I'd gladly suffer indigestion for it.' Mrs Eliasberg's famous tongue-click had a multitude of meanings, and this particular click was that of a person hard done by.

'What if I move your chair over here by the window?' suggested Elias. 'Then you can get some sun on your face.' If she clicked at him once more, he'd take her chair and throw it out the window. With her in it.

Immediately, he was ashamed of himself. Why couldn't he be kinder?

He leaned his head on the window frame and focused as hard as he could on the solid stack of scores behind him. Mahler's Fifth; think of Mahler's Fifth! In his mind, he opened the stiff green cover and looked at the first page.

Instantly, there it was, catching him, stopping his fall. The low repeated notes of the trumpet — full of hope, or foretelling tragedy? The possibility of both was there in that urgent, repeated brass voice. Then the lift to the minor third and the rise to the octave — and then the descending notes, the repeated fall, the rising up again. And the crash! That beautiful, all-encompassing, full and worldly *sound*, shutting out critical faces and marching feet, ominous news, guilt and fear. All of it gone, gone —

'What?' Distantly he heard something behind him. He turned, but the breeze from the window was full in his hair and Mahler was still crashing in his head like the sea. He saw that his mother's mouth was moving, yet he could hear nothing except the trumpet, falling in brassy rain onto the embroidered tablecloth. His hands had floated up off the windowsill, were moving in the air, giving shape to what he was hearing.

'What did you say?' he said, dazed.

'I was saying —' His mother's voice came from a great distance away. But just as the string melody emerged, sweeter than a nightingale, he returned to his real life: caged in the front room of his apartment, listening to his invalid mother. He shut the window, closing out the wind and the possibility of what lay beyond the city — sights he'd never seen, music he'd never heard — and he turned, with customary self-imposed politeness, to his mother.

'I was asking,' said his mother, 'whether you might begin thinking about children? You're not a young man any more; thirty-five has been and gone. And before the Germans or the English blow this world to smithereens, I'd like to see a grandchild with your dear father's face.'

'Mother,' he pointed out, 'I don't have a wife yet. Not even a suspicion of a wife.'

She waved a dismissive hand. 'Surely in the orchestra? There must be plenty of girls in search of a handsome husband. A nice viola player, a pretty flautist?' She stopped in sudden concern. 'But perhaps a musician is not the best choice for a wife. They can be temperamental, so I'm told.'

Elias saw his chance. 'Yes, they can certainly be temperamental — all the more so if I'm late to rehearsal. What woman could love a man who's unable to be punctual?'

'You're right!' Mrs Eliasberg rolled her chair over the uneven floor and seized his gloves off the music cabinet. 'Put on your outdoor clothes! Don't waste your time here with me.'

Elias accepted his gloves. 'Let me put your chair here by the window. Is the sun in your eyes?'

'No, no!' His mother waved him away. 'I'll be perfectly comfortable. If you will pass me my sewing basket on your way out, I can begin darning your socks. It's not a good start to a courtship if the man has holes in his toes.'

All the way down four dark flights of stairs and out the front door, Elias kept a steady pace, walking as a soldier would, head erect, feet straight. At the intersection where the trams swung around with a clanging of bells, he turned, shielding his eyes against the sun. His mother's white handkerchief waved from the window, and he lifted his heavy briefcase in a kind of salute.

Once around the corner, he broke into a much faster walk: almost a run. *Dignity*, he reminded himself, sweating a little between his shoulder blades. *Dignity must be maintained at all costs*. There was the news-stand, directly across the street. Elias was blind to anything but the stack of newspapers displayed at the front.

'Morning.' The man in the kiosk was casual, almost insolent. The stub of a cheap cigarette stuck out the side of his mouth like an errant tooth. 'Anything else?'

'Nothing.' Elias stepped away from the kiosk and shook open the newspaper — and there it was.

'Angular . . . More farce than comedy . . .' The sun was so bright the words were almost impossible to read. 'A light-hearted romp in which style is sacrificed for the sake of vigour.' He felt almost sorry for Prokofiev. Always, when it came to the critics, the inevitable fall from grace.

But this was not what he'd been looking for. His eyes raced on down the column. 'But of course,' he murmured slowly. 'What did you expect.' He folded up the pages, once, twice, three times, until the paper sat in a hard wad under his arm. He crossed back over into the shade and leaned against the wall of an apartment block, pressing against the cold stone as if its strength might seep into him.

'Aha!' Someone emerged from the doorway on his left. 'If it isn't Karl Eliasberg!'

Blinking, Elias turned to see Sollertinsky beside him. 'Good morning to you, Ivan,' he said, as evenly as he could manage.

'And a good morning to you, too!' Sollertinsky was still bundling his tie into a clumsy knot. For such an eminent lecturer, not to mention Artistic Director of the Leningrad Philharmonica, he looked rather a mess. 'At least I hope it's a good morning. I'm off to buy a newspaper to see what damaging words that dung-beetle Druskin has written about my orchestra.'

Elias swallowed so loudly he thought it must be audible over the clatter of the trolley cars. 'In fact, I've just read that very review.'

'Oh! How scathing was it?' Sollertinsky pulled his collar down over his untidy tie and squinted at Elias.

'Not at all scathing, Sir.' Elias bit his lip; not even Sollertinsky's sartorial flaws could save him from undue deference. 'That is, Prokofiev didn't come off so well, but Mravinsky — well, yet again Mravinsky has saved the day.'

'Is that so?' Sollertinsky spied the newspaper clenched tightly under Elias's elbow. 'May I?'

'Of course.' Elias shoved the paper at him as if it were red-hot.

Sollertinsky smoothed out the paper. '"Only Yevgeny Mravinsky and his skilled musicians could rescue the music from charges of flimsiness",' he murmured, scanning the review at top speed. '"His stick technique is as modest as it is commanding." *Nice!* "Barrow-loads of self-confidence, which translates to complete authority." *Very good!* "Leningrad is fortunate to call a conductor of this calibre our own." *Well!*' He straightened up, although the newspaper stayed bent like an old pin in his hands. 'Who would have thought such warmth of feeling could be hidden in Druskin's heart, eh?'

'Indeed.' Elias tried to smile, though he felt as if his face would crack with the effort. 'Quite a review from such a tough nut.'

With a gallant flourish, Sollertinsky offered the ridiculous-looking newspaper back to him, but he waved it away. 'Please, keep it. I've read enough already.'

The birthday

Happiness or the lack of it always stopped her sleeping. Tonight, it was happiness. She lay in bed, looking at the way the moon painted tiger-stripes on the wall, and she made herself stay that way while she counted her breaths.

By the time she reached forty — *in* and *out* — she couldn't help noticing she was breathing faster than usual. The sheet was hardly rustling, so shallowly were her lungs working, so eager was her heart.

'Kitten breaths,' she told herself severely. 'You're cheating!' When she reached the allotted fifty breaths, she added ten more as penance, though by now the longing to roll over was almost unbearable. 'You're a born teacher!' Papa always said, when he watched her copying out a lesson all over again because of a small ink blot on the last line. 'I've only ever known one other person with such an insistence on perfection.' He laughed as he said this, but he sighed too. 'Perhaps it's not necessary to be quite so strict with yourself. Life is a hard enough taskmaster, you know.'

Sonya had started to notice that Papa often sighed. Also, that the end of his beard was fraying away in wisps because he pulled it when he was writing. And another thing — their apartment was not like other people's. It was strewn around with piles of paper, and dust-balls skittered under the sofa like mice. Secretly she thought that if Papa were a little more orderly, there would be fewer grey streaks in his brown beard and fewer lines on his forehead.

Now, breathing deeply, she'd reached sixty, so now — now! — she sat up and looked. There it was, leaning against the window: only one day known, but two centuries perfect. Its neck was graceful in the moonlight, the scroll bending towards her like the head of a swan.

From what she'd heard, Aunt Tanya hadn't wanted her to have it. 'Are you sure you've thought this through, Nikolai?' Her aunt had pulled Papa into a corner and they stood there, too close, wedged between the piano and the tall fringed lamp. 'She'll drop it,' hissed Aunt Tanya. 'She'll smash it. She's too small for it.'

'She'll treasure it,' contradicted Papa. 'She'll master it. She'll grow into it.'

It was true, Sonya was still a little short for the cello, but if she placed a cushion on her chair and stretched her neck (imagining herself as one of the tall buildings on Nevsky Prospect), and if she made her arms as long as possible (thinking of orang-utans in the zoo) — well, then she became bigger than her years, and her birthday present was a perfect match.

'It's foolish,' said Aunt Tanya, her cheeks even redder than usual. 'A genuine Storioni! To think of giving such a valuable instrument to a mere child!'

'There is nothing *mere* about Sonya.' Papa had sounded quite angry. 'At any rate, I can't help thinking that you're objecting for entirely the wrong reasons.'

'Such as?' Aunt Tanya's neck was slightly mottled.

Sonya had stopped cutting up small blocks of sausage and placing them on squares of bread; she moved into the doorway to get a proper look.

'You're scared that I'm forgetting —' Papa cleared his throat. 'That I'm trying to replace —' He stopped and slammed his hand down on the piano, making the metronome ting and start to tick prestissimo. 'As if!' he said, silencing the metronome and Aunt Tanya with one angry hand. 'As if I could ever forget her!'

'Look!' Sonya nudged Konstantin, who'd come early to help with the party food. 'Look at Aunt Tanya's neck!' She stared, fascinated, at the blotches above her aunt's collar, merging like the pools of blood under the pigs hanging in the market. 'Oh, would you just look at that!'

But Konstantin was too busy unwrapping candies, cramming several into his mouth at a time.

'Talk about pigs,' she said, though in fact no one had been talking about them, it was only in her mind that she'd taken a quick trip over the bristle-covered cobblestones to see the bloated bodies hung in rows. 'You're no better than a pig!' she repeated severely, looking at Konstantin, who stood with drifts of coloured *fantiki* wrappers at his feet like a sturdy oak that had lost its leaves. 'What about the Shostakoviches? You'd better leave some sweets for them.' She snatched the brass bowl away from Konstantin and took it into the living room, where she placed it on the sofa and covered it with a cushion.

'Why are the Shostakovich kids coming?' Konstantin trailed after her. 'They're nothing but babies.' His ten-year-old face was shiny with sugar and radiant with scorn.

'They're sweet,' said Sonya. 'It's not their fault they're young. As for Mrs Nina Shostakovich, she's the most beautiful woman in Russia.' She looked over at the window standing open to the hot afternoon. The light through the glass formed a perfect white square on the carpet, marked with a shadowy cross. 'The most beautiful *living* woman,' she corrected herself.

Konstantin took a step closer. He'd forgotten his ill temper and the sudden removal of the sweets, but the sugar rush was still in him. 'You're beautiful,' he said. 'I could make you a damn good husband when I'm older.' His mouth hung open, showing strings of brightly coloured spit between his lips.

Sonya moved backwards until she was stopped by the piano. *Wham!* Her bottom landed on the keyboard in a muddled mess of notes. The discord made her wince. 'Konstantin Kushnarov! Don't swear! Besides, I'm only nine. Nine years and three minutes, to be precise.'

At that moment the doorbell rang, Papa and Aunt Tanya stopped their heated whispering and the birthday — which had looked in danger of collapsing — was saved. In came the Gessen children (Papa called them Gessen One, Gessen Two and so on) and Boris the Caretaker's Son and the four Shostakoviches, all at once. For a while Sonya could hardly hear herself saying 'Thank you' and 'Welcome' every time someone wished her happy birthday.

Maxim Shostakovich, tiny in his black fur coat, was holding tightly to his mother's hand. His small round head swivelled like a parrot's as he surveyed the room. 'You see,' Sonya hissed to Konstantin. 'I told you he was sweet.'

Konstantin looked jealous. 'Why are you wearing that fur coat?' he said to Maxim. 'You can't be cold, it's not even three weeks till midsummer.'

'He always wears it to parties,' said Galina. 'There's nothing wrong with that.' Her hair had been parted perfectly straight down the middle and braided into two long gleaming ropes. Like Maxim, she had an unblinking stare, which was now trained on Konstantin.

'You both look beautiful.' Sonya spoke quickly. 'I'll get you some sausage.'

When she came back from the kitchen she was pleased to see that Galina was mingling, but Maxim, his coat still buttoned up to his neck, continued to hold onto his mother's hand.

'Something to eat?' Sonya held out the plate, reaching up and then down to make allowances for mother's and son's differing heights.

Mrs Shostakovich reached for a piece of sausage-bread with her free hand and bit straight into it: her teeth were large and square like a horse's. 'Mmmm. Delicious.'

'Deelicious,' echoed Maxim.

'I made it myself,' said Sonya. 'At least, I cut it into pieces. The butcher made the sausage specially, when he heard we were having a birthday party.'

'I hear you got another special present.' Mrs Shostakovich's dark hair was piled high above her white forehead. 'A real treasure.'

Sonya nodded. 'It used to belong to my mother. She died when I was very young, not even as old as Maxim.'

'I know,' said Mrs Shostakovich. Her eyes were the same clear brown as her amber beads, and tiny pearls studded her ears. She drew Sonya aside. 'Could you help me out?' she whispered. 'Maxim's a little shy and that's why he has to wear his fur coat, even inside.'

'To make him braver.' Sonya understood; she often put on her enamel locket with the pressed violet when she needed protection. 'I'll look after him.'

'Thank you.' Mrs Shostakovich smiled and accepted a cranberry juice from Aunt Tanya, who was still a trifle red in the face. 'To Sonya!' she said, raising her glass.

'To Sonya!' said the five Gessen children, and Boris-from-the-Basement, and Galina of the shining braids, and Konstantin who would never, in a million years, be allowed to become Sonya's husband. And the red rose on the windowsill bobbed in the wind as if to say, *Many Happy Returns*.

'To Sonya!' said her father and her aunt, and Mr Shostakovich came across to shake her hand. 'To your health and happiness,' he said, bowing as if she were a real lady. The sun glinted off his big glasses so Sonya couldn't see his eyes, but his voice sounded serious. 'I hadn't realised Nikolai Nikolayev had such a grown-up daughter.'

'I'm only nine,' admitted Sonya. 'Nine years and —' She looked at her wrist-watch. 'Thirty-three minutes.'

'A perfect age,' said Mr Shostakovich. 'Neither too old nor too young.' He took a mouthful of cranberry juice. 'Do you think your father has any vodka?'

'I know he does. He was drinking some the other night with Mr Sollertinsky.'

'Ah. If Mr Sollertinsky was here the other night, perhaps there is no vodka left? Rumour has it that Mr Sollertinsky could drink the Neva dry.'

'Dmitri!' Mrs Shostakovich's eyebrows lowered alarmingly.

'A joke,' said Mr Shostakovich hastily. 'Nothing more.' He turned back to Sonya. 'Perhaps later you'll play us a tune on your birthday present?'

Sonya flushed. 'With pleasure.'

'The pleasure will be all ours,' said Mr Shostakovich.

As the afternoon slunk away, the room began filling up with a strange orange light. Sonya, weaving through her guests with plates of food, felt as if she were swimming in a magic pond. Or perhaps it was more like diving into one of the beautiful beads around Mrs Shostakovich's creamy neck, which reflected back the low sun.

Maxim sat, small and grave, on a cushion in the corner. He'd taken off his coat but kept a close watch on it, resting a hand on its sleeve. Sonya kept him supplied with lemonade and sweets rescued from under the cushion that, for a while, Aunt Tanya had been sitting on.

'How could she not notice she was sitting on a big brass bowl?' whispered Galina.

'Because she has a big brass bottom,' snorted Konstantin.

Sonya laughed a little at this, and Konstantin grinned, looking wicked and handsome under his party hat. But Sonya already knew she could never marry a person who made such bad jokes.

Every now and then another guest, usually someone who worked with her father at the Conservatoire, slipped in. The chattering voices grew louder. Someone started to play the piano and, in spite of Mr Sollertinsky's recent visit, plenty of vodka was brought to the table. Then one of the Gessen children yawned, and so did another Gessen, making Mrs Shostakovich look at the clock on the mantelpiece and talk about taking the children home to bed.

'All in good time, my dear.' Mr Shostakovich, his tie a little askew, appeared at Sonya's side. 'May I,' he asked respectfully, 'see the Storioni now?'

The cello lay on its side in the shadowy bedroom. Sonya's heart gave a leap when she saw it: it was so beautiful! Carefully, she picked it up and offered it to Mr Shostakovich, who ran his hands admiringly over its red-brown front and curved back.

'A very fine instrument,' he said. 'I saw your mother play it, many times, before you were born.'

'Did you?' Sonya could hardly imagine what the world had been like way back then. 'Where did she play?'

'In the Philharmonia Hall,' said Mr Shostakovich, cradling the cello as if it weighed no more than a baby. 'Beautiful. Quite beautiful.' It wasn't clear whether he was talking about the cello, or Sonya's mother, or the concert hall with its soaring white pillars.

'I haven't played it much yet. Just a little this morning, before I started preparing for the party.'

'Does it like you?' Mr Shostakovich looked at her intently.

'Does it — what?'

'Has it taken to you? It doesn't matter if it knows you — it will come to know you. But it's very important that it *likes* you, and vice versa.' The curl at the front of Mr Shostakovich's hair sprang free from its waxy coating and bobbed in front of his face. 'A long time ago I used to accompany films at the Bright Reel Theatre, and you know what? The piano hated me! Every day, we battled. Every evening, we fought.' He gave a sigh. 'It was a disgusting job. Fighting the piano was like working with a person you detest day after day.'

Sonya stared at the gleaming cello. 'When I took it out of its case this morning, the first thing I did was pluck the A string.'

'And?' Mr Shostakovich sounded intensely interested. 'How did it sound?'

'Like —' Sonya shut her eyes for a second. 'Like a voice.' Opening her eyes, she saw Mr Shostakovich's glasses shining full in her face. 'It seemed to say something, only I'm not sure what.'

Mr Shostakovich nodded. 'In my opinion, the A string is the least informative of the four strings. If approached wrongly, it can hold its secrets forever.'

'So you think it likes me?' Sonya could hardly dare to hope.

'Definitely.' Mr Shostakovich passed the cello back to her. 'No doubt about it. Would you consider playing a tune for your guests, if I accompany you?'

'How about an adaptation of Fauré's Elégie?' suggested Sonya. She'd been practising this for the past year on her borrowed half-sized cello; last week, she'd finally learnt it by heart.

'A perfect choice for a birthday.' Mr Shostakovich looked grave. 'The passing of time is a serious matter.'

As soon he played an A on the piano for Sonya to tune to, everyone — even the fidgeting Gessen children — fell silent. 'A captive audience,' said Mr Shostakovich. 'That's what we like!'

Sonya felt a little nervous, but the light had grown even softer, candles were burning, and her father was looking happier than she'd seen him for a long time. How she loved him! 'Fauré's Elégie, an adaptation,' she announced in a slightly squeezed voice. 'For my father.'

'Ready when you are,' said Mr Shostakovich from the piano.

Sonya straightened her back and pressed her feet against the floor. The cello leaned into her. *I'm ready too*, it said in a woody whisper. Sonya placed her left hand in position and laid the bow carefully across the strings — no squeak, no twang.

Before this she'd seen the Elégie as a silvery kind of piece, clear-cut, almost icy. But today, in the hushed moments before beginning, she saw it differently. Fauré's familiar notes were transformed: they hung in the air, round, opaque, like ripe golden fruit. How odd! Already, the cello had changed her way of seeing. She took a deep breath, nodded to Mr Shostakovich, and the first note dropped into the silence, perfectly pitched and as sweet as honey.

And soon it seemed to Sonya that the cello was singing by itself. All she had to do was place her fingers on the strings, and the song sprang open, phrase after phrase floating out as if she'd unlocked a secret world with a magic key. Then, with a sigh — was it from her or the cello? — the bow drew a last husky stroke across the string, and there was silence. She let her arms fall by her side; they were aching from the effort of embracing a cello slightly too large for her. She gave the cello a quick stroke on its smooth back. *Thank you*, she said. *You were wonderful.*

Mr Shostakovich sprang up from his stool and clapped wildly. The room dissolved into applause, and Sonya's father held her so hard she heard a button on his shirt cracking. 'You were wonderful!' he said, just as she'd said to the Storioni. 'You were marvellous.'

The light faded, and people began gathering up their things, and Sonya went to stand by the front door. 'Goodbye,' she said, shaking hands with her guests. 'Thank you for coming.' To Galina, she said, 'You're lucky. I'd like a little brother just like yours.'

'Yes, he's all right.' Galina took Maxim casually by the hand. 'We might come and see you again one day.'

'Please do,' urged Sonya, and to Mr Shostakovich she said, 'Thank you so much for accompanying me.'

'I should be thanking you. A fine performance.' He bowed low so that his lock of hair bounced forward. 'You have a very talented daughter,' he said to Sonya's father. 'Don't, for God's sake, allow her to become a teacher. Let her play, whatever happens!'

'Humph!' Papa pretended to be offended. 'Just because you consider yourself a poor teacher doesn't mean the entire profession is useless! Some consider it a noble way of making a living.' He put a hand on Sonya's shoulder. 'But I agree that she's brilliant.'

'It was one of the nicest parties I've been to,' said Mrs Shostakovich. 'If one wants good company, one should always go to nine-year-olds' birthday parties — never to official functions.'

Much later, in her bedroom, Sonya lay back and watched her father who was, most unusually, tidying things away. 'Is Mr Shostakovich famous?'

'Oh, yes.' Her father bent down to slot books into the shelves. 'Very famous.'

'Those books go on the top shelf,' Sonya told him. 'And are you?'

'Am I famous?' Her father looked over his shoulder. 'No, not really. And we should be glad about that.'

'Why? Is it difficult to be related to a famous person? Galina said her father doesn't always pay attention. Sometimes he sits at the piano for a long time and then he gets up and slams the door, or shouts. After that, Galina's mother takes her and Maxim and they all go to stay with their grandparents, for something called a respite.'

For some reason, her father laughed at this. 'Well, that's one reason to avoid fame. And there are plenty of others. Life isn't easy for people with a high public profile.' He paused and then cleared his throat. 'You should try to sleep now. Concerts are quite tiring, if I remember rightly from my performing days.'

'Could you put my cello over there?' said Sonya. 'I want to see it when I'm lying down.'

Her father propped it up against the wall, where it seemed to lean in a tired but graceful way. 'Is that all, your Excellency? May I help Aunt Tanya with the rest of the washing up now?'

After the door was closed, Sonya waited for sleep. She tried to close her eyes, but they kept flying open, as if her happiness was too great to box away. So she simply lay there, looking over to where the light-blue sky gleamed on the wooden scroll of her cello. She wished the world could stop right here, because at this very moment everything was perfect.

Nikolai, grieving

There had been a time when Nikolai thought he would go mad with grief. Crossing at street corners, he didn't bother to look; he simply stepped out into the blaring, weaving traffic and trusted to fate. If he was taken away, so be it.

Since that terrible night in January, he hadn't been able to see properly, anyway. Far from the expected darkness, a glaring light had appeared in the centre of his vision. The only way he could see was by glancing out of the corner of one eye, barely turning his head, as if not really wishing to look at all. Thus the world was presented to him in slivers: distorted trees, bent lamp-posts, the thin corners of buildings.

He walked through those months like a blind man, feeling the streets through the soles of his feet. His boots wore thin, and finally wore out. 'Why don't you get some new shoes?' Tanya's tone was halfway between anxiety and a scold. 'You look like one of the men down at Finland Station.' To get her off his back, Nikolai pretended he was saving the money for something he couldn't yet talk about. The truth was, it was easier to walk now that his boots had become a second skin: just as a mountaineer traverses the lips of a cold windy crevasse on a rope, hand over hand, so Nikolai felt his way with his feet. But with every uneven cobblestone, every dip of a gutter, he thought he might fall, plummeting thousands of feet into a blue icy silence.

'Are you ready yet?' Sonya stood in front of him, her hair tied back in a red ribbon and her cardigan buttoned. Her feet were in a dancer's first position, together at the heels, turned out at the toes.

'Your shoes are very shiny! Positively gleaming!' Nikolai returned from the past with a double-edged shock: pleasure at the sight of Sonya undermined by a sharp regret. The passing of time was not altogether a blessing. He closed his eyes, trying to recapture the pale oval face, but it had gone. There were days now when he couldn't remember the colour of her hair and, desperately, he would search the world outside the window for the exact shade to bring her back to him. On other days he realised that he'd never looked carefully enough at the curve of her neck or the shape of her feet, so that these, too, were slipping from his memory.

Sonya was looking at her shoes. 'I spat on them,' she confided, 'because I couldn't find where Aunt Tanya had put the polish.'

'Aunt Tanya is an exceedingly tidy woman,' agreed Nikolai. 'Sometimes I think she'd like to tidy away the grass and the trees, and probably the Neva River. Nature is a little too unruly for Aunt Tanya.'

Sonya glanced at Nikolai's desk. Every drawer was bulging open and scores were piled high, teetering like stacks of pancakes. 'I suppose there's a place in this world for every type,' she said diplomatically.

'You'd make an excellent politician,' said Nikolai. 'Perhaps we should send you to America — you'd be President in no time.'

'No!' Sonya ran to him. 'I can't leave you. I belong here in Leningrad. This is where I belong.'

Her arms tightened, noose-like, around Nikolai's neck, and the familiar panic rose in him, as strong as it had ever been.

'Don't make me go away!' Sonya was breathing fast and her forehead was slimy with sweat.

'I was only joking, Mouse,' said Nikolai quickly. 'It's not a good time to go anywhere with the spreading of this wretched war.'

His words appeared to calm Sonya. At the mention of separation, it was as if her heart had flown apart, fragments hammering in her wrists and temples. Now, almost instantly, her pulse slowed to normal. 'The war,' she said, with unmistakable relief. 'As long as this war goes on, we all have to stay put. No one will go away — not you, not Aunty, not the Gessen kids or Maxim Shostakovich. Am I right?'

'You are.' Nikolai kicked off his slippers. 'I'll go and comb my hair, and then it's time for some fun!'

In the bathroom, he leaned on the washstand and breathed deeply. 'Eight years and five months,' he said, staring into the cracked basin. 'Eight years, five months and three days.' His whisper slipped into the slimy web of hair and soap at the bottom of the bowl, and was gone. When he looked in the mirror, his eyes were watery, and he wiped them with a greyish towel.

Shostakovich had been the only one to whom Nikolai had been able to tell the shameful truth, partly because of the way the composer sat in on rehearsals: implacable, impassive, seemingly emotionless. Even when hearing his music mangled, his face betrayed nothing. There he sat for twenty or thirty minutes, listening to Mravinsky wrestle with the Philharmonic: starting, stopping, reprimanding the bassoonist or chastising the flutes. And still he would sit in the fourth or fifth row, as silent and immobile as a wax cast, as if the torrent pouring from wide-open brass mouths, from bows and wrists, had nothing to do with him.

Occasionally, on days when his favourite football team had lost a match or he hadn't slept, he would break his customary silence. 'That solo must be pianissimo!' he would shout. 'Pianissimo, I said!' The contrast between the delivery of his request and what he actually wanted might have provoked a joke or two, if the combination of Mravinsky and Shostakovich hadn't been so formidable — and if the Great Hall of the Philharmonia hadn't had acoustics (it was said) that enabled a fart from the percussionist's backside to be heard by an eighty-year-old in the back stalls.

'It's not marked in the score.' Mravinsky, defending his orchestra, regarded Shostakovich steadily. 'See? No dynamic markings at all.' The greater Shostakovich's rage, the calmer Mravinsky remained. He was generally considered to be the only person in the world, with the exception of Shostakovich's wife, who was not afraid of the composer's sharp, though short-lived, tempers.

Shostakovich would stride to the podium and scribble on the score. 'It must have been omitted. To be true to the music, I should write *pppppp*. To be kind to your musicians, I will settle for *pp*. I'm sorry if it's difficult to play, but there's nothing I can do about it. High G, pianissimo, end of argument.'

Such detachment, combined with such certainty! It was as if the man was able to separate completely: from his own work, from his family, from life itself. His students, piqued and fascinated by this, had nicknamed him 'the man from Mars' — and it was this same quality that made Nikolai believe he could unburden himself to no other person but Shostakovich. For months he'd remained silent, not wanting to risk condemnation.

But one evening in May, thin, weak, with shaking hands, he'd met Shostakovich in the Summer Garden and they'd taken a walk. The long promenade was crowded, mostly with couples strolling quietly under the full canopy of the lime trees. Nikolai looked down as he talked, scuffing the toes of his blistered boots.

Shostakovich listened all the way to the end of his story before speaking. 'You're afraid of loving *too much*?'

Above them swallows darted and turned in mid-air. Nikolai ducked his head away from the shadows and sank down on the nearest bench. 'I was the one who wanted her to have the child. She was uncertain — she was always uncertain — but I begged her!' His words came out in a loud embarrassing cry, and he closed his eyes, remembering that evening. Sitting by the window, she appeared to him in silhouette. Her profile was etched against the bright light: the small rounded chin, the tilted nose, and eyelashes so indecently long they were the envy of every woman in Leningrad. 'Your career will always be waiting for you,' he'd reassured her. The truth was, at that moment he scarcely cared about her brilliant career. Her career wasn't going to provide him with a replica of that profile, that straight back, that soft but intense voice.

'That was all I wanted.' He wiped his eyes. 'I loved her so much, you see. I wanted to be sure that a part of her went on, even after we'd both departed. I didn't think of the danger.'

'She died of influenza,' said Shostakovich.

'Yes, but weakened by childbirth!' Nikolai could hardly breathe. 'Because of illness caused by childbirth, and depression after child-birth —'

'And now you're trying not to love the baby? I have to tell you, my friend, it seems slightly illogical to me.'

'Not illogical. Ironic, perhaps. If my love destroyed my wife, it's going to do the same to my daughter. I can't allow myself.' Nikolai put his head down on his knees. 'To tell the truth, I can't bring myself to look at her. I can't go near her.'

It was the worst admission he'd ever made, and it was true. When Tanya called to him to come quickly (Baby was smiling! Baby was pointing!), he pretended not to hear. He would bend stubbornly over the papers he was correcting, or turn up the radio to cover the murmuring in the next room. At night he paused beside the closed door, but the handle felt resistant to his touch. *Keep out*, it warned. *You are the carrier of danger and death*. Then he turned away from the quiet breathing within the dim room, calling to Tanya that he had to go back to work, he'd forgotten something; and then he would stride for hours along the canal, crossing every bridge he came to, back and forwards in a meaningless trickery of a route that seemed to offer escape but led nowhere, especially not away from himself. When he arrived once more at the apartment door, he was slick with guilt, as if he'd visited a whorehouse and sunk, finally, into depravity.

'I don't want to love her,' he said, looking at Shostakovich who was sitting upright beside him. His profile was as sharp and bold as if it had been hacked from the side of a mountain, and Nikolai waited numbly to hear himself condemned.

A few small boys ran across the avenue, kicking a ball, sand flying up behind their feet. Nikolai leaned back on the bench and felt the slats dig into his back. He was skin and bone, as Tanya was always telling him when she removed his untouched soup and bread.

At last Shostakovich spoke. 'You can't choose whether or not to love.'

'What?' Nikolai, lost in a spinning world of memory, had forgotten everything: where he was, what they were talking about. He stared at the leafy trees and the tall blowing grass, turned his face to the sun wheeling high in the pale-blue sky, tried to remember what season it was.

'It's impossible to choose, when it comes to love. I tried it once myself.' Shostakovich spoke decidedly, like a sixty-year-old man rather than one not yet thirty.

'You did?' Nikolai knew a little about Shostakovich's stormy past, but he wasn't sure if it was seemly to admit this.

Shostakovich sighed. 'As a teenager, I loved a girl called Tatyana Glivenko, and she loved me. Then she began loving me more than I loved her. She wanted to live with me, but I wouldn't let her, because by then I had met Nina Varzar. The die, to speak in gambler's terms, was cast.'

Nikolai stared. He hadn't expected the story to begin so far back, when Leningrad was still Petrograd and the fiery Nina wasn't even on the scene.

'Do you think I wanted that?' Shostakovich looked a little defiant. 'Do you think I *wanted* to fall out of love with Tatyana and in love with Nina Varzar?'

Nikolai scuffed his feet.

'Of course I didn't.' Shostakovich answered himself. 'Especially because I never intended to marry so young. There was still plenty of living to do, but how could I go on fishing when I was well and truly caught myself?'

Nikolai shrugged and opened his mouth, but Shostakovich held up his hand. 'I loved Nina. That was it. And then, as you may have heard —'

Nikolai gave a tactful, non-committal shake of his head.

'As you may have heard,' repeated Shostakovich, staring into the middle distance, 'I stopped loving Nina. For quite a time. Yelena Konstantinovskaya came on the scene. My God, she was something.' He whistled under his breath. 'Take my advice, Nikolai. Never get involved with a woman able to speak twelve languages, and each one of them with the tongue of an angel. When you're in bed with her, it will drive you wild, and when you're in an argument, it drives you crazy.'

Nikolai remembered that summer well: he'd just taken up his own appointment at the Conservatoire, and his new intimacy with the city's musical circles meant he was more than usually aware of what was going on around him. Everyone had known of the affair, but no one mentioned it, for Nina Varzar was well liked. Yelena would glide up the stairs of the Maryinsky Theatre, her hair piled high, exposing the white nape of her neck that invited kissing — or biting. People whispered in the foyer below, and Shostakovich waited at the top of the stairs, pale-faced, expressionless. Only the way in which he took Yelena's elbow, so their hips brushed against each other, suggested the intimacy between them.

'After that particular storm,' continued Shostakovich, as if relating an epic tale passed down through generations, 'there was once more a port of calm. Miraculously, I fell in love with Nina again; fortunately, she agreed to have me back. For a second time our love blossomed, and so it was on with the show!'

Dizzying circles of midges swam on the evening air, but Nikolai sat motionless. He hadn't expected such confessions — nor had he expected to feel so much lighter inside.

'My point is this.' Shostakovich returned to the present. 'You love, or you don't love. You can't order the weight of that love, as you can a packet of tea. Nor can you decide on its temperature: hot, cold, mild, indifferent. If you love your child — and I'm almost certain you do — you simply have to give in to it. And be glad that you're capable of loving.' His voice faltered a little, making Nikolai glance at him. 'Of course I love Nina.' Shostakovich sounded almost indignant. 'But not, perhaps, to the extent that most women would wish. You, on the other hand, were the ideal husband, and will very likely be the ideal father.'

After that evening, the white flickering had gradually cleared from

Nikolai's vision. By the end of the summer, he was able to look at his daughter quite steadily, could pick her up and kiss her, and soon even Tanya was convinced that it was safe to give up temporary guardianship of her dead sister's child and visit — as previously arranged — on a daily basis only, to cook and clean. 'About time,' she said, trundling around the apartment, packing her meagre possessions. 'I was wondering how long you were going to stay in that mood.'

Yet Nikolai's 'mood' had never entirely left him. At times, such as this morning with Sonya's arms around his neck, his fear of love was nearly enough to overwhelm the love itself. It felt like an impairment that he would struggle with for the rest of his life — not crippling but exhaustingly constant.

'Come on!' Sonya danced ahead, occasionally turning to admonish him. 'Slow old Papa!'

'I'm out of condition. Sitting around all day teaching lazy students to scribble sonatas isn't the best exercise.'

'Perhaps if I run backwards you can keep up,' offered Sonya.

'Perhaps if I hop —' Nikolai raised his left foot off the ground — 'you'll realise that I'm wearing my seven-league boots. All the better to catch you with!' Hopping, watching Sonya running backwards, he crashed into a lamp-post. 'Care to dance?' he said to the metal pole, making Sonya giggle.

'Thank you! I'd love to.'

Nikolai unwound himself from the lamp-post, and saw a slim dark figure beside him. 'Oh! Nina Bronnikova! Good day!' He'd been half-hoping to see her, knew she lived somewhere in this block — but this was certainly not the ideal way of meeting. He tried not to blush. 'Of course I'd rather dance with you than a lamp-post, though I fear you're used to more athletic partners.'

'Not at all,' replied Nina Bronnikova, smoothing back her dark hair. 'You'd be surprised at the clumsy oafs admitted into the Kirov these days.'

'You're in the Kirov?' Sonya stared at the woman's narrow shoulders, and her muscular legs clad in black stockings. 'Oh, I've always, *always*, wanted to be a ballerina! But Papa says dancers are stupid and I'd be better off being a musician.'

Once again, Nikolai felt close to blushing. 'I wasn't referring to anyone specific,' he mumbled. 'Certainly not you.'

A slight smile crossed Nina Bronnikova's face. 'Your papa is probably right,' she said to Sonya. 'On some days, even I consider dancing to be a stupid profession.' And with that she walked away, feet turned slightly outwards, elbows tucked into her slim waist.

Sonya stared at her longingly. 'She's wonderful. Is her name Nina too? Like Mrs Shostakovich?'

'That's right.' Nikolai's forehead was throbbing where it had connected with the lamp-post. 'But she's not at all like Mrs Shostakovich. Quite the opposite.' He'd never seen Shostakovich's wife in one of her legendary rages, but he had no problem imagining it, whereas Nina Bronnikova seemed as cool as water.

'I've never met a real ballerina, I've just seen them from afar. They look much bigger up close.' Sonya peered at Nikolai. 'Are you all right? Your face is red.'

'I expect it's the sun. I've been indoors such a lot this spring, my skin's not used to it.'

'You need to get out more,' agreed Sonya. 'Shouldn't we go to the country this summer? Galina Shostakovich said they might be renting a dacha near Luga. It's only a few hours by train. She said we should go as well, because when visitors are around Mr and Mrs Shostakovich don't argue so much. She said —'

'Sonya,' interrupted Nikolai. 'You shouldn't repeat everything other people say. It can be very embarrassing.'

'But they're not even here! I wouldn't say it to their faces. Give me some credit, *por favor*!'

This last phrase was a favourite of Sollertinsky's; Nikolai could hear the rich satirical tone behind Sonya's bird-like voice. 'Let's get ice cream,' he suggested, heading for a kiosk.

By the time they reached the People's House, the midday sun had rolled high above their heads and the stone buildings were bleached against the backdrop of blue sky. Excited screams came from the direction of the roller-coaster. Nikolai wished he hadn't eaten most of Sonya's strawberry ice cream; his stomach rolled in anticipation.

'Two tickets, please.' Sonya stood as tall as possible in front of the booth, and counted out her birthday money saved for the occasion. 'You're sure you want to do this?' she asked Nikolai, chewing on the end of her long dark braid.

'I'm sure,' said Nikolai, taking a deep, surreptitious breath.

Once they were strapped into the carriage, he focused on thinking about household finances: the most boring subject he could come up with, and the only possible way to ward off terror. The man working the switch shouted, while Nikolai shut his eyes and started adding. Thirty extra roubles to Tanya this month, for looking after Sonya while he waded through appalling student orchestrations of Mussorgsky —

The carriage lurched, and his eyes flew open. They were nearly at the top of the first loop, and he saw the track thrown carelessly in front of them, like coins from the hand of a drunken gambler. *Coins*, he thought desperately, shutting his eyes again. *Kopeks, roubles.* Thirty roubles for Tanya. A hundred roubles for Sonya's new winter clothes —

'Why are your eyes closed?' Sonya's voice pushed through the chinks of his counting.

He opened one eye and looked sideways at her. 'Just working out some bills in my head.' It was almost the truth.

'Papa!' Her voice rose. 'This is meant to be a treat!' The car was at a temporary standstill at the top of the loop; wind whistled in Nikolai's ears, voices floated up from the ground, and screams came from those swooping in front of them. Was this like the moment of complete clarity before facing an execution squad?

Suddenly, they were flying, screaming, shrieking into nothingness. Sonya's braid flew behind them, Nikolai's eyes streamed with tears. As they churned over the bottom of the loop and back on an uphill gradient again, he felt relieved that at least he hadn't been able to see clearly what was happening.

Sonya's hand crept into his. 'That was fun, wasn't it? Are you ready for another one?'

'Of course!' Nikolai wiped his palms on his trousers and gave a forced smile.

After more ice cream, courtesy of Sonya's birthday fund, and then some fried cutlets — 'in the wrong order, but who cares,' said Nikolai — they left the crowded Nevsky Prospect and wandered home along the narrow back streets. Windows stood open to the heat, and ragged tomcats lay at a distance from each other, too hot to bother with hissing or hostility.

'Phew,' said Sonya, when they reached their own front steps. 'That was quite a day.'

'Thank you for taking me out.' Nikolai opened the front door and felt the cool breath of the hallway on his face.

'You're welcome,' said Sonya formally.

Aunt Tanya had already finished the day's chores and gone home, but the cello was waiting for them, leaning against the sofa as if it, too, had succumbed to the heat.

'I haven't done my practice today.' Sonya sounded guilty.

'Consider it a rest day,' said Nikolai. 'Even professional musicians take days off.'

'Did Mama?' Sonya picked up the cello, and the C string gave a low gentle *boing*.

'Even Mama! Although not many, I have to admit.' He remembered there had been times when he'd forcibly unwrapped her hand from the bow, and days when she'd played so long it took hours for the dents in her fingers to disappear.

'I'll check that she approves.' Sonya disappeared into her room with the cello.

Nikolai lay on the sofa and stared at the broken edge in the moulded ceiling. He could hear Sonya murmuring away as she usually did in the evenings, telling her mother what they'd done that day. A tiny tear squeezed out the corner of his eye, running lightly down the side of his face and into the green cushion.

The price
of furniture

Eliasberg had always listened at doors. He understood why the State functioned like this; it was the only way to find out the truth. The problem was, he didn't rate the intelligence of Stalin's information-gatherers at all highly. This was where the system fell down.

Listening in to others had become a habit. He couldn't remember a time when he hadn't been standing in a hallway, leaning towards a wooden panel as if it were about to sing small confidences to him. By listening at doors or below windows (a necessary subterfuge, which he'd never considered as eavesdropping), he'd heard many useful things. Things that had lodged in his skin like burrs, inflaming him, driving him to succeed — and turning him into the professional man he now was.

'Why must Karl Elias always creep around in stockinged feet?' His father, seeing his eleven-year-old son soundlessly passing the kitchen door, had flung down his wrench. 'If there's one thing I'm good for, it should be putting shoes on the feet of my family.'

'The cobbler's children,' ventured Elias, 'always run barefoot.' He'd heard a teacher say this about ginger-headed Boris, son of the famous botanist Boris Berlovich whose sharp eyes had discovered a rare form of ground moss on the day of Svetlana Stalin's birthday (her name had been bestowed upon it). 'Talk about the cobbler's children!' the teacher had exclaimed, watching Boris the Younger scrabbling blindly about in the undergrowth, searching for a bright white ball not two feet away from him, while the rest of the class watched in impatient silence. Naturally, Elias had remembered this, for out of the twenty contemptuous children he was the only one to whom this saying was applicable, and he was puzzled as to why the teacher had aimed it at short-sighted Boris.

His father looked still more aggrieved. 'Cobbler? Why does Karl Elias use such a word in this house? Has he not noticed the sign hanging outside his own home? Makers —' He began hammering at the leaky pipe, punctuating his words with bangs. '— Of. Fine. FOOTWEAR!' At the last blow, the pipe flew apart like a worm chopped in two by a shovel. Even this disaster didn't throw Mr Eliasberg off course. Once started on the topic of his profession, he was unstoppable. 'If Karl Elias is to take over the family business, he must learn that there's a world of difference between a man who mends and a man who *makes*. Cobbler, my arse. I am an artisan!'

'Please! Mind your language!' Elias's mother entered the room, and the fray. It was rare for her to criticise her husband, but she felt strongly about bad language.

Elias shuffled his socked feet. Somewhere outside there was sun to be found, and the quietness of a Saturday afternoon, and an empty alley in which to kick a can. But his mother had caught sight of the ruined plumbing. 'Heavenly stars!' she exclaimed, turning to Elias. 'Run upstairs and get Vladimir the Carpenter. He knows a thing or two about pipes.'

'We don't need no Vladimir,' protested his father.

'*Any* Vladimir,' corrected his mother. 'Karl Elias, go!'

'Do as your mother says.' His father looked both grumpy and relieved. 'What do I know? I'm only a cobbler.'

Mr Eliasberg's self-pity had seeped into everyday life like strong bitter tea, and it was even stronger on the days when letters arrived from Uncle Georgii. George was the lucky one, the brave one, the one who'd sailed for the United States in time to escape violence, upheaval and poverty under the guise of opportunity for all. Occasionally Elias retrieved one of Uncle George's letters from the bin, where it lay buried under potato peelings and tealeaves. 'Exciting experiments . . . in the field of . . .' He deciphered the blurred violet words with difficulty. 'Working with an eminent scientist . . . by the name of —' But the flimsy paper disintegrated in his hand.

On these black-letter days, his father would disappear, like Mephistopheles, through a trapdoor in the kitchen floor and into the bowels of the building, where he laboured on fine boots for the city's most beautiful ladies. Moody tappings shook the foundations of daily existence, making Elias's desk shudder and his neat sums wobble. Concentrating, he held his tongue between his teeth so that when his father suddenly shouted he jumped and tasted his own blood.

'Why will Karl Elias not come and help his poor father?' Most of Mr Eliasberg's questions started with 'Why' and revolved around his son. Why was Karl Elias so silent? Why did he spend so much time at the library?

Elias had his own question that he phrased equally repetitively, but silently, for fear of receiving a lashing. 'Why,' he shouted inside his own defiant head, 'do you always address me in the third person?' At times his voice rang so loudly inside his skull that his ears could hear nothing except his own protest.

It was strange but true. Every time his father used his name in this unthinking way, a small part of Elias was slivered away. By the time he was eleven, he felt almost invisible. When he was twelve, he learnt, by listening through his bedroom door, that he might indeed be a spectre sooner rather than later. For the doctor told his weeping mother that her son couldn't be expected to live past fourteen years of age. Tuberculosis would carry him off.

After the doctor left the house, Mrs Eliasberg sank to the floor outside the bedroom door. Elias knew this, for by now he was adept at interpreting what, in theatrical circles, were called 'noises off'. First the rustle of skirts. Then the creaking of floorboards on the landing. And, finally, a puff of air from crushed lungs. As he stood barely two feet away from his mother, separated from her grief by a panelled wooden door, he felt curiously optimistic — more alive, in fact, than he had for a long time. Was it true his demise might actually leave a small dent in someone else's heart?

But it was by checking in at the living-room door later that evening that he received the really useful piece of information, the one that kept him alive, sending defiant blood between his heart and his brain, shrinking the swelling on his neck. For his parents were discussing what they might sell to raise the money to send him to a sanatorium where his blood would be cleansed and his life saved.

'It must be a substantial sum,' stressed his tearful mother. Once again her skirts rustled, but this time, obviously, she was swivelling to assess the items of furniture in the room. 'What about the bookshelf?

'The only piece of good furniture my parents left me?' queried Mr Eliasberg. 'The only good piece they ever owned?' The familiar contempt weighed down his voice. Having sprung from the loins of men who'd all worked in shoeing — first equine, then human — he'd never forgiven any of them. Grandfather, father, uncles, cousins, all were blamed for apprenticing him to a craft which they saw as honourable and he saw as a stigma. 'No,' he said. 'The bookshelf stays.' Elias heard him lean on it with a possessive elbow (squeak of cloth on polished oak) and then kick it (crack of leather on wood).

'What about the table? And all four chairs?' Already Mrs Eliasberg sounded defeated by the potential cost of saving her only son.

'Where do you propose we eat? In the gutter?'

A pause. On his side of the door, Elias wiped a film of sweat from his forehead and shifted from one weak leg to the other.

'How about the best china?' His father sounded a little brighter.

Now it was Karl's mother who demurred. The tea set was dear to her heart, the only possession in which she could take pride when entertaining. For some minutes Elias listened to his parents tipping the scales back and forth: the value of his health against various household items. His feet burned with cold, and his face burned with an emotion impossible to define. As he dragged his way back to bed, he felt a new strength in his limbs, and he clenched his hands under the chilly sheet.

'I will live!' he declared, spitting over the side of the bed into a basin, staring at the bubbling mix of blood and saliva. Then, propped up against his lumpy pillow, he wrote a list headed 'Karl Illyich Eliasberg's Ten Commandments'. They included:

> *Surviving, to prove them all wrong*
> *Not becoming a Shoemaker or any other kind of tradesman*
> *Never valuing Material Possessions over Art or Life*

During the following months Elias recovered, thus achieving the first of his commandments. 'Inexplicable,' exclaimed the doctor. 'A miracle.' He sounded almost annoyed: predicting bad news and then being robbed of the outcome can leave one feeling faintly ridiculous.

Though never strong, Elias proceeded to grow steadily upwards and increasingly inwards. He refused point blank to learn the shoe trade (thereby achieving his second commandment). To kneel in the dust of life, dealing with objects that came in contact with the base earth — this was not for him! He considered becoming a pilot — 'A pilot?' queried his mother in alarm — and a general, until he realised he disapproved

51

of organised killing, whatever the cause.

And then one Sunday, after performing a solo in a youth-choir concert, he was approached by a distinguished grey-haired man. Did Karl Eliasberg play an instrument, asked the man, as well as sing? Yes, Elias did; the neighbour across the landing owned a piano and she'd taught him for many years.

'Would you mind playing something?' asked the grey-haired man, with just the right mix of authority and diffidence.

The dilapidated church echoed like a cave as Elias walked, with booming uncertain steps, to the piano. He started with a Bach prelude, which was all he could remember under duress. The notes fell starkly and too loudly into all that empty space. They seemed like stones hurled off a cliff, some flying in arcs, others aimed more deftly — but as they piled up together they achieved their own amassed validity. He started his favourite Beethoven sonata with more confidence. *Boom, boom-be-boom!* The low bass notes spread out impressively, while his right hand lifted the melody higher and higher towards the roof.

When the final repeated chords had dissolved, the grey-haired man applauded. It was a reaction that seemed incongruous in a church, even a disused one, but Elias flushed with pleasure. He couldn't remember the last time someone had listened to him so attentively, nor the last time he'd been praised. After the grey-haired man had asked several questions — where did Elias live, what was his age, how was his father's financial situation? — he asked the most significant question of all. Was Karl interested in trying for a scholarship for the Conservatoire?

Elias was taken aback, but as his father had developed pneumonia and was unable to work, and his mother had begun serving pancakes consisting mainly of coffee grounds — 'Yes!' he said. 'I'd be most interested.' At the very least, a scholarship would entitle him to extra grocery rations. At best, it would set him free.

An almost inescapable legacy

During his first two terms at the Conservatoire, Elias noticed his father's cheeks becoming hollow and heard the breath rattling in his lungs. Instead of pity, he felt hatred. His contempt for his dying father grew with every new technique he learned and with every conversation he had with fellow students.

His father had taught him nothing, prepared him for nothing. He hadn't shown Elias how to act around artists, nor coached him in the art of conversation. He'd sung neither hymns nor gypsy tunes, lullabies nor operas. He'd never even *been* to the opera. He hadn't owned a decent suit, had never knotted a casual scarf around the throat like Professor Steinberg, nor worn an expensive jacket so carelessly that it ended up a nonchalant second skin.

Even Eliasberg's highly honed skills of observation were not enough to save him. When he wore a long fur coat to the end-of-term recital — as he'd heard the famous Professor Glazunov had, when performing for Artur Schnabel and other esteemed visitors from the West — laughter started up at the back of the auditorium. It didn't stop until he'd finished all three of his chosen Etudes, an interminable journey, at the end of which no recognisable vestige of Chopin remained.

Stumbling from the stage, he locked himself in one of the rehearsal rooms on the first floor. When the coast was clear, he crept back down to the empty auditorium and lay down in the wings behind the curtains, which smelt of mothballs, pressing his hot face against the cold floor.

After some time he heard footsteps on the stage.

'Extraordinary decision to wear that coat.' It was Professor Steinberg. 'Shoulders, arms, spine, all restricted. Whatever possessed him?'

'Pretensions, I suppose.' Professor Ferkelman pushed in the piano stool with a screech. 'He's completely out of his depth.'

'Socially, you mean?' Steinberg's voice grew more distant. 'His work's certainly up to scratch.'

'His own worst enemy.' Ferkelman's voice, too, was further away. 'Tries too hard to fit in . . . stands apart.'

When Elias finally reached home, he found his father sleeping. He stood over the bed, looking down at the diminished figure that had once — strange to remember! — represented authority. The body jutted through the threadbare sheet: haunches like a withered fox, a sharp march of ribs, one wasted arm lying across a rasping chest.

'You've given me nothing but disadvantage,' he said in a low voice. 'You've taught me only what I don't want to become. You have bestowed on me all the disadvantages of a narrow-minded, straight-laced upbringing. A life of endless scales and five-finger exercises, with no higher goal.'

He put his face close to his father's, staring at the sunken cheeks and the stubble pushing through the yellow skin. The camphor fumes and the stuffy darkness made him as breathless as his dying father. 'You pretended to be creative, but you were nothing but a craftsman,' he said, backing away from the bed. 'You were born and will die a bootmaker.'

That night he lay awake for a long time, hearing tomcats shrieking in the alleys and the monotonous trolley cars rattling by. Where did he belong? Not here in this family with its wafer-thin layer of culture, nor in the corridors of the Conservatoire, among those who referred to Mussorgsky as casually as the latest football scores and somehow knew the right time to discuss each.

Where do I fit in? He tossed and turned on the mattress. Being neither educated nor ignorant, he had ended up in no-man's land, where rules couldn't help him nor background support him. 'I am an outsider,' he whispered. 'I am outside.'

The sharp embarrassment of the afternoon, the guilt at not doing justice to Chopin, the needling pain of the professors' comments: these seeped out of him like black ink and disappeared into the darkness. Nothing could comfort him, apart from the chilly austere knowledge that he was *other*, and therefore less likely to be tainted or influenced.

Not until he saw the first dirty streaks of dawn over the railway station did he know what to do. 'The dilettantes were right to fear,' he said slowly. What he intended to achieve could not be bought by the wealthy or pulled down by philistines; it existed above social status and scorn. It was the only untouchable thing — and the only way to become untouchable.

When he emerged, bleary-eyed, from his room, his mother was in the hallway, her eyes and nose streaming. His father had died. Karl Elias was the new head of the family.

He stood there impassively, feeling her body shake against his. Should he announce his new-found resolve? It seemed neither the time nor place. But as he stared over his mother's head, he saw a clear-cut future before him.

The road to professionalism wasn't easy. He attended classes on days when the air inside the Conservatoire felt too cold to breathe, or when Professor Steinberg turned up an hour late and all the other students had left, grumbling. Stubbornly, he sat on, playing two hands of a four-handed transcription to keep himself warm. Occasionally he was joined by Dmitri Shostakovich, who took the melodic part as a matter of course, playing fast, loudly and with flair. Rather than looking at the sheet music, he seemed to look past it, into a cavernous place behind the written notes that Elias could only guess at.

'A professional?' repeated Shostakovich, on one of the rare occasions when they exchanged more than a basic greeting. 'Of course! I've been a professional since I began playing. Since the age of nine.' He buttoned his thin coat around his thin torso and marched away to the library. Elias watched him go with an odd feeling in his stomach: an envy so strong it almost amounted to anger.

When Elias was knocked from his bicycle, cracking three vertebrae and suffering nerve damage to the third and fourth fingers of his left hand, his mother wept for days. His brilliant career as an instrumentalist was over! He was washed up before he had begun! Elias had no time to lament; he was too preoccupied with recovering, and then he was too busy reassessing his career. After lying on his back for three and a half weeks, he limped into Professor Ferkelman's office, and emerged an hour later with a new major.

Some would consider it making the best of a bad situation but, looking back, Elias saw it as a turning point. Standing on the podium was like facing the world alone, which was, after all, what he was used to. Years later, stepping in front of the Leningrad Radio Orchestra for his first rehearsal, he wished with equal measures of scorn and regret that his father could see him. The grinding years of hardship, apprenticeship and the utmost loneliness had paid off. He was a real conductor, with his own musicians. The orchestra stretched before him, a sea of restless movements and indistinct noise. When he tapped the side of his music stand with his brand new baton, he felt as if the small noise might shatter his body.

Night watch

Unsettled by the news of the German evacuation, exhausted from teaching, Shostakovich was unable to sleep. He twisted over and over in his bed until he was wound tightly in the sheet like an Egyptian mummy.

The treachery of the body! On nights like these he wanted Nina, her long toes twined in his and her cool rounded stomach against his back. He bitterly resented her — for not being there, and for making him need her.

The clock on the mantelpiece struck two. Two and a half minutes later came the tinny chime from the church on Kovenskiy Pereulok, and one minute later a more commanding clang from Kazan Cathedral. He threw the pillow off his head and onto the floor. Why in God's name was it impossible for Russians to fix anything? For three years, since the night of Maxim's birth when he'd first noticed it, these clocks had been predictably out of time.

'I'm bored.' He spoke to the whispering dust on the floorboards, to the creaking springs of the wedding bed given to him by his mother (an attempt to prove she didn't mind her son marrying a most unsuitable girl). 'Bored, so bored, at our petty and predictable human ways.'

Somewhere in the house a door slammed. He stiffened and watched the branches tap at the window. Who could be up and about at this time, except composers and drunkards? He knew he was watched — for all he knew, Stalin's men were watching right now, crouched in one of the buildings opposite. For some years he'd kept a bag in a cupboard on the landing: two clean undershirts, a toothbrush and razor, pencils and score paper. 'I won't let them have the satisfaction of a public removal,' he vowed to Nina. 'I won't have my children remembering their father being forcibly taken from his home.'

The knife-edge danger of being public property, the possibility of falling from grace at any time — these were constant fears. The stifling irritation of daily existence was another problem altogether.

'There's nothing new under the sun,' he'd complained recently to Nina.

'You're always saying you need a monotonous existence to work properly.' Annoyingly, Nina had the abilities of a court lawyer, reproducing his most sweeping pronouncements as evidence against him.

He shrugged away his own words. 'It's not healthy, being able to predict what will happen.'

'What will happen?' she asked, mocking him slightly.

'I will crank out another movement of a piano quartet, my students will surprise me with their stupidity. Maxim will learn a few more words, Galina will learn another way of tricking her grandmother at cards. Hitler will continue his march. Churchill will continue to be exasperated by Roosevelt. Stalin will stick his head more deeply in the sand.'

But in the past few days the heaviness had become altogether more than this. On the surface, life proceeded at its usual pace, but Shostakovich felt as if some menace lay clenched under the city, ready to uncoil and spring.

Was that a rat scrabbling in the wall beside the bed? He thought he felt something run across his face — rasping claws, a dragging leathery slither, a foul breath mixing with his — and he shivered. His insomnia was like a plague; already the fever was starting in his joints. He dipped his finger in a glass of water and smoothed the moisture over his hot eyelids. 'Sleep now,' he said, as if he were talking to Maxim.

But his mind was stretched as tightly as rope. Out of nowhere came Herr Lehmann, the German diplomat who had fled the city, marching with his family along a wide road. Legs bent in perfect unison, swinging out and back, joined by a single note — was it a repeated C? — which moved their limbs like strings on puppets. Their feet pointed straight ahead, never deviating from the black-ink markings on the road. (Five parallel markings: now it was recognisable as a musical stave.) The Lehmanns moved unerringly forward, turning only their heads as they peered from side to side, searching for their home country.

A pattern started up in his head, rising and falling in regular peaks. 'C to G,' he muttered. 'C to G.' Trapped in an endlessly repeated progression, he could neither struggle awake nor escape, and he was filled with dread. 'Steady,' he mumbled. 'Focus on what you know.' But the white moulded ceiling, the mantelpiece clock, the glass of water: all had vanished. Thudding boots shook the bed, and he saw the machine-like movement of a hundred bodies, flashing teeth, the sun glancing off the curve of an eagle's beak. Through the din emerged Sollertinsky's mocking voice. 'Don't you understand? The Germans are evacuating.'

Helplessly, Shostakovich watched the lines of people marching away. When one of the women turned, he thought he knew her. 'Nina?' But as she began striding back towards him, her face blurred and coarsened. 'You remember me,' she hissed. 'They call me Lady Macbeth of Mtsensk.' And she leapt at him, and her hands were around his throat, and he choked and screamed — and woke.

Sweat lay thickly on his body, the sheet was wet through. He pulled on his trousers and coat, and shuffled towards the piano. At last the room was silent, and the strange low light of the night sun showed nothing but empty corners. He bent over the piano, resting his forehead on the wood, then laid his hands on the keys.

The repeated nightmare pattern was still there, absorbed in his fingers. He picked it out with his left hand and grasped a pencil with his right. Seizing a new sheet of paper, he licked the tip of the pencil and began to write. Halting yet unerring — it was like following a sunken road, covered for centuries by soil and grass, that was slowly revealing itself.

God, he was tired. Damn Sollertinsky and his unsettling news. Damn Nina for being neither goddess nor whore nor mother figure, but some mixture of the three, making him worship her, lust for her and need her. Damn the tyrannical, homely, grounding ties of family. And above all damn himself and all his neurotic, unavoidable tricks that had to be fought through before he could begin composing. More than anything he wanted to sleep, but the marching notes were clustering in his veins.

Only when a dog barked — three, four, five times — did he look up. The light filtering through the trees was bright gold. The bed was a tangled mess of sheets and pillows washed up against the wall. Morning was here. Throwing off his coat, he crashed across the mattress and fell into sleep.

In Sollertinsky's office

L ate afternoon, and the dust motes were swirling in the sunlight. Sollertinsky's meeting with an attractive student was about to end — though not as pleasantly as he would have liked.

'I'm afraid,' he said reluctantly, 'that I really cannot alter your grade.' He watched as Lydia's huge eyes began to brim with tears. 'Of course, had I the power to make such a decision single-handedly, I would be delighted to do so.' This was true: Lydia's presence in class was a joy. She sat in the front row, looking at him as if his lectures were enthralling; her sweaters were so tight it was difficult to imagine how she wrestled them on each morning. 'Delighted,' he repeated, tearing his gaze away from her breasts, which were rising and falling in delectable distress.

'So,' gulped Lydia, 'I am stuck with a — with a —' She seemed unable to voice the grade scribbled on her paper, and she bowed her head so that Sollertinsky could see the nape of her neck tapering into the depths of her astounding jumper.

'Remember, there's always next term! If you spend the summer studying, that might make all the difference.' Although he tried to sound encouraging, he doubted whether she would be allowed back to the Conservatoire. For someone so pretty, she was remarkably untalented.

'Forgive me.' She raised a streaky, doe-like face. 'I shouldn't cry in front of a lecturer, especially such an important one as you.'

'Oh come,' said Sollertinsky. 'I've seen plenty of students cry in my time. There's nothing wrong with tears.'

'You're very kind.' Lydia's voice was as trembling and luminous as the dust dancing in the air behind her. 'I'm afraid I must look a mess.'

'Not at all. Many women are at their most beautiful after crying. Their faces have a newly washed look, a kind of purity.'

For the past ten minutes, he had been thinking longingly of the brandy stowed behind his leather-bound copies of Beethoven's orchestral works. Now, as Lydia gave a small but radiant smile, he was no longer sure if he wanted her to leave. There was a short, anticipatory silence, during which he became uncomfortably aware of his second wife's scrutiny from the photo frame on his desk.

He cleared his throat self-consciously. 'Will that be all?' He sounded like a grocer wrapping up spring greens for a favoured customer. 'Anything else I can help you with?' Not, of course, that he had helped her at all — nor, on this fine Monday afternoon, had his concentration been aided by her tearful face and delicious body. He walked to the window, casually turning his wife's photograph away so her steely gaze was trained on the *Dictionary of Musicology* rather than himself.

'Nothing else,' said Lydia, showing little sign of vacating her chair.

Sollertinsky kept his back turned. Below him students were spilling out onto the Conservatoire steps. In the street, mothers and children walked hand in hand; a tram clattered past, swaying on its domino-tracks. The light was so bright that, when he turned back to Lydia, for a second he could see nothing at all.

'I hear that you're good friends with Mr Shostakovich.' Lydia's voice filtered into his dazzled vision. 'And that there will be a performance of his Sixth Symphony in a fortnight?' She stopped, her desire for a ticket — and perhaps something more — hanging in the air.

'I'll see what I can do.' But he spoke automatically. He'd just noticed a line of smoke creeping under his door, rising in a spiral against the panelled walls like a snake lured by a charmer's flute. 'I meant to say,' he corrected himself, 'although I'd like to offer you one of my tickets, it isn't de rigueur, considering my position at the school, and your —' Just in time, he stopped himself from saying *considerable allure*.

The strong tar-smoke was familiar. Reluctantly, he held out a hand to Lydia. 'Allow me to see you out.'

As she paused beside him, she pushed her shiny hair behind one ear, and he caught the tempting scent of rosewater and skin. Nonetheless, he opened the door, and Lydia stepped out onto the landing, keeping her eyes fixed on his face so that she failed to see the figure sitting at the top of the stairs. 'Oh!' she cried, almost falling.

'Careful now!' The man grabbed her shapely ankle with one hand, while plumes of smoke poured from his loosely rolled cigarette. Lydia coughed. 'Excuse me!' she said, sounding genuinely flustered. 'I didn't know it was you. That is, I didn't see you!' With a flurry of hair and heels, she departed rapidly, less *femme fatale* than embarrassed teenager.

Sollertinsky watched her disappear down the curved stairwell before he spoke. 'Dmitri Shostakovich,' he said, holding out both hands. 'You may not be as comely as my last visitor but you're welcome all the same.'

Grasping the stair rail, Shostakovich pulled himself to his feet and picked up his books. 'It's about time you finished your *tête à tête*. Did you want your old friend to die of chain smoking?' A pile of grainy butts lay in a bottle top on the floor.

'You smell like a bonfire,' said Sollertinsky. 'Care to come in for a spot of Beethoven?'

'Absolutely!' Shostakovich followed him back into the office. 'Did you fail that girl?'

'I had no choice. Fortunately for her, her looks will compensate for her astounding lack of brains. Once she gives up this musical nonsense, she'll find a husband who — the lucky sod — will keep her in clover for the rest of her life. But now, on to more important matters.' He reached behind Beethoven's Second Symphony and extracted the brandy bottle. 'To whom shall we toast? Pretty girls with large — ahem — I mean, pretty girls with little brain?'

Shostakovich swirled the brown liquid in his glass.

'You prefer to drink to something worthier?' queried Sollertinsky.

'Yes. To sleep!' Shostakovich swallowed the brandy in one gulp and held out his glass for more.

Sollertinsky tilted the bottle with careless finesse. 'What *have* you been doing to yourself, my friend? I thought the Romances on Verses were wed and put to bed?'

'Nowhere near.' Shostakovich's eyes were red-rimmed. 'They went cold on me. Now I'm onto something else altogether.' He lay back in his chair. 'A kind of march, I think.'

Sollertinsky groaned. 'Not a march. Well, I have to support you, whatever nonsense you're up to. But whatever will Mravinsky say?'

'I don't care what Mravinsky says.' Shostakovich looked mutinous. 'Let him stick his baton where the sun doesn't shine. Anyway, I might not let him near it — whatever *it* is, whenever *it* is finished.'

His words held no truth: everyone knew that Yevgeny Mravinsky, at the helm of the Leningrad Philharmonic Orchestra, was the only conductor Shostakovich trusted, and it had been this way for the past three years, ever since their roaring battles over the Fifth Symphony, when Shostakovich had sat stony-faced in the fourth row, refusing to offer suggestions, and Mravinsky sat at the piano, thumping out every melody at the wrong speed until he'd finally provoked Shostakovich into action. By the fifth rehearsal, metronome markings had been written into the score and a firm friendship had developed, cemented by Mravinsky's being awarded the All-Union Competition for Conductors with Shostakovich's symphony.

'Anyway,' added Shostakovich, in a kind of protestation, 'there was a march in the Fifth! At least, the hint of a march. And I haven't done one since.'

'So you're entitled to a march. Whatever lights your fire. But I fear for your domestic harmony. I don't expect your mood will be improved by working on a march.'

Shostakovich swigged another mouthful of brandy. 'I don't know what's wrong with me. Some kind of foreboding.' He looked sombrely into his glass. 'What will we do if the rumours are true and the Germans are planning to double-cross us?'

Sollertinsky walked back to the window. 'I don't know. At any rate, we'll be told what to do — or it will be "suggested" to us. Since when did we have what's commonly called a choice?'

Shostakovich joined him at the windowsill, gazing out at the crowded pavements, the bustling women with their baskets, the buildings throwing long shadows across the streets. 'What will be, will be. But I promise you, I won't leave Leningrad willingly.' Sighing, he suddenly became practical. 'I promised Nina I'd be home before Maxim's bedtime. What's the time?'

'Twenty-five past six,' said Sollertinsky, without looking at his watch.

'Damn! Are you sure?'

'I'd bet my monthly salary on it.' Sollertinsky pointed to a figure rushing across the square. 'Karl Eliasberg. He always hurries but he's never late. As regular as a Swiss metronome and twice as reliable. Do you know, I bumped into him last week and he dropped a score of Mahler! Rather incongruous for an old stick insect like Elias — but apparently he has a passion for the music.'

'What?' Shostakovich was picking up his books, and dropping them again, and knocking papers off Sollertinsky's desk, and finishing his third brandy.

63

'*Mahler*,' repeated Sollertinsky. 'Elias must know there's no hope of performing that German music — not now, possibly never again. Still, he seems almost as obsessed with it as you are.'

'I can't think about Mahler right now, nor Karl What's-his-name-Berg. I absolutely must get home.'

'Calm down! I'll see you out!' Sollertinsky placed the nearly empty brandy bottle back in its hiding place. 'Cheers, Ludwig. Don't drink it all in our absence.'

As they were leaving the office, they heard a door slam and quick footsteps on the landing above. Shostakovich peered up the stairwell. 'Hello there! Many thanks for the other night!'

'You're welcome! It would have been less of a party without you.' It was Nikolai.

'Party? What party?' queried Sollertinsky. 'Could there possibly have been a party in Leningrad to which I was not invited?'

'Sollertinsky missed a delectable performance, did he not?' Shostakovich started down the stairs beside Nikolai. 'A beautiful young cellist. Played like an angel.'

'Who?' Sollertinsky pricked up his ears like a hunting dog. 'Does the angel attend the Conservatoire?'

'She's a little too young for that,' said Nikolai.

'And a little too young for *you*, Sollertinsky,' said Shostakovich.

'It's my daughter.' Nikolai relented. 'The occasion for the party was her ninth birthday.'

'You spoil all the fun, Nikolai,' said Shostakovich, striding ahead across the marble foyer. 'Here was Sollertinsky, anticipating a new quarry.'

'Please.' Sollertinsky looked injured. 'I'm a married man with two children.'

'In that case,' said Shostakovich, 'I wonder why *you* are never required at home for bedtime stories? Here I am, about to run for a tram that I'll miss, forcing me to sprint alongside it as I did for most of my youth, being too weak to push into a crowded car, and in spite of sprinting I'll be late, Maxim will already be in bed, Nina will be angry, I'll slam a door, Maxim will cry, and I'll wonder why, in heaven's name, does my married friend Ivan Sollertinsky never suffer such a scenario?'

Sollertinsky gave an elaborate shrug. 'When she met me, my wife sensed that I had excellent genes. In this matter, at least, I didn't let her down. What more can I say? You, on the other hand, promise too much and you can't always deliver.'

'Oh, I can deliver.' Shostakovich set his jaw determinedly. 'I always deliver, I promise you that.'

'You look done in,' said Nikolai. 'Go home to that family of yours and have an early night.'

Shostakovich gripped his hand. 'I meant what I said the other night. About Sonya. She's got a bright future ahead of her and you must take care of that at all costs.' He peered across the square. 'Not a tram in sight. Damn. I won't get home in time to prevent Maxim conducting.'

'What?' exclaimed Sollertinsky. 'Your son has started conducting?'

'With anything he can lay his hands on. Pencils, knitting needles — he must be discouraged. I'll never consent to having a conductor in the family.'

Nikolai watched Shostakovich set off at a jog across the square. He turned to Sollertinsky. 'Is he serious?'

'Alas, I fear he is. At least half serious. His dislike for the baton-wielding race is rivalled only by his despising of orchestras. And the profession of teaching, of course.'

Suddenly Shostakovich, already some distance away, stopped and turned. 'Football!' he called.

Nikolai shielded his eyes against the sun. 'What's that?'

'Football! Tickets! Get some for next week?'

Nikolai waved. 'I'll take care of it!'

'Plebeian pastime,' said Sollertinsky pleasantly. 'Don't know what you see in it. Fancy a drink?'

'Maybe one,' said Nikolai. 'Then I've got to get home.'

'Don't tell me. Parental duties.'

'The very same,' agreed Nikolai.

The first fight

The orchestra was at its worst when the weather was hot. The rehearsal-room windows were too small and too high up to let in more than a trickle of air. Today, before the musicians had even started playing, sweat was running down their faces and painting large wet patches under their arms. Those who were already warming up were pausing, mid-arpeggio, to scrabble for handkerchiefs or flap sheets of music in front of their faces.

Elias stepped onto the low platform and began straightening his score. It didn't matter how many hundreds of rehearsals he had taken over the past decade. In the moments between entering the room and the sounding of the first note, he felt like an impostor, about to be sent, red-faced, back to music school.

'Good morning,' he called over the messy riffs of violins, and flutes emitting single repeated notes like ships entering a channel, and the low hum of gossip about who was sleeping with whom and which government official had been seen at the opera drinking champagne with the new young star of the Kirov. 'Only sixteen!' he heard. 'Young enough to be his granddaughter.' There were hoots of laughter, and the shrill rise and fall of a clarinet playing a passage that had nothing to do with what they were currently rehearsing.

'I trust you're well?' he said to nobody in particular. His voice was overly careful, and he despised himself for it. Apparently when Mravinsky walked into a rehearsal room an instant silence fell.

'Let's start with the second movement,' he said, rapping repeatedly on his stand until he'd gained a mutinous hush. But even once the musicians started playing, his control was flimsy. He'd kept his jacket on to make himself feel more authoritative; this was a mistake. Whenever he raised or lowered his arms, drops of sweat ran like mice inside his shirt-sleeves.

Outside the trams rumbled by, shaking the floor: a reminder that the whole of Leningrad was built on waterways and over unstable marshes. The orchestra felt similarly unstable, lagging a quarter and sometimes half a count behind. Soon Elias's arms were trembling with the effort.

'Crisper articulation!' he ordered. 'Make it more extrovert.' Each time he swallowed he could taste the fried egg he'd had for breakfast, mixed with the sour bile of insecurity. 'Pay attention!'

But the players' eyes remained fixed on the music. The strings turned the melodies to mush, the brass was coarse, the woodwind as shrill as a wife long out of love with her husband.

Finally Elias stopped them and marched to the piano. 'At bar one hundred and thirteen, you must pick up the pace. Or have you lost your collective memory, so you no longer know the meaning of *poco più mosso*?' Setting the metronome going, he picked out the melody with his right hand. 'Hear that? More like a dance, less like a bloody funeral procession.' Leaving the metronome on, he returned to the podium. Down in the street a dog began to bark, and it continued barking against the beat. Laughter started up in the strings, and spread through the ranks.

The only thing to be grateful for was that no outsider was witnessing the debacle. 'We'll take it from the start of the oboe solo.' Elias tried to sound assertive. 'Bar one hundred and sixty, please.'

The strings began obediently enough, hacking out a ragged accompaniment. But from the woodwind section — nothing. Elias glanced down at the score, half-hoping it was he who'd made a mistake. The notes clustered mockingly on the stave, but there was no corresponding sound. The violas and cellos sawed on, minus a soloist.

Now, more than ever, the ground seemed to be shaking under his feet. He grabbed the sides of his stand to steady himself. 'For God's sake, stop!' he shouted, so loudly the orchestra instantly halted. For the first time that day real silence fell, as taut as a soap bubble — and as fragile.

Elias wiped his forehead with his handkerchief, and forced himself to look up.

He could hardly believe what he saw. Alexander was lying back in his chair with his eyes closed. He held his oboe loosely across his body, and the way he was reclining meant his pelvis was tilted towards the ceiling in a half-insolent, half-indifferent gesture.

'You!' Elias had never spoken with such rage. The other musicians straightened in their chairs.

Slowly, ostentatiously, Alexander opened his eyes.

'You deliberately missed your entrance.' Elias tried to ignore the fact that his legs were shaking. 'Are you going to grace us with your genius, or should I give your solo to someone more dedicated?'

Alexander waved a languid hand. His freckled face was pale, and his eyelashes were almost invisible against his pink lids. 'I'm hung over. After all, it's midsummer, and I am a reveller. At midsummer, those who have friends revel and those who don't —' He paused in a theatrical way. 'Suffice to say, this morning I have other things on my mind than dry professional concerns. Last night I had wine in my veins. And in my bed . . .' Lasciviously, he licked the reed of his oboe. 'I don't mean to make you envious. Truly, I'm sorry that my flesh is weaker than yours and my life is more varied.'

Elias dropped his eyes to the score. The notes blurred into a sickening black mass. 'I don't care how much you've drunk. Nor how many teenage whores have been in your bed in the name of midsummer revelry. What you do in your free time is your own business, but what you do in rehearsal is not. If Leningrad weren't so sorely lacking in oboists, I'd remove you at once for not being up to the mark.'

Alexander sat up, flushing pink around his nostrils. 'I'm the best!' he hissed. 'How dare you talk to me in that way?'

With his hands behind his back, Elias drove the point of his baton into his palm. 'You're not the best.' His voice was like a whip; he wanted to hurt as much as he was hurting, and he ground the baton deeper into his hand. 'None of you is the best,' he said, staring around with hatred. 'You're second-best, the lot of you. If you weren't, you'd be playing for Mravinsky. This is an orchestra of losers, myself included. We're nothing but understudies and reserves, sitting on the bench of life, hoping to be called to action. In the meantime we butcher the music that grants us a livelihood! We kill the music we're supposed to love!' He stopped, aware of a tiny movement from old Petrov, the concertmaster. Glancing down, he saw bright beads of blood falling onto the scratched floor.

'You're all excused from rehearsal. Anyone who is late on Monday will be permanently dismissed.' He stood stiffly, hands behind his back, and watched the players shuffle out the door. No one looked at him as they passed.

Only Alexander paused, so close that Elias could see the sweat on his heavy eyelids. 'You can't sack us.' Vodka fumes leaked from the pores of his skin. 'You're not in charge of appointments; you don't even have the power to choose the repertoire. Everyone knows you're nothing but a puppet to the committee.'

Elias wanted nothing more than to punch him, to smash the bridge of his sneering, arrogant nose. For a second Alexander's face disappeared in a streaming mess of blood, his eyes purple slits, his cheekbones sagging, his teeth splintering. 'You're ridiculous.' Elias looked away dismissively. 'You're nothing but a fish.'

'A what?' Alexander lurched. 'A *fish*?'

'You heard me. You're a big fish in a small pond. An oboist in a second-rate orchestra in a cold swampy city that's been forgotten by the rest of the world. No one will remember you or thank you for what you've done. Do you think we're the ones who make history? We're simply ciphers. *These* men —' He smacked his hand down on the score, leaving a smear of blood on the page. 'They're the ones who'll be invoked long after their bones lie in the grave. Tchaikovsky, Sibelius, Prokofiev, Shostakovich — these men are the ones who will be revered for what they've given the world. Your sweat, your aching back, your blistered fingers: do you think anyone cares? You're not a god, Alexander, however you strut and preen. No one will make pilgrimages to your altar. You will die as you've lived — a mediocre musician, and an arsehole of the first degree. In that, at least, you excel.'

Alexander dropped his mute with a clang, and Elias watched him scrabbling on the floor with a loathing so strong he felt it would rot his guts. *Would that I could mute you*, he thought, wrapping his handkerchief tightly around his bleeding hand. *Would that, in the middle of your tirades, I could shove that mute so far down your throat that you gag.*

He said nothing more, simply watched, as if from a great distance, the figure of the oboist weaving away from him. At the door Alexander stumbled, spat, then disappeared.

Elias looked at the globule of spit lying on the floor. Elongated, fizzing with bubbles, it looked like some malevolent living organism. He wiped it up with his blood-stained handkerchief and threw the ruined cloth into the bin by the door.

In the dressing room, only old Petrov remained, sitting straight-backed in a chair, combing his fingers through his wispy beard. Elias nodded to him and began packing up. His hands were trembling so badly he couldn't even bundle the shuffled edges of the unbound score inside his briefcase.

'I heard what you said to the Principal Oboe,' said Petrov finally. He always spoke of the other musicians like this — Third Cellist, Fifth Bass — as if by doing so he could exert control, if not over the individuals, at least over his own emotional responses to them.

'Did you?' Elias went on straightening the score.

'I was listening at the door,' admitted Petrov. 'There are times when the concertmaster needs to know what's going on. For professional reasons.'

'I suppose so. But this problem is more personal than professional, I fear.'

'You're right. Your pedantry annoys the Oboist. Intensely.'

Elias gave a short bark of laughter.

'Let's say exactitude,' modified Petrov. 'The Oboist doesn't like being pulled up on detail. Regardless of that, whether he likes you or not, you're the one in control. I approve of what you said to him.'

'It's so ludicrous!' Elias sank into a chair. 'He insists on fighting these battles, day after day, while half of the world is engaged in real war. Mothers sending their sons to face the bayonets, tanks crushing bodies into the mud — who knows where it will end? But as long as Alexander's precious Leningrad is safe, as long as he can strut the streets, and ride half-price on the trams, and jump the queue in the movie theatre because everyone knows his foxish face, then Alexander is happy!'

'But not, perhaps, for much longer.' A small tear squeezed out of the corner of Petrov's rheumy eye. 'Better to be prepared for the worst than be tripped and thrown down a mine-shaft when you least expect it. I'll say this for you, you strike me as someone who's never avoided walking on the dark side of the street.' His hand strayed to his jacket pocket. 'Care for a drink?'

'No, thank you. I never drink during the day.'

'Very wise.' Petrov swilled from the flask and wiped his mouth with his sleeve. 'Everyone should have rules of personal conduct. That way, when one breaks them, it feels like a special occasion.' He heaved himself to his feet. 'If it's any consolation, it's common knowledge why the Principal Oboe is being such a bastard at the moment — although it's no excuse.'

'It's plain and simple.' Elias shrugged. 'Alexander hates me. He's always hated me, and he will hate me to the grave.'

Petrov looked surprised, and his thin arms floated out slightly from his sides. 'I thought you knew! The Oboe is in love with the Second Flute, hence he's strutting like a wild cock. Once she snares him, he'll become a regular chanticleer. You'll see.'

Left alone at last, Elias laid his head on the cracked table and cried. His tears, unlike Petrov's, were no involuntary leaking from eyes weakened by poor nutrition and reading badly copied scores in half-light. They were tears of exhaustion, and of loneliness deeper than a well. *I'm nearly forty years old*, he cried inside his head, *and I've never known what it is to be happy. I'm nearly forty, and I have never loved.*

When he raised his head, the buttery light had slid across the wall: how much time had he lost in self-pity? He reached for his handkerchief before remembering it was in the bin, covered in his own blood and another man's spit. He dragged his sleeve across his wet face. 'Idiot. Fool. Blubbering like a woman.'

His father had never cried — at least, not in front of Elias. Perhaps that explained the guilt that lay so heavily inside him? He stared at his reflection in his highly polished briefcase. The small dents in the leather made his face look battered; his cheekbone was caved in on one side and his left eye disappeared into his hair. And suddenly he was back in the hallway of the old Dimitrovsky Pereulok apartment, hearing his mother screaming so hysterically that the hair rose on the back of his neck. His grandfather was being carried in from the street by strangers, his head lolling, his neck bent at a strange angle. The men passed so close to Elias that he could have touched his grandfather's bleeding face. There was a gaping hole where his nose should have been, bones gleamed through the flesh, and his eyes were two black swollen welts. 'He was attacked near the station,' said one of the men.

Mr Eliasberg appeared, to stare impassively at the wrecked body of his father. 'We found him in a pool of blood,' explained the unknown man, and Elias's shrieking mother was led away to the kitchen by a neighbour while his father ordered that the body be carried into the back room. (The 'body'! As if it were no one he knew!). And then the door of the back room slammed, leaving Elias alone in the hallway. Kneeling, he put his fingers in the pools of blood, and he was still crouched there when his dry-eyed father reappeared. 'What the hell are you doing?' he barked. Elias looked up at him with bloodied lips, for he'd heard that if you tasted the blood of someone you admired you absorbed their attributes.

He remembered the taste as if it were only yesterday. His grandfather's blood had tasted of metal, like the railings of the Pantelimonov Bridge that he walked over every day to the market — there was no trace of courage and bravado in it. Instead, it had sent terror into him. He imagined its darkness spreading through his guts, poisoning his stomach, seeping into his brain and eventually driving him mad.

'Is Grandfather dead?' he'd quavered. Death had never been explained to him, but he knew that it had entered their house. 'Go outside and play,' ordered Mr Eliasberg, roughly wiping his son's hands with an old workshop cloth. And Elias had gone to sit on the front steps with fingers that smelt of boot polish and were stained brown instead of red.

No, his father hadn't cried, not even on seeing the broken body of his own father, a victim of random violence. When Elias asked him timidly why he hadn't shed tears, his father had shrugged. 'Tears?' He sounded as if he didn't fully understand the word. 'You can't bring back the past, nor change the present, with tears. What use are tears?'

What use indeed? thought Elias. Why cry over a row with an oboist, when all it had done was make him late?

Outside the light was as bright as snow. He stood at the top of the steps for a moment, dazzled, before setting off blindly. *Wham!* He collided with a dark shape racing up the steps towards him. His briefcase flew out of his hand and hit the ground, the clasp burst open, and pages of Tchaikovsky soared through the air.

'Oh, hell!' He looked despairingly at his score, pages scattering like butterflies. 'Bloody, bloody hell!'

'Hell, indeed.' The newcomer was none other than Dmitri Shostakovich. 'Please forgive me! I was in such a hurry, I failed to see you.' He ran back down onto the pavement and began gathering up great handfuls of paper, oblivious to the fact that he was blocking passers-by.

'No matter.' Elias tried to sound light-hearted. 'The music is in no more of a mess than it was in the hands of my orchestra.'

Shostakovich gave a crack of laughter. 'Oh, it's you!' he said, as if he hadn't been aware of Elias's identity until now. 'It's the conductor, Karl —' He paused, pulled out a large handkerchief and sneezed heartily.

Please, thought Elias, with a disproportionate desperation. *Please don't forget my name, not today.*

'Karl Eliasberg!' Shostakovich removed his spectacles and wiped his eyes. 'Eliasberg, the radio-master!' He bent down to tug at a page pinned under the boot of a stout woman at the tram-stop. 'If you please!

Kindly release the music of one of the world's greatest composers. His work does *not* belong under your heel.' Wiping the dusty sole-mark off the page, he handed a messy sheaf of paper to Elias. 'Here. I hope that constitutes an entire symphony.'

Elias took the tattered bundle and tried to speak, but his tongue refused to work.

Shostakovich coughed. 'I'm in rather a hurry, as you may have noticed from my hasty arrival. I'm simply dashing in to pick up some tickets left for me by Nikolai Nikolayev.'

'Nikolai —' stuttered Elias, glancing over his shoulder. 'He is no longer — that is, I was the last —'

'Yes, yes,' said Shostakovich, slightly impatiently. 'But he was recording here earlier today. I'm hoping — though not expecting, as Nikolai's mind is as cloudy as a March morning — that he's remembered to leave my tickets with the doorman. Tomorrow is a most important match. And if I miss it I will be most annoyed.'

'M-m-match?' Elias could have bitten his tongue out.

'Football, of course.' Shostakovich stared up at the glinting windows. 'Not just one game, but two.' With alarming rapidity, his attention switched back to Elias. 'I don't suppose you want to come, do you? Zenith is playing the Moscow Locomotives. Dementiyev has been drafted in from the Dynamos and he's in top form!'

'It's d-d-difficult,' said Elias.

'Difficult? The game's right here in Leningrad! Half an hour's journey at most.'

'It's my mother. She's a semi-invalid. It can be a bore, but as her only son —'

'You *are* a Zenith supporter, I hope?'

'Certainly,' said Elias in an uncertain voice. 'That is, I don't know much about the sport but, were I to support anybody, it would be Zenith. If I ever made it to a match, I would be Dement . . . Dementi . . . that man's biggest fan.'

Shostakovich nodded. 'Zenith is the absolute best. One night when my wife was away, I invited the whole team to my home for supper. We had a tremendous time. One of them even knew how to play guitar.'

'Is that so?' Elias managed a small laugh. 'Remarkable!' He was trembling slightly. This might be his only chance to speak to Shostakovich on such intimate terms; he must do it now, yet it felt as risky as sticking his hand into a fire. 'Will you permit me to say something I've long wanted to say? I wish to t-t-t—' But at this point his tongue seized up altogether, and he was eleven years old again, standing before his father who was shouting at him for stuttering like a ninny.

Shostakovich blew his nose, as if allowing Elias time to recover. Seconds dragged by. 'You wished to tell me —?'

'S-s-imply to s-s-say —' He bit the inside of his cheek; blood welled inside his mouth. 'Your Quintet! The power of your Quintet. The beauty! To capture such passion in such a restrained form. It is quite miraculous.'

'Oh! Thank you! Thank you, indeed, for such praise.' Shostakovich bent his head — perhaps in gratitude? — yet he sounded as if he wished he were somewhere else.

Now that his tongue was working, Elias couldn't stop. 'Your performance in the Moscow concert was miraculous. I travelled there overnight simply to hear you play. What a performance! So long since you'd played the piano, let alone one of your own works, but no one could rival you. Not Lev Oborin, not Sviatoslav Richter! Even if they'd rehearsed for a month of Sundays, if they'd slept with the score under their pillows — not even then could they know the notes as intimately as you. From where I sat, it seemed that the notes were pouring out, impromptu, from somewhere inside you.' He stopped for breath, feeling immense relief.

What had he expected to see on Shostakovich's face? Recognition? An acknowledgement that the second-rate radio-master, Mr Eliasberg, was worthy of sharing the secrets of a great composer? *What*, he asked himself bitterly, *did you expect?* For somewhere in the middle of his outpouring, it seemed, Shostakovich had stopped listening. He was glancing into the street, then up at the blank windows of the Radio Hall; he was shading his eyes, shuffling his feet, rummaging in his pocket. *He hadn't listened.* And when he looked at Elias the sun glinted off his glasses and Elias was shut out. Blinded, winded, wounded. Alone again.

'You really must excuse me.' Shostakovich spoke from behind his shield of glass. 'I'll be in terrible trouble if I'm not home soon. Once again, I apologise for —' he stared at the dirty score in Elias's arms — 'for that.'

Abruptly he turned on his heel and was gone.

At the
fish market

Elias made his way down Nevsky Prospect, trying not to think of anything at all. 'I hate him,' he muttered over and over again. 'I hate him.' His sweaty palm slipped on the handle of the briefcase, now filled with a crumpled mess of pages that he'd have to smooth out and press under heavy books once he'd put his mother to bed.

He'd reached the crowded marketplace of Gostiny Dvor before his breathing returned to normal. Entering the Clock Line, he pushed through a mass of people, not looking at faces. 'An arrogant human cannonball,' he mumbled, experiencing again the moment of collision, the wind knocked out of him, the briefcase flying from his hand. 'I hate him. An arrogant son of a bitch who happened to have been born with a gift. *I hate him.*'

'You want to buy?' Someone was pressing closely to his side: wrinkled face, glazed eyes, toothless open mouth.

'I hate him,' he said again to the old woman pushing a handle of candles at him.

'What's to hate?' queried the crone. 'These are quality candles, damn your eyes.'

Elias shied away. 'No candles. I'm not here for candles.' He hurried on, straightening his jacket, attempting to remember that he was a professional working man. But there was a lament inside him: something had been lost. How could he ever listen to the soaring lines of the Quintet with the old appreciation? Even now, though the day was cooling, his cheekbones burned.

Fish, he thought. *Got to buy fish. Don't cry. Fish.*

Turning into the Haymarket, he came face to face with none other than Nina Shostakovich. It took all his willpower not to turn and run. *Don't say it!* he thought desperately. *Don't say, I hate your husband!*

'Mrs Shostakovich.' He wiped his free hand on his jacket. 'How do you do?'

'Hello, Mr Eliasberg.' Nina's grip was cool and smooth. 'How are you? I haven't seen you for a very long time.'

'My mother's unwell. She's in what you might call a decline.'

'I'm sorry to hear it.' A small straight line appeared between Nina's brows. 'Is it serious?'

Elias thought of his mother's hands pushing him into the kitchen, pulling him away from his work. 'Let's say that it's been serious ever since she decided she no longer wished to cook, clean or queue for food. The decline has already lasted an eternity, it shows no sign of ending, and it often results in me arriving so late at the fish market that there's nothing left to buy.'

Nina laughed. 'You're not so late. At least, not too late for codfish.' She grimaced at the dry grey curls protruding from her basket.

'One might say,' joked Elias a little nervously, 'that one is never late *enough* when it comes to codfish.'

'Indeed.' Nina laughed again. 'Our domestic help, Fenya, often buys cod, and my husband loathes it. On the days when I come myself, I remember there's often no other option.'

'In these deprived times, codfish is as ubiquitous as the common cold,' agreed Elias, 'and seemingly as unavoidable.'

'In fact, I've got too much here for one household. You're welcome to some, if it would help to make you a little more . . . punctual.'

Elias stiffened. 'Punctual?' He'd heard the jokes told at his expense: how the Conservatoire staff watched from their windows, commenting on how fortunate it was that Leningrad had such a stickler for time, considering the unreliable reputation of the civic clock keepers. It was said that Ivan Sollertinsky wouldn't start gathering up his lecture notes until Elias appeared around the corner of the press building, and that he departed for his 9 a.m. class at the precise moment Elias's coat-tails disappeared behind the Pushkin fountain.

But there was no gleam of humour in Nina's brown eyes. She looked as calm as she had in the days when Yelena Konstantinovskaya had usurped her place at Shostakovich's side, causing opera-goers to stare and housewives to gossip on their doorsteps. 'I'll get some extra paper from the vendor for you,' she offered.

'Thank you! But no, thank you!' As always, Elias became flustered in the face of kindness. 'However hungry she is, my mother won't touch codfish. Anything dried creates mayhem with her gums. It gets —' he stuck his finger in his mouth to demonstrate — 'schtuck in the holsh.'

'Well, one evening when there's something a little tastier than cod on our table, you and your mother must come for supper. I'm sure my husband would like to hear more about where you studied.'

'Most kind of you.' Elias flushed. 'In fact, I studied at the Conservatoire here in Leningrad. With your husband.'

Nina's eyebrows shot up. 'Is that so? He often talks about his fellow students from that time, but I've never heard him mention you. Surely you didn't study under Maximilian Steinberg?'

'Rimsky-Korsakov's son-in-law? Indeed I did. A little conservative in his methods, but a fine teacher.'

'I don't remember you being at the reunion party for Maximilian's students. Were you there last year, in our Bolshaya Pushkarskaya apartment?'

'Ah, no.' He shuffled his feet and looked over the heads of the shoppers with a desperate nonchalance. 'I must s-s-s- . . . I must *confess*, I didn't have the pleasure of attending that party.'

'I hope you were invited. I thought Dmitri had extended invitations to all his ex-classmates. If you were overlooked, I offer my belated but most sincere apologies.'

'Overlooked?' echoed Elias vaguely. 'Perhaps I was. Or perhaps I received the invitation but had a particularly busy work schedule at that time. Now I come to think of it —' He clapped his hand to his head in what he hoped was a convincing way. 'Mother was ill. Yes, that was it. She had a mild dose of pneumonia last summer.'

'The party wasn't in the summer, it was in the autumn.' Nina looked slightly annoyed, although certainly not at Elias. 'Well, you must come for supper soon. I'll invite you myself. But now I must get home to my husband. He's in bed with a bad head-cold.'

'But I've just —' Elias's mouth fell open. *Don't stand there catching flies!* he heard his father shout, and he flinched, waiting for a ringing slap on the ear.

'Yes?' enquired Nina.

'Are you sure he has a cold?'

'Having Dmitri cooped up in the apartment is no daydream, I assure you,' said Nina tartly. 'He's a nightmare when he's ill and a nightmare when he's working on something new, and at present we're putting up with both. The problem is he doesn't know how to rest. At times I think he'll work himself to death.'

'The burden of genius,' said Elias in a low voice. 'The world will never realise how much it owes them.'

'You think Dmitri is a genius?' Nina sighed. 'Time will tell. In private he's no different from anyone else, apart from being a little more short-tempered and a little less talkative —' She broke off, waving over the heads of the nearby women haggling over lace. 'Nina Bronnikova!'

A slim dark woman emerged from the jostling crowds. Nina Shostakovich kissed her on both cheeks, and turned to Elias. 'May I introduce Miss Nina Bronnikova, a dancer with the Kirov. This is Mr Eliasberg, who leads our Radio Orchestra. Perhaps you already know each other?'

'I don't believe so.' Nina Bronnikova's black hair gleamed in the late sunlight. She stepped aside for a stall-holder, moving with a sinuous grace that reminded Elias of a fish. *Eel! Dinner! Mother! Shopping!* His thoughts were a jumble. There was an angel in the Haymarket! What did one say when introduced to a beautiful angel in a black shawl? But the moment for saying anything had long gone.

'We were just discussing my husband,' said Nina Shostakovich. 'Mr Eliasberg tells me he is a genius.'

'Most of Russia would agree.' Nina Bronnikova smiled. There was a tiny scar above her mouth, running parallel to her lips.

'Most of Russia doesn't have to brew tea for a genius with a head cold. Nor explain to a genius why he has to eat codfish four nights in a row. Nor prevent him from attending a football match tomorrow, at which he will shout himself hoarse.'

Elias felt it was time he said something. 'Oh, of course! Football!' He'd intended to sound authoritative, but his voice came out more like a croak.

Nina Shostakovich and Nina Bronnikova swivelled, in beautiful unison, to look at him. 'You're a football fan?'

Elias cleared his throat. 'The word "fan" might be overstating it. But I do take an interest. The game tomorrow is shaping up to be a good one.'

'Are you a Zenith supporter like most of the men I know?' Nina Bronnikova's expression was unreadable as the sun blazed behind her.

'Indeed! I never miss a home match, as long as my work schedule permits.'

'Is that so?' Her voice emerged, cool and direct, from the heart of the fiery glare.

'The Moscow Locomotives don't stand a chance.' A new confidence flooded through him. 'Dementiyev is the one to watch at present.'

Nina Bronnikova pulled her shawl around her shoulders. 'How sad! It's now a definitive truth. When it comes to the brutal sport of football, Ivan Sollertinsky is the only man in the world with his senses about him.'

Nina Shostakovich laughed. 'And that's despite the fact Dmitri wasted a considerable portion of his youth attempting to persuade Ivan that football is an art.'

Elias flushed. 'I suppose I'd better get on, or there'll be no supper tonight.' But as he stepped back, he stumbled against the stall behind him, put out a hand to steady himself, and felt it sink into a rubbery mass of cheap caviar. 'Oh, hell,' he said for the second time that afternoon. 'Well, goodbye! Please don't feel obliged to shake hands.' He tried to laugh. 'You may have already heard that I'm a bit of a cold fish.'

Nevertheless, the two Ninas shook his hand politely before walking away together. Nina Shostakovich's feet pointed straight ahead, as if plotting the most direct route home to her husband, and Nina Bronnikova's toes turned outwards, her shining head tilted to catch what her friend was saying. Elias also strained to hear over the cries of the fishmongers. 'Nikolai Nikolayev?' he heard distantly. 'Yes, a wonderful man. Tragically widowed. Devoted to his daughter.' It sounded like a recommendation for a job — or an epitaph.

He began wiping his hands clean with some old sacking. 'Here lies Nikolai, a man devoted to his daughter,' he recited. 'Here lies Shostakovich, devoted to work, fame and football. Here lies Eliasberg —' He prised a fish egg from under his fingernail. 'Here lies Karl Elias —' But he couldn't finish his own epitaph. What was he devoted to?

'Are you going to buy some of this, now you've put your mucky hands in it?' The stall-holder stood behind the box of caviar, his arms folded.

'I might as well,' shrugged Elias. 'Everything for sale these days tastes like rubber. I suppose your fish roe is no worse than anything else.'

The fisherman scooped up some of the tough yellow balls. 'You shouldn't worry.' His leather skull cap was so tight it pushed his eyebrows low over his eyes, and he peered at Elias through a mass of grey hairs.

'Worry about what?' Elias felt worried about everything: his career,

his mother, the hatred of his colleagues, the probability of dying alone —
'I'm sorry, what did you say? I'm a little distracted today.'

The fishmonger thrust a damp parcel at him. 'That girl. The black-haired one. She has the same effect on everyone. I've seen it before. Even the best man turns into a blundering idiot — you didn't stand a chance.'

'Thanks,' said Elias, without rancour.

'No offence. It's just that she's a real looker, and a ballet dancer into the bargain.'

'Yes, I know she's a dancer. That explains the good legs.' His stomach lurched with surprise. What was he doing discussing women's legs with a fishmonger?

'An odd coincidence,' said the fishmonger, 'considering Pyotr Dementiyev's nickname.'

'Who? What nickname?'

'Your Zenith footballer.' The fishmonger started pouring the unsold roe into a sack. 'He's so quick on his feet, they call him The Ballerina. Tell the girl that, next time you see her. It might get you a head start with her.'

Elias watched the river of yellow roe disappearing into the dark sacking mouth. 'I won't be seeing her again. I don't move in those sorts of circles.'

'What d'you do, then?' The man swung the sack onto the cart behind him.

'I'm a conductor,' mumbled Elias.

'Trams? Or buses? Must get a bit tiring, that.'

'Tiring? It's exhausting,' said Elias in a heartfelt voice. 'Although most people think it simply involves waving your arms about.' He gestured with the squishy package. 'Thanks for the supper.'

'Nice that you dropped in on my stall, so to speak.' The man cackled and shoved an extra parcel at Elias. 'Take this. On the house. Can't get rid of it.'

'Cod!' said Elias weakly. 'Thank you very much.'

In fact, he meant it. Somehow this cancelled out other things: Alexander and the fight, the collision with Shostakovich, and the realisation that he didn't know what could possibly be written about him after his death.

'My mother will be delighted,' he said.

The turning point

Nikolai had woken feeling out of sorts. His throat was sore and his eyes smarted. He sat by the open window, a half-drunk cup of coffee in his hand and a half-written pile of reports beside him, listening with half his attention to the Gessen children tormenting a stray dog in the alleyway below. *So I am half a person still*, he thought. *After so many years, I'm still living in a half-hearted way*. Was it this that made his stomach clench? Or the fact that he'd slept badly, with images of war seeping into his dreams?

'Hold it down!' The orders drifted up from the alleyway. 'Tie the string around its tail.' Nikolai sighed, pushed his reading glasses up on his forehead, and lit a cigarette. Was it a universal instinct, this attacking of the vulnerable and the weak? Recently he'd tried to curb his obsessive reading of the newspapers, his compulsive listening to the radio. It was impossible to ascertain what, exactly, was happening in Europe, but one war was much like another: the toll on ordinary people, the burning and looting, the casual atrocities. It would be easier to stop hunting for facts, but he couldn't disengage. Avoiding looking the world in the face as he'd done for so long had brought him nothing but pain; now he'd become addicted to knowledge. 'To be apprised of the worst,' he told himself, 'is to be prepared for the worst.' Yet he wasn't sure if he fully believed this.

Today there was an ache behind his eyes that took him back to those floating white days with the coffin open in the front room and the baby crying in the back one, while he wanted only to dive into the anonymous city, leaving the mess of his life behind him. And now the whole world was in a mess. Down in the alleyway the dog yelped frantically, and he was about to shout at the Gessens to leave it alone when Tanya arrived, with bread under her arm.

Nikolai started. He'd hoped to tidy up before she arrived, although he knew this was ridiculous, a misplaced sense of courtesy like trimming his beard before going to the barber. 'Breakfast?' he said, in answer to her query. 'Thanks, but I've already eaten.'

'You've eaten nothing.' There were two days of dirty dishes stacked on the sideboard, but Tanya was practised at assessing domestic chaos and was perfectly able to see that not one of the plates had been used that morning. 'You're not starting up all that nonsense again, are you?'

'Starting a cold, perhaps.' Nikolai coughed. 'My throat's a bit sore.'

'You smoke too much.' Tanya removed the ashtray from the windowsill and the cigarette from his hand. 'No wonder your voice sounds like gravel under the wheels of a cart.'

A great howling rose up from the alleyway, and Sonya came flying out of her room. 'What are those Gessen pig-dogs doing?' She leaned so far out the window that Nikolai, alarmed, grabbed hold of her dress.

'Stop it, you kids!' she shouted. 'Leave the dog alone or I'll tie tin cans to your own sorry arses!'

'That's enough!' Tanya pulled Sonya inside and slammed the window. 'The entire neighbourhood doesn't need to hear you cursing.'

'I don't care.' Sonya crossed her arms. 'I won't tolerate cruelty to minors or animals.'

At the sight of her stern, incongruously rosy face, Nikolai's stomach gave another lurch. He gripped the edge of the table, watching his scolding sister-in-law and his small angry daughter. What was wrong with him today?

The ensuing silence was broken only by the sawing sound of Tanya slicing up hard rye bread. Sonya's cheeks were puffed out; she looked as if she might explode. Nikolai crossed the room in a semblance of nonchalance and struck a few chords on the piano.

Still no one spoke. He picked his way through a Boccherini minuet. Each note, even those imperfectly executed, fell like a small pickaxe, chipping away at the frosty atmosphere, easing the pressure. Once he'd finished the tune, he addressed Tanya's formidable back. 'I thought I might take Sonya to Daimishche tomorrow. This city heat is enervating.'

'Daimishche?' Sonya, who'd been slouching in a chair, sat upright. 'Oh yes, let's go to the dacha!'

'You could bring back some butter,' grunted Tanya. 'Can't get it for love or money in town.'

But already Sonya's face was clouding over again. 'I ought to stay here. I must protect the neighbourhood from those Gessen children.'

'I'll have a word to them,' promised Nikolai. 'I'll tell them no more tin cans and no more tails. Then will you come to the country?'

'Oh, definitely!' Sonya hopped towards him. 'I'm a Daimishche rabbit!' She banged into the table, knocking Nikolai's reports onto the floor. As she bent to pick them up, Nikolai did the same, and their heads bumped together with a resounding crack.

'Shit!' said Nikolai.

'Papa!' Sonya drew back. 'You always tell me not to use that word.'

'Neither you should,' said Nikolai, examining his glasses. 'Except in dire circumstances, such as when you've nearly broken your spectacles and you still have fifty-five reports to write. Or —' Catching sight of a note sticking out of the papers, he snatched it up and groaned. 'Or if you've promised to deliver football tickets to a famously irascible colleague and have forgotten to do so!' He reached for his jacket and found the tickets still in his pocket. 'I'll have to call him right away. God knows how we'll manage to meet at the stadium in all the crush.'

'Stadium?' Sonya, surreptitiously slurping his cold coffee, put down the cup with a clatter. 'You're going to the football? With Mr Shostakovich? Oh, couldn't I come?'

'Football isn't a game for children,' said Tanya, standing with a spatula in her hand. 'Especially for hooligans who broadcast bad language through the whole neighbourhood.'

'Oh, go fry yourself!' said Sonya.

'Sonya!' said Nikolai sharply.

Sonya bolted for her room, slamming the door so hard that the half-full coffee cup fell off the table and onto the divan.

'Blast!' Tanya frowned. 'Excuse my language. I don't know what's come over me today.'

'Midsummer madness?' suggested Nikolai, going to the kitchen for a cloth.

'I'll clean that up,' said Tanya. 'You concentrate on getting Mr Shostakovich's tickets to him and Sonya out of her room.'

'I don't know which task will be more difficult,' said Nikolai ruefully.

Shostakovich sat drumming his fingers, waiting for Nikolai to call. He could, of course, have telephoned, but there were some things it was wiser for a man not to do the day after his wife had returned from market to find water pouring from the sink, cushions on the floor, two children running amok, and a husband who, though left at home slightly ill and fully in charge, was nowhere to be seen. He flinched at the memory. Racing up the stairs sweaty and empty-handed (damn Nikolai's sieve-like memory; damn the radio conductor and his unbound score; damn the Leningrad trolley cars and their unfailing lateness). Hearing, even from the landing, Nina's voice cracking out commands — *Galina, fetch the mop! Maxim, pick up the cushions!* — and, in an even sharper voice, *Where, exactly, did your father go?*

Hovering in the stairwell, he'd imagined only too clearly what would have happened on Nina's return: the bedroom door flung open, and his wife's outraged expression at the empty bed and the untouched dandelion tea.

'Well?' she'd repeated to the children. 'Did your father say where he was going?'

'Say you don't know,' murmured Shostakovich, peering in the keyhole. 'Remember what I told you.'

'Papa went . . . to the Radio Hall,' stammered Galina.

Goddamn it! Shostakovich smacked the wall with his hand. Why couldn't his children tell a small white lie for the sake of domestic peace?

'*Really?*' Nina had said icily. 'And did he say why he had to go there?'

There was a short silence as Galina realised she'd put her small patent-leather foot in her mouth. 'No.' She was almost certainly shaking her head. No, she didn't know why Papa had rushed off to the Radio Hall when he was ill and supposed to be resting.

'Maxim!' Nina's voice was even sharper. 'Why did your father leave you to flood the bathroom and demolish the living room?'

'Foot!' piped Maxim, sounding frightened. (This was fully understandable: Shostakovich's own palms were sweating.) 'Foot, foot —'

'Football? He went to pick up football tickets?'

Shostakovich had never seen a volcano but it seemed an appropriate image for this moment: shaking, shuddering, great burning streams of lava and ash pouring forth. Gloomily he realised that a pall would hang over the domestic landscape for some time.

'That's right!' Galina and Maxim spoke in unison. 'Football!'

It had taken all his courage to walk into the apartment, spreading his empty hands as if returning without tickets somehow made him less guilty. It had better be a good game, he thought now, staring at the silent phone. A bloody good game to compensate for the trials of yesterday evening. He could still hear the clashing of pans, the roaring crash as Nina poured a box of cutlery onto the table in front of him. 'You want your dinner?' She dumped down a pile of plates with such force that the bottom one smashed into long white shards. 'Here's your dinner, you poor sick man.' He'd received a leaking paper parcel on his lap. 'Cod!' he said, coughing. 'Thank you very much.'

At last! The phone was ringing. Nina stood at the bookshelf, ostensibly searching for a textbook, her back rigid. 'I'll get it,' he said, snatching up the receiver as she disappeared into the bedroom, slamming the door.

'I'm so sorry.' It was Nikolai at last, apologising profusely. 'Truly sorry. My bad memory seems to be getting worse. Senility lurks just around the corner.'

He never made excuses, simply admitted to the mistakes he'd made — a trait that Shostakovich, master of excuses, admired and envied. *Why can't I be bolder and more honest?* he thought. *More like other people?* He hadn't done a stroke of work on the new piece for several days, and the guilt and unease were becoming severe. 'Tell me you have the tickets,' he said, cutting through Nikolai's apologies, 'and all will be forgiven. To be honest, I'm eager not only to see Zenith in action but also to escape —' he glanced at the bedroom door and lowered his voice — 'the domestic madhouse.'

'You too?' Nikolai laughed. 'Perhaps it's the summer solstice. You have my sympathy, and very soon you will have your tickets. Where shall we meet?'

Sonya softened sufficiently to open her door a crack and say goodbye. 'I'm sorry I don't have a spare ticket for you,' said Nikolai, realising he had spent a good part of the morning apologising.

'You would have taken a cursing hooligan with you?' She still looked a little dangerous, her chin lifted in a challenging way.

'I'm always happy to have an extra hooligan with me,' he assured her. 'The more hooligans, the merrier.'

'Even if there were a spare ticket, I'd be too busy to come to the stadium. See the tasks waiting for me?' She stepped slightly to one side, displaying teetering stacks of books all over the floor. 'When you get back, my library will be arranged in alphabetical order.'

Nikolai looked suitably impressed. 'And your toys?' he asked, peering at the piles of fur and porcelain.

'They'll be housed in the cubbyholes I used to keep my shoes in. I'm putting them under the bed.'

'You're putting your toys out of sight?' He felt a little disturbed at this. 'Won't you miss them when you go to sleep?'

'They need sleep, too. These white nights are really wearing them out.' She gave him a kiss. 'Be careful at the match. I'll see you when you get home.'

As he stepped out into the street, the pain behind his eyes crashed in again, far worse this time. The sun turned the windows into blinding mirrors, and he put his hand over his eyes and swayed. The sound of a radio drifted from the window of the basement.

Out of habit, he strained to listen. Over the last few days he'd heard rumours that only added to his unease. But he must hurry. Shostakovich would be waiting. Running his finger under his collar, checking for the tenth time that the tickets were in his breast pocket, he forced himself to walk away.

From the end of Donskaya Street, he could see the small dark figure of Shostakovich pacing about in his usual manner, circling his favourite bench.

'I'm so sorry!' he called, as soon as he was in earshot.

But, far from looking annoyed, Shostakovich's eyes were bright with anticipation. 'I feel like a truant!' His cowlick fell over his forehead, and his face was tinged with pink. 'I shouldn't really be here.'

'Trouble at home?'

But Shostakovich appeared to have forgotten whatever it was that had made him sound so cowed on the phone. 'No,' he said, waving his hand, 'simply that I have a whole stack of composition papers to grade, and I've promised Venyamin Fleishman that I'll look over his working notes before next week.'

'Fleishman? Is that the skinny blond boy that every female in the Conservatoire is in love with?'

Shostakovich nodded. 'Not that he notices the girls falling at his feet. Poor innocent that he is.' For a second, he looked almost wolfish and his eyes glittered; it was easy to see why many of the wealthiest and most beautiful women in Leningrad had fallen under his spell. 'He's enormously talented but overly modest, and sorely lacking in confidence. So I've got him started on an opera, based on a Chekhov story I gave him.'

'Chekhov! Then I hope you'll also teach him the writer's riposte to critics.'

'*When you're served coffee, don't try to find beer in it!* Yes, he'll need to develop a thick skin with the Leningrad vultures descending on him. Nevertheless, "Rothschild's Violin"! It's the perfect framework for an opera.' Shostakovich looked torn, as if he wanted to rush back home and immediately begin lecturing his promising student on his favourite writer.

Nikolai glanced up at the sun, already high above them. He thrust the tickets under Shostakovich's nose. 'There are times when it's imperative not to work. And today is one of them.'

'You're right. We mustn't be late! Come along.' Shostakovich set a cracking pace as they rounded the corner into Mandelstam Street. 'The highlight of the football season awaits!'

'Speaking of seasons,' said Nikolai slightly breathlessly, 'I'm curious to see what Eliasberg will make of his orchestra this year. I overheard the beginning of their rehearsal yesterday and it sounded like a dog's dinner.'

'Eliasberg?' Shostakovich's eyes were fixed on the high green roof of the stadium. 'Oh, the radio conductor? I don't really know his work. Mravinsky is quite enough for me to handle.' He shaded his eyes, peering at the main entrance ahead of them. 'What's going on there? It looks like chaos.'

'Dmitri! Nikolai!' The shout came from behind. It was Sollertinsky, sprinting towards them, his large jacket flying out like a cape.

'What the hell —?' Shostakovich stared. 'Sollertinsky, *running*?'

Gravel flew from Sollertinsky's feet. His breath came in great rasps, audible even from some distance away.

'Changed your mind?' called Shostakovich. 'Realised at last that Zenith is worth sprinting for?'

But Nikolai seized his arm, his heart hammering as though he were the one running. 'I fear — oh, God, I fear the worst.'

Then Sollertinsky had reached them, sweat pouring down his face. He bent double, struggling for his breath. 'I — followed — you,' he gasped. 'Knew — you — were — coming — here.'

Shostakovich stiffened. 'What is it?'

Sollertinsky's chest heaved as he straightened up and stood to attention. 'It's just been announced. Hitler has attacked. Russia is at war with Germany.'

PART II

Summer 1941

The Cossack and
the dead boy

When Dmitri Shostakovich was eleven, back in 1917, he'd seen a boy killed right in front of him. The city had become a mess, a bad and dangerous place, and his mother had tried to keep him home as much as possible. But for the past year attending music classes had become a routine, and he liked routines: they were the only way to make progress. What he didn't like, however, was the director of the music school.

'He treats me with a total lack of respect,' he complained to Mariya, as she sat on her mattress combing her hair.

'You're eleven years old.' Mariya was fourteen, and annoyingly aware of her superior age. 'Mr Gliasser is a grown-up and an expert. You should listen to him.'

'He may be fully grown, but I don't believe he is an expert.' Dmitri snatched the saucer of warm candle wax from Mariya, who was preparing to rub it through her hair. (Her inherited frizzy hair was only one of a list of teenage grievances against her mother, Sofia Vasiliyevna Shostakovich.)

One by one, Dmitri stuck his fingers into the molten wax and held up their white tips. 'Gliasser plays Bach like a moron. Like a machine. Even on my worst days, I play Bach better than that old man.'

Mariya grabbed the saucer back. 'He's better than my teacher. He has a great reputation.'

'He *had* a reputation,' corrected Dmitri, 'forty or fifty years ago. He relies too much on the past. It's always Fux this, Bellermann that and

Yavorsky the other. He takes his music from text books. That's a dead-end.' He marched over to the piano in the corner of the room. 'I was playing the opening to my Chopin Prelude like this —' With sticky wax fingertips, he began picking out the B Flat Minor Prelude. 'And he said if I continued that way I would fail my exam. Then he told me to play like *this*!' Sitting up straight on the stool, he shut his eyes so as to better remember Gliasser's pious expression, and felt his body transform into his teacher's. His arms became stiff, his fingers turned to wood and, on the pedals, his feet shrivelled to those of a seventy-year-old. Because this was a special knack of his, the keys also changed under his touch, as if responding to a different person.

'You shouldn't mock your elders.' But Mariya was laughing, sounding less annoyingly adult and more like herself.

The door crashed open and Dmitri swivelled on his stool, though his hands continued pounding through the Chopin.

'Dmitri, what on earth are you doing?' His mother was in the doorway, her arms folded, her eyebrows lowered. 'That's no way to treat Chopin.'

'I'm being Gliasser, Mother.'

'He's being precocious,' said Mariya, turning traitor once more, and kicking the incriminating saucer of wax behind a chair.

'You're lucky to have such a teacher,' scolded Sofia Shostakovich over her son's mechanical playing. 'Your father and I don't make these sacrifices for you to mock your elders and betters.'

'Exactly what I said.' Mariya wandered to the window, hoping for a glimpse of Goga Rimsky-Korsakov, who was sixteen and handsome.

Dmitri stopped playing and began peeling the wax coating off his fingers. 'Gliasser is a dinosaur. He's the past, and I'm the future. I'll give him until next June to prove his merit.' He looked up to see his mother's mouth fall open, like a frog waiting for flies. 'What's wrong? I'm only speaking the truth.' He pushed the stool back with a loud squeak. 'Don't worry. Gliasser has a perfectly wonderful Bechstein, and I won't give that up in a hurry.'

So he went on attending lessons throughout the long winter, as the streets of Petrograd descended into chaos. By February, his father was lying ill in the small room at the back of the apartment.

'Just a little throat trouble,' his mother told Zoya, who wanted to hear one of her father's gypsy songs. 'But there isn't enough air in his lungs for singing.'

Conditions were bad enough inside; outside, the frozen streets were being set alight, and shop fronts smashed so the pavements glittered with glass and ice.

'Don't go to class, Dmitri.' Sofia Shostakovich was mending Mariya's tights, which were more holes than wool. 'Stay home today.'

Dmitri placed his books on the table with a determined thud. His mother was a fine pianist and a good teacher, but she was an amateur. Already it was clear — she didn't understand what was needed to get to the top. The only way you could improve at something was to do it every single day. And as heartily as he despised dusty old Gliasser, at present there was no better option. 'It's cold today!' he said, bending to put on his overshoes. This was not simply small talk; his fingers could barely work his feet into the stiff rubber.

'Didn't you hear me?' His mother's voice was more definite, catching at his ankles, hobbling him before he could make it out the door. 'You're too young to understand. There are changes afoot. It's dangerous out there. The city's no longer safe to walk in.'

'I won't walk, I'll run.' He avoided her gaze. 'I'll run straight to school. How else can I become the b — breadwinner?' He'd nearly said 'the best pianist in Petrograd', but he realised that naked ambition wasn't the best way to win over his mother. With a gravely ill husband and three hungry children, Sofia Shostakovich's fear of the financial future seemed his most likely ally.

Zoya ran out of the back room, her creamy cheeks mottled like marble. 'Da won't tell me a story, either! No songs, no stories. What's wrong with him?' She collapsed on the floor and pushed her face into the folds of her mother's skirt.

Dmitri felt suffocated. He wanted nothing more than to turn his back on it all, to race out into the chilly stairwell and breathe air uncluttered by family ties. He stood scraping his foot against the shoe rack. 'Da will get better,' he said to no one in particular. The metallic scraping was almost the same pitch as a cello's A string. He felt a brief lifting of his heart, like the waft of air when a heavy winter curtain is raised. *Scrape, scrape*. Yes, definitely an A. If he experimented with tempo, this could be a possible beginning for —

But Zoya had started to cry, and his mother dropped Mariya's stockings in a jumble of loose threads. 'It's just the cold winter we're having,' she said soothingly. 'The cold factory Da's been working in. Once the spring comes, he'll improve.'

Dmitri forced himself to step towards his crying sister and his lying mother; then he stopped, wavering towards the back bedroom. The door was half-open and he peered inside. There was a brown blanket nailed up over the window — his mother's attempt at keeping in the meagre warmth from the burzhuika, and keeping out the minus-twenty-degree breath of the world outside. The light was muddy and dull. And there, as if at the bottom of a dirty pond, lay his father, his thin shoulder hunched under a thin blanket, his head barely visible. His breath sounded like a saw labouring through wood, producing much noise with little effect.

'Father?' But Dmitri's voice had almost entirely deserted him. He tried again. 'Father?'

His father didn't seem to have heard. Dmitri backed away into the main room and seized up his books. 'See you tonight,' he said quickly, and with shameful relief he stepped onto the landing.

He banged and jumped his way down the stairs, taking two at a time. *It's all right*, he reassured himself. *If you're going to become a professional, nothing must get in your way: not faintheartedness, nor politeness. Not family illness, nor pity.* At the front door he looked out at a familiar desolation. Charred metal girders lay crossed over each other like bones in a charnel house. Along the street a car burned dully, the flames muffled by falling snow. From the direction of the city came shouting, the blowing of whistles and bursts of gunfire. *Neither looting nor rioting must put you off*, he said, pulling his furry hat over his ears, *nor political protests. These things mustn't sway you.*

His mother was right — he didn't really understand what was happening, but he knew that people were fed up with being hungry, with queuing at bakeries for hours and camping outside butchers' shops to get scraps of offal fit for dogs. Petrograders had reached the end of their tether, as Mariya would say — reduced to eating mouldy bread, no longer remembering the taste of butter or eggs! His stomach rumbled; all he'd eaten was half a cup of watery porridge. His mother had watched him shovelling it into his mouth, while Mariya frowned into her bowl and Zoya screwed up her face. 'Your father will soon be back at work,' she'd said. 'This unsettled time will soon be over.'

'Soon we'll be dead of starvation,' muttered Mariya, whose kindly teacher at the Conservatoire sometimes gave her extra bread, which she brought home to break into five pieces.

Turning up his collar, hooking his leather book-strap over his shoulder, Dmitri set off. He wasn't sure how much longer classes would continue; there was a looseness, a nervousness in the air that affected even the orderly regime at the Conservatoire. As he rounded the corner into Nevsky Prospect, he stopped and gasped. Before him was a wall of backs. The street was filled from one side to the other with people pushing slowly forward, looking more like one heaving body than separate human beings. He hesitated and then darted into the ranks, ducking under elbows. Twice, right beside him, he saw revolvers clasped in large reddened hands.

He straightened up, took a gulp of icy air. 'What's happening?' he asked the woman next to him. 'Please, tell me what's happening.'

'This is the day!' She barely glanced at him. 'Today we're going to break them!'

At the edge of the pushing crowd, a window splintered into a shower of glass. The people roared in response.

Up ahead, three shots rang out. The woman grabbed Dmitri, her rough fingers gripping his neck. Saliva hung from her lips; her mouth was a dark cavern, her teeth broken and blackened. 'Go home! Children should have no part in this.'

He shrank away, suddenly scared of her frenzied excitement. 'Let me go!' He wrenched free of her hands, and ran, twisting through the crowd — but he made his way towards the front, rather than retreating.

When he saw the teenage boy fall, he felt as if he, too, was falling. He was so close! Close enough to see the stubble on the boy's chin, to smell his sweat and hear him shout in a cracked voice, 'Bread for the workers!' But the Cossack was looming before them. The sabre swung high, glinting against the grey rain of snowflakes — then it carved through the air like the downwards stroke of a violin bow, masterful, precise, perfect.

Cleaved through the shoulders and neck, the boy fell without a sound. Blood leapt from his mouth, staining his teeth. Within seconds, the crowd was swarming around him, hiding his body from view. But already Dmitri was racing away through the screaming women and the cursing soldiers, dodging the boys with slingshots and the girls hysterical with fear.

When he stopped, he was in an empty alley. He crouched behind a stack of crates and pressed his head against the rotting planks. Hiding there, he could hear the heavy beat of a drum. Where was it coming from? It was some minutes before he realised it was the thump of his own horror-struck heart. He lay against the wall of wood, and the high keen of what sounded like a flute came from his own mouth.

He stayed there until the cold struck through his overshoes and socks, driving upwards through his legs. Pulling himself upright, he found that he could barely move. He wiped his cheeks and pulled his hat back down on his head, then peered out from the alley to plot an alternative route. Composition class might still be on, in spite of the chaos that had descended on Petrograd. He glanced back towards Nevsky Prospect, to where smoke was smudging the sky. 'This year or next year, or in ten years' time,' he promised the dead boy, 'I'll write down your story in music. You'll have your Funeral March. I won't forget.'

Trying to lie

Elias was bored. Part of him marvelled at this: how could he be in a city so galvanised into action, yet feel so stultified? On the outskirts of Leningrad, ditches had been dug; in the city, bunkers were being built and guns mounted on rooftops. That morning he'd passed a dozen men digging around the base of a large statue, while others laboured along, ant-like, carrying planks of wood. Were they building a protective wooden shelter for the statue? Did they expect looting — or bombs? Elias, too intimidated to ask, had simply skirted around them and rushed on his way. Already, he felt like a shirker and a fool.

Here he sat, in the familiar low-ceilinged room, listening to his mother's droning voice, while fear was seeping from the open drains, swamping the marketplaces and the drinking halls. All the same, he felt his face would split from yawning, that his eyes would grow bloodshot from the pressure of his boredom.

'I've always been afraid of June. Everything bad happens in June.' His mother rocked in her chair, which wasn't intended for this purpose; its legs thumped unevenly on the floor. 'Your Uncle Peter died in June, and your Aunt Ester also. Your dear father avoided a June death by a mere twenty-four hours. And now — now we have a June war on our hands!' She rocked so vigorously at this latest grievance, she nearly toppled backwards.

'Mother,' said Elias, 'I don't know if it has escaped your notice, but your chair has no rockers.' *And you*, he felt like adding, *are completely off yours*. Did she really believe that Hitler and his Luftwaffe were acting in accordance with her calendar of superstition?

His mother ignored him. 'I've always felt nervous on entering June. I hold my breath until it is over. The trouble started, of course, when they adopted the Gregorian calendar. All that to-ing and fro-ing, mucking about with dates and names. It wasn't good for stability.'

'Yes, Mother, let's blame Lenin. He's a convenient scapegoat for so many things — why not this mess into the bargain?'

'Karl! No Russian person can be blamed for this war! How can you say such a thing.' She looked as if she'd like to scrub out his mouth with soap, just as she had done when he was eight and he'd called his aunt a greedy pig for scoffing the weekly cake ration in one sitting.

'We have to stop this bickering.' He took a deep breath. 'There's no knowing what the future holds. But, naturally, I'm concerned about you. On my way home from work, I made some enquiries about the new evacuation policy. They say —' He forced himself to go on. 'Apparently there may be trains to transport the elderly out of Leningrad as early as next week.'

It was suddenly quiet, so quiet he could hear the cartilage creak in his tired neck. 'It's for the best,' he said. 'Surely you can see that.'

His mother looked both stricken and mutinous. He got up and tried to put his arms around her. It was a long time since he'd been so close to her; her body felt like an unevenly stuffed mattress, her shoulders slumped, her torso heavy. The smell of her damp wrinkled skin made him weak with remorse and fear.

'I refuse to leave you.' She clutched him tightly. 'We should stay together at all costs. We're family.'

'We're part of a wider family now.' Even to his own ears, Elias sounded like a propaganda poster. 'We're all citizens of Leningrad, and we must draw on that united strength.'

His mother looked at him as if he were mad. 'We have nobody but each other, you stupid boy! Nothing but this!' She gestured at the faded blind, the shelves bending under piles of scores, the motley collection of china. 'This is our home, and I don't want to leave it. I won't.'

Elias had never been able to stop himself from voicing unwelcome facts. ('How will you snare a wife if you can't pay compliments?' his mother had asked more than once.) 'It may not look like home for much longer,' he said.

'What do you mean?'

'Our city's in a vulnerable position. If the Germans attack from the west and the Finns from the north-east, we'll not only be cut off but also locked in. In effect, we'll be trapped in our own homes. What comfort will china plates be to you then?'

'But our army's so strong,' quavered his mother. 'Surely our men will stop the Germans and keep our possessions safe?' She glanced nervously at the door as if, at any moment, Nazi soldiers might burst in and carry off the cabinet Elias's father had made to display his finest samples of boots.

Elias walked to the shelves and pretended to search for a book. He couldn't bear to look at his mother's expression any longer. He sensed that, whatever happened in the months ahead, the time would come when he would be haunted by her face.

'Maybe they will keep us safe,' he said, clearing his throat. This was as close to a lie as he could come.

Brandy, talk and the twelfth of July

The air was layered with cigarette smoke and subdued conversation. Shostakovich sat staring at a long scratch on the tabletop. 'I can't believe they turned me down. How could they?'

'Because,' suggested Sollertinsky, 'they don't want one of Russia's most talented sons shot to pieces?'

'Simply because of my eyesight!' muttered Shostakovich. Removing his glasses, he peered at the headline of Sollertinsky's *Pravda*. The characters were unruly, sliding to the edge of his vision. '*Ev* — ' he muttered. '*Ac* —' But it was like trying to catch smoke rings. As soon as he shoved his spectacles back on his nose, the letters sprang into neat legible rows. *Evacuation Planned for Leningrad's Children and Elderly*.

He tossed the paper aside. 'With half the city gone, the other half will be needed to fight. I'm going to reapply. They can't be idiotic enough to refuse me twice.'

'It's you who's being idiotic,' contradicted Sollertinsky. 'What good will it do letting you run about with a gun? You couldn't hit an omnibus from ten feet, let alone a German. Let those citizens fit for the army do their job, and we'll do ours. There's plenty for cultural men to do in times of strife.' He took a large swig of brandy, and Shostakovich knew what was coming: the tale of how Sollertinsky had once watched a grand piano — 'a first-rate Koch' — dragged from a bourgeois household and hoisted onto a lorry. 'Whereupon I, not a day over fourteen, was also hoisted aboard,' reminisced Sollertinsky, 'to be joined by an eighteen-year-old songstress called Ludmila. Then all three of us — the singing beauty, the piano and myself — were driven to military headquarters where we performed our hearts out, thus donating our cultural knowledge to raise the morale of Mother Russia.'

A smattering of applause came from the nearby tables, and glasses clinked. Shostakovich, despite his familiarity with the story, joined in the toast. 'To the well-endowed Ludmila and the mighty arm of the artist.'

'To Ludmila,' echoed Sollertinsky, misty-eyed. 'Magnificent in more than the voice department.' He gestured to the barman for another bottle. 'We have a lot to discuss,' he said, as if an excuse were needed.

'And you've made your point.' Shostakovich tilted defiantly on his chair. 'Nonetheless, I'm not convinced that artists can't be men of action. Look at Venyamin Fleishman. He's already been accepted into the guard of the Kuibyshev District.'

'Fleishman isn't a proven talent,' shrugged Sollertinsky. 'He's still a student. He's had nothing published and nothing performed. Moreover, Fleishman doesn't wear prescription spectacles.'

'He's already set down the beginnings of a first-rate opera. One day *Rothchild's Violin* will be heard in the best concert halls in the world.'

'And one day you'll acknowledge the facts. You're too blind for the battlefield, and I'm too fat.'

Shostakovich laughed reluctantly. 'Regardless of facts, I'm going back for another try. I've already made a second appointment for an eye test.'

'I expected nothing less of you.' Sollertinsky sloshed more brandy in his glass. 'Your extreme pigheadedness warrants a new toast.'

'As if you need an excuse! You toast as readily as a dog farts.' It was a poor joke, and unnecessarily sharp. But for some reason he was struggling to keep up with the flow of witticisms. As familiar as it was to be sitting at his usual table, bantering with his old friend, it felt somehow wrong.

'Feeling under the weather? Your wits seem a little dull.' Sollertinsky, in spite of numerous brandies, seemed to sense his friend's mood.

'The advantage is yours,' replied Shostakovich. 'You have all the time in the world to sharpen your wits, for you do little else.' Again, he sounded more acerbic than he intended. But the sight of Sollertinsky cracking jokes, apparently disregarding the mounting chaos in the streets, made him envious — and also afraid. Did he really want to push his way out onto a violent and bloody battlefront?

Sollertinsky chose to disregard the insult. He dug Shostakovich in the ribs and gestured out the window. 'Look there.'

It was Karl Eliasberg, walking across the cobbled square with his pigskin briefcase clasped in his hand. As if sensing he was being watched, he quickened his pace, throwing his legs out in front of him in an almost military style.

'They say,' mused Sollertinsky, 'that Eliasberg has walked the same way every day of his life.'

'What, to the Radio Hall?'

'He's walked the same way since the day he was born,' cackled Sollertinsky. 'With his head up his arse!'

Suddenly the door flew open so violently that the windows shook and the lunchtime drinkers looked up in alarm. There, framed against the light, was a young man with a scrubby beard. His cheeks were flushed and his eyes startlingly blue.

'Who's that?' Shostakovich felt alarmed.

'I've got no idea,' said Sollertinsky, frozen in mid-laugh, the bottle poised in his hand.

'It has begun.' The young man's voice was harsh, the death-croak of a raven. 'It's all over for us.'

Sollertinsky put the bottle down with a crash, and an arc of brandy flew in the air. 'What's happened?'

'The Volchov pocket has been smashed,' announced the young man. 'General Vlasov is captured. The Germans are advancing towards the Luga River, and in a couple of days they will be not seventy miles from our gates. We are doomed.'

The truth about Nina Varzar

Once, Shostakovich had walked along a street into the setting sun and thought he was walking into the end of his life. The low orange dazzle of light, the silhouettes of the lamp-posts: these seemed so strange that, in those moments, he could conceive of nothing beyond them. But his feet had gone on rising and falling, just like the sun. And soon the world settled back into its usual patterns, alternating between the mundane and the dramatic.

He remembered that evening more as if he'd dreamt it than lived it. He thought of it with the fierce longing of a soldier, hands clenched, thinking of safety and home. For a second, the world had opened up to him. He could have stepped through and been rid of it all, the constant demands of the body and the never-ending pressure to succeed. The pressure to be the best, to play Chopin's third Ballade more tenderly and Beethoven's Appassionata more brilliantly than either had ever been played — and then to remain at the piano, long after the audience had gone, composing a work to put both Chopin and Beethoven in the shade.

His dream had been one of escape. And it wasn't until he met Nina that he could say, quite truthfully, he was glad he hadn't disappeared on that unearthly evening. Glad that the sun had been pressed below the horizon and he'd been restored to the ordinary streets of Leningrad, a little out of breath, out of sorts, relieved, disappointed, resentful.

The things that first struck him about Nina Varzar were her ferocious intelligence and her lack of deference. How tired he was, already, of deference! Tired of searching for truth behind every face, of standing

103

in concert-hall foyers and listening to a chorus of approval from his acquaintances — *Dmitri Dmitriyevich! Allow me to pay my respects!*

Behind Nina's pale face there was nothing but a seeming indifference for his reputation. She discussed other men's music but not his, offered opinions on others while remaining oblivious to what they thought of her. After the pretty mincing girls who usually gathered around him, laughing too loudly at his jokes, stifling him and breathing his air, Shostakovich found her irresistible. Towards the end of the party, a little drunk, he'd drawn her behind the Steinbergs' curtains and kissed her. The clash of her slightly crooked teeth against his! The heat of her breath! Even now, many years later, he felt lustful at the memory. The velvety dark, the chilly windowpane, the keen blade of Nina's intelligence: these things convinced him that he was a man first and foremost, and a composer second. The relief of shedding the official mask had brought tears to his eyes. After they returned to the crowded room, he'd excused himself and had gone to the bathroom to wipe his spectacles with slightly trembling hands.

When she'd finally agreed to marry him, as the spring rain ran down the window, her 'Yes' had the clarity of an oboe. Turning his head on the pillow, he heard their future. There it was, mapped out in a series of arpeggios, rising and falling with stormy certainty.

'Dmitri?' she'd said. 'What are you thinking?' But he couldn't explain, could only mutter how happy he was, while the wild music merged with the rain. Once the fights began — with plates flung against walls and the servants hiding in the kitchen — the sounds were more like clashing cymbals and snare drums.

'Just because you're a talented composer,' Nina would say, throwing on her coat, 'doesn't mean you're a talented husband. Just because you're beloved by the people doesn't mean you're loveable.' She'd storm off to find her own place in the laboratory lit by yellow flickering lights. Often she stayed away all night, working alongside colleagues who talked about physics rather than ranting about domestic mess or excessive noise. Returning in the morning, she'd refuse to speak to him. His throat would ache and his eyes smart with the effort of remaining silent and retaining his pride.

After their long separation, before the children were born, there were nights when he no longer expected to hear her key in the door. He didn't even try for sleep. Instead, he sat up miserably over his orchestration, drumming his pencil on the desk to fill up the silence. He could no longer hear what he wrote. The lines were sullen before they reached the stave, refusing to speak separately or work together. In bars of rest, he waited without hope for her footsteps.

'I can't live without you,' he said, having lurked outside the laboratory building for two hours, waiting for her to leave work. This was the truth — for how could a man live without sleep, and how could a composer continue without sound? His reflection in the glass laboratory door was a mess: his eyes were red-rimmed from wasted working nights, and from mornings spent awake on a lonely mattress.

Nina looked at him with no sign of softening. 'I'll come back to you, but only on my terms.'

The sheet-ice in his head cracked and he could hear again. The soft rain dented the ground, the leather soles of his shoes squelched. 'I can work again!' he said with relief. And then it seemed wholly right, as he stood there in his sodden coat, that he and Nina should be together for the rest of their lives.

The rages continued, of course. He'd never known such fights. Doors slammed, windows fell like guillotines. Nina was fiercely combative, could freeze him like the hardest frost and burn him with a look. More than once, as payback for her temporary desertions, he disappeared for a night of drinking. 'Nina is a gift,' said Sollertinsky, even while encouraging him into vodka-induced disarray. 'You should be more careful of her.' Shostakovich, losing count of the drinks he'd had, would slump over the table, hoping she was missing him.

Today, walking through a city preparing for a German invasion, he wondered how to break the news to Nina. He felt guilty, as if his negligence alone had permitted the breaking of the defence lines. Had he been too preoccupied with his work to keep an eye on the bigger things? Now that he'd raised his eyes from his music, it was too late. The enemy was inexorably advancing, and the surface of everyday life was tearing apart.

The brandy sloshed uneasily in his stomach. He hoped the caretaker of their building had already alerted the residents to the news, or that Fenya had heard it at the market. He didn't want to be the one to announce it.

As soon as he shuffled in the door, it was clear that Nina knew. She sat at the long scrubbed table, sewing an ear back on Maxim's teddy bear. 'An early casualty of war,' she said, in lieu of a greeting. 'To be precise, a tug-of-war.' Her hand was quite steady.

'Nothing's certain yet.' Shostakovich inhaled as he kissed her forehead, so she wouldn't smell the brandy on his breath. 'Look at what our tanks did at Pskov. Everyone says the Germans are underprepared for our strength.' Anxiously, he rolled a pencil between his palms. 'We could push them back. We could still crush them.'

Nina re-threaded her needle. 'There may be a chance that we can all get out. There's talk of evacuating prominent citizens and their families, perhaps to Tashkent.'

He dug the pencil into the table and felt the lead snap deep inside the wood. 'No. Absolutely not. I won't desert. I couldn't live with myself.'

'Allow me to help you.' She looked up sharply. 'Rather than thinking in terms of desertion, think of it as saving your children's lives.'

When he opened his hand, the pencil fell away in two halves. 'Nina,' he said. 'The only woman I've ever known who stands up to me.' He returned to her end of the table and kissed her on the mouth. Her lips were as warm and full as they'd been on that first night, but her hands stayed in position like a surgeon's, the silver needle in her right hand and her left hand on the head of the wounded bear.

'You've been drinking.' She spoke into his mouth. 'And you haven't slept with me for weeks. Not even in the same room.'

The combination of accusation and desire was too much; he drew back. He wanted her desperately, but he needed to work.

Galina ran into the room. 'Can we eat? I'm starving!'

'Yes, it's lunchtime.' Nina started tidying away her sewing.

'Papa!' Maxim ran in circles around him. 'Look!' He dived under the table, and a moment later emerged with a gas mask over his face.

Shostakovich stepped back. 'Where the hell did you get that?' His son looked horrifying, a tiny body swaying under an enormous bovine head. 'Take it off. Take it off now! It's not a toy.'

'They're issuing them at military headquarters,' said Nina. 'Eugene used our ID cards. He managed to get one for everybody in the building. It's better to be prepared.'

'There's one for you, too, Papa.' Like a dog wanting to please its master, Galina brought over an armful of heavy rubber masks.

'Put them back in the box, Galina,' said Nina. 'You heard what your father said; they're not play-things.'

Straight-backed with disappointment, Galina walked away again, her long braid swinging like the pendulum of a clock. 'Don't shove, Maxim. Be careful. They are not toys.'

'Nottoys,' repeated Maxim. 'Nottoys.'

As they chattered on — 'The breathing holes should face the left. No, not like that!' — Shostakovich stopped listening to their words and heard the counterpoint in their voices. Was it two violins, or a violin and viola? The first line soared away and fell back: a yearning for distance, a desire for intimacy, until, for one perfect second, both strands became one —

'What did you say?' he said, startled.

His children stood in front of him, and beside them was his wife, a ladle in her hand. All three faces displayed a similar exasperation. For a second, he had no idea who they were.

'Mama was asking if you'd like some cabbage soup.' Galina spoke slowly and deliberately, as if he were deaf.

'Galina asked if you'd teach her some more sonata after lunch,' said Nina.

'Maxim ask if he can go to Grandma,' chirped Maxim.

Shostakovich felt a tightening in his chest. 'Sorry! I just drifted away for a minute. Thinking about something else.'

'Obviously,' said Nina. 'Soup?'

'No soup, no thanks,' he babbled. 'You know how I feel about lunch before work. Not good for the mental faculties.'

'Sonata?' queried Galina, without much hope.

'Grandma!' demanded Maxim, going red in the face.

Shostakovich took a deep breath. 'I've got an excellent idea. Why don't we ask Fenya to take you to Grandma's this afternoon? Then Grandma can help Galina with the sonata. She's a far better teacher than I am.' *Masterfully done!* he heard Sollertinsky say wryly.

Galina's shoulders drooped. 'I wanted you.'

'A brilliant plan.' Nina clashed glasses about on the table. 'Flawed by the fact that Fenya hasn't been coming to us for over a week. Nor will she be returning in the foreseeable future.'

'She's been . . . drafted?'

'The city's forming a female construction brigade. Fenya will have more important things to do than cook for us.'

'Poor Fenya! She'll be worn to the bone!' Shostakovich sounded shocked. *Don't lie, you're envious!* laughed Sollertinsky. *You want a piece of the action yourself!*

'I expect digging ditches is no more strenuous than visiting your mother,' said Nina, tying a napkin round Maxim's neck.

Shostakovich backed away towards his workroom. The warmth in the kitchen, the babble and the steam, the information, accusations —

'I have to work,' he said faintly. And then defiantly, 'I must work. I have work to do.'

Without waiting for a reaction, he closed the door and marched to his desk. Once there, he sat for a minute, staring at the compositions waiting to be graded. In despair, he laid his head on the pile. When would life stop getting in the way of music? The scribbled lines of his students' notations stretched before his eyes like undisciplined soldiers.

The horseman

'I won't go,' said Sonya.

It was mid-morning and a breeze was blowing, lifting the leaves on the plane trees so their silver undersides flashed like the bellies of trout. There was a similar nervous quality to the sunlight; it slipped down the gleaming onion-shaped domes as if, for today at least, it wanted to go unnoticed.

It was barely ten minutes since they'd left the house, but already Nikolai could feel sweat running between his shoulder blades. He stepped aside to avoid a line of female factory workers pushing laden handcarts towards the outskirts of the city. They kept their eyes trained on the ground, anticipating bumps in the cobblestones; their sleeves were rolled up to reveal muscular arms. The rumbling wheels drowned out the rest of what Sonya was saying, but Nikolai could see her lips forming words that were definitely defiant.

Finally the procession of carts reached the other side of the square and the racket died away. But now Sonya wouldn't move at all. She stood like a donkey, feet braced on the stained stones. 'I'm telling you, I won't go,' she said, stamping her foot. Nikolai had never seen anyone do this except on the stage, and he was surprised at the level of rage it conveyed. There was nothing remotely theatrical about it; it was as if Sonya's white-hot anger needed an outlet and had conducted itself, like lightning, through the nearest object.

'Sonya, it's not for you to decide.' He sounded sterner than he'd expected, considering his sorry state: streaked shirt, dripping hair and sinking heart. 'You're a child, and children don't make decisions on such matters. It's already been decided for you by —' He hesitated. 'By the officials of Leningrad. By the Chief of Staff, and the Chief of the General Staff, and the leaders of the army, and the leader of the Party — and, well, just all the important people you can imagine.' He hoped he sounded sufficiently authoritative to stop further argument. If he let it slip that, even before the announcement of planned evacuations, he'd decided to send Sonya out of the city to her cousins, he'd be lost. 'Pskov!' she would exclaim in horror. 'Pskov is just a little town! Mama would never have wanted me to go there. They don't even have their own ballet company.'

Sonya said nothing. She stuck out her bottom lip.

'It won't be for long,' urged Nikolai. Why was it that parental lies came so easily, when children were rigorously trained to tell the truth? 'It mightn't be for long,' he corrected himself. 'You have to remember that Leningrad may not be safe to live in for a while.'

'I don't care! Do you think I'm a sissy? I suppose Gessen One blabbed to you about me rescuing that baby blackbird.'

'I never listen to the Gessens, from One to Five. You know that.' He put his arms around her, but it was like hugging a small unyielding tree.

'What about Aunt Tanya?' challenged Sonya. 'Are the generals sending her away, too?'

'Aunt Tanya is needed here.'

'For what? Cleaning? I can clean. Why don't you send Aunt Tanya off to Pskov instead of me?'

'Tanya isn't cleaning,' sighed Nikolai. 'She won't even be helping us out any more. She's going to work with some other women, building blockades.'

'Blockades? What are they?'

'Obstacles to keep the German tanks out.' *Supposedly*, he added to himself. He'd seen the small forest of concrete pyramids sitting in the fields to the south-west of the city, backed by spindly wooden fences. If the Panzers got that far, they'd roll through with little more than a bump. 'Can't we walk while we talk?' he pleaded. 'I have to be at the hospital by twelve.'

'All right.' But Sonya looked stern. Clearly, the battle was far from over.

They walked along the Moyka Canal in silence, but everywhere around them was shouting, hammering, the falling of timber, the constant clatter

110

of wheels. The entire city was an anthill of activity, its citizens marching out in lines to dig and build. The energy infected Nikolai — not with a desire to be part of the action, but simply to believe it wasn't all in vain. Leningrad, city of vapours and mist, built by dogged dreamers who'd balanced stone towers and gilt domes on top of quaking marshes! *Foolhardy*. He slapped his feet harder as he walked. Foolhardy and foolish. This had been a doomed city long before Hitler had set his sights on it.

Sonya led the way over the Antonenko Bridge. She walked in a perfectly straight line but the parting in her hair was crooked, zigzagging to the left and the right. As if aware of Nikolai's gaze, she spun around. 'Can't you walk a bit faster? If you're going to be on time, we've only got four minutes to visit the Horseman and leave again.'

'Perhaps your watch is fast? By my calculations we have at least five and a half minutes to spare.'

Sonya ignored his half-hearted joke. She passed St Isaac's Cathedral without a sideways glance, though normally she liked to walk up the steps and scrape her feet on the small iron oxen by the door. But when they reached their destination she gave a gasp. 'The Horseman!'

In front of them was the familiar bronze statue of Peter the Great. He sat astride his huge rearing horse, face averted from the city he'd founded, eyes fixed eternally on a far horizon. His sword had a greenish hue towards the hilt, but its tip was bright from the touch of many hands and the bent fetlock of his horse had been stroked to gold.

'What are they doing?' Sonya spoke in a half-whisper.

The Czar and his horse stood as high as ever, but scurrying around the base, hacking away at the earth, were men and women with shovels and pickaxes. They'd driven poles into the ground, and were hammering a wooden platform on top of them. Immediately below the rearing horse stood an officer of the Home Guard. In spite of his shining brass buttons and his wide chest, he appeared puny, insignificant, as if he might be crushed by the giant hooves.

'They're putting a shelter around the Horseman.' Nikolai stared at the bent backs and straining forearms, the jolt of shoulders when a shovel hit rock.

'So that the Germans can't hurt him?' Sonya's hand crept into his. 'What would they do? Steal him?'

'Maybe. Or smash him up.'

Suddenly a pile of wood tipped off the platform and slid, with a roar,

111

all the way down to the bottom of the earth mound.

'Incompetent fools!' shouted the officer, hitting the statue with his whip. *Wham! Wham!* The strokes rang out over the grunting and hammering. 'How the hell can we keep out the Germans with clumsy bastards like you as defence?'

'He doesn't need to hit the horse!' said Sonya indignantly.

'Nor abuse the men like that.' Nikolai had just realised who the officer was: Vladimir Lisin who, many years earlier, had married a friend from Nikolai's student days. Just three months after her wedding, Anya Lisin had pushed her way out onto the attic windowsill, balanced there for a second, then hurled herself into the street. Her skull had cracked, her delicate ribcage smashed, but her disappointed heart had gone on beating for several hours afterwards, as if rebuking the brutish Lisin for as long as possible.

'We should get on,' he said abruptly.

But already Lisin was slithering down the dirt mountain, his spurred heels digging into the ground. For a second it seemed his cold gaze would pass over them, then he gave a start of recognition. 'Nikolai Nikolayev? Am I right?'

'You are.' Nikolai's throat clenched with dislike. 'But we're just on our way.'

'To —?' asked Lisin, as if it were his job to oversee the movements of every citizen in Leningrad.

'Papa has a hospital appointment,' announced Sonya. 'We mustn't be late.'

'A worthy attitude.' Lisin slapped his boot with his riding crop. 'Punctuality wins ground. Lateness loses wars.' He laughed, revealing crooked and stained teeth.

Sonya stared up at him. 'My father's going for his medical examination for the army, and I must go home to pack my bags. I'm leaving Leningrad soon.' There were bright spots of red on her cheekbones.

'You won't be leaving right away,' said Nikolai, squeezing her hand. 'But Sonya is right. We have places to go. Please excuse us.'

'How's your wife?' Lisin seemed reluctant to return to work. 'I remember seeing her years ago in a performance by the Leningrad Philharmonic. Tchaikovsky, if my memory serves me right. Such beauty, such talent! Is she still playing?'

'My wife is dead.' It had taken Nikolai four years to say this sentence without hesitation, and five to achieve it without a break in his voice. Now his words sounded as flat and chilly as the flanks of the metal horse.

'Dead?' Lisin flushed. 'I'm sorry to hear that. Such a looker! Such a gorgeous woman, dead!'

Nikolai clenched his right hand in his pocket. He wanted to smash Lisin to the ground, topple him like a tree in front of the labourers he'd been swearing at — and let them cover him over with soil and suffocate him.

'My wife was indeed beautiful.' He spoke as coldly as he dared. 'As, I believe, was yours. The difference is that my wife was taken from me, whereas yours —' He paused. 'Well, of what value is life, when living is a hell?'

'How dare you speak to me like that!' Lisin's face was florid but his eyes were as pale as a wolf's. 'What do you know about my marriage? *What do you know?*'

Several women stopped their digging to listen. Their half-curious, half-blank stares reminded Nikolai of cattle. *So this is what we are reduced to*, he thought. *Before they've even marched into our streets, the Germans are reducing us to animals.*

'Come on,' he said to Sonya. 'Come away quickly.'

'How dare you?' Lisin was almost screaming. 'You'll soon know about living hell, damn you. The Germans will get you! You'll be punished!'

Nikolai couldn't remember the last time he'd felt such rage. He spoke loudly over his shoulder, not caring if the staring workers heard. 'Be careful on whom you wish that fate. Even the Third Reich doesn't look kindly on men like you.'

Once they reached a small deserted square, he stopped and took a deep breath. 'That's a man whom it's better to stay well clear of. Remember that, Mouse. If you ever see him again, put your head down and walk away.'

'Why was he so angry?' Sonya was breathless. 'How did his wife die? Did the Germans kill her?'

'Nothing like that. The Germans were still our friends back then. Maybe one day —'

'When I'm older, I suppose —'

'Even I don't like thinking about it, so I'd rather you didn't have to.'

'He used very nasty language. The Nazis seem to bring out the worst in people. Whatever will happen to Aunt Tanya? She was cross enough before the war.'

'In some families,' explained Nikolai, 'the eldest child ends up with the lion's share of the responsibility. Aunt Tanya was a lot older than Mama, so she had to look after everything and do most of the chores. I suppose that's why she comes across as a bit —' He had a sudden heart-wrenching vision of Tanya, scarf knotted around her face, driving a pickaxe into rock-hard soil.

'A bit bossy?' suggested Sonya.

'Efficient,' modified Nikolai. 'And now she's being efficient for the whole of Leningrad.'

'God help her, wherever she is now,' said Sonya cosily.

'Sonya!'

'What?' Sonya looked defensive. 'I'm just saying what Mrs Gessen said about Grandma Gessen.'

'Grandma Gessen died of pneumonia. Aunt Tanya is ditch-digging somewhere near the Forelli Hospital. There's a slight difference.'

'I'm sure Mama's glad to be in the sky right now,' mused Sonya, 'rather than down here being ordered about by horrible men.' She walked in silence for a minute, and then caught Nikolai's elbow. 'Oh, no! I have to go straight home! I can't come to the hospital.'

'It's just up ahead.' Nikolai pointed past a line of trucks piled with concrete pillars. 'Anyway, I don't like you walking on your own.'

'But I haven't done my morning practice yet, and it's nearly afternoon.'

'Is that all?' He was relieved. 'Can't you just add some time onto your afternoon session?'

'No, it's not the same!' She stepped blindly into the street, narrowly missing an oncoming bicycle

Nikolai pulled her back onto the pavement. Her heart was beating so hard her whole body was shaking. 'The check-up won't take long,' he said, though he suspected this was another lie.

'You don't understand! Morning practice has to be done in the morning, afternoon practice in the afternoon and evening practice after dinner. Otherwise everything goes wrong.'

'What goes wrong?' He began to feel concerned. 'You mean your playing?'

'Not just my playing. Everything!' She flicked her braids back with desperation. 'Things will not be . . . safe.'

Nikolai felt a chill run through him. What did she mean, things would not be —

'Greetings, Nikolai Nikolayev and Sonya Nikolayevska!' Shostakovich stood in front of them, dressed in a jacket and tie, his cowlick slicked

114

back off his forehead. 'Where might an esteemed violinist and a promising cellist be heading on such a fine day?'

'Mr Shostakovich!' In a second Sonya's anxiety disappeared. 'Papa's going for his medical exam, although he's promised he will try not to fight in the war. And I'm going home to do my practice.' She fished her key out from her dress, the sunlight catching in the silver chain.

'You have your own latch-key!' Shostakovich recognised the importance of this instantly. 'When were you entrusted with that?'

'Only this week. Aunt Tanya isn't home any more to let me in. I could have had one for a lot longer, though. I never lose things.'

'If more Russians had your responsible nature,' replied Shostakovich gravely, 'our country wouldn't be in this pickle.' He looked at Nikolai. 'So you're volunteering? According to Sollertinsky, there's no need in the world. You'll be evacuated before it comes to that. The Philharmonia and the Conservatoire are two of the cultural jewels in our Great Leader's crown.' Behind his glasses, his eyes glinted with contempt.

'Sollertinsky could be right.' Nikolai nodded. 'He always seems to know what decisions are being made behind closed conference doors. All the same, I'm going through with the medical exam as a kind of . . . superstitious precaution.' This was as close as he could come to explain his motives, even to himself.

'I fully understand. Sometimes intuition is the only voice worth listening to. It's impossible to know or predict what will happen.' Shostakovich glanced up at the sky. 'Although Nina wants us to leave, I feel I have to stay for as long as possible. These are my streets. Leningrad has provided the ground bass to my entire life.' He took off his glasses and rubbed the lenses on his sleeve. Unmasked, he looked both vulnerable and determined — much as he might have at the age of nineteen, accepting applause for his First Symphony from an enraptured audience.

'But can you continue to work? In the midst of all this upheaval?'

'I've finally forced them to take me — a four-eyed bat — into the Home Guard.' Shostakovich looked satisfied. 'I intend to hammer and dig and build until there's no breath left in me. No doubt I'll still be required to compose rousing tunes for the purpose of raising morale. But twenty-four-hour service is nothing more than I owe. I'd be nothing without Leningrad.'

'I suspect the feeling's mutual. The whole of the city takes pride in your achievements.'

For a second, Shostakovich looked testy. 'It's nothing. It's my job.' He shuffled his feet. 'Well, I must be going. There's no time these days for real conversation. Action — this is how it'll be from now on. Possibly for a lamentably long time.'

'I must go, too.' Sonya pulled up her socks in a decisive manner. 'My cello's waiting, and I've got a lot of tidying to do.'

'Tidying?' Shostakovich looked approving. 'We could do with you in our household. Things are too often in a state of chaos, especially now we no longer have our domestic help. I suppose you're completely quiet when tidying?'

'My quietness is one reason that Papa calls me Mouse,' agreed Sonya. 'By the way, who's the bossy one in your household?'

'The bossy one?' Shostakovich considered this. 'I think you could say that every member of my family is bossy. Myself, certainly, and definitely Mrs Shostakovich — not to mention my mother and Galina. Maxim is probably the least bossy, which is why he'll make a second-rate conductor. He's not enough of a dictator to be the best.'

'He's three years old,' laughed Nikolai, clapping Shostakovich on the shoulder. 'You may yet be spared the agony of having a conductor in the family.'

'What's wrong with conductors?' enquired Sonya.

'Nothing at all,' said Nikolai. 'One of Mr Shostakovich's best friends is a conductor.'

'Unfortunately,' said Shostakovich to Sonya, 'your father's telling the truth. May I escort you part of the way home?'

'Thank you.' She tucked her hand under his arm a little primly, more like a grown woman than a nine-year-old girl. 'I'll be holding my thumbs all the way home,' she promised Nikolai, 'for good luck with your examination.'

'Good luck, indeed,' said Shostakovich. 'Though I expect you'll have no problem today. You'll be pronounced either fit to fight or fit to toil. The difficulty will come later, when they want to remove you from the city altogether, telling you that preserving Leningrad's culture is more important than preserving Leningrad itself.'

'One hurdle at a time. At any rate, such conflicts of duty and conscience have dogged us long before this crisis.' Nikolai spoke smoothly, but he felt a stab of anger at the way Shostakovich seemed to consider himself exempt from such pressure. Did he really believe the authorities would allow one of Russia's most esteemed composers to stay behind, digging ditches, while lesser talents were removed to safety?

He watched Sonya parade away on the arm of Dmitri Shostakovich, possibly the most famous man she'd ever encounter. The upward tilt of her face suggested that she was engaging in polite conversation, possibly enquiring about Maxim's extreme shyness, which seemed to prey on her mind, or Galina's ambition to become a world-class ballerina. But at the corner of Dominkovskaia Street she turned to check that Nikolai was still watching, and raised her free hand in the air to show him that she was holding her thumb for luck.

The secretive nature
of the Elias men

Elias's father, although talkative, had been a secretive man. He was a shoemaker who'd hauled himself up by his bootlaces to reach a platform of unshakeable self-satisfaction. If his acquired veneer had chinks in it, if his grammar let him down or his table manners slipped, he refused to acknowledge these things. His armour was one of suppression, hammered out over many years.

An accomplished craftsman, he was an artist in one area only: the art of hiding things. Hiding his background, hiding his weaknesses, hiding remorse, nostalgia and grief. By the time Karl was born, Mr Eliasberg was already adept at ignoring anything that revealed the person he'd once been.

Often he strode about the house naked. The more physically open he was, it seemed, the less emotion he felt obliged to reveal. One of his few pleasures was bathing. As late as October, when the sky was leaden, he'd coerce his wife — who didn't care for swimming — and his son — who couldn't swim — into providing an unwilling audience. Karl and his mother would sit on their coats, on a carpet of dank leaves, watching as Mr Eliasberg pulled off his over-shirt and trousers and rushed for the water. After interminable splashing, he'd rise up from the weed-filled shallows, his hairy legs streaming and his pendulous balls hanging behind a penis shrivelled with cold. At this point Karl would avert his eyes and begin talking about anything, anything at all, so he didn't have to look at him.

'What's the problem with Karl Eliasberg? Is he offended by the human body?'

Nearly thirty years later, Elias could still hear the braided emotions in his father's voice: exhibitionism mixed with self-regard and scorn. It wasn't the human body that had made his ten-year-old self squirm, simply the fact that it was his father's body. In full view of his mother! Sitting there on her darned coat, her arms folded against the biting air! The shame of it all had seeped into his soul, just as the chill seeped into his bones.

Elias remembered this now, as he stood self-consciously in a makeshift cubicle, his shirt lying limply over the screen and his braces in shameful loops. 'You can keep your trousers on,' the doctor had said, before beginning his barrage of tests. Elias had flushed with relief. He couldn't remember the last time someone else had seen his legs. He stood sucking in his breath, and avoided looking in the mirror that hung on the cloth wall.

The stethoscope felt icy on his left breast. He couldn't control his shivering, and he knew this wasn't entirely from the cold.

'Try to relax.' The doctor was well trained in remaining expressionless. 'We don't want to push up the heart rate before we've recorded it.'

Why, wondered Elias, did he say 'we'? It wasn't the doctor who was subjected to indignities, not the doctor who had rough sticks thrust onto his tongue and a light shone in his eyes.

'We're very thin, aren't we.'

The doctor's comment buzzed against Elias's ribs, sounding almost like a reproach. *Judgement follows me wherever I go*, he thought. Like a tick burrowing into his skin, it was, and had always been, the bane of his life.

The doctor continued to move the chilly metal mouth over his chest, murmuring and scribbling on his notepad.

'I'm a conductor,' announced Elias suddenly. He wasn't sure why he said this — except, perhaps, that he was beginning to find the silence in the screened-off cell acutely embarrassing. But his information turned out to be not irrelevant after all.

The doctor raised his head with interest. If Elias was a conductor, that accounted for the imbalance of muscles between the two sides of the body, particularly in the biceps and triceps. 'Mind you,' he added, 'that fellow Mravinsky is a muscular brute all over.'

'Hmmm.' Now it was Elias's turn to murmur. Was he supposed to respond to this?

'Mravinsky may look angular,' explained the doctor, 'but it's my opinion this has something to do with the length of his head. His skull is extraordinarily long and narrow, and his high forehead adds to the impression of leanness. In fact, he has the chest of a carthorse, and his arms would do a wrestler proud. My wife has quite a passion for him — as, I believe, do most of the women in Leningrad.'

Elias's forced laugh turned into a cough. 'You're right. Mravinsky is quite the film star. One stands in awe of his physique, not to mention his technique.'

'Some of us are born to lead,' agreed the doctor, 'and some to follow. The important thing is to find your place early in life and accept it. Envy does terrible things to the body. I've seen people eaten up by it, like some kind of canker.' He slid his pen into his top pocket with the confidence of a man who has long known his place in life. 'Are you resident with an orchestra yourself?'

Elias squared his shoulders and tried to forget that his torso was covered with goose bumps. 'Yes, I am. The Radio Orchestra.'

The doctor appeared unimpressed. 'I don't go to concerts often. It's more my wife's thing. When we do go, it's to the Philharmonic, on account of Mravinsky, of course.'

'Of course,' repeated Elias. 'Why not see the best, especially if it's a once-a-year occasion?' He noticed there were small rye crumbs hanging in the doctor's moustache, as well as what looked like a smear of egg on his shirt.

'Music will be taking a back seat for a while,' said the doctor. 'Along with most of life's other little pleasures, I'm afraid.' Yet he didn't sound particularly regretful.

Elias began buttoning his shirt. If the doctor were a member of the Radio Orchestra, he would tell him to leave. 'Your presence is no longer required,' he would say. 'You may return only when you can prove your diligence is equal to your calling.' He felt like informing the doctor that he had a total of a hundred and six musicians in his charge.

'I must go.' The doctor sounded as if he'd lost interest in Elias and his profession which was important only in times of peace. 'I've got another thirty-five men waiting to be examined.'

'What now?' Irrationally, Elias felt abandoned.

'Your notes will be assessed, and if possible the results presented to you before you leave the hospital.'

Too late, Elias understood that the shape of his future was scribbled on the sheet in the doctor's left hand. 'Could you tell me —?' he began.

But the doctor was gone, hurrying away to his thirty-five waiting men, or perhaps, en route, to a bowl of cabbage soup in the hospital canteen.

Elias sank onto the hard wooden chair, cursing his pride. Why did he always alienate others, however friendly they were? He was so damned quick to take offence, even when none was intended. And now he'd even fastened his shirt wrongly, so the tails hung unevenly over his knees. Mechanically, he began undoing the buttons.

'Karl Illyich Eliasberg?' A stout nurse peered around the screen.

'Yes, I am Elias!' He sprang to his feet, crossing his arms over his bare chest.

She barely looked at him. 'You're to wait in the main hallway. The health officers will assess your case and call you when they've reached a verdict.'

Clumsily, hastily, he launched himself after her, his tie trailing. 'Can't you tell me if I've passed?' He cringed, both at his ingratiating tone and his choice of words. *You're not hoping for top results in a composition exam, you fool!* In fact, if he 'passed' this test, his only reward would be a rifle in his hands, boots on his feet, and a terror more complete than anything he'd ever experienced.

Still, he drifted like a child behind the nurse.

'I can't say.' Her feet slapped on the cracked floor. 'But from what I've seen and heard —' she pushed through the door — 'you're not fit for much.' And with that they emerged into a hallway crowded with men, many of whom turned to stare at the formidable-looking nurse pursued by a half-dressed, bespectacled weakling. 'I can't say,' she repeated, scanning the corridor. 'It's not my job.'

Elias trudged to the end of the corridor. His head was down, but he was sure all eyes were on him, pitying him. The war had ripped open the small safe world of Leningrad, but nothing else had changed. Keeping his eyes fixed on the ground, he concentrated on small tasks: re-knotting his tie, straightening his collar. Soon the desultory conversation, the roll-call of names and the clash of the swing doors merged into a muddy shade of grey that was close enough to peace.

After a long time he heard his name being called. His heart tripped and started up again, out of time. This was it. He forced himself to look up — and saw a bearded face, tired eyes, a slightly grubby collar. It was Nikolai.

'I thought it was you at the end of the line! What a surprise!'

Elias let out his breath. 'Yes, it's me, I'm afraid.'

'Don't apologise.' Nikolai shook his damp hand. 'I'm glad to see someone I know. I can't tell you what an ordeal my day's been — even before I reached this hellhole.'

Stupidly, Elias stood pumping Nikolai's arm as if trying to produce water from a well. He found it hard to let go.

'Have you had your medical yet?' Casually, Nikolai extracted his hand from Elias's grip and wiped it on the seat of his trousers.

'Hours ago. At least, I think it was hours. I seem to have lost track of time.' Was it this that was making him feel so odd? Normally he could estimate the time of day to the nearest minute.

'Surely your position will give you exemption from —' Nikolai looked down the dingy hallway, where men stood leaning on walls or slumped on the floor — 'from this mayhem and what it will lead to?'

'I believe so. For a while, at least. But I've heard of others — others who haven't allowed their positions to protect them. I feel I should follow suit.' It wasn't usual for Elias to volunteer information, but today his tongue was behaving as unpredictably as his hands. 'Our musical colleagues, for example. Some of our most esteemed colleagues have tried not once but several times to pass the medical. I find this . . . inspirational.'

'You're not talking about Shostakovich, are you?'

'Oh, he's one example,' said Elias diffidently.

Nikolai frowned. 'I'm extremely fond of Dmitri, and his music is ground-breaking — but I don't know if he's the best person to emulate. He operates entirely within his own moral system, and effects his own self-imposed duties with little thought of the consequences.'

Elias looked up at the high windows, at the swaying cobwebs and the pigeon droppings spattered on the dusty glass. He half-closed his eyes against the sun (he couldn't see, he didn't want to see). 'But Shostakovich has such purpose! He's someone I ad-ad-admire. Someone I t-t-try to —'

But before his stutter could grow worse, and before Nikolai could voice any other unwelcome opinions, a clerk with a pencil-thin moustache approached them. Mr Eliasberg, he announced, had emphysema of the left lung and had been given a Grade 4 rating, meaning he would not be required for military service in the immediate future.

Elias stammered out thanks to the clerk, and a farewell to Nikolai, and he reeled from the building. The warmth of the late afternoon washed over him; the air felt like silk. He leaned on the stone balustrade until his legs felt strong enough to carry him. Once in the street he proceeded in his usual composed manner, but his bearing was that of a liberated man, and his relief was so profound that he began whistling under his breath. He stopped only when he remembered that, although he felt as if the war was over, the worst was still to come.

The march

All day the sky had looked like the ground. In the morning, the clouds lined up in neat undulating rows, like a freshly ploughed field. Later they dispersed, merging into each other so that by mid-afternoon they resembled an endless grey stretch of sand. The world, it seemed, had inverted.

Shostakovich — looking up, wiping his hands on his trousers — remembered his first trip to the sea. He'd been five, sickly, wrapped up in rugs. It must have been summer then, as it was now. Through a crack in the cart, he'd seen fields bristling with flax, heard the seed-pods popping, and smelt their honeyed sweetness. When the horse had stopped suddenly — at a gate or a ford — he hadn't been able to stop his stomach heaving, and a mess of chunky bile dribbled out over the blanket. *He's a bad traveller*, someone had said, mopping him up with paper that scratched his chin. *Dmitri's always been the delicate one*. The next thing he remembered was being lifted out of the cart, salt air sweeping through his lungs, clearing away the smell of horse-shit and the heavy yellow scent of hay. 'The sea!' he'd cried, and he left his rugs lying on the sand and headed towards the vast expanse of ocean. Glittering, unpeopled, it was infinitely more inviting than the cosy dacha behind the dunes, with its rounded rose bushes, a jug of cornflowers on the windowsill and a bubbling pot on the fire.

Recently, he felt as if he'd lost sight of the sea. He'd allowed himself once more to be wrapped in rugs (institutional, familial) so he could no longer reach that enormous, necessary loneliness. Loneliness was undoubtedly a vital part of it all, though not always easy to achieve. He winced as he remembered the previous night (the pain was far sharper than that of the reddening welts on his hands). 'I'm working, goddamn it!' he'd shouted. 'Get out of my room!'

Nina's mouth had become smaller and tighter, as if trying to suppress the drama that always surrounded her husband. '*Your* room! *Your* home, *your* children. Everything is yours until it demands something of you, at which point you disappear like a snowflake in a fire.'

She was right. He'd recognised this even in the midst of his desperation to be left alone. How deftly she exposed his character! As neatly as gutting a fish: no squeamishness or mercy, in with the blade, and there were his innards, spilled out for the world to see. Yes, he admired her astuteness — but he wished she'd get the hell out of his working space.

Slowly, ostentatiously, she gathered up her books, walked from the room and closed the door.

Shostakovich watched the door handle; when the latch reached its resting position, there was a click. The noise both sealed him off and liberated him.

'Alone at last,' he said loudly enough for Nina to hear. 'Finally, alone!' She understood the reasons for his fierce demands — why, then, did he always have to fight for his rights?

And so, with the added pressure of having to prove himself right, he'd written all night, and had turned up for work with the Home Guard with heavy eyes and a body that was already intolerably weary.

'You look tired.' It was Boris Trauberg, the oafish pianist whose appointment at the Conservatoire had been opposed by both Sollertinsky and Shostakovich. He'd spent the last twenty minutes poking ineffectually at the sides of the trench, sweating profusely, making no progress at all. 'Little wonder you're exhausted. Ditch-digging is no occupation for men like us.'

Shostakovich spat on a callus on his hand and looked at Boris's shiny face. He resented being placed in the same category as a toad, even by the toad himself. 'I was working last night. If I look tired, it's because I only had a couple of hours' sleep.'

'Working?' Boris looked annoyed, as if he'd hoped war would level all creative differences. 'Can we expect another hit for the people — a new national anthem, even?' He closed his eyes and hummed a few bars of the Internationale rather badly.

'I believe our leader remains happy with the current version,' replied

Shostakovich. 'Until he commissions a new one, I'll continue working on my own compositions. Of which —' he bowed over his shovel, as if Boris the Toad were worthy of respect — 'of which I can't speak for superstitious reasons. I'm sure you understand, from whatever it is you're working on.' Knowing that Boris had as much artistic ability as one of Sollertinsky's pug dogs, he waited with interest for a response.

Boris stared suspiciously at him. 'I'm keeping in practice, if that's what you're implying. It would be foolhardy not to. We'll only be doing this donkey's work until planes are organised to lift us out of here.'

'I'm surprised you're in such a hurry to leave the city that's offered you such great opportunities. After all, your professional career took root in Leningrad's Conservatoire and your future is flourishing on its soil.' *Greatly helped*, he felt like adding, *by the fact that you're a distant cousin of the cultural minister*.

'But I won't be leaving the Conservatoire.' Boris pursed his rubbery lips. 'At present I am digging *for* it, and soon I will be evacuated *with* it.'

'The Conservatoire will remain,' said Shostakovich. 'Musicians and composers will come and go. But the Conservatoire will live on in its permanence and greatness — exactly, one hopes, as Mother Russia will.' He spoke as sarcastically as he dared. Opposing the Toad's appointment had been risky enough, considering the status of his third cousin. Implying that the Red Army might be at a disadvantage — poorly armed and undertrained, lacking in supplies, and especially in expertise after the purge of Tukhachevsky and other experienced generals — well, such an implication might be enough to send Boris bleating to the Kremlin.

'You speak the truth.' The Toad chose to interpret his words as complimentary. 'We're nothing but bricks and mortar in the great wall of national culture.'

Shostakovich winced. There was no reason in the world to voice such sentiments unless facing a jail sentence or worse. 'A shabby assortment of bricks,' he said, glancing at their companions. A few were digging in a desultory way, but most had thrown aside their tools and were sitting in the shade, engaged in earnest discussion. They might as well have been in a lunch restaurant, he thought, or the staffroom of the Conservatoire. The sight of Horowitz waving his puny white arms as if delivering a lecture on nineteenth-century orchestration, and of Possokhov's skinny ankles protruding from his suit trousers, made his heart sink. Boris was right. These men belonged in concert halls and lecture theatres. As defence workers, they were as useless as babies.

A young officer strode up beside them. 'What's going on here? Why are you wasting time gossiping?' His voice had only a thin veneer of authority. With his smooth chin and round blue eyes, he looked young enough to be one of their sons. 'Well?' he snapped.

Boris gave an ingratiating smile. 'We were discussing Comrade Shostakovich's musical contribution to this confounded war. He was about to elaborate on his work in progress.' He glanced sideways at Shostakovich. *Now you have to tell me!* said his treacherous smirk.

The officer gave a start at Shostakovich's name and his right arm jerked, as if suppressing a salute. But he'd been trained to overlook individual attributes in favour of the wider causes of Party and Country. 'We're not here to talk music. We're here to dig! The ditch has to reach the hospital walls by evening, and we'll stay here until it does.'

Boris ducked his head deferentially, but once the officer's back was turned, he winked. 'We may be hollowing out the ground,' he whispered. 'But we're filling in time, if you get my meaning.' Slithering into the shallow trench, he jabbed at the rock-hard earth with his shovel. A tiny rivulet of soil, not even enough to fill a thimble, ran over his borrowed boot.

The officer turned back to Shostakovich. He opened his mouth, but any awkward apology was drowned out by a blast of martial music. Around the corner of the Forelli Hospital appeared a long line of men marching in an unsteady way, three abreast. Some were in threadbare uniforms, but most wore their own thick trousers and jackets.

'Volunteers from the Kuibyshev District. Just look at them.' Again, the officer's voice was a tangle of emotions: contempt mixed with what sounded like pity.

Shostakovich stared at the ragged men. 'They're scarcely armed! There's barely one rifle between five of them.'

The young officer remained silent. Perhaps it was more than his life was worth to comment on the decision to send men to the front line armed with home-made hammers and swords made from melted-down printing presses.

The volunteers laboured on, their eyes trained straight ahead. As the final rank approached, Shostakovich dropped his shovel and started forward.

'Fleishman? Is that you?'

The man at the end of the row turned, and a fleeting smile appeared on his face. He raised his arm in greeting but continued to march.

'Fleishman! Stop!' Shostakovich took a useless step forward. The ditch between them was narrow, but the space was uncrossable: one was a civilian, the other had become a soldier.

'I know him!' he cried, turning to the officer. 'He was my student.' Already Fleishman's thin back was disappearing into the distance, his shoulders squared inside an overly large jacket. 'One of my more promising students,' he added. 'He was writing an opera.'

'Operas won't win the war.'

'Neither will sending untrained, unarmed boys to the Front.' Shostakovich was hot with anger. 'They'll never come back alive. They're doomed, every one of them.'

The officer stiffened. 'Just dig the bloody ditch. Finished by nightfall, I said!' He strode over to the men sitting beside the bushes in their incongruous suits and neat leather shoes. Picking up Possokhov's books, he threw them in the air. The blue covers spread like wings, releasing a few loose pages which the officer stamped into the dust.

Miserably, Shostakovich bent to his work. His blistered palms felt as if they would bleed.

Suddenly there was a rush of air beside him. 'Mr Shostakovich!' It was Fleishman, his normally pale cheeks blotched with red. 'I can't stay — I'll be court-martialled, or worse.' His hands were trembling as he shoved a crushed mess of pages at Shostakovich. 'Could you look after this? It's not finished, which is why I was taking it with me. I thought I might have time, in the evenings —' He stopped. 'But when I saw you here, it seemed as if it was meant to be. Could you take care of it until I get back? Perhaps have a quick look at it?'

Shostakovich grasped Fleishman's thin wrists. 'Of course I will. In the names of Chekhov and Fleishman!'

Despair swept over Fleishman's face. 'I'm sorry the score's in such a mess. And there's a dreadful aria in the second act that you'll probably pull to pieces. Remember it's in its early stages, and I have a lot of work to do when I . . . If I —' He pulled away. 'I must catch up with the guard.'

He was gone as quickly as he'd arrived, a gangly figure with patched boots. Shostakovich sank down in the trench, staring at the notes: hundreds of them running over crooked staves, accompanied by scribbled stage directions and crossings-out and over-scorings. It was like looking into someone else's brain: a mass of information gathered over years of listening and learning, half-followed threads, half-exposed themes.

'What's that you've got there?' Boris sidled up. '*Rothschild's Violin*. What's that?'

'None of your business.' Shostakovich spoke curtly, but he felt like crying. 'Nor should it be mine. Unfortunately, one result of this war is that we're all forced to do things for which we're not even remotely qualified.'

Although the comment wasn't directed at him, Boris looked offended. 'We all know you're a genius, Dmitri, while the rest of us are merely artisans. But how will your precious talent save us when the Germans come marching in, raping our women and smashing the skulls of our children? Will your symphonies stop the bullets that are already flying in the streets of Moscow?'

Shostakovich removed his glasses, so that Boris's face became a round pink blur. He wiped the grit out of his eyes. He was about to tell Boris to get back to the only work for which he was fit, grubbing around in the dirt. But as Boris's voice hammered on, a tinny tune emerged from the insults. Just as he grasped it (a mindlessly repetitive tune, but there was something there) and was trying to memorise it, annoyingly Boris stopped.

'You were saying?' Shostakovich gazed away in a casual manner. 'Something about my worthless opera, its neurotic quality, its excessive number of notes? But surely you're simply quoting the famous *Pravda* editorial, Comrade. Have you no views of your own?'

The ploy worked. Instantly Boris started up again, his voice chipping away like the pickaxes behind them. 'Your conceited nature obstructs your music . . . Your ego is larger than what you write . . .' And once more Shostakovich heard the tune.

Pizzicato, that was it! A pizzicato refrain rising from a melancholic E flat melody like a puppet rising from a heap of toys. Unseen hands pulled on the strings (slowly, relentlessly) until the puppet was marching. The wooden tune spread from the strings to the woodwind, and battled repetitively against the snare drums. 'Idiotic,' said Boris's voice from amid the growing din. 'Arrogant. Imitative.'

'Exactly!' The words burst out of Shostakovich. 'You're right! The themes of fascism. It will be a *fascist march*.' As he put his spectacles back on, the Toad's face leapt into focus.

'What did you say?' Boris glared. 'Did you call me a fascist?'

'Not at all, my dear Boris!' Shostakovich was blazing with excitement. 'To tell the truth, I've never felt more kindly towards you than now. Do

128

you have a pen? I seem to have dropped mine during the digging.'

Boris stuck a hand into his shapeless trousers and drew out the tiny stub of a pencil. 'Here. But be sure to give it back. It still has some wear in it.'

'Certainly, my good fellow. In such uncertain times, you're wise to take care of your belongings. One never knows where the next pencil will come from. Perhaps the pencils of the entire nation will be sequestered for fortifications.'

Boris, looking nonplussed, trailed away, and Shostakovich glanced around for the officer, who was haranguing a respected music historian for sitting against a handcart, reading. Furtively, he scribbled a few lines on the back of Fleishman's manuscript. True, the pencil was as blunt as Boris's wit and it wrote as badly as Boris played the piano — but it was enough. He'd captured it!

He longed for evening, for the slowly creeping ditch to reach the hospital grounds and for the officer to dismiss his incompetent volunteers. As soon as he got home, he would begin writing.

Counting down

Once again, Nikolai was shut out of Sonya's room. He sat staring at the familiar contours of the door: the crack where Sonya had thrown her overshoe, and the polished handle which warned, *Keep out! You're not wanted here.*

He obeyed, though he was desperately aware of each minute ticking away on the kitchen clock. Sixty minutes. Fifty-nine, fifty-eight, fifty-seven. He gnawed at his thumbnail and wiped the blood off on the tablecloth. 'Sonya! How are you getting on in there?' He tried for nonchalance, but his voice was ragged.

No sound came from behind the door. Over the past week, Sonya had become increasingly silent, her chatter drying up like a creek-bed in summer. Wordlessly, she'd watched Nikolai chopping onions, scrutinising him so intently that he became flustered.

'Do you want to crack the eggs?' he'd asked. 'You know I'm useless at that.'

Her black-pebble eyes were inscrutable in her round face. She shook her head and watched him smash the egg, sticking his thumbs in it, mashing shell into the yolk. 'You see?' he pointed out. 'You should have done it while you had the chance!'

Peering into the bowl, she'd picked up a fork and extracted the splinters. But still she said nothing.

They sat down for dinner with the politeness of strangers. Sonya moved carefully about on her chair, positioning it so that the seat was lined up exactly with the edge of the table. Finally seeming satisfied, she gave a small nod. 'It's a pity Aunt Tanya couldn't be here,' she said, moving her water glass one inch to the right.

'She could probably do with a square meal,' agreed Nikolai. 'Goodness knows what she's surviving on. Cabbage and water, I expect.'

For the past two weeks, Tanya had been working in a fortifications brigade to the south-east of Leningrad, sleeping on straw, working twelve-hour days hacking ditches from the stony ground. The skin on her face had roughened and her hair was harsh, as if her body was taking on the properties of the dry earth. 'We wash in the stream,' she said. 'Sometimes we have to crap in the fields.' (The Tanya of old would never have undressed in front of other people, nor used a word like 'crap'. Nikolai had never liked or admired her more.)

'If Auntie were here, she could eat all this.' Sonya looked at the food on the table with an obvious lack of enthusiasm.

'More potato? You'll be glad of it tomorrow.' He regretted the words as soon as they were spoken. Quickly, he dumped another lumpy spoonful onto Sonya's plate.

Sonya clicked her tongue, the way her mother used to do when annoyed. 'Not there!' She pushed the mash away from her tiny portion of stringy pork. 'The potato should go *there*.'

It was then that Nikolai noticed. Sonya had arranged her food in separate portions with clearly delineated edges, ensuring the red beet didn't bleed into the cucumber, nor the salty cucumber juice seep into the meat. He felt disturbed at the sight. How long had she been doing this? Ever since his medical exam and the vague classification he'd been given (he was fit, he could fight; he was a valued member of the musical elite and therefore not eligible to fight), his head had felt cloudier than ever.

For dessert there were blueberries, which he'd procured from a secretary at the Conservative in exchange for a ration of sugar. 'Are you sure, Professor Nikolayev?' she'd asked. 'Shouldn't you be thinking about food that will last? The memory of blueberries won't be much comfort when the autumn comes.' Her hand wavered over the twist of sugar, her derision for impractical academics warring with her good heart. 'Don't you have a child?'

'I have a daughter,' said Nikolai. 'But I've provided for her for nine years now, and in spite of my useless ways she's never gone without bread or potatoes. Blueberries are her favourite, and are now hard to come by. Thank you.'

'Thank my nephew. He's the one who risks his life getting out to the woods and back through the checkpoints.' The secretary had headed quickly for the door, before she could be overcome by her better self.

Nikolai piled the berries into Sonya's favourite cut-glass bowl, and carried them to the table with a professional flourish. 'For Miss Sonya Nikolayevska! The kitchen was informed that this is your favourite dessert.'

'No, thank you.' Sonya looked distantly at the bowl. 'I don't feel like blueberries.'

'No?' Nikolai tried to fluff them up with a spoon but instead mashed them to a pulp. 'Not even berries handpicked from the outskirts of the city and smuggled past many greedy soldiers?'

'Not even then. But thank you all the same.' Like someone eating in a hotel dining room, Sonya folded her napkin neatly over her smeared cutlery. She surveyed Nikolai's inept attempts at festivity: a candle wedged in a bottle, a drooping rose filched from a Conservatoire windowsill. 'I'll clear away now,' she said, with a slight frown.

Once the dishes were done, she suggested that he might like to read while she straightened up the apartment.

'But you straightened up last night,' he protested. 'Things couldn't be straighter.' This was quite literally true. The high-backed chairs, the rectangular table, the tea trolley with its few pieces of china: everything was positioned at a perfect right angle to the walls. Cushions lay on the sofa in symmetry; curtain-cords were neatly tied. Even Nikolai's battered music stand stood to attention.

'It's important to do it every night.' Sonya patted the end of the sofa as if summoning a dog. 'Sit here and you'll be out of the way.'

He pretended to read the noticeably thinner *Pravda* while watching Sonya out of the corner of his eye. There was something odd about the way she tackled her tasks, methodically yet somewhat illogically. She dusted each shelf once, then retraced her steps and ran the cloth over them several more times. Cleaning the drinks cabinet, she touched each corner repeatedly, murmuring, 'Two, four, eight, twelve.'

'Darling?' He tried to sound casual. 'What are you counting?'

'Nothing. Don't watch me, watch your newspaper. It's your job to keep an eye on the war.'

He looked disparagingly at the editorial. 'This paper tells us nothing, because apparently we're supposed to know nothing.' Nonetheless, he rustled through the paper as ordered. Between rustles, he could hear

Sonya's small concentrated puffs of breath, which nearly made him cry.

When she disappeared to dust the bedrooms, he threw the paper aside. Nothing but unconfirmed Soviet victories on vaguely specified fronts, and governmental exhortations to be vigilant against traitors and spies. Indecision swelled inside him, making it hard to breathe. Was he being responsible — or was he simply wrong? After all, Shostakovich was stubbornly staying on in Leningrad, keeping his children by his side. But when it came to matters of principle, Shostakovich was almost obsessively romantic — a lunatic, according to Tanya, who heard tales from Fenya about the disarray in the Shostakovich household (lamps burning all night, bolted study doors, children running wild in the staircase, and Mrs Shostakovich sleeping on the sofa because her husband needed creative space). Yes, Shostakovich had the certainty of the truly selfish, whereas Nikolai was certain of nothing.

'Certain of nothing,' he muttered, 'except that tomorrow I'll be forced to part with the most precious thing in my life.'

That night he didn't sleep at all. Instead, he concentrated fiercely on images: Sonya's round eyes when she heard about the treasures removed from the Hermitage and shipped to Sverdlovsk ('A thousand miles away? A million?'); the flush on her cheekbones when she laughed; the wispy arrows of hair at the back of her neck. Her rounded forearms when she played the cello, the dents in her right thumb from the bow, the calluses on her left fingers from the strings. He tried to file the pictures in his head, while knowing this was useless.

'How long will it be?' he whispered. 'How long until it's safe to bring her back?' The window rattled, the clock clacked on towards morning, and he covered his head with his pillow. But he registered the passing of time in his nervous blood and his quick, uncertain heart.

The morning was much the same as any other. Sounds that had once been strange — marching boots, blaring loudspeakers, the wail of sirens — were already familiar. They blended with the noises of a more ordinary past — clanging dustbins and barking dogs, and the Gessens arguing in the back yard. The warm smell of porridge spread through the apartment, but it provided little comfort. Soon Sonya pushed away her bowl and disappeared back into her room.

'Make sure we haven't left anything out of the suitcase,' called Nikolai through the closed door. 'Did we remember stockings and mittens? I'm sure you'll be home before the end of summer, but just in case . . .' He looked around for something to do, began pouring leftover milk into a

133

flask, adding water to make it last longer. But his hands were shaking so badly the milk ran down the bottle and over the bench.

He gave up and sat staring at the closed door until the ticking clock could no longer be ignored. 'Sonya, the train won't wait! Can I help with anything?'

'I'll be five minutes.' Sonya's voice was distant but very definite.

Walking softly to the door, he laid his ear against the wood. He could hear her talking — was she saying goodbye to her dolls? Every now and then her voice rose in an enquiry, and then paused as if waiting for an answer. Nervous sweat prickled under Nikolai's arms. He'd give her sixty seconds, and then he'd go in.

When the door flew open, he jumped back guiltily. Sonya stood there with her red winter coat around her shoulders. In her right hand she held her small battered suitcase, and in her left was the cello. 'We've got a minute or two to say goodbye to the Gessens,' she said. 'It's only polite, don't you think?'

He was so dismayed he could hardly speak. 'Sonya, you know you can't take the cello.'

Her mouth fell open, forming a small shocked circle. 'But I must! How else can I do my practice?'

'You're only allowed to take the minimum. Warm clothes, food for the journey, that's all. Practice isn't important right now.'

'You're a musician, how can you say that?' cried Sonya. 'Nothing is more important than practising. You sound like a stupid person.'

Suddenly Nikolai felt furious. 'Do you think I make the rules for this bloody war? If you carry the cello on the train, it will be taken off you before you're ten miles out of Leningrad. It'll be smashed up for firewood, or given to an official as a bribe. How will you feel then?'

'But if I go without the cello, how will Mama find me?' She swayed in the doorway. 'I told her that as soon as I reach Pskov, I'll play, "Song Without Words" so she'll know exactly where I am.'

Nikolai's anger drained away. 'Mama always knows where you are, with or without the cello. What about before your birthday, before the cello was yours? What about before you even started to play?'

'I won't go,' said Sonya, staring at the floor. 'I won't go without it.' Her fingers were stiff and unyielding, gripping so hard to the case that Nikolai had to uncurl them one by one. Glancing desperately at the clock, he shoved the cello inside the bedroom door and picked Sonya up.

'We have to leave now! You're going to miss the train and it's your last certain chance to get out.' He blundered to the door, Sonya's suitcase banging against his back, and fumbled with the handle.

'Put me down.' She turned her head away on an unnatural angle, as if she couldn't stand looking at him. 'Put me down. I'm not a child.'

———◆———

The train station was chaotic, like an overfull stockyard; on every platform there was a crush of bodies. Women with large busts and loud voices shouted out names. Children with parcels of food dangling from their wrists cried and clung to the railings. Old women hovered protectively beside their piles of belongings.

Nikolai approached the nearest official. 'Where do the unaccompanied children leave from?'

The woman glanced at her list. 'Second platform.' She wiped a drip off her nose with her sleeve.

Sonya looked at her with distaste and followed Nikolai to the inner side of the platform, sticking closely to the railings, touching every second bar with her left hand.

'There's the meeting point,' he said. 'I can see it. Hold onto my jacket, now.' He began forging through the crowd of children; it was like wading through waist-deep water.

Sonya dragged behind him. 'You mustn't —' she began, but her voice was lost in the blast of a train whistle.

'What did you say, Mouse?' Nikolai tried not to look at a group of mothers fighting over a dropped packet of food.

'You mustn't let anyone else touch the cello.' Although the heat was growing, she looked frozen, her mouth like a small crack across ice.

'Of course I won't!' He tried to concentrate on what she was saying, but already he could see children being hoisted onto the train.

At the end of the last carriage, another woman was ticking her way down a list. 'Name?' she rapped out.

'Sonya Nikolayevska,' said Nikolai, peering at the clipboard, pointing.

The woman moved the clipboard away. 'Yes, Number 78. Is she wearing her number?'

'A number! She doesn't need to wear a number. She's perfectly capable of speaking for herself.'

'I'm nine years and five weeks old.' Sonya's voice rang out over the shrieking and crying. 'I've been able to write my name since I was three.'

The woman ignored her. 'They all need numbers or they can't get on.'

Sonya's face flared with hope. 'I don't have one! Can we go home?'

Nikolai's stomach lurched; part of him wanted nothing more. 'I wasn't informed about the need to label my child,' he said, looking directly into the woman's eyes. 'In any case, it's irrelevant. She's going to be met by her cousins in Pskov.' *Don't argue with me*, he thought, *or I'll snatch that clipboard out of your fat bureaucratic hands and smash it over your head.*

Angrily, the woman crossed off Sonya's name. 'It's up to you. If anything happens to Number 78, it won't be my fault.'

'What will happen to me?' Sonya grabbed Nikolai's hand. 'Will I be bombed? Will I be . . . killed?' Her palm was slippery with fear.

Nikolai was no longer shocked at the anger he felt; it was touch and go whether he'd punch the woman in her officious mouth. Instead, he bent down and smoothed Sonya's hair off her hot face. 'Nothing bad will happen to you,' he assured her. 'You can take off your coat as soon as you're on the train. It won't be long now.'

Sonya leaned into him for a few seconds, breathing in, breathing out. 'The Germans will be sent packing,' she recited, as she and Nikolai had practised, 'and Leningrad will be peaceful again, and I can come home.'

'Exactly,' he said, but his stomach was churning with guilt and terror.

A whistle blew as if signalling the start of a race. Sonya looked nervously over her shoulder. 'Does that mean I have to get on?'

'I'm afraid so.' Nikolai's heart was beating so hard he felt sick. 'Got your . . . got your bag?'

The clipboard woman tapped him on the shoulder. 'Get her on at once! The train will leave in one minute.'

Suddenly, Sonya was gripping Nikolai's arm and tears were streaming down her face. 'Please, Papa, don't make me go! I'll help more around the house, I'll dig in the fields with Aunt Tanya. Please don't make me go!'

'My darling. My Mouse.' Nikolai could hardly speak. 'But I might be leaving Leningrad myself, you know that. It's better for us both to be safe, so we can meet up later on.'

'When?' Sonya was crying so hard that her face and hands were wet, and she clung to Nikolai's arm as if it were a life-buoy. 'When?'

'Get her on!' The woman seized Sonya's left arm and shook it. 'Stop crying! Do you want to be left behind?'

Nikolai tried to free himself from Sonya's grip, while the woman grasped her around the waist. For a moment the three of them were caught in a bizarre tug-of-war: the woman pulling Sonya backwards, Nikolai pulling away, and Sonya held tight between them.

With the final blast of the whistle, she gave up. Her arms and legs went limp, and the official was left holding a bundle of red coat and jumbled limbs. 'About time!' She heaved Sonya up the steps, and handed her and her suitcase to an open-faced woman who drew her back into the crowded corridor. The door slammed, the train screeched.

Nikolai was shaking all over. Moving to one side, he tried to catch a glimpse of Sonya's red coat through the slatted windows. A mass of tousled heads and flushed faces — but none of them belonged to Sonya. The train had swallowed her whole.

He couldn't wait for the final moment, the grinding, roaring, smoking departure. He turned, trampling on feet. 'Sorry. Sorry.' Pushing through the crying women, he made for the exit. Once in the street, he stood with his hands on his knees, gasping for breath.

On the walk home, it felt as if gashes were opening in the soles of his feet and his strength and endurance were pouring away through them. By the time he reached the apartment, he could hardly stand. He sank down on the living-room floor, then crawled along the wall to Sonya's door. Turning his head carefully, as if the movement might shake his eyes from their sockets, he looked into the room, and the hairs on his arms stood on end.

All her possessions had been taken off their shelves and out of their cupboards, and were lying in precise rows on the floor. Overshoes and slippers stood with their toes pointed towards the door, as if awaiting marching orders. Pens, pencils and rulers were arranged in lines like surgical instruments. Dresses and pinafores had been folded and stacked in piles of exactly the same height.

Nikolai pulled himself up and stumbled into the room. He trod on something soft: the body of a cloth doll, which had fallen forwards out of its line. The hair on its china head had been cut short — so short that patches of naked white porcelain were visible. He turned to the toys ranged against the wall. Every one of Sonya's treasured dolls had had its hair hacked off. Beside the last shorn doll there was a paper bag with a neatly taped top. In small block letters were the words, 'HAIR. PLEASE DISPOSE OF.'

Holding the bag close, as if it contained some last explanatory note, he blundered to the window. The sun struck the bronze weathercock across the street and ricocheted back through the glass. Shielding his eyes, he pulled down the blind so the room was plunged into semi-darkness. He lay down on Sonya's bed, pulling his knees up to his chest like a dying man.

How could he not have seen what was happening? He remembered incidents from the past weeks. Sonya turning a key several times in the lock, then running back up the stairs to check once more that she'd locked the door. Sonya walking in a crab-like way along a street, touching a fence or a railing every ten yards with one hand. Sonya insisting on crossing the canal at every second bridge, even if it was partially blocked with wood and twisted wire. 'We can't get over that,' Nikolai had objected, looking at the fortifications on the bridge over the Griboydov Canal. 'We must,' she'd insisted. 'We must walk on the other side of the canal for the next two bridges, and then cross back again.'

He clenched his fist under the pillow, thinking of the large, chaotic Ustvolskaya household in Pskov. Four cousins under the age of ten, rampaging through life, breaking china, bouncing on chairs, throwing belongings in untidy heaps. What would happen to Sonya, with her obsessive rituals and painstaking systems built up to control an uncontrollable world?

'Sonya, forgive me,' he whispered. 'Forgive me.'

Out in the living room, the clock ratcheted on. With every passing minute the pistons of a train hammered out unending circles, carrying her further away from Leningrad, further from her home and her self-made safety. From the street came the frenzied sounds of a city preparing for war; beside the bedroom door lay the long silent body of the cello. Nikolai closed his eyes, but tears slid under his eyelids and ran, hot and heavy, into Sonya's pillow.

Into the limelight

Elias walked the length of Nevsky Prospect without stopping. Heavy tanks rumbled over the patched streets, instructions blared from speakers on the corners of buildings, defence troops poured through the centre of the city. But Elias felt both untouched and untouchable, protected by a brand-new confidence.

Was this how other people felt? If so, it was wonderful! To see the sun glance off the burnished dome of Kazan Cathedral and not wince; to pass a group of men and not look for derision in their eyes. *I'm normal*, he thought, with a lurch of his heart. Although he tried not to whistle, occasional snatches from the *Eroica* Symphony escaped from his lips.

After all, it wasn't as if anyone had *died*. No one had been snatched from their homes by midnight henchmen or bayoneted in their beds by German soldiers. They were simply being sent to Siberia, which many would see as a lucky escape —

Yet, if he were strictly truthful, he felt like the lucky one. Leningrad seemed to belong to him in a way it never had before. If only his father were alive to see him now, striding the greatest street of Russia's most cultural city, marching like a man, walking on air all the way to the entrance of the Radio Hall.

Inside, he found a few orchestra members already in the rehearsal room, their instruments leaning against chairs. They nodded when he entered — but no one seemed to notice the glow that hung about his head, nor to realise that, since they'd last seen him, he'd been transformed into a braver and more engaged human being. Slapping his briefcase down on the desk, flinging his jacket over a chair, he couldn't wait for a decorous entry into the conversation.

'Have you heard the news?' he blurted.

'What news might that be? Seems as if something important is happening every minute of the day at present.' Andrei Kholodov was a quiet man whose drooping moustache gave him a permanent air of melancholy, even when smiling. Today, however, he wasn't smiling. Holding his clarinet close, he related his own news: that his Jewish neighbours had been arrested that morning. 'Even the children were taken. Do you know what the supposed crime was?'

Elias bit his lip. This was not the pleasant scene he'd been imagining. 'What was their crime?' he asked nervously.

'They'd asked for evacuation permits, fearing what the Nazis might do to them. And now they've got it from our own side. Accused of spreading rumours that the Germans will defeat us, so thrown into a cell.'

Elias's sense of well-being was leaking out of him. 'The children as well? I thought all Leningrad children were meant to be removed to safety.'

'The Jews are convenient scapegoats for everyone. Guilty as charged, from the cradle to the grave.' Kholodov picked up his clarinet and removed the reed, placing it on his tongue as if he no longer wished to talk about the fate of eight-year-old Irene whom he'd recently taught to play the C major scale without squeaking.

The room was filling up, but the atmosphere was subdued. For a moment Elias considered holding off with his own news. He opened his briefcase, shuffled a few papers about and cleared his throat. But his excitement got the better of him. 'I also have some news,' he said loudly. 'But not about unfortunate Jews or official errors of judgement. My news is about our friend Mravinsky and his Philharmonic Orchestra.'

Blank faces turned towards him. The only sound was a fly buzzing against the windowpane. 'The entire Philharmonia is being evacuated to Siberia.' He tried for a flourishing delivery. 'Which means that the Radio Orchestra will now be the cultural backbone of Leningrad. We alone will carry the autumn season!'

The only sound was a scornful laugh from the doorway. Elias stiffened; he didn't need to look around.

'You consider that a *privilege*?' Alexander swayed into the room. It was not yet midday but the vodka fumes were unmistakable. 'We'll be cornered like rats! Left behind in Leningrad to play morale-raising music while Mravinsky and his band twiddle their thumbs elsewhere, ready to replace us when we've been slaughtered in the streets. What a wonderful privilege!'

Elias tried to remain calm. 'We've been understudies for ten years. Do you really wish to remain that way? To remain a second-rate, unknown windbag for the rest of your miserable life?' A titter ran around the room, and Elias flushed with gratification. Normally, such laughter was at his expense. 'Siberia would once have been just the place for you,' he added. 'At least you'd have learned about hard work, had you been in a labour camp.'

There was more laughter at this.

Alexander sneered. 'You don't care what will happen to us. You care only about your career. Achieving fame because of a German invasion? You're no better than a Nazi collaborator!'

'A labour camp would be too good for you.' Elias spoke through clenched teeth. 'For now, whether or not it's pleasant, you're condemned to work for me.'

The ensuing silence was broken only by the persistent buzzing against glass. Elias strode to the window and flung it open. A cacophony of hammering and clattering rose up and poured into the room. 'Listen to that!' He turned to face the orchestra. 'We're at war with the Germans; we shouldn't be waging war among ourselves. Until we're called on to fight, we'll do the job for which we're trained. We're not children in a playground, nor animals scrapping in a cage. We're professional musicians, and we will play like professionals until we no longer have lips, lungs or arms with which to do so.' Glancing out the window again, he saw the roof of the Alexandrinsky Theatre bristling with guns that pointed to the sky like accusing fingers. He slammed the window shut and spoke into the newly sealed silence. 'Do you understand?'

In a corner of the room, a small patter began, spreading and growing like rain. The back-desk violinists were tapping their bows on their music stands, and Ilya Fomenko joined in with his drumsticks. The woodwind section began stamping their feet. Soon the whole room was applauding. Only Alexander stood, mute and red-faced, by the wall.

'I'd like to start with the first movement of the *1812*,' said Elias. 'Please get out your scores.' As he waited, he caught sight of himself in the large mirror. How strange! His face appeared as pale and impassive as ever — but inside he felt as if he were singing.

Meetings and partings

Sollertinsky was throwing a huge farewell party. 'A valedictory romp,' he explained. 'Plenty of food, no speeches and definitely no tears.' The location was to be his favourite restaurant, the Chvanova on Bolshoy Prospect, whose baby quails in tarragon and whiteheart-cherry sauce were unsurpassed.

Nina voiced reservations, as she so often did these days. The only thing about which she seemed wholehearted was nagging Shostakovich to leave Leningrad. 'It doesn't seem right, partying in the midst of all this uncertainty. Does it seem right to you?'

'No, definitely not right.' Shostakovich was slicking down his hair with one hand and making corrections to his score with the other. 'The Boris-tune should start with the cellos and spread upwards, not vice versa.'

Nina rolled her eyes. 'I'll talk to myself.'

Shostakovich leaned low over the desk, only to be blinded by his unruly hair. 'Damn it! Do I have to cut off this cowlick to keep it out of my way? Now look! Hair oil all over the bass.'

Nina swept over with a small pot of pomade. 'Stand still now.' In a second, the tuft of hair lay shiny and flat to the right of Shostakovich's irritated brow. 'You could always try parting it closer to the middle,' she suggested, deftly blotting the oil off the score.

Shostakovich looked at her shoulders, white and smooth under the cream lace straps of her slip. Through the thin cotton, the steps of her spine led temptingly, distractingly downwards. 'My hair doesn't work with a centre part,' he muttered. 'I look like a peasant.'

She was holding out the score, looking at the small spots of oil but not seeing what lay beneath — the swell of an E flat ascent, a drum beat as dark and constant as the sea. 'That's better.' Her nipples were also visible through her slip; suddenly, he longed to touch them, feel them harden under his fingers.

But already she was back on the other side of the room, sorting through her jewellery box. 'You should hurry. You promised to read to Galina before we leave.'

'Do we have to go?' He felt pulled in two directions: the score for his march on his left, his curvaceous wife on his right.

'Your work will still be here when you get home. Sollertinsky, on the other hand, will soon be in Siberia.' But a secretive smile flicked over Nina's lips, as if she sensed what her husband was thinking about her, and she fastened the topaz necklace around her throat with an air of confidence.

The pavements of Leningrad had become like an army training ground, cluttered with rolls of wire, old mattresses and mounds of rubble. By the time they got to the Petrogradsky district, the hem of Nina's dress was flecked with dirt. 'Sollertinsky will be too merry to notice how we look,' said Shostakovich, brushing off his shoes at the restaurant door.

Inside, glittering light played on the gleaming heads of the cultural elite. Sollertinsky stood in the centre of the room. 'Welcome!' he cried, ploughing towards them, shaking off the beautiful clinging Kirov girls as if they were gnats. 'Nina Shostakovich, as stunning as ever, in spite of our troubled times! And even my old friend Dmitri's looking smart — though he might have cleaned the mud off his shoes before entering the finest eating establishment in Russia.'

'Look at yourself,' retorted Shostakovich. 'I wonder why the Philharmonia Committee appointed an artistic director who doesn't know how to knot a tie correctly.'

'At least I'm wearing one.' Sollertinsky peered down at the loose spindly knot under his chin. 'Whatever will I do without you, Dmitri? You're the only one who dares to criticise me. Well, this may be our last supper, so make the most of it! The sevruga here is exquisite.'

The three of them threaded through bare-shouldered women in rustling silk and men with starched white collars. Clouds of perfume wafted up Shostakovich's nose, making him sneeze. He stood with his back to a pillar, watching Nina circle the table, nodding and laughing.

She appeared absorbed, but occasionally she raised her eyes, checking that he was still close by. Had she been this way when they'd first met — watchful, a little wary? Impossible to remember. There had been so much work over the years, so much necessary concentration; he'd simply toiled on, hoping that every time he raised his head from his work she'd still be there.

Thinking of his failings as a husband and a father aroused the usual guilt. *I wouldn't want to be married to me*. Turning abruptly, he collided with the woman beside him. 'Forgive me.' He reached out to steady her. It was Nina Bronnikova, nearly as tall as he was — and as beautiful as when she'd first joined the Kirov Ballet Company.

'My fault.' Her hair was coiled high on her head, emphasising her cheekbones and the slightly melancholic fall of her mouth. 'I shouldn't be loitering behind pillars! But I'm not in a partying mood, and I have very little to chat about.'

'That's hardly surprising. The extramarital activities of the intelligentsia are less absorbing when one is listening for the sound of the Luftwaffe.'

She shrugged. 'I never listened to gossip, even before the war began.'

'Nor I. Gossip distracts one from working. It's a good reason to avoid parties such as this.' He stared across the room. It had been a mistake to come. Had he learnt nothing from toiling through six symphonies and an opera? From struggling with sonatas and concertos, quartets and quintets, song-cycles, ballet scores and film scores? How did he manage to forget, every single time, that the initial stages of a work demanded constant attention?

'Speaking of work,' asked Nina Bronnikova, 'when will you be going?'

'I must stay for a while, at least.' Shostakovich took a gulp of his vodka. 'Sollertinsky is my best friend. And it was quite an effort for my wife to get me here.'

Nina Bronnikova laughed. 'I wasn't referring to the party, but to evacuation plans. The Kirov is leaving within a week.'

He took another swallow of vodka; already its effects were making him feel stronger. 'I'm not going. I intend to stay in Leningrad as long as possible. If the Luftwaffe attacks, the fire brigade will need extra volunteers.'

'You'll stay and fire-watch?' She looked surprised. 'Are you allowed to do that?'

'At first they refused to let me dig ditches. Now I've been digging ditches for three weeks. If incendiaries start to fall, how can they refuse another set of hands?'

'You have rather famous hands.'

'I've got a will of my own, even if my hands and my mind are claimed by the State.' For once he didn't glance over his shoulder to see who might be listening. 'Besides, as long as I continue providing tunes for their infernal brass bands, they have no grounds for complaint.'

'I hope my husband isn't depressing you.' His wife appeared at his side, glancing at him to check he was all right but addressing Nina Bronnikova. 'He finds the initial stages of anything difficult — although once a party warms up, he becomes its life and soul.'

'Far from depressing me, he's inspired me! Choosing to stay in Leningrad, with the Germans at our very gates, displays a sense of duty most of us couldn't hope to possess.'

'Duty?' Nina Shostakovich's eyes narrowed. 'I can't help thinking that "duty" has become the most overused word in our society, not to mention a defence of any number of atrocities. Is it one's duty to remain in an increasingly dangerous situation — or rather to remove one's children to safety? Duty to one's country also necessitates safeguarding its future.'

'We don't know if it is any safer,' said Shostakovich loudly, 'to send children out of the city. Look at the disaster that happened in June! Children put on trains, sent directly into the path of the enemy and brought back again.'

'The issue isn't only about evacuating the children,' replied his wife sharply. 'It's also about safeguarding yourself, so your children can grow up with a father.'

How swiftly the conversation had shifted from the impersonal to the personal! He felt the same longing to escape as he had when a boy. Now, too old to run and too civilised to withdraw, he said nothing and stared down into his glass.

'It's a many-sided debate,' said Nina Bronnikova diplomatically. 'Not only has the war thrown our streets into disarray, it's forcing moral dilemmas upon us. Even this party —' she gestured at the platters laden with wild boar, whole fish and golden melon — 'feels like the last gasp of the Roman Empire. A wilful denial of what is to come.'

'Yes, it seems paradoxical to enjoy such a feast,' said Nina Shostakovich, 'when the bread queues are becoming longer by the day.'

'Our country is built on such paradoxes!' Sollertinsky had arrived to join the fray. 'Contradiction lies at Russia's heart, and always has.

Refusing the privileged cards we've been dealt won't help those who are less fortunate.' He looked dishevelled, with sweat on his brow and his sleeves rolled up, but he spoke seriously. 'Take our friend Dmitri. Think of the music that would never have been written if he hadn't been willing to compromise. To duck for cover when necessary, strut when commanded, and steer the fine line between integrity and common sense.'

'You're overstating the case.' Shostakovich shook his head. 'I'm just doing what I was born to do.'

'You're too modest.' Sollertinsky's hazel eyes glinted. 'All I'm saying is that nothing is black and white, not even — or especially not — in times of war.'

Shostakovich sighed. Although he was feeling a little more sociable thanks to the vodka, he wished to God all this talk of war and his work would stop, and that he could go home and get on with his march.

Sollertinsky laughed. 'Look at you, standing here with the two most beautiful women in Leningrad! You might at least have the grace to look happy about it.'

'No offence,' shrugged Shostakovich. 'But half my mind is in my work and the other half in the trenches.'

'No wonder you're more dim-witted than usual. Gogol wrote of a man without a nose, we're talking to a man without a mind!' Sollertinsky gave him a bear-hug. 'You great dolt. I'm not accustomed to missing anything, except my wedding anniversaries and the occasional tram — but, by God, I'll miss you.'

———◆———

Arriving late — his mother had been particularly difficult to get into bed — Elias paused in the doorway. For once, this wasn't for fear of socialising with more educated, elegant Leningraders. Tonight he stopped simply to experience his new sense of self. With his feet planted firmly on the red carpet and his chest swelling, he surveyed the room.

'Good evening, sir.' The restaurateur was also scanning the room, albeit with a more professional eye. 'Welcome back. We haven't seen you in our establishment for some time.'

Not long ago, Elias would have found the man's impressive moustache and air of impatience intimidating. 'It's good to be back,' he replied.

In fact, he'd never ventured here in his life. How many times had he walked past the gilt-handled doors and longed to sweep through the crimson curtain, like one of those confident white-shirted men with beautiful women on their arms!

'Champagne?' The restaurateur gestured to a waiter hovering nearby.

'I'm not —' began Elias, but already a chilled glass was in his hand. 'Well, all right.' Usually he mistrusted champagne, both for its instant effects of gaiety and its almost immediate after-effects (a throbbing headache and gnawing pains in the stomach). But tonight everything was different.

'Your friends are on the far side of the room.' The restaurateur gestured discreetly with his head.

'Thank you.' A little bewildered, Elias glanced across the crowded restaurant to see who his friends might be. There on the carpeted podium was a grand piano, and gathered around it, like an unholy triumvirate, were Sollertinsky, Mravinsky and Dmitri Shostakovich.

He felt the sudden inconvenient need to be honest. 'To be precise, they are not —' But the restaurateur was darting away to reprimand a waiter, and Elias, taking a deep breath, stepped down to join the party. He swallowed another mouthful of champagne for courage and stationed himself beside a table laden with food. From here, through the dark-suited backs and the silk-clad shoulders, he could just make out Sollertinsky's leonine head. And Mravinsky's cool smile — and Shostakovich's face, lit up with mirth, his huge glasses glinting.

Your friends. Wasn't that what the restaurateur had said? *Your friends are over there*. How would they react were he to step onto the podium, shake hands, and lean on the piano beside them? *No*. He gripped his glass. He couldn't do it.

'It's Mr Eliasberg, isn't it?' Suddenly there she was, not two feet away from him. Her eyes were as large and dark as he remembered, and her neck as slim. The swell of her breasts (sometimes, lying in bed, he'd taunted himself with the memory) provided a pleasing contrast with her narrow ribcage.

Very carefully, he set down his glass and extended his hand.

'Do you remember me?' Nina Bronnikova smiled. 'I met you in the Haymarket back in June. On the very day, I believe, before this nightmare of a war officially began.'

'R-r-remember you? How could one possibly n-n-not remember you!'

'Oh, thank you!' She flushed slightly. 'Of course, if you dance for the

Kirov, fielding compliments is part of the job, and not always a welcome one. But what you just said — well, it's the most heartfelt I've ever heard.'

'I'm sorry if I was blunt. My mother's always telling me to become more practised at paying compliments. I've never had what the storybooks call a silver tongue.'

'Silver tongues can hide tarnished hearts,' said Nina Bronnikova.

He remembered this from the fish market: the unpretentious simplicity with which she gave her opinions. Her eyes were almost almond-shaped, slanting up at the outer corners . . . but he shouldn't stare. He should say something. Why couldn't he be more like other men — more like Shostakovich, for instance? Women seemed to hang on the composer's every word, whereas he —

Say something! he shouted inside his babbling head. *Anything!*

'Are you,' he stammered out, 'still dancing?'

She gave a slight frown, and his heart plummeted. Had she been sacked from the Kirov? Received the dreaded summons, been called up before Zagorsky for some imaginary transgression against the State? But surely the outbreak of war had stopped all that, at least for the time being! Flustered, he opened his mouth to apologise.

'Unfortunately,' said Nina, 'my Achilles tendon's troubling me. Even after several weeks of rest, it still hasn't come right. It's extremely disappointing.'

Relief at not offending her, gratitude that she hadn't incurred official censure, pleasure at her devotion to her work — all these rendered Elias joyful and thoughtless, and he drained his champagne glass recklessly. 'Is that all? I imagined something much worse.'

'Well, it's bad enough.' Now she did look offended. 'Don't you realise how hard it is to get medical services these days? All the doctors are examining recruits to be sent to the front, or piecing them back together when they're brought home on stretchers. A weak Achilles tendon isn't a top medical priority in Leningrad at present.'

'I didn't mean to belittle your injury,' he assured her. 'Believe me, I know what it's like to be prevented from working. Aspiring to be the best, yet not having the means to achieve it.' He spoke with an acute awareness of the men on the podium behind him: Sollertinsky, as bold as brass, and cleverer than anyone around him; Mravinsky tilting on a chair with the carelessness of the chosen; Shostakovich gesturing with long-fingered hands that created a magic Elias could never come close to.

'You're right, of course,' nodded Nina. 'A personal injury is nothing compared to what's unfolding around us. It's just that work is my last refuge, and not having it is almost unbearable. Without it, there's nothing to block out all this chaos. Dug-up gardens, sirens, memories of the past — not to mention the fear of what's going to happen to us all.'

'I understand,' said Elias croakily. 'I use work in the same way myself.' He was fearful of admitting the full extent of his fierce working habits. How, sitting up with a score, he'd ignore his mother's calls because he couldn't bear to be pulled away again. The way he blocked his ears and scribbled on more determinedly than ever, copying out the fifty-nine motifs of *Elektra* and a list of its different keys. 'Saved by Strauss,' he would murmur when he finally surfaced — only to find that, when he crept to the door to check on his mother, his relief was overtaken by guilt.

He stared at Nina Bronnikova. 'You shouldn't talk to me. I'm no good. I'm nothing but a lowly beetle.'

But the music had grown louder. Shostakovich's composition assistant, Izrail Finkelshtein, had been hoisted onto the podium and was pounding out a wild improvised polka.

'What did you say?' Nina leaned closer, wafting a faint scent of lilac towards him.

But the moment for confidences was gone. Something closed inside Elias as decisively as a door slamming shut in a wind. 'Simply,' he lied, 'that I don't know many people.'

'What about your orchestra? Aren't they here?'

'A few are here.' He looked around. 'But we've been depleted in the last few weeks. Some of my musicians have gone to the Front; others are exhausted from twelve-hour days of ditch-digging. We're not as fortunate as the Philharmonic. We're not considered national treasures.'

'Can you continue rehearsing?' Nina looked concerned. 'You must be anxious with the autumn season ahead.'

Elias glanced down, his eyes smarting. No one — no one at all — had asked how he felt at the sight of his orchestra splintering before his eyes. 'I'm filled with anxiety,' he admitted. 'My soloists are under par, concentration is low. Our rehearsals sound like those of a shoddy provincial brass band. Yet in six weeks we are scheduled to broadcast Tchaikovsky's Fifth to Britain!' He looked down at his empty glass. 'Can I fetch you a drink?'

But now someone else was beside Nina, touching her on the shoulder. It was Nikolai.

'Hello!' Nina's smile was radiant. 'I thought you'd changed your mind about coming!'

Elias's stomach lurched with a feeling so unfamiliar it bewildered him. Sketching a half-hearted wave at Nikolai, he looked around for another bottle of something — anything at all — though he knew he'd end up regretting it.

Nikolai looked exhausted, his forehead more lined than ever, his beard more wispy. 'I thought about staying home, but this may be the last gathering of Leningrad culture for some time. How could I forgive myself for not farewelling my friends?'

Quickly Elias sloshed vodka into three tumblers. 'A toast to departing friends. By the end of the month you'll both be gone, and I will remain. But distance has little effect on faithful hearts and minds!' He'd never spoken so boldly, and with such effusiveness.

Nikolai raised his glass, and then emptied it as if barely aware of what he was drinking.

'The sentiment's true, but not the facts,' said Nina Bronnikova. 'I'm also staying behind.'

'You're staying?' Elias's giddy heart leapt.

'I decided months ago that whatever happened I would stay in Leningrad. The Kirov's like my family, but Leningrad is my home. Once the company leaves, I'll be free to work with the other women.'

'Are you sure that's wise?' asked Nikolai. 'Quite apart from the fact that the authorities won't like it, who knows what's going to happen here? Novgorod has already been captured; the Luga line has crumbled and is retreating. If the Germans continue to advance, and if they link up with the Finns — well, Leningrad will be completely surrounded.'

'Who can say if we're any better off fleeing to Tashkent?' said Nina. 'Or anywhere, for that matter. Hitler seems to be some kind of madman, and he won't stop until he's marched across the face of the world.'

'I wouldn't talk like that, even here,' said Elias. 'My lead clarinettist has neighbours who —' At the memory of Kholodov's stricken face, he felt his new confidence faltering. 'Please excuse me.' He shoved his empty glass into his pocket and hurried away.

Behind the heavy bathroom door, he found a cool white silence. He stood motionless for a moment, staring at his reflection in the mirror, then pulled out a comb and tried to tidy his hair. 'You're a mess,' he said to himself in a severe but slightly slurred voice.

'Pardon?' An old man shuffled up beside him. 'What did you say?'

'I said, it's quite a press! I've never seen the place so full.' *That's because*, the sober part of his mind added, *you've never been here before.*

'A press indeed.' Meticulously, the old man washed and dried his hands. 'Sollertinsky always draws the crowds. If he weren't a musicologist, he'd make a successful ringmaster.' He peered at Elias. 'It's Mr Eliasberg, isn't it? Conductor of the Radio Orchestra?' He held out a chapped hand. 'I'm Professor Lopatkina from the Conservatoire.'

'How do you do?' Elias made a conscious effort to focus. 'I've seen you about, of course. Nice to meet you at last.' Once the professor had politely bid him good evening and he was alone again, he continued to stare into the mirror. Somewhere behind his high forehead and thin cheeks hovered the face of his father: larger, heavier, but with a similarly determined jaw. 'You may look a mess,' he said to his wavering reflection, 'but you belong. For tonight, at least, you're one of them.'

S hostakovich was feeling happier. He'd eaten some excellent hare seasoned with thyme, and had lost count of the vodkas he'd drunk during a rousing discussion of Stravinsky's musical merits versus his personal flaws. In addition, Prokofiev had been seen slouching from the restaurant, his face like a wet morning in March. 'Problems with his wife,' said Sollertinsky with a knowing nod. 'They say he's been dipping his fingers in the neighbouring jam jar.'

'All the better for Lina Prokofiev,' said Shostakovich. 'Who wants to be married to a goose?' It had been more than six years, but it was hard to forget Prokofiev nosing through the score of *Lady Macbeth*, pronouncing it entertaining but a trifle demented.

'Now that your wife's left the party,' warned Sollertinsky, 'I trust you're not considering following in Prokofiev's wandering footsteps.'

'Assuredly not. Those days are over. Even that beauty —' He nodded at Nina Bronnikova, who was talking to Nikolai. 'Even she couldn't tempt me. No, indeed.' He shook his head, feeling virtuous, secure, even happy. *Happy!* How could this be possible, with his best friend about to travel in one direction and other friends in another, and poor young Fleishman . . . But he couldn't think of this, not tonight. Leaping off the podium, he landed heavily on the toes of the Radio Orchestra conductor.

'Oh, I do beg your pardon!' he said. 'It seems I'm destined to keep bumping into you — quite literally.' The conductor (What was his name? Always, it slipped away!) looked different tonight: his shoulders were squarer and his gaze more direct.

'Perhaps,' replied the conductor with a half-smile, 'I'm fated to stand at the feet of the great. And sometimes under them!'

'If it isn't Karl Eliasberg!' interrupted Sollertinsky. 'Just the man we need. Mravinsky is insisting that when he invests a performance with emotion a sophisticated audience responds accordingly. As an experienced conductor yourself, what's your opinion?'

Elias looked startled. 'I must c-c-confess that I believe the opposite. A conductor may channel the emotion of the music — but he must never display it.' He glanced a little nervously at Mravinsky. 'I d-don't mean to contradict you, but such an attitude proves as much of a downfall for musicians as for conductors. We're none of us there to experience emotion. We're simply there to convey it.'

'Just what I've always said!' Shostakovich slapped him approvingly on the back. 'Musicians and conductors are tools.'

'Or do you mean fools?' Looking amused, Sollertinsky turned to Elias. 'Such is the barely disguised contempt of Dmitri Shostakovich for those who are indispensable to him. Without musicians and conductors, his music remains silent on the page. With their help, it can occasionally approach the sublime.'

'Contempt is too strong a word,' protested Shostakovich. 'It's just that I can't stand the sight of musicians swaying to Mahler, looking as if they're about to burst into tears.'

Elias nodded. 'I have a flautist whom I call the Human Eggwhisk. As soon as Schumann is placed in front of her, she begins to sway. Head, shoulders, ankles, everything must be moving — including her performance!'

Now Mravinsky, looking more handsome than ever in the warm flickering light, was nodding. 'I have several of those. Musicians who believe themselves to be the primary experience of the evening. It's tedious.'

Shostakovich looked at Elias. 'You should have come to the Conservatoire Club. Debates like this were our daily fodder. And now it's too late! Who knows when we'll gather there again?' His glasses misted over and he clasped Elias's hand.

'Perhaps, after the war —?' Elias looked a trifle overwhelmed.

'Dmitri,' said Sollertinsky, 'you're quite impossible. You find emotion repulsive in others, yet you're one of the most emotional men I know. You preach icy detachment in music, yet you're currently working on something intended to stir — and perhaps to save — the whole of Russia.'

Shostakovich swayed slightly. 'I must sit down.' He gave Mravinsky an ineffectual push on the shoulder.

'You should have thought of your need for a seat before holding forth on my shortcomings,' said Mravinsky, sitting immovably in his chair.

Elias fetched another chair and guided Shostakovich into it. 'Tell me, what is it you're working on? I'd be honoured to hear more.'

Shostakovich was dimly aware of a flicker of panic. *Too close, too close.* He swallowed some beer. 'There's really nothing to hear. I can only presume Sollertinsky's referring to my recent masterpiece, composed in response to higher orders, entitled "The Fearless Guards' Regiment Is on the Move".'

Elias's hands flew to his face as if he'd been slapped. 'I didn't mean to pry.'

Shostakovich tilted back, staring at the ceiling. 'It's a military march, designed to motivate the honourable men of the Red Army,' he intoned as if reciting a dull lecture to an equally dull class. 'It sounds passable when heard in the open air from some distance away.'

Sollertinsky glanced at Elias. 'More lubrication's needed!' he called. 'Bring us more grog! Grog's the only known cure for terminal reticence.'

Shostakovich closed his eyes and saw the outline of the chandelier in a sharp red silhouette on the back of his lids. When he opened his eyes again, he saw that Elias had moved to the edge of the podium. His neck was scarlet. Shostakovich groaned. Why hadn't he stopped drinking when he felt the fighting spirit rising up inside? All the same, he'd done what was necessary to save himself.

Dismayed, he looked at Elias's ramrod back. Nina would have known how to patch things up, but Nina was already at home in bed. 'Miss Bronnikova!' he hissed. 'Do you like dancing?'

Nina Bronnikova laughed. 'One would assume so, since I've centred my life around it.'

'I haven't been clear.' Shostakovich focused on her nose, which seemed to be the only completely still point in the moving room. 'I meant dancing as these guests are doing.'

'You look a little worse for wear to dance,' she said. 'Besides, as your wife is no longer here, I wonder if it's appropriate?'

'Oh, I don't want you to dance with me. As you've noticed, I'm barely able to stand. Would you consider —' He gestured towards Elias.

'Mr Eliasberg? Does he need rescuing?'

'Exactly that.' Relieved, Shostakovich sank back in his chair. 'He needs rescuing.'

What an idiot Sollertinsky was, blurting out details about his work in such a setting, knowing so little about it! Yet as soon as he saw his friend blundering towards him, he couldn't help but forgive him.

'So you're playing the pimp now?' Sollertinsky didn't mention what had just happened; he simply proffered a heaped plate of caviar like a peace offering. Together they watched Elias hold out his arm, slightly stiffly, to Nina Bronnikova, and lead her closer to the band.

'Better a pimp than a man who puts his foot in his mouth.' Shostakovich sniffed the caviar but the metallic aroma was no longer the smell of luxury. It merely reminded him of the bent shovel he'd wielded that day, as he'd hacked at the dry ground. 'Besides, I told the truth. I really am working on military music, as well as my own private march, and the combination's driving me mad.'

'It's not the official composing that's getting you down.' Sollertinsky put a hand on his shoulder. 'You've always had to do that, thanks to the . . . how shall I put it? . . . the *philanthropic* regime under which we've flourished. If you ask me, you're more worried about the fact that this time next week you may be watching for incendiaries from the Conservatoire roof.'

'It'll be preferable to ditch-digging.' Shostakovich spread his palms to reveal open sores. 'I'm tired of scrabbling in the dirt.'

'At least you'll be back at the Conservatoire. But on top of the building, rather than inside it!'

Shostakovich looked at Sollertinsky's blunt features: the big nose, the light blue eyes, the vast planes of his cheeks, all of which somehow made up an attractive whole. 'Yes, I'll be back there, but you won't.' The fiery vodka and the sustaining strength of the beer vanished like a sun falling into cloud. He was left with nothing but foreboding.

'I won't be around for a while,' agreed Sollertinsky. 'But no war lasts forever, you know. Perhaps we'll meet again before either of us expects it — if not in Siberia, then back at the club in better days, when you can make amends for your curtness by buying the conductor a drink.' He glanced down at Shostakovich's plate. 'May I? You're not touching that excellent caviar and tomorrow morning it will be wasted on the pigs.'

Shostakovich passed his plate. 'I'm fearful. Fearful that I'll never see you again.' He looked at his friend long and steadily.

'Just get on with that secret work of yours,' said Sollertinsky. 'Put out a few fires to satisfy your nationalistic conscience, and then meet me in Siberia. It may not be the most attractive of holiday destinations, but I hear the girls are pretty.'

She will not go

Elias woke to an unfamiliar feeling. His stomach was rumbling like a heavy cart on cobblestones, and his eyelids rasped. There was thick sweat all over his body: forehead, chest, even the backs of his legs. He rolled over and reached out for Nina Bronnikova. She wasn't there.

The light falling through the thin curtain was too bright, and the hammering and crashing from the street compounded his nausea. *Nina!* Groaning, he closed his eyes again to block out recent reality and his even more recent dream. Taking Nina Bronnikova's arm and escorting her to the dance floor (reality). Her cool hand in his sticky one, her legs moving close to his (reality). His fingers stroking her face, their lips meeting, his hands running over her bare shoulders and down to her arched lower back, her body shuddering with pleasure. *Dream. Dream. Dream.* Despising himself, he rammed his head into his pillow.

When his erection had subsided, he turned on his back and stared at the ceiling, at the large boot-shaped stain caused three winters earlier by a burst water pipe. Of course it looked like a boot; he would never escape his upbringing. Perhaps one was allowed only a glimpse into a better possible life, before falling back into the pit where one belonged? God, this nausea, the frustration and guilt — and the new resentment that throbbed like a cut. Sollertinsky had put out the bait; Elias — stupidly confident — had risen to it. And Shostakovich had thrown him back like an unsatisfactory sprat.

Nina Bronnikova. He repeated it like a mantra. *Nina Bronnikova.* The intimacy he'd felt on waking was caused by nothing more than lust and a ridiculous sense of romance. 'Do you care to dance?' That was all she'd said. He knew even then she was partnering him out of pity, but his tongue had been loosened by alcohol, as well as relief at escaping Shostakovich's unexpected attack, Mravinsky's cool stare and Sollertinsky's jokes. So they'd chatted — about what? About the dacha she owned south of the city, left to her by her grandparents after her parents were killed in a train crash. It was deserted now: dacha owners had been ordered to destroy all crops and food stores, lest they provide sustenance for the enemy. What had Nina done when she left for the last time? She'd locked the door and the garden gate, then cycled back into the city with jam jars and pickles in her basket, and a sack of potatoes on her back. At the checkpoint, the soldiers had searched her belongings and told her she wouldn't be allowed to pass this way again. 'A series of lock-ups,' she said. 'A series of retreats.' She'd clamped her mouth shut and her eyes looked sad. Quickly, Elias had told her of a recent rehearsal when Fomenko had struck the kettle drums so hard that the end flew off his drumstick, bouncing smartly off Marchyk's bald head and into the open mouth of his tuba. Nina had laughed at this, and he'd noticed that her teeth were slightly crooked, and he'd almost kissed her for her beautiful imperfections.

God, he felt ill. He tried to sit up, but the room whirled. He had to get to work. Cautiously, he reached for his watch — and a piercing scream came from the outer room.

'I won't go!' It was his mother, shouting in what sounded like genuine distress.

Just swinging his legs over the edge of the bed made fresh sweat break out on his back. Automatically, he checked the time: barely an hour before he was due at rehearsal.

'Karl! Karl!' His mother sounded panicky. 'For God's sake, help me!'

He pulled on his coat and blundered out. 'What is it, Mother? What on earth is happening?'

Olga Shapran stood in the middle of the room. She was bending over Elias's shrieking mother, pulling at her, half-lifting her out of the chair.

'What in God's name are you doing?' Elias's head felt as if it would explode.

Olga looked at him disapprovingly, taking in his bare feet and his dishevelled hair. 'I tried to wake you. You were snoring like a pig. You've got to help me — your mother's due at the station in less than two hours.'

'Today?' He glanced at the calendar above the stove. 'You've got it wrong. The train leaves next week, not today.'

'The timetable has been changed. Clearly, you've been too busy carousing to listen to the news.' Olga began pulling at his mother's shoulders again. 'Stand up. Get dressed. Do you want to be sent out of Leningrad in your nightclothes?'

'Leave her alone!' Elias's nausea was made worse by his intense dislike of the interfering Olga. 'I'll get her dressed. She doesn't need to be bullied by you.'

'Just trying to help.' Olga's mouth turned down further until she looked like a large and wily trout. 'Just looking out for my neighbours. If it weren't for me, you'd both have slept through your mother's chance at evacuation. One of you snoring from old age, and the other —' she eyed Elias suspiciously, as if sensing his lustful dreams — 'through *over-indulgence*.'

Mrs Eliasberg whimpered and shifted in her chair. 'This is my home. I won't be evacuated like a refugee. I wish to stay here, in my neighbourhood where I belong.'

'Mother.' Elias straightened her woollen shawl. 'We've been through this already. The situation's becoming more dangerous by the day. Have you looked outside recently? Your street is unrecognisable. There's a tram filled with sandbags at your intersection. Your park has become a trench. Your trees are shelters for snipers.' He went to the window and raised the blind, though vomit rose in his throat at the sharpness of the light.

His mother rolled her eyes. 'I'm too ill to travel.' She held out a wavering hand. 'See how it shakes?'

Triumphantly, Olga turned to Elias. 'You see? She's becoming infirm. Which is why we have to get her out of the house and onto that train. You weren't here for the last air-raid practice, so you have no idea what we went through with your mother.'

'No, I wasn't here. In that, at least, you're correct. I was at work, carrying out my duties as a citizen of Leningrad.' He spoke as coldly as he could, trying to ignore his churning bowels.

'Had you been here, you'd have witnessed the near-impossibility of carrying an old woman in a chair down four flights of stairs. Fortunately, *some* men were around to help — my husband, for one.'

'Yes, I understand Mr Shapran has been out of a job for some time now.' Elias gripped the windowsill. 'I'm surprised he hasn't volunteered for a labour battalion by now.'

'He's duty bound to stay with us as long as possible. He's been voted warden of this building.'

'Oh.' Already Elias was tiring of the fight. 'I hadn't realised. I —'

'You artistic types with your heads in the clouds.' Olga seemed slightly mollified. 'Lucky for you you've got practical neighbours. When the real air raids start, you'll be even more grateful we're looking out for you. Now, where's your mother's suitcase?'

'No!' Mrs Eliasberg began banging her head against the back of her chair. 'I won't go. I — will — not — go.' There was fear in her eyes, and she clutched her chair so tightly that her knuckles shone white through her skin.

'You will go!' Olga's temper returned. 'You're another mouth to feed! Another useless body to carry to the air-raid shelter!' She rushed across the room and grabbed Mrs Eliasberg by the ankles. 'See, you can't even move by yourself. You're a liability!'

'That's enough!' Elias launched himself away from the windowsill. 'How dare you touch my mother in such a way!' Grabbing Olga by the hair, he flung her sideways so she staggered against the table. His jar of batons crashed to the floor. 'She's not going. She'll stay here with me. I'll be responsible for her. If we have to endure frequent air raids — *if*, for we still don't know what the Germans are planning — then I'll carry her to the cellar. If I'm not here, Mr Shapran will do it. Is that clear?'

Olga's ruddy face was pale; her freckles stood out like crumbs on a white cloth. She nodded but said nothing.

'What a scene.' Elias glanced down at his bare bony ankles and then, guiltily, at the sparse handful of hair pulled from Olga's head. 'Being at war with barbarians turns us into barbarians ourselves. I apologise.'

Olga shuffled her feet amid the batons and broken glass. She spoke gruffly. 'Can you still conduct with those?'

'The orchestra will neither notice nor care. They rarely do what I ask, even when commanded by batons of a full length.'

A smile twitched at the corner of Olga's trout mouth.

'We're still neighbours, eh?' said Elias. 'Regardless of what the next few months may bring. We're still human beings, rather than liabilities or statistics. Now you must excuse me. I have to go to work.'

Protectively, he stood beside his mother until Olga had disappeared, then he, too, stepped out onto the landing. He made his way up the three small stairs to the blue-painted door and rapped on the wooden panels. Mercifully, there was no one in there. Bolting the door behind him, he knelt on the floor and, with his head in the lavatory bowl, was instantly, copiously sick.

The plea

Shostakovich's paper supply was running low. Three mornings in a row, straggling back to Bolshaya Pushkarskaya Street in the early morning, he'd detoured to the Composers' Union. Three mornings in a row, he was met with blank expressions and empty hands. Everything was running out. Even the farcical old plaster replicas had reappeared in the windows of grocery stores, and bread rations had been cut once again.

'But why has score paper run out?' He ran his hands through his hair. 'Now, of all times? Especially as Prokofiev's no longer in Leningrad to hog it all.'

The clerk gave an uncertain laugh.

'I wasn't joking.' Shostakovich spoke morosely. He had an increasing and not irrational fear of being stopped in his tracks. Stopped by military developments, as the crucial battle at Mga was still raging and the German lines were coiling closer around Leningrad. Stopped by Nina, demanding they leave the city. Stopped by lapsed concentration, exhaustion or illness. The music he'd written over the past weeks was like a steam train at his back, bearing down, forcing him on. It was bad enough thinking about what he still had to write, without fretting about what he was supposed to write *on*. 'Can't you give me something?'

The clerk shuffled through logbooks as if to postpone the bad news. Finally he looked up. 'It appears our deliveries have been temporarily halted.'

Shostakovich sighed. 'Please try to get me some, by whatever means you can. It's extremely important.'

In recent days the clerk, having witnessed the departure of almost all regular Union visitors, had become increasingly gloomy. The building was a ghost-ship with his puny reluctant self at the helm, and outside a fearsome storm was brewing. But now his chin lifted. 'You mean to say you're still *composing*? And it's something *important*? I suppose it'd be impertinent to enquire what it . . . might be.' His sentence ended in a nervous squeak.

Shostakovich dropped his fire helmet with a clang. 'I'm not sure. That is, I can't speak about it.' By the time he'd stooped, banged his head on the desk and retrieved his helmet, his dislike of the clerk was complete. His wife and his best friend: these were the only two who'd possibly earned the right to enquire about his work in progress. In fact, due to past experience, neither Sollertinsky nor Nina had asked very much at all. How would a spindly idiot behind a desk have any insight into Shostakovich's rough black notation?

'Just move heaven and earth to get me some paper,' he said curtly.

'I'll try, sir. I hear that you're fire-watching now?'

'Yes, I'm keeping watch on the roof of the Conservatoire.'

'How ironic!' The clerk peered at him deferentially. 'For so long you've nurtured our city from inside that building, and now you're protecting us from its heights.'

More than ever, Shostakovich wished someone else would enter the room and save him. But the Union, once full of people he wished to avoid, was dismayingly empty. 'I suppose it's ironic,' he muttered.

The clerk was beginning to look elated. Never before had the chance arisen to talk to Shostakovich at such length! 'I'm hoping to join you at your post, perhaps as early as next week. Now that most of our musical best have departed, my work here has almost disappeared. And physical disabilities prevent me from going to the Front.' He stuck out a thin leg. 'Polio. Struck when I was six. My mother feared for my life — but now, perhaps, it's saved me.'

'Your limbs, my eyesight.' Shostakovich spoke with the fearsome civility he reserved for the overly familiar. 'Any firebombs that fall on our city will be dealt with by crocks and cripples.'

'Indeed. We, too, have our part to play.' The clerk's expression was almost coquettish.

Shostakovich stepped back. The pull of comradeship, so desired by others, aroused in him a kind of physical repulsion. 'I must go,' he said abruptly. 'I've got work to do, though all too little paper on which to do it.'

The streets, bathed in early sunlight, were relatively calm. Tanks lay under tarpaulins and the trams overturned across intersections looked as if they, too, were sleeping. Sandbags were piled around the bases of statues, while boarded-up monuments floated like unwieldy arks on the cobblestones. Shostakovich knelt beside one to retie his bootlace and realised he could no longer remember what was concealed behind the boards. He'd always been in such a hurry, rushing to the Conservatoire, rushing back to the apartment.

A sudden roar made him jump. Fuel trucks with flags fluttering from their roofs — 'Defend the gains of the October Revolution!' — were rumbling across the square in the direction of the train station. Glimpsing the faces of the men behind the streaked windscreens, Shostakovich could tell that some of them were no more than seventeen or eighteen. What did the Revolution mean to them? Well, now they'd have their own battle to tell tales about — if they survived. He wiped his eyes and hurried away.

When he got home, the apartment was quiet and dark. Very quietly, he laid his helmet in a corner and pulled off his boots. The bedroom door remained closed.

He tiptoed to the side table. The top drawer was locked: was the key still hanging in the crockery cupboard? He opened the cupboard door little by little and groped along the wall. A cup spun on the edge of the shelf; he caught it in mid-air. Thank God! The door behind him was still closed — and there it was under his fingers, the small iron key, the shape of work to come. His clenched stomach eased.

No sooner had he unlocked the drawer than the bedroom door flew open, and out rushed Maxim, loud and furious in his calico nightgown. 'I *won't* stay in bed any more!'

Nina appeared, her hair in a glossy ponytail. 'Sorry. I tried my best.' Half-apologetic, half-defiant, she padded across the room and began unhooking the blackout curtains from the top windows.

Next came Galina, her face lighting up at the sight of her father. She twirled in front of him and began singing in a slightly self-conscious way. (Sollertinsky was to blame for this; ever since he'd announced that her voice was promising, she preferred singing to speaking.) 'Where was Papa all night long?' she sang. 'Does he like my morning song?'.

Shostakovich tried to smile. 'Yes, Papa likes it, but he's very tired. He's been on a rooftop all night, looking out for fires, and now he has to work on his music.'

'If I couldn't find a fire,' sang Galina, 'I'd go and join a choir.'

'I'm hungry,' growled Maxim. 'Damn hungry.'

'Don't swear,' said Nina, 'or you'll stay hungry all day.' Simultaneously she boiled water, mixed porridge and combed Galina's hair. Watching her, Shostakovich thought she looked like a beautiful, severe, many-handed Madonna.

'How did it go last night?' She looked over one shoulder as she spoke. Her enquiry was sharp-edged, as if she hoped that finally the firebombs had arrived, a bright white shower falling on the Leningrad domes and merging into a running field of fire. For as soon as the Germans began bombing, even pig-headed patriots like her husband would be forced to leave.

He thought back to the night he'd just spent under the velvet August sky. The moon, so low and large he could set it swinging like a pendulum. The familiar streets were transformed into an unfamiliar tableau, fountains and buildings like paper cutouts rimmed with light. Far away on the horizon came the occasional flash of a different light: German gunfire and the Soviet reply. But this, too, had seemed unreal, no more than an operatic effect. On the Conservatoire roof the hours had fallen away, and by the time sunrise stained the eastern sky Shostakovich had lived through several lifetimes.

He stared at Nina, dazed. 'It was quiet. Yes, extremely quiet. Perhaps our troops will hold Mga after all, and the Germans will be forced to retreat.' A melodic line hung in his head, somehow connected to the bright moon and the silence, but now it was in danger of disappearing altogether.

'Do you actually listen to the radio reports?' Nina placed the pot on the stove with a clang. 'Or do you mentally rewrite them for your own convenience?'

Galina leaned against Shostakovich's legs like a cat. 'What's that you're holding?'

Stroking her smooth head, Shostakovich felt the first waves of tiredness breaking over him. Perhaps he should lie down for an hour and gather some energy for the task ahead? 'It's something my Da made. He made it when I was a boy and he was working as an engineer.'

'What's it for?' Maxim stared at the spidery gadget, forgetting his hunger.

'It draws five lines at once. You can make musical paper with it. I need some because the Composers' Union has run out and I have to finish my march.' This last sentence was largely for Nina's benefit: an explanation without any tedious detail.

'Your march? That boom-boom one we've heard on the piano?'

'It won't end with a boom, Galya' He cast a longing glance at the workroom door. 'It will end with a sigh, and perhaps a few tears. It will end quietly — as long as I can get some quiet time to end it.'

'Are you really low on paper?' So Nina had heard his plea! Now perhaps he'd be allowed to leave the kitchen, fighting off the need for sleep, beckoning to the faint sounds he'd heard some hours earlier.

'Yes, God knows what they've been using score paper for. That numbskull Prokofiev probably took a stash to the Caucasus for scribbling his crap on. And Khachaturian took the rest to the Urals. It might as well be used as toilet paper.' He spoke lightly; winning Nina over, even temporarily, always made him feel better.

She was laying out mugs and spoons on the table. 'Are you eating with us?'

'I'm not hungry. I got something at the Union canteen.'

'Is that so?' Nina regarded him steadily. 'What did you get — white lies with onions? You're getting so thin, you need to eat.'

'Stop fussing!' He lost his patience. 'I've got a job to do. And it's a damn sight more important than perching on a rooftop, watching for non-existent bombers.'

He slammed his way into his workroom and barricaded the door with a chair. *Don't try to come in*, he prayed, opening the lid of the piano. There was no time for recriminations and apologies.

———

Much later, he raised his head. He could hear a hammering — not the thudding ground-bass of his strings, as he'd first thought. It was definitely external.

With a sigh, he went out into the main room. It was empty and tidy. The dishes were stacked away. The children's overshoes had gone from beside the door. The onslaught of knocking continued.

'Who is it?'

'Dmitri!' The voice was familiar. 'It's me! Let me in.'

Alarmed, he flung open the door. 'Nikolai! What in God's name has happened? Are the Germans inside the city gates?'

Nikolai stumbled past him and sank down in a chair, his chest heaving. He looked as if he'd run all the way from his apartment, some fifteen blocks away. 'It's Sonya! It's . . . my . . . Sonya.'

'No! Tell me she's safe. Has Pskov been attacked?'

'She never got there. I've just had word from my wife's sister. The train never arrived. At first they thought it was delayed — nothing unusual, as some trains have stood in sidings for days, waiting for the all-clear. But now —' Tears ran down his cheeks as silently as rain. 'Now it's been a week, and there have been reports of a German attack on the line to Pskov. They can't say which train was hit, but it's likely —' He stopped and laid his head on the table, crying so hard the wood creaked under the weight of his grief.

Shostakovich hovered beside him. 'You mustn't give up hope. These reports are often bullshit — ninety per cent rumour, ten per cent hearsay. You've been intending to join the Conservatoire in Tashkent, haven't you? Why not go there as planned, and surely you'll soon hear good news about Sonya.' But his head was still ringing with the notes he'd just written; the thudding of the timpani held the authority of a death march, and he found it hard to believe his own words.

'I can't go away now,' said Nikolai, lifting his head. 'I must stay here, in case she makes her way home.' He wiped his eyes and blew his nose. 'I must find something to do while I wait for her to come home. Perhaps I can work in a munitions factory. Or lend my support to the Radio Orchestra.'

'That will raise the spirits of our melancholic conductor!' Shostakovich, clumsy from thirty hours without sleep, tried for a joke. 'If Elias gets one of Russia's finest violinists to join his ragged band, he'll smile for the first time in a decade.'

Nikolai's swallow was painfully loud in the quiet room. 'I came to you not just because you're my friend. I hoped you might help me find out the truth.'

'The truth about what?'

'About what happened to the train. The Kremlin listens to you, after all. Your name's known by the top authorities, not only in the cultural department but also in defence.' He fixed his eyes on Shostakovich. 'I ask you — I *beg* you. Would you make use of your position to find out the truth about Sonya?'

A light breeze rattled the window frame; Shostakovich took off his glasses and began polishing them with his handkerchief. 'I'm so sorry,' he said at last.

Nikolai stood up in a rush, his chair crashing to the floor. 'I've offended you! If it were anyone but Sonya, I'd never ask for such a thing. I know you loathe asking the Party for privileges, that you never do it even for yourself, that you despise people who try to use your influence for their gain. I know all this, and I'm sure you hate me for presuming. But it's Sonya — it's my Sonya!' He backed away from the chair as if it were a body on a battlefield.

'Please believe me, Nikolai. If I could do anything to find her, if I could make any phone calls or send any telegrams, I would do so instantly. But from the day the Germans breached our borders, my influence has counted for nothing. I can't even get score paper to continue my work. Stalin and his generals are concentrating on military strategy, not musical matters. At present, in official eyes, I'm smaller than an ant.'

'Of course.' Nikolai's hectic flush had faded, leaving his face waxy. 'You're right. I've been grasping at straws.'

'As one does, when the river is closing over one's head.' Tears stung Shostakovich's eyes; he'd just remembered Sonya's small hand on his arm as he'd walked her home down Nevsky Prospect. Was it possible the train carrying her to safety was now a twisted mess of metal? Carriages splintered apart, fragments of bone scattered over the dry ground?

'I must go.' Nikolai sounded more definite. He picked up the chair and set it neatly in at the table. 'I'll go to the *Pravda* offices to see if anyone there knows anything. I'm sorry if I interrupted your work.'

Shostakovich kissed him on both cheeks. 'Don't mention it. I'm quite used to interruptions. You know what it's like trying to work with youngsters —' He stopped, bit his lip and rushed on. 'Even if my name were General Shaposhnikov or Marshal Voroshilov, I'd be unable to help you. Our commanders are masters of chaos, attempting to steer Russia with neither a plan in front of them nor experience behind them. Details go unnoticed, the bigger picture confounds them. We're in the hands of fools and idiots, thanks to the way the army was decimated by our own leader. You don't think the bumbling generals who survived the purge would know where evacuees are, do you, when they can scarcely locate their own brains?'

'I understand what you're saying.' Nikolai's head drooped. 'It's hopeless, of course. But nonetheless I must go on searching.'

'It's not hopeless,' urged Shostakovich, 'and you must go on hoping. Hearing Sonya play, I felt sure she was destined for a great future. I still feel that now, and my instincts are seldom wrong.'

'I have the cello. Perhaps, like the beam of a lighthouse, it will bring her home.' But Nikolai walked to the door like a blind man, hands outstretched as if to stop himself falling.

Back in his workroom, Shostakovich sat at the desk for some minutes, his shoulders heaving. Then he wiped his face on his sleeve, picked up his father's shaky hand-made gadget, and began tracing staves on the backs of old composition essays as if his life depended on it. The metal spider moved lightly and crookedly over the paper, leaving trailing lines in its wake. Page after page, rhythm soothing away thought until the chaos of the world was reduced to five clean but uneven lines.

PART III
Autumn 1941

The descent

September was cold and grey. Every day the sun hid behind thick cloud as if avoiding the sight of German tanks poised at Leningrad's gates. The urgency of the summer had been replaced by a strange lethargy growing like moss over the surface of the city. Ordinary activities were interspersed with extraordinary ones but, whether shuffling in bread queues or training for grenade-throwing, people spoke in flat voices and their faces were as dull as the gun-metal sky.

Shostakovich was feeling increasingly exhausted. His legs ached and there was a constant pain behind his eyes. 'Perhaps it's because my thirty-fifth birthday is approaching,' he said to Nina. 'I'm becoming an old man.'

'Fire-watching all night and composing all day is enough to make anyone feel old. Besides, you always feel ill when you're writing. Once you've finished this work, you'll be fine.'

'Once I've finished! The problem is —' He took a burning gulp of tea, glanced at Nina, who was grating potatoes, and plunged into an admission, hoping it wasn't a mistake. 'This is only a first movement. Although this one may be done in a few days, there'll still be a second movement to write, and then a third and a fourth.'

'It's going to be . . . a symphony?'

'I'm afraid so. You'd think twenty-five minutes of thunder and lightning would be enough. But a few days ago I was forced to acknowledge that there is more to come.' He remembered the moment with something close to annoyance. As he'd dragged a bucket of sand up the steep steps to the Conservatoire roof, suspicion had hardened into certainty. The final grumbles of the main theme, the tanks fading into the distance — they weren't final. There was more to write.

Nina gave a small sigh. Perhaps she was remembering the last stages of the Sixth Symphony, when he'd plummeted into such a severe depression he couldn't get out of bed? Mixing flour into the grated potato, she made a face. 'I could do with an egg.'

'And I could do with a scherzo,' he said gloomily. 'Then an adagio, then a finale. Wonderful.'

'You might be pleasantly surprised. After all, the Sixth turned out to be only three movements.'

He toyed with his glass, turning it between his fingers, watching the clear liquid spin inside.

'You'll be fine.' She turned from her cooking and gave him a bright smile.

Shostakovich grunted. He resented being told he'd be fine when he knew with conviction, he would never be fine again. The constant nervous energy that drove him on was giving him diarrhoea (inconvenient when stuck on a roof for hours without anyone to relieve his watch). He might die in a flurry of bombs, with his arse stuck in a bucket. A fitting end for a prominent Soviet composer! Then Stalin would regret the harassment he'd ordered over the years. 'Comrade Shostakovich?' he'd say from behind his walrus moustache. 'I'm sorry to say I hounded him to the point where he became a nervous wreck. This was before the war with Germany, of course. The Seventh Symphony was his last; his bowels were shot to pieces from the strain. The trouble began in 1936, when I misjudged his opera, and it ended, somewhat ironically, on the roof of the building where he studied. Caught by the Junkers with his pants down, shitting like a firebomb — not the way we want our greatest men remembered —'

'What?' With a jolt, he returned to the present.

Nina was beside him, taking the tea from his hands. 'Can you call the children in? We'll eat in ten minutes.' Even in the dull papered-window light, her exhaustion was plain.

'Nina,' he said earnestly. 'I know you want us to leave Leningrad, but please understand. It seems wrong to flee like rats from a sinking ship.'

She averted her face. 'That's beginning to sound like an excuse to make yourself feel better about risking your children's lives.'

'An excuse? *An excuse?* I hardly think that saving Leningrad from destruction qualifies as a bloody excuse!'

'The only thing you're bothered about saving is yourself.' Nina's voice rose. 'You can't bear to be interrupted in the middle of writing. You're scared that if we leave now, you'll lose track of what you're working on. Your music is far more important to you than your family or your country. Why don't you just tell the truth?' She marched over to the window. 'Galina, Maxim, come inside now!'

Shostakovich sank back in his chair. Of course evacuating now would pose a danger to his work. He'd managed to wrest a strange routine from the chaos around him, and if this was interrupted he wasn't sure he could go on composing. 'If they start to shell us, then we can reassess.' Stating this made him feel better: more decisive and authoritative, more like the head of a family. 'Shells,' he repeated. 'And bombs. Once these things start, it may be the right time to pack our bags and leave.'

Running for cover

For two days, all anyone talked about was the first artillery attack on the southern edges of the city. Several of Elias's musicians came to work with lurid tales passed on by neighbours, or the friends of neighbours, or the neighbours of friends.

'Like the best fishing tale,' said Alexander, 'the shells become bigger and louder with every mouth.' He alone seemed unfazed by the news that the crucial junction at Mga had fallen; that rail lines east to Tikhvin and Moscow and south to Luga had been cut, leaving one tenuous link across Lake Ladoga. In spite of the fact that bread rations had been further reduced and food supplies would barely last a month, in spite of the fact that German shells were now raining down on factories and churches, ripping up the streets and setting rooftops alight, Alexander sat back and cracked jokes — though no one laughed.

Today he was disrupting rehearsal with more stories. 'Yuri's sister-in-law was out shopping,' he said in a dramatic voice, 'and suddenly she heard a faraway screaming.'

'It was more of a moaning than a screaming,' interrupted Katerina Ginka. 'Vasily Smirnova told me it sounded like a woman in the throes of childbirth.'

Alexander looked annoyed. 'Well, it rapidly became a screaming once the shells began to fall. Suddenly they were raining all over the street and bursting on the pavement like melons. Human flesh was flying through the air and splattering over the shop fronts. One woman lost her arm and her shopping bag; another woman grabbed the bag out of the dismembered hand and ran off with it.' At this there were groans and gasps. Alexander smirked. 'As Yuri said, only a woman would think of supplies at a time like that.'

Katerina looked at him witheringly. Their love match, it seemed, had already burned itself out. 'I heard the women were wonderful. It was the men cowering in doorways, while the women went back out to drag in the wounded. Some people had their faces blown right off. There were only holes where their features had been.'

Elias had heard enough. He rapped on the stand with his baton. 'Please,' he said, trying to cover his dismay and shock, 'remember why we are here.'

'To play sitting ducks?' The proximity of death had made Alexander even bolder. 'Here we are, preparing to quack like birds for our unseen English listeners, waiting for shrapnel to tear our wings off. Is it worth it?'

Before Elias could speak, old Petrov took up the cudgels. 'Shut up. We'll keep rehearsing until shells fall on our own heads, because that's our job.'

'Thank you,' said Elias faintly. He could imagine only too clearly the writhing bodies and the boarded-up shops sprayed with blood.

'If there's any justice in the world,' added Petrov, staring at Alexander, 'the noisiest bird will get the first shell.'

'Perhaps we should look for somewhere else to rehearse,' suggested Kholodov. 'If we move to the northern edge of the city, we'll be further away from those murdering bastards and out of range of their missiles.'

'The north will become the most dangerous if they start bombing us the way they have in Moscow,' objected Fomenko. 'They won't risk blowing the shit out of their own men.'

And so the squabbling and the bickering began all over again, while Nikolai sat quietly in his usual position at the back of the violins. He'd adamantly refused Elias's suggestion that he take up the position of concertmaster. 'It would be more than my life's worth. I'd rather face German artillery than the collective wrath of an orchestra.' Now Elias was uncomfortably aware of Nikolai's objective gaze as the orchestra became more unruly, arguing over Luftwaffe tactics in the same way they fought over interpretations of minor Russian composers. It took all his new-found confidence to raise his voice and tell them to be quiet, that they were obliged to keep playing both in spite and because of this sodding war.

It wasn't until the next morning on the tram that he realised how exhausted he'd become. He sat in a trance, staring out at a city transformed. Familiar parks slashed by trenches, piles of rusty bedsteads and girders stacked across intersections. It reminded him of his father's workroom at its busiest: dismayingly chaotic, with no apparent end in sight. He glanced into his briefcase to check the neat scores knotted with string, and pens lined up in canvas holders. Reassured by order, he closed his eyes.

Suddenly the air was ripped apart by sirens. The blaring was entirely different from the sound of air-raid practices — though perhaps this was because it was fused with an unfamiliar whining. The tram halted suddenly, throwing passengers forwards in their seats. Out in the street urgent instructions were being called through loudspeakers.

'What is it?' The old woman beside Elias sounded confused; her scarf had slid forward over her face, making her look like a hooded-eyed reptile. 'What are they saying?'

'It's an air raid! A real one.' Elias's heart had leapt into his throat; he could hardly speak. 'We've got to move!'

There was a crush as people shoved their way towards the doors and out onto the street. 'Go to the Alexandrinsky Theatre! Run!' The driver's cheeks were flushed a deep crimson.

Theatre Street looked impossibly long, its brown facades and arched windows disappearing into a haze. Already the driver had taken off, a few passengers stumbling behind him. Elias glanced towards the horizon and saw black shapes sweeping in like bats over the city. He gasped, put his briefcase over his head, and ran.

Time moved in odd, unwieldy chunks. He sprinted for what seemed like an age, then found himself tumbling through huge oak doors and falling down some stairs. All of a sudden he found himself motionless, lying in pitch darkness, face down on a cold tiled floor. The body of an elderly man was pressed close against him, his warm wheezing breath filling Elias's nose and mouth.

How long were they there for? It was hard to tell; there were muffled sounds from outside, and the shifting of bodies inside — and all around was total blackness, increasing Elias's sense of disembodiment. Later he couldn't remember what he'd thought or felt. The first clear moment was the distant wail of the all-clear siren.

After some minutes, people got to their feet in silence and shuffled up the stairs. Elias was first out onto the street. There were columns of smoke rising in the direction of the river.

'I never thought it would be like this.' The tram driver was beside him now, brushing dirt and grit off his trousers. 'I never thought they'd start bombing us so early in the day — before we've even digested our breakfast.' Shaking his head, he headed back in the direction of the trolley-car.

Elias stood still for a minute longer, mesmerised by the smoky sky. He rarely had preconceived notions about anything but he was also surprised — not by the Germans' audacity, but by the fact he'd just been through an air raid and wasn't gibbering with fear.

It seemed odd, too, that life could simply go on; that the tram was still there and people were back in the streets, resuming their places in bread queues and quarrelling over who'd been first. Elias, still clutching his briefcase, boarded the tram and returned to the seat he'd been in before. But when they reached the Bolshaya Pushkarskaya stop, he wasn't sure if he could stand; his legs felt disconnected from the rest of his body. He shuffled into the aisle, using the hand-rail for support.

'This isn't your usual stop!' said the old reptilian woman, her pursed lips almost disappearing into her creased chin. 'Shouldn't you be going home, anyway, to check that your mother is safe?'

Who was she? She looked vaguely familiar: perhaps a one-time customer of his father, or an acquaintance of his mother from the days when she still had friends and went out. He bowed stiffly. 'I have an important errand to run. Besides, I'm sure my mother will be unharmed. The bombs have clearly struck the north and the east of the city, while the south side has been spared.'

'Uncaring upstart,' mumbled the woman. 'Society's going to the dogs, that's what I say, when children no longer —'

'Shut up, you old crone! It's none of your business.' Elias pushed his way towards the door. He didn't need to be reminded about carrying out his duty — particularly when that was just what he was doing.

The side streets in this part of the city seemed peaceful, as if a thunderstorm had passed and the birds were about to start singing. Elias hadn't been here before, but standing on the stone steps and looking up at the windows, he felt as if he were coming home. He paused for a moment, breathing deeply, before he climbed the stairs to the fifth-floor landing. Only when he knocked on the door did he notice that his knuckles were badly grazed and smeared with dust.

Shostakovich himself opened the door. His dark hair was standing on end, his face was pale, and a long smudge of ink marked his forehead.

There was such a racket coming from the room behind him it was impossible to hear a word he said.

'Good morning.' Elias spoke loudly, though the din made him suddenly doubt his purpose. What on earth was he doing? The old woman was right. He should be at home — this was no place for him, today of all days.

The noise continued unabated: shrieking, wailing and fitful crying. 'Would — you — be — quiet!' roared Shostakovich.

There was instant silence.

Elias stepped back. 'I'm sorry —'

'Please excuse me. I wasn't speaking to you, of course!' Shostakovich wiped his forearm over his face, so that his sleeve, too, garnered an inky smear. 'My family's upset by this morning's air raid — although I'm afraid such a circus is nothing out of the ordinary.' He looked at Elias as if seeing him properly for the first time. 'If it isn't Karl Eliasberg! Please, come in.'

The room was large and sparsely furnished, filled with a hazy light. On the sofa sat Nina Shostakovich, her sleek black head bent over two smaller ones as she spoke soothingly over snuffling breaths and small sobs. 'Good morning,' she said to Elias. 'I'm sorry for the noisy welcome.'

'Not at all. Excuse me for arriving unannounced.' Elias sounded awkward and apologetic, speaking over his shoulder as he scuttled after Shostakovich into another room.

'Pandemonium.' Shostakovich shut the door firmly and sank down on the piano stool. 'After the sirens began we went to the cellar, where we were forced to sit for God knows how long in close proximity to neighbours with whom I have no wish to spend two minutes. Now the bombs have given my wife ammunition of her own. She's adamant we must leave Leningrad within the hour.' He stared at the stack of paper at his feet and seemed to speak to himself. 'Unfinished. Unsatisfactory. Nevertheless, she wants to leave by tomorrow!'

Elias sat down in the nearest chair and placed his briefcase on his knees. 'I s-s-seem to have arrived at a difficult time. Forgive me for intruding, but I have something here that you might find useful.'

'Any time in this household is a difficult time. I can understand why Beethoven eschewed family life in favour of brief romances. Can you imagine what the *Eroica* might have become had its creator been forced to cope with two children?'

Elias coughed uncertainly. 'Speaking of the *Eroica*, I'd like the Radio Orchestra, at some time in the future —'

'The Radio Orchestra?' Shostakovich sat up straighter. 'That might, indeed, be possible — although Mravinsky seems to know how my mind works.' He peered at Elias from behind his steel-rimmed glasses. 'How are they shaping up, your orchestra?'

'The orchestra is satisfactory, considering the circumstances. Depleted in numbers owing to military commitments, but we're managing. We're currently rehearsing Tchaikovsky's Fifth —'

'Yes, yes, I know this from my good friend Nikolai. I'm not interested in your repertoire, but rather in the calibre of your musicians. For instance, what's the state of your wind section?'

'My wind section,' repeated Elias. 'My wind section?' Being alone with Shostakovich was having a strange effect on him. There was ringing in his ears and a red blur at the edge of his vision.

Shostakovich moved restlessly. 'Are they strong? It's some time since I've attended one of your performances.'

'Are they strong?' Elias could have bitten out his parrot tongue. He tore his eyes away from Shostakovich's mesmerising stare, trying to think more clearly. 'They're talented enough. Though I'm dissatisfied with my lead oboist and hope to replace him before the year's out. But with the war . . .' He trailed away. 'Everything is uncertain now.'

'I see.' Shostakovich sounded disappointed. 'The oboe is most important. What about the rest?'

'The rest I'm reasonably content with.' He was floundering. Surely his contentment wasn't Shostakovich's primary concern — but what was? 'They've been playing together for six years, so the trombones are excellent, as are the horns. And my trumpets were recently described, in a review by Semyon Shlifsteyn, as some of the finest of this century. But perhaps you read that in *Pravda* last spring?' He paused hopefully but Shostakovich was staring past him, looking rather vague. 'As for their lung capacity,' he hurried on, 'that must be the best in Russia, if the constant shouting and arguing is anything to go by!'

The joke was wasted on Shostakovich, who began tapping his pencil on the desk in a rapid, considering way. 'If only I could get word from Sollertinsky or Mravinsky. Who knows if they even have adequate rehearsal facilities in Novosibirsk? But it's been a fortnight, and I hear nothing! Nothing!'

Elias flushed with an entirely irrational guilt. After all, it wasn't his fault that Leningrad's top musicians were exiled in Siberia, nor that the postal service was more unreliable than ever, nor that the military censors had the power to intercept correspondence if offended by a minor point of punctuation. 'I, too, have had no news,' he ventured, though there was no reason in the world why anyone in the Philharmonia, let alone its Artistic Director or orchestral conductor, might write to him, even in peacetime.

'I'd hoped for something here in Leningrad.' Shostakovich scratched his ear with his pencil. 'Though, naturally, that depends on the course of the war.'

'Naturally.' Elias was beginning to feel dizzy.

'But what am I thinking?' It seemed that Shostakovich was looking at Elias properly for the first time. 'I haven't asked you about your own experience of this terrible morning. I hope you weren't harmed in any way?'

'No, not harmed, thank you for asking. I happened to be close to a shelter when the planes appeared, and nowhere near the districts where the bombs were dropped.'

'That's a mercy. Though I fear it's now obvious what German tactics will be. Not content with imprisoning us in our own city, they intend to make daily life a living hell.'

'Yes, it seems this morning was only a taste of what's to come.' Once more Elias heard the terrible whine of the planes, saw them sweeping in like a plague, blackening the sky. He groped for his handkerchief and wiped his forehead.

'Please don't mention such things to my wife,' said Shostakovich, glancing at the door in a slightly hunted way. 'I wouldn't wish to alarm her.'

'I wouldn't dream of it. In fact, I've got little time to speak to anyone, for I must hurry to rehearsal. The purpose of my visit —' But now Elias's stutter welled up again, and his tongue turned to wood. 'I h-h-heard . . . someone t-t-told me —' Giving up, he reached inside his jacket and laid the bulky paper parcel on the desk. 'I'm s-s-sorry it's crumpled. I'm afraid I lay on it during the air raid.'

Somewhat gingerly, Shostakovich removed the wrappings. For a few seconds he sat and stared, then he sprang up from his stool. 'Score paper!' he cried, brandishing it above his head. 'And so much of it! Where in heaven's name did you get it? It's harder to find than the rainbow's end!'

Elias's face burned. 'I've been saving it ever since my composition classes at the Conservatoire. I didn't need much. Never was much good at composing, you know.'

'This is wonderful! Marvellous! I can't tell you what a difference this will make. Not having to scrimp and save, especially not having to battle with this —' He waved something that looked like a large metal spider. 'How can I ever repay you?'

'There's no need.' Elias shuffled his feet under his chair. 'I'm pleased to be of service.'

'Can you stay a minute longer?' Shostakovich's face shone. 'I finished a work — at least, the first movement of a work — a couple of days ago.' But he didn't wait for Elias to answer. He snatched up some pages lying beside the piano, drew in his stool, held his hands above the keyboard for a moment, and began to play.

As the notes built up into a solid wall, Elias sat perfectly still, watching Shostakovich's slightly stubbled, concentrated face. The composer's mouth twitched as he played and he hammered at the keys as if they were made of steel rather than ivory. Sometimes his hands leapt over each other, left hand soaring over right and back again.

As the march-like theme grew louder, the piano began to shake. Sheets of paper leapt off the rack and sliced through the air. But Shostakovich was no longer looking at the music; his face was almost touching the keyboard and his glasses were suspended at the end of his nose. Then, in the middle of a savagely repeated phrase, he broke off altogether. The only sound was of plates clattering in the main room.

Shoving his glasses back onto his nose, Shostakovich sat back, breathing hard. 'The rest of it is to be a bassoon solo. A kind of elegy. But it doesn't sound effective on the piano.'

At last Elias could let go of his chair. His fingers were red and grooved from gripping the wood. 'It's . . . Oh, it's —!' But the room was blurring; quickly, he wiped his eyes. 'Is it to be a symphony?'

'Yes, though I didn't know it at first. I began it in the first weeks of the German advance.'

'A war symphony. For Leningrad.' Elias's voice sounded tiny in the aftermath of Shostakovich's bold, defiant notes. 'It will be your *Eroica*.'

Shostakovich's flush was fading. Suddenly he looked smaller and thinner, his shirt hanging loosely from his shoulders. 'Some might say that. If they're kind. But it's more likely this will be hailed as my *Wellington's Victory* — which, as you know, represented Beethoven at his most simple-minded.'

'The premiere of *Wellington's Victory* featured Vienna's finest performers!' protested Elias. 'Salieri, Meyerbeer — the audience loved it! You can't deny it was extremely popular.'

'Popular, yes.' Shostakovich shrugged.

'Like Beethoven, you've captured the very essence of war. The people of Leningrad can't help but hear that.'

'A naturalistic portrayal of battle may win popular approval, but, as Beethoven proved, it can also turn out to be an aesthetic embarrassment.' Shostakovich's shoulders slumped lower with every word. 'Do you not think,' he added, 'that this movement is somewhat reminiscent of Ravel's *Bolero*?'

'That's it! I couldn't immediately place it, but yes, it is similar to *Bolero* — the quiet start, the crescendo, the insistent repetition.'

Shostakovich began raking up the loose pages at his feet. 'That's exactly how the critics will damn me. They'll say I've copied Ravel. Well, let them say it. This is how I hear war.' He glanced around, then dumped the pages into a large saucepan standing under the piano.

'Not *only* Ravel,' said Elias hastily. 'I heard definite echoes of *Ein Heldenleben*. And perhaps a nod, too, towards the second movement of Sibelius's Fifth.'

'Really?' Shostakovich's glasses glinted in the filtered light. 'Strauss, Sibelius — and what about Tchaikovsky? Could you detect elements of him, too?'

'The *1812* did come to mind.' Elias began to feel as if he were back in the Conservatoire on examination day.

'Another naturalistic battlepiece. Interesting.'

'But of course Tchaikovsky is very much on my mind,' stammered Elias. 'In three weeks we're broadcasting the Fifth to Britain. And the *1812* has already been scheduled as part of our winter programme.'

'The final charge,' said Shostakovich in a low voice, 'will be that I'm becoming derivative of my own work. A seventh symphony necessarily carries the other six on its back. Yet how can I avoid this, unless I stop composing?' He went over to the faded divan and sat with his hands on his knees, staring at the floor. 'If only Sollertinsky were here. He could help me.'

Elias's stomach began to tie itself in painful knots. The atmosphere in the room had become chilly, the conversation sealed over like a pond in winter. Shamefully, he almost longed for the sound of another air-raid siren.

Instead the rain arrived — a squall that hit the windowpanes and made him jump. Shostakovich sprang up and pulled the saucepan out from under the piano, throwing the manuscript pages onto the floor. 'We have leaks. The water gathers on the sill and pours in somewhere about here.' He stood with the pan in his hands, eyeing up the cracked wooden windowframe.

Elias stood up. He'd been sitting still for so long that his knees clicked like an old man's. 'I should go. I insist on punctuality from my orchestra, so I must set an example.'

'What else are conductors for?' Shostakovich placed the saucepan under the sill and led the way to the door. 'Thank you for the paper. And thank you, too, for your frank comments on my symphony. It's rarely pleasant to hear the truth about one's work, but honesty is always preferable to sycophancy.'

Elias stopped in his tracks. 'I wasn't criticising! I think your symphony is m-m-m —' He dug his fingernails into his palms. 'It's w-w-won —'

Shostakovich glanced around the main room. 'Thank God. The children must be napping. Silence at last. Do you need to borrow an umbrella?'

Nina appeared from the bedroom opposite, closing the door quietly behind her. 'They're exhausted. Over-excited by the air raid.' She turned to Elias. 'Would you like some tea? It's been difficult getting hold of provisions recently, but we still have tea.'

'No tea.' Shostakovich spoke abruptly. 'He's in a frightful hurry.'

'Well, at least allow me to pour Mr Eliasberg some water. I fear we've been poor hosts.'

'On the contrary, it's been a wonderful visit.' Elias tried to smile. 'I've been privileged enough to listen to your husband's new work. A rare honour, and —'

'Work!' Shostakovich strode to the table, snatched up Elias's gloves and thrust them at him somewhat desperately. 'Yes, you must get to work, and so must I.'

Nina laid a hand on his arm. 'Dmitri, are you all right?'

'The scherzo,' said Shostakovich in a low voice. 'It's waiting. It's always waiting.'

Nina sighed. 'Well, goodbye, Mr Eliasberg. Take care. The world outside is becoming an increasingly dangerous place.'

Elias blundered down the first flight of stairs and paused on the landing. Heavy wooden boards had been nailed across the windows, so that he stood in almost total darkness. He waited for his eyes to adjust, then pulled a sheet of paper from his briefcase. In capital letters, much larger than he ordinarily used, he wrote 'MAGNIFICENT'. Then he folded the paper in half, tiptoed back up the stairs and pushed the note under Shostakovich's door.

The night of fire

The noise was the worst. Usually, Nikolai looked forward to autumn. After the temporary euphoria of summer with its blowsy white nights, the sprawling city closed itself up again and regained its dignity. He preferred Leningrad this way: the streets quiet and empty, footsteps echoing against stone walls, the chilly breath of the marshes hanging on the wind.

But this year, although the leaves were browning and the evenings were becoming cold, Leningrad was denied peace. The hammering and sawing had been replaced by far worse sounds: the blare of air-raid sirens, the high-pitched scream of artillery shells, the crack of anti-aircraft fire, the whining of fighter planes. When the Junkers appeared, their loud drone was followed by a deafening chaos. Fire roared on rooftops, entire buildings collapsed with a crashing of stone and timber.

'It's as if the very city is in pain.' Nikolai huddled against a chimney on the Conservatoire roof. 'Don't you hate the constant noise?'

Shostakovich's face was a white blur in the darkness. 'It's never been quiet in my head. So perhaps it is easier for me.'

'Not easier,' said Nikolai, resting his head against the bricks. 'Just different.' He was so tired that it was all he could do to string two words together. How long could he go on like this? At rehearsals, after sleepless nights, even placing the bow on the strings felt like too great an effort; it was as if his fingers weren't even attached to his hands. *I feel dismembered*, he thought.

'Coffee?' Shostakovich held out a tin cup. 'You look as if you could do with some.'

Nikolai shook his head. 'It gives me the shakes.'

'Not this stuff! It tastes like one part coffee and five parts mud.'

Nikolai took a swig. 'Disgusting,' he agreed, though he could taste nothing at all.

'Isn't it? Apparently one of our neighbours has started making pancakes using old coffee grounds. Nina found her going through the rubbish.'

'So we're back to this. Cabbage soup by the gallon, rotten meat in the borscht — if there's any meat at all.'

'Watered-down porridge, watered-down vodka.' Shostakovich sighed. 'Substitute sugar, substitute fat, substitute everything. One would think we'd be used to it, from the earlier days, but how quickly we forget!' He drained the coffee into his mouth, then spat over the edge of the building. 'I was about to say we can get used to almost anything, but I refuse to get used to this muck.'

It was true, Nikolai reflected; human nature was extraordinarily adaptable. What had once seemed strange — putting on a helmet, climbing to a rooftop with a pail of sand — had become routine. People who'd once sewed fine linen coats now threaded fuses into artillery shells. Those who'd suppressed their urge to pray were being officially urged to enter churches. There was only one thing to which Nikolai was unable to adjust: the terrible pain that had been with him ever since he'd prised Sonya's fingers from around his wrist and handed her into the train carriage, into someone else's arms. That pain was as raw as it had ever been, and its strength and ferocity surprised him. When he entered his apartment, it leapt upon him; when he dozed off from exhaustion, it was waiting in his dreams. It burned through his numb, sleep-deprived state like frozen metal on skin. He would never get used to her not being there, and he looked for her when he turned every corner and boarded every tram. 'I'll never get used to the absence,' he whispered, scraping his boots on the guttering to cover his words.

In spite of the vast sweeping arms of the searchlights, it was just possible to make out the delicate points of stars. 'It's quiet enough now,' said Shostakovich. 'Maybe we'll be allowed a night of silence.'

He was right. Even the muffled thud of faraway artillery was stilled. It had been a bad day, with waves of Junkers sweeping in and dropping showers of incendiaries over the city. All evening, fire brigades had been fighting the flaring white flames. Passing a local park, Nikolai had seen children frantically digging up soil and heaping it over a cluster of fires.

Shostakovich leaned back on a chimney pot, and a loose tile fell on his helmet with a loud crack. 'The Russian composer Dmitri Shostakovich,' he said in a broadcaster's voice, 'spent the winter of 1941 preventing incendiaries from falling on his workplace. The only thing to fall on him was a piece of the roof.'

Nikolai smiled. 'Perhaps the Germans feel they've treated us to sufficient indignities for one day.'

'Let's hope so. The city can't take much more heat. Do you want to get some sleep, while the coast is clear?'

The thought of lying down made Nikolai feel both better and worse. He'd spent the previous night in a chair in Sonya's room, with a rug over him; by pretending he wasn't interested in sleep, he'd hoped he might succumb to it. The trick hadn't worked. Already he knew every detail of the room, had replayed every conversation he and Sonya had ever had, but still his eyes roamed around restlessly, hoping for something new. By the time the dawn crept around the blackout blind, he was sick from nostalgia and grief.

'Well, what about it?' suggested Shostakovich. 'You going below?'

'I think I'll just grab a cat-nap here.' He pulled his helmet low over his eyes so that he wouldn't appear duplicitous or ungrateful. For fifteen minutes he tried not to think of Sonya and what might have happened to her; instead, from the small, unrestricted corner of his sight, he watched Shostakovich sitting with his shoulders hunched and his profile set. Was he thinking about his unfinished work, his scattered friends? It was impossible to tell.

Suddenly Shostakovich gave a loud exclamation. 'What the hell —?' He threw off the blanket around his shoulders and leapt up, staring across the city. 'What the bloody hell is *that*?'

Nikolai also sprang to his feet. To the south, the sky had turned a deep, sinister red. Billowing smoke plumed upwards, lit from below by a searing orange light. 'What can they have hit to cause a bonfire like that?' he asked, aghast.

Immediately, as if in reply, shouts rose from the alleyway below. 'Send for help! The Badayev warehouses are burning! All available men needed!'

Shostakovich grabbed Nikolai's arm. 'If the warehouses have gone up in smoke, we're lost. The whole city is lost. What happens to sugar when it burns?'

'It melts,' said Nikolai slowly, 'and then it solidifies. Leningrad will be left with nothing but four acres of hard candy.' The immense fire was mesmerising, horrifying, spreading along the horizon like a forest.

'Look at it — it's like a bloody beacon. It's going to attract the attention of the Luftwaffe. They'll soon be here. How can they resist an opportunity like that?'

Already lorries and handcarts were crawling through the streets, heading towards the long red line on the edge of the city. 'And what about all the other fires?' Nikolai felt a new despair.

'They'll be ignored.' Shostakovich's glasses flickered, reflecting the sickly orange light. 'The Badayev warehouses are made of wood and stuffed with food. They're the perfect fuel. If the fire brigades can't put out the flames, there'll be nothing left by morning but scorched ground.' He sounded angry, but it was difficult to tell whether his anger was directed at the German bombers or the shortsightedness of the city officials.

Silently, shoulder to shoulder, they watched as Leningrad's food supplies — flour, cooking oil, butter, lard, meat — fed the unstoppable fire. Dense black smoke stained the night sky. The sounds of distant panic floated across the city: bells, loudhailers, shouting men and barking dogs.

Then, as if set off by the chaos, the air-raid sirens shrieked into life.

'Here they come,' said Nikolai grimly. 'Moths to a literal flame.' He looked at Shostakovich's anxious face, and then at the chaos that lay before them. For the first time, he was almost glad that Sonya was no longer in Leningrad.

A kind of retreat

When Shostakovich was a boy, he'd invented an ingenious game called the Pebble. Whenever he wanted to escape household chores he took the sacred pebble from its tin and challenged one of his sisters to guess which hand it was in. Soon he had this down to a fine art, puffing up his empty fist to make it look as if it contained something, or flattening his fingers to suggest attempted concealment.

After some weeks of constantly choosing the wrong hand, Mariya began to complain. Dmitri was cheating! The cleaning forced on her by fate and the Pebble became noisy and obtrusive. She bumped her brother's chair as she swept, and scrubbed roughly over his feet as he sat reading. She flurried his pencils with her duster and wiped the piano keys when he was playing. The commotion became too disturbing; after all, the whole point of escaping chores was to gain uninterrupted practice time. Thus Shostakovich had learnt to shut himself away, not physically but mentally. A smooth second skin emerged from his spine, crept around his ribcage and sealed itself around his heart. Noise-proof, emotional-blackmail-proof, it blocked him off so he could neither hear Mariya banging the scrubbing brush on the pail, nor smell the strong carbolic soap. In this way, he was able to continue with his important composing (this was the year of his piano piece, 'Funeral March in Memory of the Victims of the Revolution') and he heard only the notes in his head.

Long after the Pebble had disappeared, along with his father (dead and buried) and the piano (sold to pay the rent), Shostakovich's ability to seal himself off saved him. When, in a narrow white bed in the

Gaspra Sanatorium, he'd lost his virginity to Tatyana Glivenko and she'd inexplicably laughed — well, then the cool skin had grown over his uncertain teenage body and saved him from mortification. When, standing at Arkhangelsk Station on an icy morning in 1936, he'd opened *Pravda* to see the headline 'Muddle Instead of Music' (not only the death knell for his opera but his first public fall from grace), again he'd closed himself off. The avalanche of criticism, composed of voices once fervent with praise, now running like dogs after Party opinion — he was a formalist, an anti-socialist, and an enemy of the people! — all this fell around him, but it didn't seep into his heart.

He'd tried to describe this to Nina. *Lady Macbeth* was, after all, dedicated to her. He'd held her in his arms and explained, in his clumsy way, how it was that the repeated blows of the critics hadn't killed him.

'I know,' she said, stroking his forehead and his rough chin. 'I see the way you do it. You simply . . . go away.'

At that time, amidst the passion of their recent reunion, she didn't seem to mind. Later, she resented his escapes, the way he disappeared into the knotted heart of his work. She called it 'hiding', while he called it a retreat.

And so it was now, as day after day Leningrad burned and the streets erupted under the shells. After the Badayev fire had raged for six hours, the warehouse cellars flowing with several thousand tons of burning liquid sugar and the Junkers returning in successive waves, Shostakovich closed off the world. For the next two weeks, he kept his head down and his ears closed. He wrote fast, sometimes right through the air raids, as plaster poured from the ceiling and books fell off shelves, and the single light bulb above the piano swung. The nights of fire-watching were filled with action — kicking incendiaries off the roof, pouring sand on flaring magnesium fires — but they seemed like relief from the pressure of existing inside his symphony.

'I'm consumed by it,' he confessed to Sollertinsky down a crackling phoneline. 'It's too much to carry alone. If only you were here!'

'You should be here, my friend.' Sollertinsky, in a post office in Novosibirsk, had waited three hours to get a connection — and a bad one at that. 'I'm not the only one who thinks you should leave Leningrad. Rumour has it that the authorities are —' His voice was lost in a maelstrom of hissing, but already Shostakovich knew enough. Any day now a Party official would give him evacuation orders that he had little intention of obeying.

The sound of Sollertinsky's voice brought tears to his eyes. 'I miss you,' he said. 'I really miss you.'

'Change your mind,' urged Sollertinsky. 'Siberia isn't as fearsome as depicted by our writers. It's not filled with convicts. We even have food — that is, if you don't mind rock-hard pies garnished with Central Asian ants. Are you getting enough to eat?'

'Enough for now.' Just that morning, Shostakovich had had to fasten his belt several notches tighter. 'But it doesn't look good. Bread rations are going to be cut again — to five hundred grams, I think.' The truth was, he was barely aware of what he'd eaten in the last weeks: a bit of sausage chopped into red cabbage, dried mushrooms in watery broth, bread with sunflower oil rather than butter. The main thing was that mealtimes were now less of a palaver, meaning he could eat quickly without losing track of the work. While he was wasting time shovelling food into his mouth, the violins were hovering in his workroom, marking time above a pizzicato bass.

The phoneline was worsening. Soon all he could hear was an odd exclamation or the fragment of a word, yet he couldn't bear to say goodbye. When the line suddenly went dead, he swore. *Goddamn it!* He'd wasted an opportunity to talk about real things, had babbled on about food rations and an air raid the previous evening which had trapped them in the cellar for two hours, when he should have been asking about Mravinsky, and whether the Philharmonic might start rehearsing his symphony, and how one might transport a score to Siberia, and how many copies could be made of what would amount to thousands of pages. 'Ivan Ivanovich!' He kicked the wall in frustration; the sound of his friend's name filled him with foreboding. Suppose he never again felt that solid arm around his shoulders, nor saw the crumpled collar and badly knotted tie, nor benefited from Sollertinsky's informed conversations on topics ranging from Sanskrit to Sophocles?

He knew he should start working again, but he felt a reluctance so strong it surprised him. *Keep going*, he commanded himself. *This is the reason you're still in Leningrad!*

Before he could begin, he heard a small knock on the door. It was Nina, who'd been gone for hours, queuing for bread. She looked closely at him. 'Is something wrong?'

'I just talked to Sollertinsky.' He noticed, for the first time, how her cheekbones stood out in her thin face. She'd stopped suggesting they leave Leningrad; in fact, she'd stopped saying much at all. But it was obvious that, every day, she was hoping someone else would help her fight this particular battle.

'Is he all right?' Nina rarely entered his workroom; this was his territory and he kept it as free as possible from the clutter of family life. But now she came over to him and laid her head against his chest.

He could feel her shoulder blades jutting through her coat, and the sharp steps of her ribs. Shamed, unprotected by work, he saw that this was also his fault. Maxim had started wetting the bed, Galina had become afraid of the dark. Single-handedly, he was destroying his family.

'You miss Sollertinsky,' said Nina. It was a statement, not a question.

'I do.' Shostakovich gave a huge sigh. 'I miss his certainty. I miss the life we had.'

Heroes

E lias was woken by the most intense pain he'd ever felt. The entire right side of his face was burning. It was as if a wire was threaded from his jaw to his ear, and it was being ratcheted tighter and tighter.

'Hell!' he said, opening his eyes to darkness. 'Bloody, shitting hell.'

As if on cue, the early-morning silence was ripped apart. Church bells tolled, sirens blared. Two months earlier, a loudspeaker had been mounted on a pole immediately below the apartment windows. ('How considerate,' his mother had exclaimed. 'Someone must be aware that I'm hard of hearing.') Now, out of that very speaker, came the repeated warning 'AIR RAID! AIR RAID!', blasting through Elias's already splitting head.

Clutching his cheek, he pulled his coat on over his pyjamas. The noise and the pain merged in a red-hot blur. *If we're not dead by the time this infernal war is over*, he thought angrily, *we shall certainly be deaf*.

Getting his mother down to the cellar was becoming increasingly difficult, for her indignation grew with each air raid. 'The Germans signed a pact,' she'd say. 'They were supposed to be our *friends*.' Recently, she seemed to have found a way of making herself heavier, so that Elias had to grit his teeth and call on Mr Shapran for help. 'You're not even trying, Mother,' he'd exclaim. 'Yes, it's all most trying,' she'd answer, sitting solidly in her chair.

Now, he could barely open his aching jaw to call out for assistance. Instead he ran out onto the landing just as the Bobrovskys' young son emerged from the door opposite.

'My . . . mother,' Elias grated out. 'Can't . . . lift . . . alone.'

'I'll help you. But we have to hurry!' Valery's blue eyes were round with fear.

By tilting the chair at a dangerous angle, it was just possible for them to jolt Mrs Eliasberg around the corners of each landing. After two flights of stairs she began to shout, flailing her arms about so that Elias narrowly missed a punch on his already smarting jaw.

'What's the matter with her?' Valery's chubby face was flushed.

'I forgot my shawl!' Mrs Eliasberg caught at the stair-rail.

'Can't . . . go back.' Elias's shoulders were burning, but he was almost glad of the new pain, distracting him from the one in his head.

'There are blankets in the cellar, Mrs Eliasberg. We can't go back.' Valery stumbled and nearly dropped his side of the chair. 'Whoops.'

Olga Shapran's face loomed below them, lit by the feeble glow of a lamp. 'Hurry! We want to close the door! Hurry up!'

'All right, we're coming. You try hurrying when you're lugging an old dragon in a bath-chair.' Valery looked as if he might cry.

'I must go back,' cried Mrs Eliasberg. 'I've left my lucky shawl behind, and the portrait of my husband isn't in its proper place. If he isn't in the shrine we're doomed!'

Just in time, Elias caught her, pushing her back in the chair and wrapping her coat tightly around her legs. 'Would you shut up, Mother,' he hissed, 'and let us get you to the cellar, or we'll all be as dead as Father.'

They sat crammed together in the dark, the door firmly bolted and their backs to the wall. The attack seemed very close. Elias felt the anti-aircraft fire vibrate through his body; the shriek of the falling bombs sounded almost human. The whole building shuddered, making even Mrs Eliasberg stop moaning and fall silent.

Elias clenched his hands. His pain blended with the noise outside, and soon it all became so intolerable that he felt as if he were not in his body at all. *Think about the symphony*, he told himself. *Remember that day in Shostakovich's study*. He concentrated on the memory of the composer's face: his flickering mouth when he reached a difficult passage, the rise of his eyebrows mimicking the upward lilt of a melody. Unclenching his left hand, Elias played out the opening theme on his knee. Had the first shift to the dominant key happened so early? Gradually, the sounds around him receded; he tilted his head back against the shaking wall, his eyes shut and his mind on the music.

He was halfway through working out the exposition when there was an enormous crash and Mrs Bobrovsky gave a piercing scream. The cellar shook violently. Elias's eyes flew open, but it was pitch dark and he could see nothing. Plaster was raining down on his head.

'After all this time,' said Mr Shapran, 'we've been hit.' He sounded amazed, as if until now the raids had simply been tiresome exercises.

'Well, somebody do something!' cried Olga Shapran.

Elias groped for a box of matches. The terrified faces of his neighbours flared into light and then faded.

'I'm going upstairs,' he announced.

'No!' shrieked his mother. 'Are you mad?'

'It's over,' he said. 'I need to know what's happened.'

Cautiously he unbolted the door, letting in a chink of light, peering up the stairs. Then he took off his scarf and wrapped it around his head.

'To ward off the shrapnel.' Olga sounded impressed.

'There *is* no shrapnel from incendiaries,' said her husband. He got to his feet and pushed past Elias. There was no way he was going to be outdone by a thin conductor in slippers.

The booming and the whine of the bombs were distant now. Mr Shapran tried the switch in the stairwell but nothing happened. 'Electricity's gone,' he said. In the entrance hall, a faint light crept through the boarded-up windows; it was barely enough to see by, but still too bright for Elias's pulsing right eye. He felt his way up the stairs. On the second landing he heard a sound behind him and turned in alarm, pushing the scarf back from his face.

'It's only me,' piped up Valery. 'I want to help, too.'

'Go back to the cellar,' ordered Mr Shapran. 'If that was an incendiary bomb, there's going to be fire. This is no place for a twelve-year-old.'

'He can come if he wants to,' said Elias. 'Boys not much older than him are fighting for us at the Front.' To Valery he said, 'Keep behind me and walk carefully.'

After this Valery followed so close he stepped on Elias's heel. 'Whoops,' he said, just as he had before, and he pushed the cracked leather slipper back onto Elias's foot.

When they reached the third-floor landing and paused at the Eliasbergs' door, a faint sound could be heard from inside. Now it was Elias's turn to push to the front. 'It's my apartment! Get out of the goddamn way.'

'No need to swear,' said Mr Shapran in his warden's tone.

The main room was undisturbed: orchestral scores on the table, dishes in the rack, enamel pans hung above the sink. But playing over the far wall was a new, ominously flickering light.

'It's in the old lady's room!' Valery rushed forward and stopped at the bedroom door. 'Holy cow!'

'Stay back!' Elias grabbed his shoulder. Mrs Eliasberg's bed was ablaze. A pillar of flames rose from her much-prized quilt, leaping towards the gaping hole in the ceiling. Without stopping to think, Elias seized one end of the mattress and tried to fold it in half. The heat was intense and he ducked his face away. 'Give me a hand, will you!' he said through clenched teeth.

Mr Shapran grabbed the other end, and together they carried the burning mattress to the window, heaved it out, and stood watching as it soared down into the yard that was already flaring with small magnesium bonfires. Falling through the misty morning, with fiery bedclothes trailing behind, it looked like a strange and beautiful bird.

'Like a phoenix,' breathed Valery.

Elias wanted to tell him that a phoenix rose from the ashes, rather than creating them, but there were more important things to attend to. He stumbled back through the singed bedroom, stamping on stray sparks as he went, and extracted a bottle from the cupboard under the sink.

'Vodka?' Mr Shapran sounded eager. 'But oughtn't we put out the fires in the yard before we start drinking?'

'Not . . . going to . . . drink it. I have toothache.' Elias drenched the dishcloth in alcohol and crammed it in his mouth. Dazed from pain and anticipating more (his mother treasured her quilt as much as life itself), he caught sight of himself in the mirror. Face covered in soot, scarf wrapped around his head, bared teeth clamped around the cloth, he looked less like a professional conductor than one of the Baltic Fleet sailors who frequented Leningrad's drinking houses. *Thank goodness Nina Bronnikova can't see me now* was his first thought.

Valery was staring at him with undisguised admiration. 'That was great! You were great. How'd you know what to do so fast?'

Elias had no idea what had prompted him even to leave the relative safety of the cellar — unless it had been to get away from the voice of Olga Shapran. The unaccustomed alcohol fumes made him light-headed; his knees were turning to water. 'Don't know,' he mumbled.

'And when you told your mother to shut up — and she did!' It was definitely hero-worship on Valery's face. 'Yesterday I ate the tiniest spoonful of honey,' he confided, 'and now Ma's hidden the jar. Maybe if I shout at her the way you did with your mother, she'll tell me where it is?'

Gingerly, Elias pulled the rag from his mouth. 'It was the toothache that made me shout. I don't normally.'

'War causes abnormal behaviour in the best of us.' Mr Shapran spoke with the certainty and weight of a philosopher. 'How about a quick nip to give us strength?'

Shrugging, Elias sloshed some vodka into a mug. It was too early to drink, but any man married to Olga Shapran deserved a break. For himself and Valery, he poured two tiny measures into small glasses. His eyes were watering, his mouth burned, but gamely he raised his glass. 'To Leningrad's finest —'

'To Leningrad!' Mr Shapran drained his mug in a single gulp.

'To Leningrad!' Valery hesitated, glancing at Elias to see how brave men drank their vodka.

Elias swallowed the last word of his toast, along with liquid tasting more like petrol than pure Siberian grain. He and Valery spluttered like disused engines while Mr Shapran reached for the bottle. 'Got to light a fire in order to put 'em out,' he said with a wink. Suddenly he was treating Elias as a comrade and an equal — not something Elias had particularly desired, but it wasn't unpleasant at seven in the morning, after a minor act of bravery.

He nodded at Mr Shapran, wiped his streaming eyes, and saw the recent past with the clarity of the sleep-deprived and the slightly drunk. *The war symphony!* He was the first person in the city to have heard it, and because of this he'd changed. The music had marched into his body and strengthened him, fortifying his resolve.

'I *am* the symphony.' He said it out loud, but Valery, having drunk his second vodka too fast, was coughing loudly and being clapped on the back by Mr Shapran. *The symphony is me.* The words seeped through Elias's red-hot tooth and into his gums, soothing his jaw. He sank into a chair, weak with gratitude for what Shostakovich had given him.

Mining the past

It was the memory of the dacha that saved him, taking him back to a place where he could hear notes again — though he had, quite literally, to block his ears, stuffing them with the cotton wool reserved for medical emergencies. These days the raids began at dawn and continued late into the night. The distant thudding of artillery was constant, muttering like thunder. Even standing in the bread queues was dangerous, with the frequent shelling forcing people to run for cover. Leningrad had become scarred: pockmarked squares, pitted stone walls and shattered houses. When munitions factories were hit, there were flaming explosions. Regardless of the chaos, Shostakovich continued to go to his study.

The dacha? It had been close enough to the city but it seemed like another world. It was the year after he'd first met Tatyana Glivenko, in the sanatorium in Crimea. She was what the French called *jolie laide*. Her face held a potential for excitement close to hysteria; it lit her peaky chin and high cheekbones to an approximation of beauty. As he watched her, Shostakovich had felt the bandages on his neck become constricting. Running his finger beneath them he felt not the familiar swellings of his tuberculosis but the girl's cool white neck — bent, at that moment, over a plate of tasteless cabbage soup. He knew he had to touch her skin, soon.

In the late afternoon, they'd climbed the tower in Gaspra, gazing at the purple smoke drifting above Ai-Petri. For three weeks fires had raged between Alupka and Simeiz; and as his arm lightly brushed sixteen-year-old Tatyana's, he felt his boredom falling away, tumbling down the tower to merge with the haze. He no longer pined for Petrograd, for its sharp winds and the drizzle on cobblestones. The connection was instant and reciprocal. As she looked sideways at him, there was a knowingness in her eyes that coloured them the same smudged violet as the smoke.

As much as Shostakovich was attracted to Tatyana, his sister disliked her. While he and Tatyana lay together, one secret night after another, he could hear Mariya turning and coughing in the next room, perhaps sensing that, on the other side of the wall, her brother (whom she'd come to look after) was getting himself into trouble. When he carried letters to the post each morning, he felt them weighing heavily in his hand. He stopped behind a stand of oak trees and carefully unsealed all envelopes addressed to their mother, reading such things about his first love that made his cheeks flare. While he'd been taking care not to worry his mother — the injections of arsenic 'didn't hurt at all', he was now allowed to expose his body to sunlight, he was recovering quickly — Mariya was writing in a deliberately anxiety-provoking manner.

'Dmitri's grown up,' she had written. 'He's got a tan, and is happily in love.' Yes, this was true enough. But then he read: 'Tatyana Glivenko is a strange girl, verging on coquettish.' And, in the next letter: 'T. is a flirt. I don't like her.' It took a large effort of will for him to reseal this envelope and send it on — but even at the age of seventeen he had a fear of altering destiny, and the censorship of letters fell into this category.

By the time summer frayed into autumn, he'd written several letters to assure his mother that he'd remained pure (which he had, in spirit). 'I won't throw myself into the whirlpool,' he promised, as his mother warned him of the many ways family life could threaten artistic talent. After a month, however, it was clear that he was head over heels in love. Everyone could see it — Mariya, Dr Elena Nikolaevna and the nurses, not to mention his mother and Tatyana herself.

By the following summer, when they were invited to the dacha in Repino, Shostakovich believed himself to be truly in love. The invitation had come from Tatyana's aunt, who'd heard the confident predictions of the Leningrad music professors. Her niece's beau was destined for greatness, perhaps as a concert pianist! 'There's a grand piano in the dacha,' she wrote reassuringly to Shostakovich's mother. 'His daily practice can continue.' She'd welcomed them when they arrived, dusty from the train ride and a walk down a lane musty with elderflowers, and she'd shown them a battered upright that had survived years of her father's folk tunes.

'It's there,' she said knowingly, 'in case you have nothing better to do.' Then she showed them to their room, a large bare space in the southern turret, with a tin bath in the corner and a huge bed in the middle of the floor. 'Everything you need!' she said, pressing a key into Shostakovich's hand — after which she disappeared down the creaking stairs and stayed out of their way for the next four weeks.

'Our own place at last!' Tatyana kicked off her shoes and bounced on the mattress, so that her braids stood up with every downwards fall.

Although no more than an hour from the city, the place had felt like an island, cut off from the burdens of duty and ambition that usually lay so heavily on Shostakovich. The nights at Repino were open and seductive, Tatyana's cries of pleasure flying like birds into the ceiling. Every morning, exhausted from lovemaking, they would lean naked on the windowsill, looking over hazy fields and sighing birch trees, and the dark bulk of a ramshackle farmhouse by the river. They ate fruit and vegetables from the garden, feeding each other with a generosity bordering on greed. Tatyana would split open a pod with her thumbnail and rake lime-green peas into Shostakovich's mouth. Shostakovich forced soft strawberries through her pursed lips, then the smaller, tarter *klubnika*, and finally a pulpy mush of raspberries, until Tatyana's chin ran red and sweet with juice. There were huge radishes, drawn from the soft ground and taken to the kitchen, trailing soil; their white biting taste was softened with salt or butter. There were cucumbers as thick as a labourer's wrist, coated thickly with honey — 'Peasant's food,' said Tatyana, biting into one hungrily.

So much food back then! Shostakovich, writing in full score and hearing the orchestra behind the piano notes, marvelled at the memory. Those same dachas now stood deserted and empty, their gardens torn up, their crops burnt and their owners trapped in the stone city.

'You love me most.' This was Tatyana at her most aggressive and insecure; her voice challenged him down the years. 'If not, why did you dedicate the Piano Trio to me?' In Leningrad, she'd sat night after night in the Bright Reel movie theatre, her eyes fixed on him as he proceeded with his undercover practice. He'd discovered that he could use his accompanist's job as a way to rehearse his own compositions; once, he'd even persuaded the manager to let in two of his classmates, a violinist and a cellist, thus providing him with a test run for his trio.

That work had failed to satisfy, its single-movement form seeming unsophisticated, its opening too obviously signalling the themes. Now, staring at the sketches for the symphony's scherzo, he realised the trio had been a forerunner to this. The resolute opening was his approach to new situations — resistant, tense, observant — and its melodic second theme was the succumbing: to the sun, his returning health, to Tatyana and love.

Trying to ignore the distant gunfire, he felt the same old magic leap inside him, an ache of possibility that was almost sexual. It was a synthesis of sound and feeling, captured in the memory of the key: that large, theatrical-looking key pressed into his palm by Tatyana's big-bosomed aunt. It could both lock them in and keep the world out — just as it had that first evening, when he'd turned it in the door and there had been a clap of thunder, the beginning of a great summer storm.

The wooden dacha had groaned in the fierce warm wind. Tatyana lay on her front on the bed, her eyes vivid. Her white cotton blouse had slipped off her shoulder and Shostakovich could see one small bare breast, peaked with a dark nipple. He'd shut the window and then pulled her blouse over her head, cupping her breasts in his hands. He liked their combined weight and weightlessness, heavy and light, like round ripe apricots.

They lay with their naked torsos pressed together, listening to the storm passing over the house. Outside, the trees were wild black shapes, bending their heads and whipping up again in a dervish dance. At one point, Shostakovich saw an apple box flying through the air, belly-up like a fish.

The few hours before this had been calm: heady, drowsy, bee-filled. 'Who would have guessed?' Tatyana's narrow ribs rose in astonishment. But of course the storm had been building all afternoon, unseen behind the hills. 'The wildness came from nowhere,' said Tatyana, whose moods did exactly this, tears springing from the mildest reproach and smiles restored by a caress.

The turn of the key, the anticipation, the banging windowpane, the rocking dacha: twenty years later these fused in Shostakovich's head. The air-raid sirens were cranking up into a wail, and he went to the door. 'Nina!' he called sharply. 'Take the children to the cellar.'

He returned to his desk. Even before the drone of the planes began, he stuffed cotton wool in his ears and picked up his pen. He willed himself back to the sweet-smelling Repino day, the warm grass, the dozing and the waking. *Remember Repino. Remember peace.*

Then, at last, he found a path into the scherzo. The lilting melody of the strings was like stepping out into a fresh country morning. This was underpinned by some stealthy, stagy, staccato cello notes — a little like the footsteps of an aunt not wanting to intrude. Next, the oboe. Lilting and soaring, it was Tatyana's voice as it used to be, before she became quarrelsome and possessive. (Dimly, he heard the roar of planes; glancing up, he saw a portrait of his grandparents falling from the wall.)

The storm? This would be easier. The first movement had pointed the way, with its uneasy C sharp minor key and its repetitive chaos. He would use brass and woodwind for the buffeting wind, crashing against barns and flattening hedgerows. And a hammering xylophone would return, slowly and inevitably, to the original key of B minor. (The light above him flickered and dimmed; the room was shaking, books tumbled off the shelves.)

Then, for a single brief moment, he could see clear to the symphony's end. As the building rumbled around him and a huge crack split the wall, he dived under the piano. But he felt no fear — only relief. That glimpse had been enough.

'Everything is resolved.' He gripped the shaking legs of the piano. 'Everything, eventually, comes to an end.' His ears were still blocked by the cotton wool; his words sounded muffled even inside his head. Just as he pulled the stoppers from his ears — BANG! He was deafened. Had he been obliterated by a Luftwaffe bomb? But it was the lid of the piano, crashing down with massive impact, setting the strings screeching like sea-witches and making him wince.

———◆———

Nina and the children had emerged from the cellar and were inspecting the damage. Mirrors and plates lay shattered on the floor, and the windows had cracked across in spite of the tape. Shostakovich sat in the middle of the debris, explaining why he'd stayed behind. 'It was the breakthrough for the scherzo. I would have lost it.'

Nina began sweeping up the mess. 'And we would have lost you.' Her reactions to danger were unvarying: humour as a defence against fear, practicality a barrier against emotion.

He watched her as she bent over a smashed geranium pot, and was filled with a sudden desire. Work often did this to him, making him as lustful as hell, yet sating him of the energy to initiate sex. And his mind was still full of Tatyana: her slanting eyes, her sudden tempers and equally sudden capitulations; her small gasps when she cried, the way she bit him when aroused.

'I love you, Nina,' he said. 'I do love you.'

Later that evening, he trudged around the Conservatoire building with Nikolai, checking the ground-floor windows for breakages. 'What a day!' He felt elated and exhausted. 'As unexpected as . . . as the second movement of a symphony.'

'So you're onto the second movement already?' Nikolai bent to retrieve a bucket of sand, half-hidden behind a barbed-wire barricade. 'Impressive, in a week during which two hundred shells a day have rained upon us.' As he picked up the bucket, he stumbled and nearly fell.

'Are you all right?' Shostakovich steadied him.

'Just tired,' said Nikolai, trying to smile. But his eyes looked like black holes in his face.

Shostakovich felt a stab of guilt. Over the past two months, his friend had changed beyond recognition. He was as intelligent as ever, capable of discussing anything from bread queues to Brahms, but somewhere in the middle of him was an unfillable void.

'I'm an idiot. Here I am babbling about my work, remaining in my room when everyone else is running for their life.' He looked around at the skyline bristling with guns and the squat concrete shelters for snipers. 'This is reality.'

'Your work is also real. You were talking about unexpectedness. About your scherzo?'

'No more of that for now.' Shostakovich stepped around the barricade across the Conservatoire entrance and sat down on the top step. 'I've avoided talking about the one topic that needs to be discussed. Have you had any news?'

Nikolai remained standing. 'No, nothing. Nothing at all.' Despair seeped out of him like ink, spreading in a dark pool around him — and, at that moment, Shostakovich realised how it was to be Nikolai. Day by day, as his hopelessness grew, Nikolai was drowning.

What is
the worst

It was mid-afternoon, and Elias was making his way home after an unsatisfactory rehearsal during which Alexander had called him a bastard and old Petrov had collapsed from exhaustion. Nikolai, more vague than ever, had fumbled his entry and dropped his bow. And they'd heard the news that several of the musicians who'd volunteered for front-line duty had officially been declared dead.

The Tchaikovsky was due for broadcast in less than ten days, and the orchestra — depleted, fatigued — needed ten times that amount of time to pull it off. Gloomily, Elias imagined how they would be heard by the world. As dismal failures rather than Soviet ambassadors, the laughing stock of Leningrad rather than the last bastion of culture. *My orchestra is like a decaying mouth*, he thought, trudging on down Nevsky Prospect. *Full of rotten teeth and gaping holes*.

When the sirens began, he was nowhere near a shelter. Along with those around him he ran as fast as he could, dodging into doorways, making for the shelter in Gostiny Dvor. But there was too little time; the sirens had sounded too late. Already the planes were visible in the sky, sweeping in from the south, wave upon wave, and he began to sweat from terror.

Just as he stumbled into the marketplace, the world erupted around him. He threw himself under a cart at the side of the square. Those who hadn't made it to shelter didn't stand a chance. Glass cascaded down in lethal showers. Chunks of concrete crashed from buildings, breaking bones and smashing skulls. It seemed as if the very air had been made of solid matter, and it was now shattering.

The noise was deafening: the crashing of masonry, the roar of the planes and the eerie whistle of falling bombs. But worst of all was the screaming. He'd never heard anything like it, and he knew he would never stop hearing it; that he would lie awake in his bed, months later, hearing the screams and seeing the cobblestones running with blood. He shoved his fingers in his ears and pressed his face against the uneven stones. A strange hot wind blew in under the wheels of the cart. He was in hell.

It was hard to tell how long he lay there, blocking out the chaos, waiting for death. As suddenly as it had begun, the raid was over. The plane engines faded to a drone, and the clatter of anti-aircraft fire stuttered into silence. Slowly, he turned his head and looked out through the bent spokes of the wheel.

It was a nightmare vision — though only the most fevered imagination could have created such terrible detail. Blocks of concrete and twisted steel strewn over the ground, canvas awnings shredded like the sails of wrecked boats. And lying amid the wreckage were dozens of mutilated bodies. Legs ripped off torsos, hands ripped off arms, some still clutching their bread rations in their bloodied fingers. The worst, though, were the severed heads, staring at the sky with open eyes.

He lay still in his small shelter which smelt of mud and mouldy cabbage. He didn't want to crawl out and confront what was waiting beyond. He prayed to someone or something he'd never believed in. *Give me strength. Help me. Give me strength.* Finally, with tears streaming down his face, he edged his way out from under the cart and stumbled to his feet.

It was easy enough to spot those who needed help; the bodies that were moving stood out from the dead. He began following the orders of a doctor, a moustached man whose right leg was drenched in blood. Along with the other shocked survivors, they ripped up coats to staunch blood, and lifted the wounded onto makeshift stretchers, covering the corpses with sacks, torn rugs and whatever else they could find. Elias worked as automatically as he could, forcing back nausea, pretending that these were not real people who had been cut down in seconds. No, this was not a mother who had been queuing for bread for her children; this had not been a boy running to snatch his baby brother out of the path of a vegetable cart.

'You'll be all right,' he said repeatedly to those still breathing. 'You'll be fine.'

Suddenly his heart began hammering so hard he thought he'd choke. 'Is it you?' His voice was clogged with fear. 'Nina Bronnikova?'

It was certainly Nina, though she was far thinner than she'd been when he last saw her. Her face was white, and her lips so pale they looked as if they'd been drained of blood. She was half-lying against a tram filled with sandbags that had barricaded the entrance to the marketplace; its metal frame had been torn in two.

'Mr Eliasberg?' She reached out for him, with hands that were covered in blood.

He knelt beside her. 'How badly are you hurt?'

'I don't know. I tried to get up, but I can't stand.' Her left calf was a mess of ruined flesh, shrapnel and blood-soaked stockings.

His stomach heaved. Quickly, he looked back at her face. 'You're still conscious. It's a miracle.'

'A miracle that anyone has been left alive,' she murmured.

'We need to —' began Elias.

But her eyes had closed, and her head fell with a thud against the side of the tram.

Frantically he felt her wrist for a pulse. Nothing. But on her neck he felt a faint fluttering. He cradled her head in both hands. Slowly, her eyes opened and she looked at him in a dazed way.

'We have to get you to hospital. Do you think you can make it over to that van?' Carefully, as if she were the most fragile of instruments, he placed her arm around his neck. 'Hold on if you can.'

She was lighter than he imagined, but he staggered as he stood up; his legs were shamefully weak. A gangly teenager stood nearby, staring blankly at them, blood trickling out from under his cap. 'Could you help me?' gasped Elias. Wordlessly, the boy stepped forward, and together they carried Nina to the nearest van. Already it was crammed with the injured, but no one objected as they laid her in the last empty space at the back.

'Nina?' Elias stroked her forehead — but she had lost consciousness again, and he was forced to step away as the engine started.

The teenager went off without a word and Elias was left watching the ambulance weave away through the broken market. He remained there long after the vehicle had disappeared, standing in the shadow of the cracked fountain: without company, without conversation, and intensely aware of the lack of both. Almost angrily, he wiped the tears from his eyes. Being alone was what he was accustomed to, after all. There was no need to cry about it.

Relatives

Aunt Tanya was installed in Nikolai's apartment for the indeterminate future, and she was as bossy and auntish as ever, though there was no longer anyone around to call her 'Aunt'. Once or twice, the title slipped out of Nikolai's mouth. His sister-in-law had always made him feel as if he were a member of the younger generation — as if he should be watching his language and hiding his cigarettes in his pocket. If he'd thought that the likelihood of being starved or bombed into oblivion might have encouraged Tanya to lower her standards, it quickly became clear he was wrong.

She'd arrived in a state of indignation and shock, her ginger hair frothing from under her hat. The apartment block in which she lived with her cousin, her cousin's husband and her cousin's father-in-law (their home, for so many years!) had had an entire wall blown off by a powerful Luftwaffe bomb.

'The front wall, too,' she stressed, as if this were far worse than any other wall. And perhaps it was, for even in normal times the street had been a busy thoroughfare, and now it was used as a regular army route, so the Katsubas' living quarters were on display to whole battalions. 'The Germans have hung out our lives like dirty laundry. Anyone might see that the dishes hadn't been washed, and that Grigori —' She lowered her voice. 'That Grigori had been eating out of the tin again.'

Nikolai's eyes widened. It was hard to believe that, only a month ago, Tanya had been sleeping in straw and washing in streams in front of other defence-line women.

'Yes, there was the tin with a spoon sticking out of it,' she said, interpreting his surprise as shock, 'for all the world to see. Anna's spent seventeen years training him out of the habit. "There are such things as plates," she says — but as soon as we're off at the bread queues, out comes the spoon and in digs Grigori. One might as well try to teach a pig to count oranges.'

Nikolai shuffled towards the door, hoping to escape the rest of the story. But non-verbal cues became invisible to Tanya on extraordinary occasions — and what was more extraordinary than arriving home to find your apartment minus a wall and your furniture spilling into the street?

'Grigori's favourite armchair was hanging on by a whisker. We nearly lost it. As for Grigori's father, where do you think he was?'

Nikolai couldn't imagine, but knew he wouldn't be permitted to leave the room before he was told.

'He was —' Tanya lowered her voice dramatically — 'on the *lavatory*!'

Nikolai suppressed a smile. 'Poor old fellow.' He knew Grigori's father slightly, having played chess with him a few times while the rest of the family squabbled over card games. 'Is he all right?'

'All right?' Tanya pursed her mouth. 'I suppose so, if you consider it "all right" to be gawked at by an entire neighbourhood with your pants around your ankles and pieces of plaster hanging off your derrière.'

'Had he not been on the toilet,' mused Nikolai, 'he might have fallen into the street along with the dining table. Humiliation's a small price to pay for a life saved.'

'I suppose we should thank God for small mercies.' Now that Tanya was permitted to speak the Lord's name, due to the Party's new-found belief that prayer might help a desperate situation, devoutness spilled from her like water from a fountain.

'I'm sure it seems a large mercy for Grigori's father.' It was also merciful, thought Nikolai, that he didn't have all three Katsubas sleeping on his floor or playing high-volume poker at his table. But it eased his mind a little that Tanya had been handed to him like some kind of universal reckoning. Having her there made things both better and worse. She treated grief like an infectious disease, sweeping it out of corners and wiping it off surfaces — something he remembered from nine years ago. Then, too, he'd felt both gratitude and irritation. But when she put away most of Sonya's possessions, stacking the dusty books in cartons and cramming the dolls into a cupboard, it was too much.

'Sonya left them like that for a reason,' he said furiously, 'and I've been careful not to disturb them. She *will* return.'

'Of course she'll return!' Tanya flushed. 'And when she does, she'll need something to keep her occupied. Such as putting her room in order.' She eyed the pencils lined up on Sonya's desk, precisely graded in colour and length. 'I see she inherited her mother's obsessive habits. When she comes back, we'll see what we can do about that.'

The relief of hearing Sonya talked about in the future tense made Nikolai forget his anger. He followed Tanya into the other room and watched her preparing to clean, rolling up her sleeves to reveal still sturdy forearms. Having been transferred out of the voluntary defence unit, she was working at the temporary hospital in the Astoria Hotel. *What a formidable sight she'd be in a nurse's cap*, thought Nikolai. Quite enough to make you run in the opposite direction, whether or not you were wounded.

Nonetheless, he admired her. He knew he'd faint if forced to enter the hospital wards, to witness the horrors wreaked by artillery barrages and shells. 'You're an admirable person,' he said. 'You make my occupation, scraping horsehair over four metal strings, seem somewhat irrelevant.'

Tanya shrugged. 'Your job is important as well. Keeping up morale and whatnot.'

This was something of a breakthrough; ever since her younger sister had not only become a musician but had married one, Tanya had been at a loss to understand the *why* — the usefulness — of such a profession. 'Of course,' she added with more conviction, 'you're also fire-watching.'

Privately, Nikolai found working with the Radio Orchestra far more of an ordeal than battling with fires. When he stumbled from the Radio Hall at the end of each day, his ears rang from Alexander's curses and Elias's rebukes, clashing in contrapuntal disharmony with Tchaikovsky's sublime chords. More than ever he ached for the days before the siege, those ordinary days when he could leave the Conservatoire feeling calm and satisfied, and look forward to seeing Sonya. Now, instead of going home, he would hurry away to replace Tanya in the bread queue, so that she, in turn, could go to her official work, fuelled only by tea and some solidified sugar meted out from the Badayev warehouse disaster.

He dreaded the hair-raising stories she told when she returned to the apartment, sometimes only a minute or two before the ten o'clock curfew. Maimed children with limbs ripped off by shells. Pregnant women on stretchers, their stomachs blown away to reveal dead foetuses. Bleeding men arriving in pairs, using each other as crutches. Tanya described these things matter-of-factly, as she chomped through her small ration of dry bread. There were few things that put her off her food or brought tears to her eyes, whereas Nikolai, listening to her, found his eyes watering compulsively. Usually he lay back in his chair and draped a menthol-drenched handkerchief over his face, citing blocked sinuses from inhaling cinder dust as an excuse.

The day after the bombing of the Gostiny shopping district, Tanya was more than usually keen to talk. 'Hundreds were caught unawares, you know. The warning came too late.'

Her face looked blurry viewed through the handkerchief. Could he, just this once, ask her to keep her gory stories to herself?

'You wouldn't believe the human damage.' Tanya slurped her tea. 'One man was brought in with no nose, no eyes, no mouth: just gaping cavities in his face.'

Nikolai inhaled sharply, filling his own nose and mouth with fabric. He sat up, coughing. 'Our conductor was there, apparently. But he wouldn't speak of it at rehearsal today. He looked terrible, as if he were still in shock.' Rearranging the handkerchief over his face, lying back again, he concentrated on tuning out most of Tanya's voice.

Then, from a great distance, he heard a few words. 'Dancer. Beautiful. Ruined.'

'What?' He sat up too fast. For a dizzying second he saw three or four Tanyas. 'What did you say?'

'A dancer was brought in from Gostiny. Shrapnel all through her leg. I talked to her this evening — she was with the Kirov before the war began, you know.' Tanya's voice rang with importance: Nikolai wasn't the only one to brush shoulders with the cultural elite!

'What did she look like? Black hair, black eyes? A pointed chin?' *Please*, he thought desperately, *please say no*.

'That's right. Now, what was her name? The same as the wife of your hoity-toity composer friend, the man with the specs.'

'Nina.' Nikolai groaned. 'Nina Bronnikova. I know her. Was she badly wounded?'

'Well, she won't die,' said Tanya. 'But it's safe to say she won't be doing much dancing.'

'Ever?' He remembered Nina's strong shoulders and slim hips, her kindness to Sonya, her composed serenity at Sollertinsky's party.

'She's still young.' Tanya sounded determinedly positive. 'There are plenty of other things she can do — get married, start a family. Even if she ends up with a limp, at least she's got a pretty face. She should be able to get a husband.'

'What a blessing.' Nikolai's voice was sharp.

'Isn't it,' agreed Tanya, who'd never been good at detecting sarcasm.

He went to stand by the covered window, feeling suffocated. He longed to pull down the black sheets, rip off the strips of tape and lean out into the cool September night. Ever since Sonya had gone, his lungs had seemed incapable of taking a deep breath. And now — now Nina was hurt, too.

'Terrible mess they've made of the Astoria.' Tanya clicked her tongue. 'Soldiers traipsing mud all over the stair carpet, vagrants sleeping in the main entrance, everything scratched and broken. Nothing like a top hotel any more. I don't know what . . .'

But Nikolai had stopped listening. His claustrophobia was growing. Trapped in his blacked-out apartment, trapped in the city — and worst of all, trapped in his own mind. Shamefully, alarmingly, he began to long for a violent release.

The gift

Shostakovich woke to the rattle of anti-aircraft fire and an intense feeling of doom. He lay studying the long crack above him that now looked as deep as a crevasse. A few more bombs, and the whole ceiling might split in two. He imagined the upstairs neighbours crashing down into his workroom, and caught himself hoping that the buxom eighteen-year-old daughter would land on his bed, rather than her formidable mother.

Galina came flying into the room. 'Happy Birthday, Papa! Maxim and I have made up a poem for you! But we'd better tell it to you in the cellar because the bombers are arriving at any minute.'

Shostakovich shuffled after her into the main room. 'Old age and illness are now officially within sight,' he said, wincing at the icy air.

Nina was bundling Maxim into his coat and overshoes. 'Some people would consider you to be in the prime of life,' she said, giving Shostakovich a kiss.

'The majority of people know nothing at all about the strain I am under.' He hitched up his pyjamas and belted his coat firmly around his waist. 'Writing all day in half-light, with no heating and no rest — an impossible job, even without the Nazis. Before most composers reach my age, they've already gone to their graves. Think of Mozart! If I were Mozart, this would be my last birthday.'

'I hope you'll cling to life, at least until tonight,' said Nina. 'Izrail has gone to a great deal of trouble to get hold of extra vodka.'

Any hopes Shostakovich had had of keeping his birthday low-key, and

211

his mind focused on his work, were dashed as soon as they entered the cellar.

'Mr Shostakovich!' Irina Barinova's voice rang out of the darkness. 'We've heard today is a special day for you. May all your anniversaries be more peaceful than this one!'

Shostakovich sighed. 'How did you know?'

'I'm sorry,' whispered Nina. 'I told her.'

'How's the new work going?' Irina wasn't allowing Luftwaffe bombs to deter her from gossip. 'Will your work soon be coming of age, also?'

Shostakovich took Maxim by the hand and groped his way to the long bench against the wall. He clamped his mouth shut and listened to Nina fielding queries. Yes, the first and second movements were completed, and the third was under way. Yes, they were hoping for a premiere performance by Mravinsky and the Philharmonic, in spite of the fact they were currently fifteen hundred miles east in the depths of Siberia.

By breathing in the scent of Maxim's hair, he remained calm. It was imperative to keep the adagio steady in his head. Although he was a week in, and possibly halfway through, it was by no means secure. Neighbourly exclamations rained down on its surface, muddying the opening woodwind chords and the searing violin melody. He would never have admitted it (except, perhaps, to Sollertinsky), but he was glad when the distant thundering of guns was joined by the loud swishing of incendiaries, drowning out the chatter — and he was even more glad when a crash shook the cellar, releasing showers of plaster and stopping the talk altogether.

'Will the house fall, Papa?' Maxim leaned closer, puffing from concern.

'Not this time,' reassured Shostakovich, half-listening to the violin that continued to soar far above the bombers and their tilting, lethal wings.

After the roar of the planes had faded, and before the all-clear sounded, the conversation started up again. Now, to his relief, it revolved not around his work or his birthday, but the dire state of affairs in Leningrad. Lack of food, lack of information, the lack of help from Moscow: these issues kept the residents of the Bolshaya Pushkarskaya house occupied for some time. Of all the voices, Irina Barinova's was the shrillest and most carping; it drove into Shostakovich's head with a force greater than the loudest bomb blast.

He reached for his notebook, but realised he was wearing only his pyjamas and his overcoat. 'Galina,' he whispered urgently, 'can you remember something for me?' Galya had the best memory of anyone he knew, which proved useful on those frequent public occasions when he was approached by someone whose name had slipped his mind.

Galina pressed her ear against his mouth. 'Of course I can.'

'B and B flat clash, reversed and raised a fifth.'

'B, B flat clash. Reverse, raise fifth. I've got it.'

And with that the all-clear siren blared at last, and the door was pushed open, and they were free to straggle into the grey light and up the stairs for breakfast.

'Sorry for my silence,' he said to Nina, swishing his spoon around in porridge that consisted largely of water. 'It's just that I can't stand their gushing.'

'They're proud of you, that's all.' Nina poured out cups of the thin black liquid that they continued to call coffee. 'Most of them heard your radio broadcast last week. They want to show their support.'

'They'd support me better by leaving me in peace. I don't know how you cope with them all.'

'Papa, stop talking — it's time for your presents!' Galina was bursting with excitement. 'Now, what would you like most in the whole world?'

Shostakovich surveyed the items in front of him: a saucer of smoked lard, a chunk of hard black bread, and two cigarettes that had to last him all day, procured (not without guilt) by trading in a silk scarf Nina had given him on his 1936 concert tour.

'What I'd like most is an enormous pork chop carved from the fattest pig in the world, served with porcini mushrooms and a white gooey sauce of imported cheeses.'

Galina's face fell and Maxim looked concerned. Behind them, Nina gestured widely with her hands.

'Of course, that's not what I *most* want,' he amended, staring at his wife who was moving her arms in scissor-like movements. 'What I'd really like for my birthday is . . . erm, a picture made by you?'

'Really? Pictures?' Relieved, Galina rushed to the cupboard and pulled out a roll of newspaper. 'That's just what we have. However did you guess?'

Shostakovich spread open the two sheets of newsprint cut into lopsided stars. Between the holes, he saw remnants of his published radio broadcast from the previous week. 'Dear colleagues and friends . . . An hour ago I completed the second part . . . I shall be able to call it the Seventh Symphony . . . the dangers facing Leningrad . . . All of us are soldiers today . . .'

He held the paper up to the dim light. 'They're beautiful pictures.

Even the paper-cutter who visited our house when I was a child couldn't do better! Let's put them on display immediately.'

Galina and Maxim had barely taped their cuttings over the already partially covered windows before they became fretful and tired. These days they had sudden jags of energy, and bursts of confidence followed by fear. Shostakovich knew just how they felt. When the symphony was going well he felt invincible; on those days, he refused to go down into the shelter, staying at the piano and listening to the Luftwaffe ripping open the sky. Yet, on less successful days, he dived into the cellar with his stomach churning; then, shaking and covered in sweat, he was more than glad of the darkness.

'Why don't we all have a lie-down,' suggested Nina, sweeping up crumbs and clearing away plates.

However closely Shostakovich watched her, he couldn't tell how much of a strain it was for her to remain so calm. The Varzars had always had a veneer of assurance, so that even in the most perilous of situations they seemed impervious to harm.

'But what about your poem!' Galina turned in the bedroom doorway. 'Those bombers were too loud for us to tell it to you in the cellar.' She motioned to Maxim, and they stood with their feet aligned like miniature soldiers. She began reciting in a loud sing-song voice, with Maxim's tiny hum trailing behind:

Mama says when you were young
That you could be quite naughty.
You're bigger now, and well behaved,
Because you're nearly forty.

Forty! Shostakovich couldn't help but wince. He grabbed for one of his two precious cigarettes.

Galina raised her head from a low, synchronised bow. 'I know you're only thirty-five. But forty rhymed.'

'Of course.' He laid the cigarette back on the table. 'Thank you both very much for going to all that trouble. It's a splendid poem.'

Only after Nina had led the children away for a nap did he realise he'd forgotten to ask Galina for another, quite different recitation. How had it gone? He forced himself to think his way back through the events of the morning. The unwelcome crush of bodies in the cellar, the dry taste of dust. The shuddering walls, the crashing blows, Maxim's compulsive starts, and Irina Barinova's voice grinding on about long queues, the flimsiness of ration cards and which parts of his radio broadcast hadn't been helpful in raising morale.

Suddenly, as he remembered Irina's voice, the progression was there. The harping, repetitive clashing of B and B flat, reversed, then raised a fifth. He smacked his hand on the table, making his cup rattle in its saucer. 'Thanks, Irina, you grumpy old witch!' Tiredness and depression fell away. He went to his workroom and closed the door.

It was late afternoon when he stopped. Raising his head, cracking his aching neck, he realised he could barely see the notes in front of him. For the past week there had been no electricity at all and already his eyes were strained. He lit a candle and held the small flickering circle over his work, scanning what he'd done. Sighing, he picked up his pen again — only to hear loud greetings and laughter from the other room. For a small, wild second, he considered plugging his ears and continuing work. To stop now seemed more of an effort than ploughing on and setting the powerful chordal theme against the relentless Barinova motif.

He tiptoed to the door and put his ear against it. Was that the reedy laugh of Izrail Finkelshtein? Perhaps he could call him in for a quick chat? Izrail was one of the most intuitive composition assistants he'd worked with, and his opinion might be helpful. He put an indecisive hand on the door handle before remembering that he was, in fact, meant to be celebrating his birthday. Returning to the piano, he gathered up the papers, laid his pen on top of the pile and blew out the candle. He stumbled through the darkened room and out into the beginnings of a party.

Rivals

Nikolai was more animated than he'd been for quite some time. Standing in the rehearsal room, he pulled off his gloves and shook his thin hands to get the blood flowing.

'Of course, the food was nothing special, if you think that only a few months ago it would have been a Krug-and-caviar birthday party.'

'So what did you eat? Insubstantial fistfuls of bread, like the rest of the city?' Elias busied himself with unnecessary tasks, tapping the stone-cold stove as if this would miraculously produce heat, polishing his already gleaming baton.

'Oh, no!' Nikolai's voice almost had a glow to it. 'Of course the food was simple, mainly black bread and potatoes. But Nina Shostakovich had managed to make a kind of cranberry cake, and other people brought whatever they could — there was even some candy! As for Izrail, he'd got his hands on enough vodka to fill the Neva.'

Elias said nothing. He watched the musicians shuffling in, pinched from cold and hunger.

'Afterwards —' Nikolai swished his bow through the air in a cloud of resin — 'after dinner, we heard some of the new symphony!'

'The Shostakovich symphony?' Katerina had been eavesdropping and her wan face lit up. 'Some people have all the luck!'

Nikolai nodded. 'We went into his study, he hesitated for only a moment, and then he sat at the piano and played straight through the first movement, barely looking at the score. It was pretty long, too — twenty-five minutes, at least.'

'Only the first movement?' asked Elias nonchalantly. 'I thought he was further on than that.'

'I haven't finished yet! Just as he reached the final bars of the march, the sirens began to sound, but he begged us to stay and hear the rest. Nina and the children went to the shelter, but most of us stayed. The bombers flew in over our heads, but on he played, as if he were possessed! And so we heard the scherzo through to its beautiful end.'

Now Elias understood the dreamy look hovering behind Nikolai's eyes and the smile playing on his lips. Jealousy flooded through him. 'That was a strange thing to do,' he said. 'Putting one's guests at risk like that.'

'He didn't decide for us, we chose to stay. How could we not?' Nikolai spread out his hands. 'It was musical history in the making. Nobody's heard a bar of it before!'

'Is it really a symphony for Leningrad, as he says?' An avid group was clustering around Nikolai. 'Will it tell our story in years to come?'

'It's difficult to tell,' mused Nikolai. 'Anything composed in response to such extreme circumstances is a complex thing. But from what I heard last night, I believe it'll be extraordinary. At any rate, it's miraculous to compose a symphonic work of this scale in the middle of such hardship — not to mention performing it as he did last night, playing without error for more than half an hour with an air raid raging.'

'Not so much miraculous as foolhardy,' muttered Elias. But no one was listening to him.

Nikolai seemed oblivious to the fact that rehearsal should have started four minutes ago, and that in three days the shambles that was the Radio Orchestra would be broadcast on international airwaves. 'Dmitri's always been capable of rising to the occasion,' he continued. 'As his classmates, we saw that from the start, isn't that so, Elias?'

'Shostakovich is talented.' Elias spoke dismissively. 'No one can deny that. But he's certainly not averse to showing off. Perhaps you don't remember his odd behaviour at Glazunov's soirée in our first year at the Conservatoire?' He looked around to make sure he had the floor. 'After a foxtrot had been played, Shostakovich pretended to be offended by it. Which gave him an excuse to set to and, then and there, re-orchestrate the whole thing in front of the guests.'

Nikolai looked taken aback. 'Yes, I was there that evening. But he was challenged to do that. I remember it well.'

Elias fixed his eyes on the painting hanging above Nikolai's head, a dreary 1820s oil of the Pantelimonov drawbridge. He felt as black as the thick-painted water. 'He flaunted his talent in the middle of the room, and went through his paces like a show pony.'

'He was *challenged*.' Nikolai spoke more sharply. 'What was a man to do?'

'How about saying no?' Elias kicked his stool, leaving a scar on the already scratched floor. 'That was his problem — that *is* his problem. Shostakovich never says no.'

The musicians, who'd been momentarily energised by Nikolai's story, fell silent. They drifted away towards their chairs, their shoulders hunched.

Nikolai slid off the table. 'Sorry to hold up proceedings,' he said under cover of tuning up. 'You were probably wanting to make an earlier start.'

Elias shrugged. 'It's understandable that you're excited after what you experienced last night. To hear the mythical Seventh Symphony, even in piano reduction, is a great privilege.'

'I thought you might even be at the party.'

'I'm not a particular friend of Shostakovich.' Elias gave a second, more emphatic shrug. 'We're nothing but acquaintances. In truth, I barely know him.'

'A pity. You'd have enjoyed the performance as much as anyone, particularly as you may conduct it one day.'

'Not while Mravinsky lives and breathes!' Elias gave a forced laugh. 'We all know he's the apple of Shostakovich's eye. Besides, with a first movement as huge as the march, do you really think we could cope?' He glanced at his scraping, blowing bunch; more than twenty chairs stood empty.

'Yes, the first movement's vast. It sounds like a great beast waking up, uncurling itself, preparing for attack.'

Elias flicked through his score. 'Did any parallels spring to your mind? Any particular composers?'

Nikolai laughed.

'I only ask,' added Elias quickly, 'because Shostakovich is well known for referencing other works.'

'And I only laugh because, even before he began to play, he made a disclaimer to that effect.'

'Really? What did he say?'

'He said —' Nikolai paused. '"Forgive me if this reminds you of Ravel's *Bolero*."'

'And did it? Did it remind you of Ravel?'

'You know what?' Nikolai wedged his violin under his chin and began tuning up. 'It did. Not only Ravel, but also Richard Strauss.'

'The battle scene from *Heldenleben*! Yes, the third theme is most reminiscent of that. Did you also hear traces of Sibelius's Fifth? Not at all obvious, and masterfully done — the subtlest of allusions, really.'

Nikolai lowered his violin and stared at him. 'Yes, there were echoes of Sibelius in the third theme. I agree with you. But how do you know that? When were you —?'

He was interrupted by a loud burp right beside them. It was Alexander, thinner and pastier than ever, clutching his oboe in unsteady hands. 'When you've finished gassing about Leningrad's most eminent citizen,' he said with ostentatious politeness, 'I'd like a private word with our eminent conductor.'

Elias stared at Alexander; his breath was strong enough to lean on. 'You're drunk. Do you really think it's acceptable to come drunk to rehearsal? I trust you're still capable of playing.' He turned away, but Alexander seized him by the shoulder.

'I wanted to ask you for some time off. My sister's contracted diphtheria, everything at home is in a mess. I must be excused rehearsal for the next few days.'

'Must?' Elias frowned. 'Who are you to say the word *must*? The only thing you *must* do is the job you're paid for, which is playing in this orchestra. We have a broadcast on Sunday! How do you expect me to find a replacement at such short notice? There probably isn't even another oboist alive in this cursed city.'

Alexander stepped closer, making an obvious effort to focus, although his eyes crossed with the effort. 'Come on, Karl. You know how it is to be underprivileged. You and I, we're the same. We've had to work our way up to our positions. We've never had maids, we haven't been given big apartments like Dmitri Shostakovich, we don't ignore people like he does. So stuck up he won't give a man the time of day! You and I need to stick together.'

Elias felt such distaste for Alexander that his skin crawled. 'Shostakovich doesn't ignore people. He's short-sighted, not stuck up. He's . . . he's wonderful.' Where were the words coming from? Now he'd started, he couldn't stop. 'Shostakovich is one of the greatest composers Russia will ever have.'

Alexander lurched. 'But he's derivative — you said so yourself. Everyone knows he steals material and buries it deep in his precious music, hoping no one will notice. That's not wonderful, that's plain stupid!'

Elias's heart sank. It was true — he'd publicly denigrated Shostakovich. And the result? The man he least respected in the world was siding with him against the man he admired more than any other. 'Shostakovich is a master of quotation.' His voice was uneven. 'That's always been one of his gifts. Now take your seat. We're running late as it is.'

'Shostakovich is a coward!' Alexander remained standing, though he swayed as he spoke. 'He pretends he's stayed on to defend Leningrad, but do you want to know something? He was about to leave at the end of August, when Kozintsev and the film studios were shipped out, but the planes were full. My cousin told me! Too bad for Shostakovich that he crept to the authorities too late.'

Was it true? Looking away, Elias caught Nikolai's eye.

Nikolai gave a tiny nod. 'For the safety of his children,' he said, over the heads of the orchestra. 'At the insistence of his wife. Dmitri himself was most reluctant to leave.'

Receiving this unexpected, unwanted information filled Elias with fury. 'He's neither a copyist nor a coward. And I will not give you time off, Alexander. If your sister's ill, she must go to a hospital. What would happen if I gave leave to everyone with a sick or injured relative? I'd have no orchestra left!'

'My sister has dysentery, you heartless bastard!'

'Two minutes ago she had diphtheria,' said Elias. 'Make up your mind. If you're placing her at death's door, you might at least decide what disease you're killing her with.'

The orchestra sniggered, and Alexander turned purple. 'All right. It's me. I'm exhausted. I can't go on like this — the air raids, the shelling, the cold. I'm not getting enough food, I can't sleep. I need a rest.'

Elias stared at him in disbelief. 'Do you think it's different for anyone else in Leningrad? Didn't you hear Shostakovich's radio address? Whether we're artists or artillerymen, at this point in time we're all soldiers — and that includes you.'

A sneer spread over Alexander's face. 'Shostakovich, Shostakovich. It's always Dmitri Fucking Shostakovich. I believe you're in love with him. Do you hear me, comrades?' He spun around to face the orchestra, his oboe hitting a chair with a sharp crack. 'Did you hear? Our conductor's in love with the famous composer!'

It was Elias's turn to sway. 'Sit down. Sit down and play.'

But instead Alexander leaned on a pillar and leered at him. 'You're a bastard. And I won't play.'

A sharp twang came from the string section, making Elias jump. A violin string, tightened too far, had snapped, and it curved in the cold air like a whip. He surveyed his musicians with their deathly pale faces and sunken red-rimmed eyes. The sight filled him with horror. He stepped closer to Alexander.

'You will play. It's your duty.'

'Get fucked,' said Alexander. 'You're a dictator and a cunt.'

A purple haze washed over Elias's eyes. He could no longer see the drunk oboist, nor the open-mouthed musicians, nor the cracked walls and the broken windows. Instead, he had a horrifying vision that he couldn't place: a marble slab, a white neck, veined eyelids wrapped over swollen eyeballs.

'Karl?' It was Nikolai's voice, calling from the back of the room. 'Are you all right?'

Elias stepped back, his vision clearing. 'Get out,' he said to Alexander. 'Leave.'

'First you order me to play, now you want me to leave?' Alexander sounded incredulous.

'You're a drunkard and a liar. If you look at your oboe, you'll see that you've damaged it, and your oboe is the only reason I've tolerated you for so long. We'll be better off without you. Go to hell.' In the back of his mind, he heard distant horns starting up: the prelude to a march.

After Alexander had stumbled out the door, the relief was so over-whelming that Elias also stumbled as he walked to the podium. But behind him he heard a welcome sound. Petrov was clapping. With his weak hands and chapped palms, the sound of his approval was tiny. But it was applause, nonetheless, and soon it spread from player to player until every member of the orchestra was clapping.

The thief

Nikolai walked home with his bread ration hidden inside his coat. There had been a scuffle outside the bakery: a woman pushed against the wall by a teenager, the bread snatched from her hand. When Nikolai himself emerged from the bakery, the woman was still sitting empty-handed on the muddy curb. No one had helped her; the rest of the queue had said nothing, done nothing, simply stared as if they had no connection to thief or victim. The crime, the indifference — neither was out of the ordinary. By now everyone had learnt that survival meant looking after yourself. But, trudging along the gritty street, Nikolai felt both sad and wary.

Just as he turned into Belinsky Prospect, it began to rain, a low slanting rain that was almost snow. He turned his collar up and put his head down. Within minutes his violin case was slippery and wet; he tried to hoist it onto his shoulder but found he didn't have the strength.

He struggled on through the mud, avoiding the potholes left by the rumbling tanks. He was only dimly aware of others toiling along beside him, moving as slowly as possible to save energy. The whole of Leningrad was grinding to a halt, winding down like a clock with no key.

As his tiredness had grown, he'd become less certain about what to do. For the well connected, there was still the occasional chance of evacuation. Being flown over enemy lines, or crossing Lake Ladoga to reach the last unbroken railroad linking Leningrad to the rest of Russia — both were risky. But they were the only two ways of escaping this living hell. Now, peering through the sleet, Nikolai saw the future more clearly than he had since the first shock of the invasion. The German Army had a stranglehold on Leningrad, and it was choking the city to death.

Realising this, he tried to convince himself that sending Sonya away might have saved her life. But, as always, his brain cried out: *You made a mistake! Whatever the situation was or will be, Sonya belongs with you.*

Only the previous week he'd felt her absence more keenly than ever when he'd arrived, alone, at Shostakovich's apartment. Galina had opened the door. 'Where's Sonya?' Her face fell. 'You should have brought her! There are too many grown-ups at this party. We wanted Sonya to come.'

He'd been shocked at the sound of her name. 'She went away for a while. To stay with her cousins.'

'Don't you miss her?' Galina shook her head. 'I do. I admire Sonya enormously, she's so cultured. And Maxim's quite in love with her. When's she coming home?'

'When this horrible bombing stops, I hope.' As he stepped inside, tears sprang into his eyes, and he was glad that the room was lit only by candles.

Galina had been the first person to say Sonya's name for a long time. Even Tanya had stopped mentioning her — had she given up all hope of a return? Others referred to her absence obliquely: had Nikolai received any News about the Situation? Recently he'd begun talking aloud to his dead wife, the only other person who'd loved Sonya as fiercely as he did. 'Tell me if she's still alive,' he would say as he lay in bed. 'Please give me a sign. Is she somewhere in Leningrad?' This was his greatest hope as well as his greatest fear: the possibility that Sonya had been brought back to the city but not returned to him, that she'd been hideously damaged in some way and was lying, unidentified, in a hospital or an orphanage. God knows he'd searched. Had gone to all the authorities he could think of, both medical and bureaucratic; had asked all possible connections for any leads. During his search he'd seen maimed children, the sight of whom he couldn't forget: bodies torn through by shells, left without voices, sight or wits. But not one of the bandaged young girls who stared blankly at him from a makeshift ward had been his.

He stumbled on, his overcoat wet through. If he could get home without imagining he saw Sonya, then, in spite of the bread thief and the icy rain, this would have been a bearable day. It was the quick appearances that ruined him, a glimpse of her face on a street corner or through a window — and then the subsequent vanishing. Sudden hope and its equally sudden removal left him shattered, blinded, with no strength to go on.

Soon the sleet was so thick he could barely see a foot in front of him. *If he could just make it home.*

Rounding the corner into what he thought was Tarasova Street, he collided with someone. 'Sorry,' he said, glancing up.

It was a woman, thin-faced, dark-eyed under her hood. She, too, mumbled an apology and hurried on. Nikolai stood still for a second, then turned. 'Nina Bronnikova — is that you?' But his voice was weak, and already there was a wall of water between them; she was nothing but a hunched shape inside a long coat, disappearing into the sleet.

When at last he reached his building, the final effort of climbing the stairs was too much. Step by step, he made it to the first landing, then, even more slowly, to the second. Finally he was outside his own apartment, leaning his soaked head on the door. He let himself in very slowly and quietly. He'd begun to feel that if he did everything as silently as possible, the spectre crouching over him might leave him alone. *Nothing good lies in store*, it whispered with dank breath — and he believed this with all his ruined heart.

The effort of removing his boots left him breathless, and he sat down on the floor. Only when he realised that the bread would be as soaked as his clothes did he force himself to get up, take off his heavy overcoat, and place the small sodden package on the table.

He drifted like a sleepwalker towards Sonya's door. Because it was now also Tanya's room, he rarely went in there out of respect for her privacy. But the deprivation was like an intense and constant homesickness, a longing for a country belonging to his past. And today he was weak; nostalgia flooded over and through him, swamping him. He gave only a tiny rap at the door before pushing it open.

Tanya was standing in front of him. 'Nikolai! I didn't expect you home so early.' A guilty tide of red rushed up her neck and into her face.

In her arms, she held a cello. *The* cello. Sonya's cello.

'What are you doing? What are you doing with Sonya's birthday present?'

Tanya stepped back, still holding the cello. Its wooden body stuck out on an awkward angle. 'We both know what's happening, Nikolai.' Her voice was as rough and muddy as the Leningrad streets. 'If we don't act now, we're going to end up starving to death.'

He stood in the doorway and stared at her. Her feet were planted firmly on the threadbare carpet where his daughter had learnt to crawl; her fingers had tightened compulsively around the cello.

'How dare you.' His voice was flat and expressionless. 'How dare you. You were planning to steal Sonya's cello and barter it for food.'

'Not steal.' Tanya gave a shrug. 'Someone at the hospital offered us tinned food. *Tinned food!*'

Nikolai laughed incredulously. 'You're holding an eighteenth-century Storioni, Tanya. Do you realise that? After this siege is over, you'll be left with a guilty stomach, empty arms and a niece who will never forgive you.'

Tanya spoke in her most reasonable voice. 'Nikolai, you know you're hopelessly impractical. If you intend to go on working, you'll need more than a handful of bread to get through the winter. Soon the supply barges will be frozen off the lake and we'll have even less food than we do now. Do you really think anyone will want a cello then? The doctor at the Astoria won't take this cello off our hands when rations are cut to nothing and there are riots in the streets.'

'It is not *a* cello.' He felt like hitting her. 'Nor *this* cello. It's Sonya's cello. And you'll put it down, now.'

Tanya shook her head and hitched up her burden, making the C string twang against her hip. 'We must act now,' she said, as if reading a propaganda pamphlet. 'We must stock up on canned food that will last. The doctor has tins of red cabbage. He has green cabbage. He has beans!'

'He can shove his cabbage up his arse and shit it out again, before he lays one finger on Sonya's cello.'

'It was my sister's cello first.' Tanya's cheeks flamed. 'And before that it belonged to our father. You didn't know my sister for as long as I did, and Sonya hardly knew her at all. I'm the one who knew her the longest, so I should decide what happens to this.' She shook the cello as if it were a difficult child.

Nikolai had never felt such anger. 'You're despicable. I've given you a home, and this is how you thank me? You know how special that cello is, what it means to Sonya and to me — yet you're willing to palm it off to a quack with an eye for the black market who will pass it on for far more than a few tins of beans. I promised Sonya that her cello will be here when she comes home. Put it down and get out now, before I force you to do so.'

Tanya gave a strange, loud laugh. 'Take your stupid cello,' she said, throwing it on the bed with a loud rattle of strings. 'Die of hunger — see if I care. As for your daughter, we both know she's never coming home. You're living in a dream world. Sonya is dead.'

She marched past him and through the main room, leaving the apartment door open behind her. Her crying echoed up the stairwell, and was followed by the bang of the heavy front door. As if in immediate response, an air-raid siren started up.

Shaking all over, Nikolai sat down on the bed. 'Sonya isn't dead,' he whispered. 'She'll come back.' There was a long scratch down the front of the cello, and he rubbed at it carefully with his cuff.

Outside the sirens wailed, but the blood hammering in his ears was far louder. He felt weightless, as if he'd lost connection with the physical world. 'I think I'd better lie down,' he said, moving the cello gently to one side of the bed, and stretching out beside it. He concentrated on breathing deeply. As his heartbeat slowed and his nerves settled, he became aware of a tiny rustling sound beside him. It was coming from the cello.

Raising himself on one elbow, he looked around him. The room was already dark. He got up, lit a candle and tilted the cello towards the flickering light. Peering through the carved holes into the instrument's wooden cavity, he could just make out what appeared to be many white paper rolls the size of a cigarette or a child's finger.

He ran to the kitchen, seized up another candle and a knife, and returned to the bedroom. With shaking hands, he managed to manoeuvre one of the rolls from the cello's body. Even before he'd finished unrolling the paper, he could see it was covered with Sonya's neat miniature printing.

Dearest Mama, today was a good day and a bad day. Papa and I met an angry soldier who hit the Bronze Horse. Mr Shostakovich walked me home. He said you were one of the best cellists in Leningrad. I told him I only got to know you after you died.

Now his hands were shaking so violently that extracting the scrolls through the narrow curved slots seemed impossible. Out in the street, the sirens were screaming and loudspeakers blared. The house shook with frantically banging doors and running footsteps. Ignoring it all, he worked on until there was a small sliding pile of notes on the bed beside him.

Mama, I'm writing to you because I'm not sure you can hear me any more. The tanks are so loud in the streets.

Today I played scales, no pieces. I want my fingers to be strong like yours. Papa said my C major was very good.

We had air-raid practice today. The Germans make everyone scared.

The low drone of the bombers had started, but Nikolai read on. His eyes stung, though once or twice he actually laughed.

I have to go to Pskov soon. I don't want to but the Generals are making me go. I hope the cousins have learned not to eat with their mouths open.

Now the planes sounded as if they were right above the house; the whole world was shuddering. He stood up, still reading desperately — and at last he found what he needed.

Do you think instruments remember people? I do. Sometimes when I pick up the cello it wants to tell me about you. Now it has to remember me too, because I'm leaving tomorrow. But I'll ask Papa to guard it with his life. Anyway, I'll be back in Leningrad soon. Respectfully, Sonya.

At that moment, there was a sharp screaming sound, followed by a thundering roar. The whole building rocked. Books were thrown off shelves and pictures crashed to the floor. Suddenly Nikolai was surrounded by splintering glass and cracking wood. He ducked his head and fell to his knees by the bed, clutching the scrap of paper in his hand.

Orders

Shostakovich sat and stared at the stack of paper in front of him. For the past four days he'd barely left the room, moving feverishly between the desk and the piano. His eyes hurt and so did his right hand. But the previous night, around this time, he'd finished the adagio.

The elation had been short-lived but real. Flinging back his head, stretching his arms, he'd briefly congratulated himself. He'd done it — and in only twelve days, too. How proud his mother would be! How she would crow, clap her hands, and say, 'Dmitri, you're a living marvel!' But she'd always been inordinately proud of him; if he did nothing more than brush his teeth, she'd pronounce he'd done a better job than any man in Russia.

After a few minutes, he'd realised how cold he was. In spite of his two pairs of socks, his feet were numb and his fingertips were white. Almost instantly, the old fear had started up again. He could barely remember where or how he'd started; the entire symphony had become cloudy, a muddle of themes, secondary themes and reiterated secondary themes. Where were the clean lines of the original idea?

He got up from the desk and paced along the wall, catching sight of himself in the small mirror as he did so. Red-eyed, stubble-chinned, he had the same gaunt look as a drunkard or a tramp. He couldn't bear to glance at what he'd written; already, the certainty of the final bars had left him. To end by returning to the first subject — was this satisfying or merely predictable? He felt exposed and alone.

He opened the study door. 'Nina?' But everything was quiet, both inside the apartment and out in the street. He peered around the blackout blind and through the criss-crossed tape, but there was no one about — the night-time curfew meant only the most foolish or desperate ventured out this late. 'I miss voices,' he whispered. 'I miss ordinary life.'

He needed to talk to someone. The sense of anti-climax was as predictable as it was inevitable — though no easier to handle because of that. 'Ivan Ivanovich. Where the hell are you when I need you?' Restlessly he wandered around the room, taking a swig of cold unsweetened tea, spitting it out in the sink. He clattered a few glasses together and restacked a few plates, and soon, as he'd hoped, Nina appeared in the doorway, her hair in a long braid.

'Sorry! I didn't mean to wake you!' It was a lie. Just the sight of her made him feel better.

'Is something wrong?'

'On the contrary. Not ten minutes ago, I finished the third movement! It's even — well, let's say it's satisfactory.'

'That's wonderful! Quite worth being woken up for.' Though she still looked half asleep, Nina went to the cupboard and took out glasses and a bottle of vodka.

'Three down, one to go.' But as he sat down at the table he felt so tired he had no idea whether he could pick himself up again and launch into that most difficult of things, a symphonic finale to not only recap but also surpass everything that had gone before.

'To the war symphony.' Nina raised her glass.

'To the end of war,' said Shostakovich, refilling his.

Later, giddy with exhaustion and vodka, he led her into his workroom to show her the score paper spread out on top of the piano. She bent her head to scan the notes (did she hear anything of what he'd heard?), and he was at once distracted by the sight of her — the swell of her breasts under her nightgown, her nipples hard from the cold. How could he live so close to her, yet not notice her for weeks on end? He'd done it again: treated her as nothing more than a wife and mother, the provider of meals and manager of accounts, the staver-off of unwelcome attention and the smoother of social waters.

'You're so beautiful tonight!' he murmured. 'And I'm a blind fool.' He pulled her hair out of its braid so it fell in a smooth black rush. 'Why do you still love me?' He led her to the divan then, and slipped her nightgown off over her head. She remained silent, but pulled him to her so closely it felt they would never separate again. 'I'm sorry,' he said, under his breath. 'I'm sorry for my absences.'

When, much later, he woke in the still-dark morning, under a rough grey blanket, Nina had already gone — but his depression had disappeared, too, so he could fall back into a deep and peaceful sleep.

———

Now, he was at his desk again, the lust and the loving of the previous night almost forgotten, his stomach as empty as his head. At lunch, Nina had suggested that he rest for a day or two, but he'd shaken his head. 'I must get on.' He'd pushed away a lukewarm cup of borscht, made with no meat, very little beet and large amounts of cabbage water. 'Who knows what will happen in the near future?'

For most of the afternoon he'd sat in his study but not written a note. Two trips to the bomb shelter within five hours — and he realised, with dismay, that the interruptions hadn't been entirely unwelcome. He had no idea how to continue. How could he follow such unearthly, funereal music with anything at all, let alone a fourth movement that might inspire the starving Leningraders and satisfy the clamouring Party officials?

'What the hell do they expect from me?' He jabbed his pencil into the desk. 'What do they want — and, more to the point, what do I want?' This, he knew, was the whole problem. He'd made the fatal mistake of inviting in an audience before the work was completed. Had become conscious of the way other people might hear it, and now craved further applause — that rapturous applause offered to him on his birthday, as his friends praised his magnificent march and his lyrical scherzo. 'The movements sing of Leningrad today and of Petrograd in the past!' Izrail had had tears in his eyes. And Shostakovich had murmured 'Yes', though whether his assistant's words were true was beyond knowing.

'Between them, they have created a monster,' he muttered — but the accusation was directed at himself. Now, when he needed encouragement once more, all he could hear was silence.

The longer he sat there staring at his work, the more unbearable it became. He could think of only one person who might help. 'I'll do it,' he said suddenly. 'I'll call him.' He sprang up and went to the door.

Nina was sitting at the table. She wasn't reading one of her scientific papers, nor was she sewing or counting food coupons. She was simply sitting and staring at the table top, looking as if she, too, were carved from wood.

He sat down at the other end of the table, waiting respectfully, picking at his thumbnail. Finally he spoke with attempted brightness. 'What are you thinking about, sitting here all alone?'

'If you must know, I'm scared.' When she looked up, her face was so bleak that his heart lurched.

'But I'll take care of you. You know that. I'll take care of you all.'

'The children are getting so thin. And everyone says rations are going to be cut again. Soon it will be winter — and what will we do for heating?'

'Nina, it was my decision to stay. So it's my responsibility to solve our problems.'

She gave a half-smile. 'You don't understand. They're not our problems any more, but the problems of the entire city. We've been so lucky until now. Privileged, most of the time, with the dacha, the car, the extra food. Don't you see that even your position won't save us now? Leningrad is running out of food and fuel. Already people are dying in the streets. Fame counts for nothing.'

His face began to burn. 'I'll call Party Headquarters tomorrow. I'll see what can be done. I realise I've been focused on the symphony, but of course you and the children are more important. Please don't worry any more!'

Nina said nothing, simply laid her hands on the table in a hopeless gesture. The only sounds were the distant knocking of anti-aircraft guns and the faint splutter of the candles.

After some time, Shostakovich cleared his throat. 'Just one thing. I need to get hold of the conductor. Do you know if he has a working phone line?'

'Who, Mravinsky?' Nina looked puzzled. 'Or do you mean Samuil Samosud?'

'Neither. I'm talking of . . . oh, you know —' He rapped the table with his knuckles. 'That tall thin fellow with the Radio Orchestra, quiet man, big glasses, doesn't speak much.'

'Karl Eliasberg? Whatever do you need him for?'

Shostakovich picked wax off the candle and fed it back into the flame so the light flared and Nina's shadow-profile leapt on the wall. 'With Sollertinsky gone, there's no one I trust to judge my work. The adagio, for instance — is it too funereal? And the way the symphony is developing overall. I can't tell if there's a shred of merit in it.'

'Judging by the general reaction the other night, I think you can rest assured on that point.'

'But that's just it — it was a *general* reaction. A chorus of approval.

And you know what Meyerhold said about that.'

'No,' said Nina, 'I have no idea what Meyerhold said.'

'That if your work pleases everyone, you must consider it a total failure.' He slumped in his chair. He could hear the playwright's voice as clearly as if he were in the room, though it was three years since poor Meyerhold had disappeared, removed for failing to please the 'Everyone' who counted.

'The people who liked your work were hardly ill-educated,' said Nina. 'They represent some of the finest musical minds in the city. Didn't you see Nikolai's reaction? Even in the midst of his grief, he was uplifted by what he heard.'

Shostakovich shook his head. 'Nikolai's an admirable musician. He's greatly talented, both as a violinist and a teacher. But he expends too much energy on making other people feel good.'

'Is that such a bad fault?' asked Nina, slightly reprovingly.

But already his mind had returned to Elias's visit earlier that month — was it only a few weeks ago? Already it felt like a lifetime. Such an odd tension surrounding the man, such a mix of reserve and resolve in his face. Even as Shostakovich had thundered through the march with his back to the room, he'd known how Elias would be sitting: muscles taut, nerves strained, critical faculties alert. What had happened after Shostakovich had finished playing? He couldn't remember much of the ensuing discussion, he'd been so keyed up from performing as well as steeling himself for work on the next movement. Nonetheless, there was something about Elias that was implicitly trustworthy. Certainly, he was an oddity, and gauche in the extreme. (That note under the door! Even now, it made Shostakovich smile.) But he had an inner severity about him that Shostakovich identified with. If one didn't like something, it was one's duty to say so, whether or not it caused offence.

'I need the conductor,' he repeated. 'He's the listener I need.'

'Who knows if he had a telephone before this chaos started?' said Nina. 'And even if we could find a number for him, and even if you were able to get a connection — well, it's far too late for phone calls.' She came to stand beside him, stroking his hair. 'Why don't you try to sleep? You can go to the Radio Hall tomorrow and find him.'

Shostakovich sprang up, away from courtesy and common sense. 'No. I need him now. Not tomorrow.'

He went back to his workroom and paced about. No music in his head and no help at hand! It was intolerable. He dragged on a third-rate cigarette, bitter makhorka tobacco sprinkled with nicotine and rolled in wafer-thin newspaper. How could he pass the dragging hours until morning?

'Dmitri?' It was Nina, knocking at the door. 'You have a phone call.'

He didn't know whether to feel relieved or annoyed. 'Didn't you tell them it's far too late for calls?' But he ground out the foul-tasting cigarette and went back out into the main room with sudden hope. 'Is it Sollertinsky?'

Nina shook her head, with an expression that was half apprehensive and half something he couldn't identify. He picked up the receiver warily. 'This is Dmitri Shostakovich. With whom am I speaking?'

'It's Comrade Kalinnikova.' The voice was tinny, sharp and unmistakably authoritative. 'From the Leningrad Party Committee.'

Then he realised what he'd seen on Nina's face had been hope, as well as nervousness at how he might react.

His conversation with Kalinnikova was brief and largely one-sided. He answered in short unemotional phrases, as he was expected to. 'Yes, I understand. Yes, I'm willing.' After a couple of minutes he asked, 'And is there any chance of taking my mother or sister?'

When he hung up, he turned to look at Nina. It was a long quiet look, implying that she'd got her wish at last, and that he was immensely grateful for the sacrifice she'd made but nonetheless he thought it had been worth it.

Finally he cleared his throat and spoke. 'You'd better get the children's things together immediately. We are to leave by plane tomorrow morning, for Moscow.'

PART IV

Winter 1941–
Summer 1942

The crawl

Looking back, Elias thought of the winter as a long tunnel. Darkness so complete there was no rest from it. Cold so intense his bones felt frozen to their very centre. But worst of all was the hunger, for it reduced human beings to animals, fighting in the street for food, grovelling through piles of rubbish for scraps, and dying where they fell.

He could feel himself slipping. The civilised exterior he'd built up so painstakingly over twenty years was crumbling, and there was nothing he could do to stop it. The process had begun that day in December, shortly after what had proved to be the final concert, when he'd closed the official orchestral logbook for the last time. Even writing had become an effort. With a hand so cold he couldn't feel what he was doing, he picked up his pen; its weight felt enormous, dragging down onto the page. Clumsily, he managed a few lines in child-like letters. 'Rehearsal cancelled from today. Nebolsin dead. Malko dead. Petrov too ill to walk. Orchestra can no longer work.'

And from the moment he'd closed the book, everything became a blur. As long as he'd been in front of the orchestra, it had seemed as if he could fight off starvation and fear. Keeping his musicians motivated, though one by one they were collapsing from malnutrition and disease, had driven him on. But at one point during the performance of the *1812*, he'd known they were in serious trouble. The faces in front of him were deathly pale and covered in welts; many had a greenish tinge. During bars of rest, the players put their heads between their knees, or laid down their instruments as if they were made of lead. Each time he raised his arms to bring in a section, he feared there would be no response.

After the concert was over, no one said a word. The musicians barely looked at each other as they packed up, their heads bowed with exhaustion. The cloths in which they used to wrap their instruments were now used to bind hands and feet blistered from cold. They left silently: without farewells, without talk of a future. Only Nikolai raised a parting hand to Elias, giving him a weak but encouraging smile. There was no energy left for emotion.

Elias walked down the corridor very slowly, stopping several times to lean against the wall. His shoulders burned, and his teeth chattered from a deep-seated chill. That was it, he thought. After what the sharp-eyed assessors had just witnessed, an official order to abandon rehearsals was only a matter of time. But already he and his orchestra were done for. Tchaikovsky's victory overture had been played by an orchestra of defeated men.

As he headed home through streets blackened with frost and fire, he felt his little remaining strength leaking away. By the time he got back to his apartment block, he'd lost everything he'd ever struggled for: position, status, respect. He was back where he'd started, and his vision blurred from the shame and tragedy of his loss. He sat in the icy stairwell for some time before he could make it up to his own front door.

'Have you brought the bread?' His mother's voice seemed to be whispering down the years, an echo from a pre-Revolution St Petersburg, when he'd run errands in a world he'd known nothing about.

'There's no bread today, Mother,' he answered like a dutiful boy.

In the long winter weeks that followed, he crawled through the days half-blinded by grief and rage. The frozen city splintered under the German shells, and bodies piled up at the sides of Nevsky Prospect. Stick-thin women stumbled to the Neva and drew water through holes drilled in the ice. Because Elias's vision was failing, he tried to make sense of the disintegrating world by listening to it. What sounds did he hear? The grating of sled-runners loaded with corpses. Huge explosions as mass burial pits were created with dynamite. The howls of stray dogs and cats, slaughtered by Leningraders desperate for meat.

Most of all, he remembered the sound of his mother's breath, rasping through the icy apartment. He would pause at the door, exhausted from the long haul of the stairs, and listen for her breathing, terrified that while he'd been gone her heart would have stopped. But then he heard it, hoarse, irregular, sawing the darkness in two. And her voice also reached him, creeping out from the heap of moth-eaten wool on her bed. 'Karl Elias? Is that you?'

Sometimes, if he had any energy left, he'd make a joke. No, he would say, it was the delivery man, bringing cod-liver pâté and lingonberry sauce. The first time he'd said this, his mother laughed — the first laugh he'd heard for a long time. But as her flesh melted off her bones and her mind grew cloudier, she stopped hearing what he said. She simply asked, over and over, for food. In fact, there was nothing but soup, usually made from grey cabbage and water boiled on the tiny oil-fuelled stove. The stench from the hard leaves was unbearable; it seeped into the walls and bedding, and when Elias lay down in his clothes to sleep, he smelt it in his hair, and it made him retch.

'This tastes odd,' his mother would croak. 'Did you make it the way I taught you?'

'Yes, Mother,' said Elias, spooning cabbage water into her mouth.

'You must always put the meat in at the same time as the onions. That's the trick, to spread the flavour through.'

When the sirens began, they no longer went to the cellar; she couldn't make it, and he no longer cared. They simply stayed where they were, Mrs Eliasberg lying in her bed and Elias sitting next to her. Even walking a few blocks to queue for food or buy water seemed an insurmountable task.

On a day when the temperature fell to minus twenty-five and the air cracked with cold, he stumbled down the stairs and knocked on the Shaprans' door.

'Who is it?' Olga's voice was wary. In a city where you could be beaten and robbed for a small hunk of bread, it was better not to trust anyone.

The cold was so intense it sat in his mouth and stopped his tongue; he tried several times before he could make a sound. 'It's me, Karl Elias.'

Olga opened the door slightly, keeping her body behind it like a suspicious official who might close a barrier at any moment.

'I've come to ask a favour.' He spoke very slowly. He'd blacked out that morning, and there was a low ominous buzzing in his ears.

'Of course you have. Why else would a person come knocking these days?'

Elias pulled his hat lower over his ears. 'I was wondering if I might borrow some lard, or a little sunflower oil? I've given all we had to my mother, and I find I'm close to collapse. A tiny amount of protein would help me get to the bread queue.'

Olga stared at him expressionlessly.

'I couldn't help noticing,' ventured Elias, 'that you and Mr Shapran seem —' His brain was working as poorly as his tongue; he didn't know how to phrase it tactfully. 'You look healthier than most people. I thought, therefore, that you might be in a position to lend me a very little oil, which I promise to pay back with my next ration card.'

Olga flushed, and she gripped the edge of the door. Her hand was thinner than before, but far from skin and bone. 'What are you implying? Do you think we're cheating the system? Using fake ration cards?'

'No, of course not.'

'Perhaps you think we're cannibals?' Her eyes were full of dislike and distrust. 'Cutting flesh off bodies from the roadsides and boiling it up for soup, or buying human meat-cakes from the black market?'

Elias, who hadn't even heard of this practice, began to shake. 'I'm s-s-sorry. I'll leave.'

'Yes, you'll leave! You'll leave me and my husband alone! Some way to thank us for our help, especially after Mr Shapran saved us all from the incendiary bomb.' She slammed the door, and Elias half-fell against the wall.

'Pssst!' A small sound came from above. 'Pssst!'

Dazed, he looked up. There was Valery Bobrovsky, staring at him through the stair railings. His hair stuck up like feathers and his boyish face was pinched, but his eyes gleamed in the old way. 'I'll tell you something,' he hissed. 'They eat rats.'

'Who eats rats?'

'Mr Shapran and his missus. They trap them out in the back alley at night. Mice, too. I seen them.'

'*I've* seen them,' corrected Elias automatically.

'You, too?' Valery nodded. 'Then I guess you know why they're surviving all right. Mrs Shapran makes soup from them. Guess she doesn't want you to know they're virgin-eaters, huh?'

'*Vermin*-eaters,' said Elias, starting slowly back up the stairs.

'And last week I saw Mr Shapran strangling that ginger tomcat that's been hanging around,' said Valery. 'The mean old bastard!' He extracted his head from the railings and got up, dusting off his knees. 'I'd better go. I'm not supposed to be out these days without saying where I am. I hope your ma's all right.'

Back in his apartment, Elias stumbled to the bedroom. The cold in there was so intense he recoiled: they'd used only the main room now for many weeks. Under a stack of cartons, he found a small jar, still almost full. He rarely used hair oil, reserving it for concerts and other special occasions; the last time had been at Sollertinsky's leaving party, and that seemed an eternity ago.

He moved slowly in the semi-darkness of the kitchen, boiling water and stirring in two spoonfuls of hair-oil. After adding a tiny pinch of salt, he sipped it. It wasn't as bad as he'd feared.

'Is that sausage soup?' queried his mother. 'Don't hog it all for yourself.'

After she'd been fed a few spoonfuls, she nodded slowly. 'Much better. See how the flavour's improved by putting the meat in first?'

Resolutions

Nikolai knew he would eat the whole of his bread ration as soon as he left the bakery. It seemed impossible, today, to save it till he got home: to cut it into three thin slices and make them last for the next twenty-four hours. He shoved Tanya's share deep inside his pocket and stepped into a doorway. There had been too many violent attacks recently; it wasn't safe to eat where people could see you, nor to linger for long in public places.

He bit off a chunk of the bread, then crammed the whole crust into his mouth. It tasted mouldy; recently the city's bread had been made out of grain dredged from the lake, salvaged from supply barges sunk by German bombers. But the sensation of having his mouth full was compensation enough for taste. Chewing hard, breathing through his nose, he shifted from foot to foot to keep warm. The wind was icy, the wall damp. He swallowed the last morsel. It had taken him two minutes to eat a whole day's worth of food.

Turning up his collar, pulling down his hat, he plunged back into the driving sleet. The snow underfoot was so heavy that every step was an effort. Over the past weeks he'd felt himself shrinking by degrees, so that even his feet, layered in socks and bound with rags, slipped around inside his boots. When he curled up in bed, his knees grated against each other and his hipbones jutted painfully through two pairs of trousers so he could never lie comfortably.

Shostakovich had written to him, begging him to get out of Leningrad. 'For what it's worth,' he wrote, with typical self-deprecation and naivety,

'I'll add my weight to an official appeal. You can stay here in Kuibyshev with us. Until then, I'm sending you some coffee.' The letter had arrived minus the coffee. Nikolai kept the scribbled page in his shirt pocket; its rustling was strangely comforting. But never once had he considered leaving the city.

Around him people moved like sleepwalkers. Some towed sheet-wrapped corpses towards the already full cemeteries, rolling them off the sleds, leaving them at the gates without looking back. He passed a vacant lot where bodies were stacked in piles, half-covered in snow. Quite dispassionately, he looked at their frost-blackened faces, their stiff outstretched arms. He felt little emotion these days, only a dogged determination to make it through to spring, when he would begin searching for Sonya once more.

At Sennaya market, a handful of women were scanning public notices on the wall, hoping to exchange china, cutlery, jewellery — anything that had once been precious and was now worthless — for rice, oil and smoked lard. Most of the notices were weeks old, ripped and barely legible. Somewhere among them, he supposed, was Tanya's offer: her father's collection of lead soldiers in return for coffee substitute.

'Keep them,' he'd said, when she first suggested this sacrifice. 'You might have sons some day.' He doubted this — Tanya had always had the trenchant air of a spinster and seemed to consider all men idiots — but small miracles did sometimes occur.

'It's a significant collection of soldiers,' she said slightly huffily. 'Papa succeeded in attaining complete regiments, from the Napoleonic war onwards.'

'Well, exchange them if you must,' said Nikolai, although it was common knowledge that even grand pianos had been traded for nothing more than a few slices of black bread. What Tanya was doing, he knew, was more significant than offering up a family treasure for a pound of dried lentils. Ever since the day she'd been caught red-handed with the cello, she'd been different: nervous, apologetic. Often she tried to give Nikolai some of her rations — half a spoonful of sugar, a slice of bread — as if these would make up for the moment when she'd shouted that Sonya was lost forever. Now the cello, wrapped in newspapers and an old blanket, was hidden somewhere Tanya would never find it. Leningraders were chopping up furniture and burning books to keep themselves warm: Nikolai would go to his grave before telling anyone where the Storioni lay.

He walked on past the market. Ahead of him was an elderly woman hauling a sled on which was slumped a half-conscious old man. 'The ice road will save us,' she said over her shoulder. She slipped to her knees, got up, and laboured on. 'We'll all be saved by the ice road.'

Nikolai fixed his eyes on the sled-runner tracks, using them as a guide. He'd heard about the ice road from Tanya, who'd heard about it at the hospital. As soon as Lake Ladoga was frozen solid, convoys of trucks would be able to cross the ice more regularly, and bring food and fuel into the dying city. 'And then,' Tanya had said, as surely as if it were fact, 'everything will improve dramatically. No one expected a siege, after all. The authorities were taken by surprise. But they'll get things running smoothly again once the lake's frozen.'

Nikolai was less certain. True, flatcars laden with grain had been sighted rolling through the deserted stations. But he'd also heard that German pilots were dropping parachute flares over the lake to light up the Russian convoys and then bomb them. And Ladoga's icy surface remained treacherous, with cracks opening up under the weight of the three-ton trucks. Blizzards drove vehicles off course, so the drivers got lost and froze to death. *Rations might be slowly increased*, he thought. *But not soon enough to save us.* The city was ruined, wreathed in black smoke, and people were shuffling in hundreds towards their death.

Nearing Troisky Bridge, he passed the old couple without a second glance, heard the woman gasping and the man coughing deep in his lungs. With a shock, he realised how much he'd changed; how, through these hellish months of deepest winter, he'd been driven by a new fierceness. Something to do with grief, but an entirely different grief from that which had felled him nine years earlier. Sonya might be missing, but until she was pronounced dead he would fight. For the first time in his life — and, ironically, through loving someone else — he'd learnt to put himself first.

Already the small amount of energy from the bread had dissipated. Up ahead the bridge rose into the swirling mist, as insurmountable as the steepest mountain. He refused to let himself think of Tanya's rations lying in his inner coat pocket. It was not his, it was not food, he was not starving.

Reach the post on the top of the bridge, he told himself, *and then find another marker to aim for.*

As he drew closer, he saw that what he'd believed to be a lamp-post was the dark figure of a man. And when he was closer still, he saw the man fall against the railings and slide to the ground.

He trudged on at a snail's pace; his legs would move no faster, nor would his brain allow him to try. But when at last he reached the crest of the bridge, he stopped and looked down.

'Are you all right?' It was difficult to speak; his lips were as stiff as boards.

The man's face was covered in blisters, and his eyes rolled. He opened his mouth, revealing bleeding gums and crimson-stained teeth. 'I'm dying,' he rasped. 'Please — help — me.'

Nikolai looked at him for a long moment. Finally, with an effort, he bent and dragged the man to his feet. His body was lighter than Sonya's had been, and his mottled wrists as thin as the neck of a violin.

'Stand.' This was all he could say. 'Stand.'

But once more the man collapsed against the bridge, slithering onto the muddy ground. His face had the same lime-green tinge as the snow-laden sky.

The breath of the frozen water rose up through the bridge, seeping through the soles of Nikolai's boots. Dangerously, murderously cold, it spread into his legs, filling them with a fierce iron-ache. 'I'm sorry.' He bent towards the man. 'I can do nothing.'

'Don't leave me.' The man gripped his ankle with a raw bleeding hand. 'Please don't leave me.'

For a second longer Nikolai stood still. Then he stepped back, wrenching his boot out of the man's feeble grip. 'I must go.'

He trudged away without looking back. The icy wind made his eyes stream so that he could hardly see to walk.

Attending to business

He hadn't remembered there were so many stairs, nor that they were so steep. He counted the number of steps he had to tackle to reach the first landing. Already, he'd climbed six from the street to the front door, and another four to the sliding glass window, and his knees were shaking.

Ignoring the custodian's stony stare, he leaned on the ledge. 'I am Karl Illyich Eliasberg,' he announced. 'Of the Radio Orchestra.'

Remembering who he once was gave him a temporary strength; he started up the stairs again like a child learning to climb. Right foot, then left foot; feet together, start again. At last, chest heaving, he reached the brass-handled double doors. Beside them was the same paint-stripped, straight-backed chair that had always been there. It had never looked so inviting.

He sat there for thirty minutes, then forty, then fifty. His tailbone pressed painfully against the wood. Shifting his weight, he cursed the Party's habit of always making their minions wait.

After an hour, or an eternity, the secretary appeared. 'This way.' Unsmilingly, he ushered Elias into the ante-chamber. Here, at least, the chairs were a little more comfortable and the furnishings less depressing. The building itself was a bomb-damaged wreck, its facade crumbling and its front steps cracked. But the entrance hall — clean, cheerless, entirely lacking in character — looked just as it had before the war. And in the ante-room there was still carpet on the floor, curtains at the tall windows and paintings on the walls.

Here the air felt clammy, almost overheated. He wiped the sweat off his forehead, and sniffed quickly and anxiously under each arm. He'd been trying to clean himself once a week but, with no soap and little water, he'd resorted to a mixture of ashes and sand gathered from the street. *Scouring myself with the ruins of my city*, he thought — but it seemed important to continue with such rituals, however inadequate. Nikolai, unkempt even before his daughter had gone missing, had slid into complete disarray, whereas Elias continued to shave every second day, using a dry blunt blade that removed a good deal of skin as well as hair.

After the secretary had emerged from the inner chamber for the second time and ordered him to keep waiting, he'd had enough. The week's meat ration had consisted of sheep's guts, discovered in an outlying warehouse and processed into a repulsive jelly. It was completely indigestible, and his stomach was roaring. With more than a touch of acerbity, he pointed out that it was now well past midday.

The secretary frowned. Comrade Zagorsky had been a busy man before the war, but now he was busier than ever. Karl Eliasberg would be called once more pressing matters had been dealt with.

How, wondered Elias, could the Head of the Arts Department manage to be busy? The city was wrecked and its people starved, while the only surviving arts institution was the Musical Comedy Theatre, expressly ordered to continue its capering for the benefit of the soldiers. Perhaps Zagorsky was occupied with sticking his fingers in long-distance pies, telling the Opera and Ballet Theatre what to rehearse while they remained in exile in the Ural Mountains.

'My appointment,' he said to the secretary, as his stomach rumbled ominously, 'was for 10 a.m.'

'A ten o'clock appointment does not guarantee a ten o'clock meeting,' snapped the secretary. Straightening his uniform, flicking imaginary hairs off his sleeve, he disappeared again.

Yet if I'd turned up now, thought Elias, *I would have been sent away on account of my lateness.*

As the hands of the clock crawled on, his nervousness grew. He'd been told nothing, except that Yasha Babushkin would also be attending the meeting. What could the Director of the Radio Committee possibly want to discuss four months after the disbanding of the orchestra? Could a conductor be demoted from a non-existent position? Stripped of an orchestra no longer together? For the hundredth time he polished his glasses, and tried not to gnaw on his split, yellowed fingernails.

The secretary emerged like a jack-in-the-box. 'Comrades Zagorsky and Babushkin will see you now.'

Elias sprang up, discovering too late there was no blood in his feet. He toppled to the floor, nearly landing on the secretary's well-polished shoes. 'Sorry,' he mumbled, getting up and shoving his glasses back onto his nose. 'My circ-circ-circulation is no longer what it was.'

The secretary had been trained not to register concern, whatever the circumstances. 'Please hurry. We mustn't keep our esteemed comrades waiting.'

'No, indeed. Wasting any more time would be unpardonable,' said Elias tartly. In spite of his tingling feet and the carpet threads hanging off his trousers, he managed to enter the inner chamber with a suitably authoritative air.

The meeting was over in less than ten minutes. The huge door clanged shut, and Elias found himself back out on the street under a leaden sky. But for once he barely noticed his surroundings as he ploughed through the slush and the mud, skirting around corpses half-covered in snow.

He dug his fingernails through his threadbare gloves and into his palms. Only through pain could he believe he was awake, that he'd really heard what he thought he had. 'How about that!' he repeated to himself. 'How about that!'

At the top of Nevsky Prospect, his short burst of nervous energy ran out. By the time he reached the Griboyedov Canal, he had to rest every few minutes, and outside the military canteen his legs gave up altogether. He held onto the railings, breathing heavily, his head bowed. He knew he mustn't linger too long or he'd lose all feeling in his hands and feet, and would never get moving again.

'Karl Elias? Is that you?'

The voice was familiar but not immediately identifiable. Coughing, Elias raised his head and found himself looking into the pale watery eyes of Alexander, his one-time Principal Oboe.

'My God, I hardly recognised you,' said Alexander. 'You were always on the thin side, but now . . .' He trailed off as if not wanting to cause offence, though this was hardly the Alexander of old. He, too, had changed; his hair had been neatly trimmed, and he wore a uniform under his patched leather coat.

'Have you joined up?' Elias had heard nothing of Alexander for the past six months. Whether from tact or ignorance, no one had mentioned him since the day he'd stormed, drunk, from the rehearsal room.

'Yes, the anti-aircraft unit. What about you? You look shot to pieces, if you'll pardon an all-too-prevalent expression.'

'I'm over-tired, that's all,' said Elias, trying to recover his dignity. 'I've been at Party Headquarters all morning, on Radio C-C-Committee business.' Suddenly he began shaking violently and his vision blurred. Alexander became nothing but a long thin streak against a hazy background.

'Stay here,' said Alexander, striding away.

There was little else Elias could do. He managed to stay upright by holding tightly to the compound railings; the frozen iron burned through his gloves and seared his fingers. *You've just been handed a future*, he tried to remind himself. But in the strangeness of the present moment — his body shutting down on him, his thoughts becoming hazy — this no longer seemed important, or even real.

Then he felt his right hand being uncurled from the fence and wrapped around a tin cup. 'Bean soup from the canteen.' It was Alexander. 'It's bloody disgusting, but it might help.'

The warmth alone was enough to bring him back to a half-living state. Silently, desperately, he drank the watery soup, scooping out the beans with his fingers and cramming them into his mouth. When he'd finished he took a deep breath. 'Thank you,' he said. 'I think you may have just saved my life.'

'It's nothing. Here, take this.' Alexander glanced towards the canteen, and shoved something into Elias's pocket. 'I'll lose my own bread rations if they see me.' Elias tried to thank him again, but he waved his hand dismissively. 'You would have collapsed otherwise. And probably never got up again, by the skeletal looks of you.'

Elias ignored this. Sensation had returned to his hands and feet, and with it came a heady relief that made him feel dizzy, expansive — and forgiving. 'I don't suppose . . .' he began. 'Is there any chance you want to come back to the orchestra? I could get you exemption from service.'

'The Radio Orchestra?' Alexander stared at him. 'I thought that was all over. Finished. Kaput.'

Should he tell? He hadn't been forbidden to, exactly. 'The orchestra's been ordered to regroup,' he blurted out. 'The Arts Department is planning a season of symphonic concerts to raise morale in the city — and we've been ordered to perform them.' He felt the same combination of elation and fear as he had earlier, standing before Zagorsky's desk.

'I've got no idea how many of our musicians are still alive, but I'd be glad to have you back, if you care to come.'

Alexander gave a fleeting smile. 'I see. Even drunks and bastards are preferable to dead men.' But he didn't speak with venom. Perhaps, thought Elias, this was as close as he could come to an admission of guilt? 'Even if I didn't like artillery work,' said Alexander, 'which I do, there isn't any way in the world I could be your First Oboe again.' He pulled off his glove and held out his right hand. All four fingers were missing, and the back of the hand was a swollen mess of shiny skin. 'A shell attack in December. But I can still manage the guns.'

'I'm so sorry.' Elias swallowed hard. 'As for the orchestra's sake — well, it's a pity. I have a feeling we will sorely need you.' He waited until Alexander had replaced his glove, then shook hands with him a trifle awkwardly. Turning away, he felt the bread Alexander had stolen for him weighing down his pocket. 'By the way,' he said, turning back, 'how's your sister?'

'My sister? I don't —'

'She was suffering from diphtheria last year. Or was it another illness beginning with D?'

Alexander clapped his hand to his forehead. 'Oh, yes, that sister. You'd hardly believe it but she made a miraculous recovery. She's the picture of health now. That is —' He bit his lip. 'She's starved like the rest of us, of course. Very thin, not able to get out much.' He peered at Elias. 'You sly dog! You know!'

Elias gave a small smile. 'Give her my regards.'

Revelations,
after snow

Nikolai ran his hand over the ice-cold wall, then looked up at the ceiling. A steel girder had crashed through one corner of the room, revealing a splintered piece of sky. The windows were either cracked or broken, and the chilly spring winds whistled in from every side. 'They expect us to rehearse in here? And perform *that*? Did they even listen to the broadcast from Kuibyshev?'

Elias, too, was dismayed by the state of the room. 'Perhaps they can provide us with some heating,' he said, trying to focus on practicalities so as not to panic at the thought of the overwhelming task that had been handed to him. He'd managed to pick up the premiere of the Seventh Symphony on his battered radio set, huddled beside the bed where his mother lay unconscious. For over an hour he'd barely moved, filtering out the crackling of the radio, fighting towards the music below. His brain had absorbed every upbeat and dying fall; his fingers longed to pick up a baton. 'I've missed it,' he confided to his mother, whose breath was rattling in her lungs. 'Oh, God, I've missed it.' Then — 'I have missed *him*.'

Nikolai was looking worried. 'It's Shostakovich's most enormous symphony yet. They must be crazy. What do they think you are, a magician?' He looked over his shoulder as he spoke, in a parody of the old pre-war caution. But they were alone. The door swung on one hinge, and the corridor was deserted, strewn with glass and dead leaves. 'I suppose it's that damn political commissar. If we manage to play the Seventh, we'll boost not only Leningrad's morale but Zhdanov's career into the bargain.'

251

'Zhdanov has already got hold of the score. It was flown in from Moscow last week.'

'Over Nazi lines?' Nikolai raised his eyebrows. 'He must be serious, then.'

'It's no longer even a subject for debate. It was already a decree before I set foot in the Party office.' Elias spoke matter-of-factly, but ever since he'd learned of his appointed task he'd been lying awake at night rigid with terror and desire. Never before had he been offered such a chance — and never before had so much been at stake. For a moment he was almost glad that Shostakovich had been forced to leave the city. The thought of the composer sitting in on rehearsals, listening intently to Elias's interpretation of his Seventh Symphony, made his stomach lurch.

'At least Dmitri will be a happy man,' said Nikolai. 'It's only right that the Leningrad symphony should be played in Leningrad. If not for the siege, of course, it would have been premiered here by —'

'By Mravinsky.' Elias gave a small smile, trying to suppress the old jealousy. 'By Mravinsky, and the esteemed Philharmonic.'

'Well, everything's different now! I know you'll do a fine job.' Nikolai began peeling mouldy carpet off a pile of rusted music stands. 'Do you know how many of the orchestra are still . . . still with us?'

Elias swallowed hard. On the list of musicians he'd been shown, twenty-five names had been crossed out in black: officially dead. Fifteen were circled in red: the only ones known for a fact to be alive. 'I'm not sure yet. I've asked military headquarters to register anyone capable of playing an instrument.'

'Men from the Front? At least they'll be adept at marches.' In spite of his attempt at a joke, Nikolai looked exceedingly doubtful.

'We need ten horns. Six or more trombones, six trumpets.' Elias spread his hands. 'Even if we can dredge up those numbers, will they be strong enough to play?'

The room was freezing, in spite of the weak sun creeping through the streaked windows. 'We should go.' Nikolai was shivering. 'We'll be spending all too much time here over the coming weeks.'

'Yes, and I must report to the Smolny Palace,' said Elias, 'to beg the generals for the loan of some of their trumpet players.'

On the steps of the Radio Hall, they paused and looked down at the street. *You think we're buying human meat from the black market?* Elias heard Olga Shapran's voice ringing in his head. *You think we're cannibals?* Now that the spring thaw had come, her words had a new and horrifying meaning. Even worse than seeing people killed by bombs or starvation was realising what had happened to them afterwards. As the grubby blanket of snow was drawn away, it became apparent that many of the corpses had been dismembered.

Severed legs with chunks of meat cut out of them, and women's bodies with the breasts sliced clean away. Torsos with cuts across their backs and stomachs, filleted like sides of beef. Flesh had been stolen from the dead to feed the living. These were the gruesome lengths to which some Leningraders had gone to stay alive.

Surveying the carnage, Elias felt utterly despairing. He covered his face with his hands. What use was art in the face of this? Was Shostakovich's music nothing but a beautiful mask to disguise the savagery of human nature?

'Seeing this doesn't exactly inspire one to perform for Leningrad, does it?' Nikolai spoke sombrely, as if looking directly into Elias's divided heart. 'But what else can we do?'

A new front

Elias blinked and swayed. The April sun — longed for and dreamed of for so many months — was no friend. It did nothing to stop his shivering, and it stung his weak, smarting eyes.

He rubbed his hand over his face. Slowly the glare through the window receded, and he saw fifty or more musicians staring up at him, their faces devoid of expression. And now a hollow-cheeked man in military uniform was getting to his feet, holding his trombone over his shoulder like a rifle. Was he saying something? There was such a ringing in Elias's ears he could hear nothing at all.

Suddenly, out of the roaring static, emerged a familiar voice. *How can I ever repay you?* For a second Elias saw him as clearly as if he were in the room — Shostakovich, his eyes shining behind his glasses, his hands clutching a sheaf of paper on which the rest of the Seventh Symphony would be written. Relief ran through Elias's veins and into his fingers, feeling almost like warmth. He had a job to do.

'I'm sorry if I seem vague.' He spoke not just to the standing trombonist but to the entire room. 'I've been having trouble with my hearing lately, along with my circulation, digestion, nervous system and general mental well-being — as, perhaps, have most of you.' As an icebreaker it wasn't much, but the watching faces relaxed a little, and mouths lifted into what, in better days, would have been smiles.

'I was asking, sir,' said the trombonist, with the formality he might use when addressing a senior military officer, 'where you'd like us to start?'

Elias's hands tightened around the score. It was thick as a bull's

254

neck, it looked impossible to penetrate. But just as panic threatened to overwhelm him, Shostakovich spoke again. *This is how I see war!* Only now did Elias hear the doubt beneath the composer's defiance and, strangely, it steadied him.

'Let's start at the beginning,' he said, letting out his breath. 'What better place to start?' He signalled for an A, but although the oboist (another unknown military man) pursed his lips and blew, there was no sound. Swaying in his chair, blowing again, at last he produced a note, as thin as a birdcall from the depths of a forest.

So this is my allotted weapon! Elias watched the makeshift orchestra tuning up. There was old Petrov, who had somehow recovered and survived the winter, though he was nothing but skin and bone. And Nikolai, lifting his bow as if it were made of concrete — but so many musicians gone! Their replacements, still unknown to Elias, handled their instruments with the jerky mechanical movements of wind-up toys. Within three months, with this roomful of skeletons, he had to produce an inspired rendition of the largest ever Shostakovich symphony! If he hadn't been so tired, he might have laughed at the absurdity of it.

Tuning up, warming up: the processes that had once seemed interminable were over in less than a minute. Then the room was quiet once more, while far away the restless mutter of gunfire continued, as familiar and constant as hunger.

Elias raised his arms. Pain flared in his back, and his shoulders trembled. 'Friends,' he said, although he knew fewer than a quarter of them. 'Friends, I know that you're weak, and you're starving. But we must force ourselves to work. Let's begin.'

He brought down his baton. The musicians stirred, seeming ready to play — but nothing happened. It was as if, moving as one body, they were paralysed from nerves, fear, or extreme fatigue. This was as bad as Elias's very first rehearsals, when he'd been so green and nervous the orchestra resisted his every move. There was no derisive laughter now, just an unnerving silence. Exhaustion seemed to be spreading through the room.

'Comrades!' He thought back to the way Shostakovich's hands had pounded at the piano keys, hammering out the opening to a work he wasn't yet certain about. 'Comrades! I command you to raise your instruments. It's your duty.'

The musicians sat upright; their eyes flickered towards him. He raised his arms again. Over the sea of heads, he caught sight of Nikolai, gripping his violin with his bony left hand. His eyes were fixed on Elias with the intensity of someone about to go over the top into battle.

Elias looked away before sentiment could weaken him. 'Let's begin.' He brought down his arms.

He'd heard the first chords of the symphony so many times, playing them out in his imagination as he lay in bed, clutching his coat around him. The reality was completely different. A few straggling chords, the inadequate rattle of a snare drum, a tiny tapping of bows on strings. It was the smell of food without taste, or the promise of sustenance without delivery. He was grasping at thin air.

He rapped on his music stand, and the musicians straggled to a halt. Already the mouths of the woodwind and brass players were reddened, their scabby lips bleeding. Some of the faces raised to Elias had the white-green tinge of the dead. Then, as he watched, the lead flautist slid out of his chair and onto the floor.

'What shall we do with him?' The second flautist knelt beside the collapsed man, calling his name in a voice high with fear.

'Take him outside. Lay him in the corridor. Cover him with a coat.' Was the flautist alive or dead? He had no idea, no energy to find out.

It took three percussionists to drag the man out. The disruption seemed to go on forever; the rest of the orchestra simply sat where they were, many of them with their eyes closed. They were bundled in threadbare scarves and overcoats, and wore woollen gloves with the fingers cut off, but most were shivering. Elias stared fixedly at the page in front of him. The black notes looked like heavy chunks of granite.

It was time to start again. He took a deep breath. 'This isn't good enough. You're making a mockery of our great composer. The music must be barbaric, it must be brilliant. Remember, you're fighting off the enemy!'

But the musicians before him were neither barbaric nor brilliant; they were close to collapse, incapable of fighting off a horde of mosquitoes, let alone brutal invaders. The symphony crawled instead of marching.

In the bars before the trumpet solo, he closed his eyes and heard the blaring, defiant notes of the symphony's premiere. Muted by distance, squeezed flat by the radio waves, but magnified a thousand times by the knowledge that, in far-off Kuibyshev, Shostakovich was listening to the performance. Raising himself on his toes, Elias brought in the trumpet with a downward sweep of his arm — and opened his eyes to see the trumpet player sitting with his head bowed and his instrument lying on his knees. The insubstantial strings frayed away into silence.

'Why the hell aren't you playing?' Elias almost shouted from a sense of grievance and loss.

The trumpeter spoke without raising his head. 'I'm sorry, sir.' He spoke in a muffled voice but his exhaustion and despair were clear enough. 'I can't play the solo. I don't have the breath.'

'If you have the breath to speak, you have the breath to play.' Yet Elias, too, was a little out of breath. The air seemed too cold to inhale, and once drawn into the lungs was hard to expel. 'You must try. Shostakovich doesn't write music to be performed by men who give up.'

Obediently the trumpeter raised his instrument and began. The desperate look in his eyes made Elias feel wretched — but when, after only a few bars, the man fell back in his chair, he felt even worse. *This is what you're here for,* he told himself. *You're not here to save individuals, but to save the city!* Even though he was trying to encourage himself, it sounded dismally like Party propaganda.

He lowered his baton. 'You're all dismissed. I'll see you back here tomorrow.' The rehearsal had taken half an hour to get under-way, and it had lasted less than fifteen minutes. 'Don't be late,' he added.

Day after day, the orchestra returned to the chilly, dusty room. 'From now on,' announced Elias, 'rehearsals will run for three hours, beginning at ten and finishing at one.'

'Three hours! That's impossible,' objected Katerina Ginka. Her cheeks were hollow, and all traces of ruddiness had drained from her face, but still she had the strength to argue. 'We can't play for even three minutes without fainting — or dying.'

Elias flushed. The flautist who'd collapsed had been taken to a military hospital and no one knew if he'd survive. *It wasn't my fault*, he protested silently. *The man was skin and bone, he had pleurisy, he'd been giving all his food rations to his wife*. Yet the sharp bite of guilt made him snap at Katerina. 'There's one word I won't tolerate. *Can't* is no longer a part of the Radio Orchestra vocabulary.'

He waited, expecting protests. Would any of the original members dispute the fact that a mismatched bunch of amateurs was now the Radio Orchestra? But no one said a word; even Katerina looked defeated. 'And if anyone is late,' he continued, 'whatever the reason, they'll lose their bread ration for the day.'

There was a muted gasp. Petrov's eyes watered, Katerina opened her mouth and then closed it again.

'Now, from the top,' ordered Elias. Even this brief exchange had left him exhausted; raising his baton felt like a monumental effort.

It wasn't until he heard the first sawing of the strings that it hit him. Under the music he heard the rasping of breath, deep and harsh, the very same sound he'd heard that morning as he'd tried spooning cabbage water into his mother's mouth. The musicians ploughed on, while he lowered his arms and stared at the score with unseeing eyes. He'd only just realised the truth. His mother was dying.

The missing

Judging from the infrequent letters that made it over enemy lines, past the censors and into Nikolai's hands, Shostakovich was safe but not happy. He'd been given a larger apartment, four rooms and a bathroom, thanks to an unusually helpful Comrade Zemlyachka, yet still he felt claustrophobic. His extended family had been evacuated from Leningrad at last, but he'd discovered that they were incapable of discussing anything but food rations. What's more, Kuibyshev was hellishly provincial: there was no one with whom he could talk about work. 'I'm surrounded by babies, the bourgeoisie and ballet dancers,' he wrote. 'And the dancers aren't even pretty.' As Nikolai looked at the fretful inky scrawl, he could imagine Shostakovich clearly: frowning, shoving his pencil behind his ear, while around him assorted women-folk (mother, sister, mother-in-law, sister-in-law, niece, daughter, wife) chattered about bread, butter, potatoes, confectionery and coffee.

Although Nikolai longed to see him again, he was glad that Shostakovich had avoided the grim slide into winter and its gruesome consequences. Leningrad was no longer the city its exiled citizens had known. It had been ground down to muddy foundations, and the return of light and warmth had done little to restore it.

Shostakovich hadn't forgotten Nikolai's own personal burden. 'We're praying for good news,' he wrote at the end of every letter. 'Don't give up hope.' But sustaining hope was becoming increasingly difficult. Every day that passed was another step away from Sonya, and the enormity of losing her became more real. The only relief lay in work. After rehearsal each day, Nikolai stayed behind to help Elias copy out scores for all the musicians who had to return immediately to their military posts. It was a dull, monotonous task but, for as long as it lasted, it deadened the pain in his heart.

Elias had become more than usually silent. His fingers were callused from hours of holding a pen; his eyes were a mess of red spidery lines. Something seemed to be worrying him — but perhaps it was simply the pressure of having to conduct a symphony whose reputation had already grown to massive proportions.

'Premiered in Kuibyshev, clamoured for in America, broadcast all over the world. Such a tremendous success already!' But Elias sounded more anxious than pleased.

'Nominated for a Stalin Prize, what's more!' pointed out Nikolai, trying to bolster Elias's confidence. 'You can imagine how pleased Shostakovich is about that.'

'Yes, that's an accolade he might choose to do without. But have you any idea how he feels about . . . about the work itself?' There was something diffident and indirect about the way Elias spoke, like a cat sidling up to a wall.

'Actually, from what I've gathered, he's not altogether pleased.'

Elias put down his pen. 'In what way?'

'He can't say much in his letters, of course, for fear of interception. But it seems he's dissatisfied with the fourth movement — he says it suffered from being written in a different place. And it wasn't helped by having to break for two months while they were evacuated and then relocated from Moscow to Kuibyshev.'

'I suppose parts of it are more efficient than inspired,' Elias admitted. 'But symphonic finales are notoriously difficult, particularly with a first movement of such power and enormity.' He paused for a moment. 'Not that it matters — the quality or otherwise of the finale, I mean. I doubt we'll make it that far.' A look of despair swept over his face.

'We'll get there!' said Nikolai, trying to sound confident. But it was impossible to deny that the orchestra was struggling. 'Perhaps we should try again to find a pianist? It would help no end in supporting the weaker sections.'

'Coincidentally,' said a voice from behind him, 'that's exactly what I've come about.' A woman stood in the doorway, her slight frame swamped in an overcoat, her hair pulled back under a shabby hat. But there was something familiar about her posture, and the tilt of her head, that made Nikolai catch his breath.

'Nina Bronnikova? Is it really you?' He pushed his chair back, forgetting that his back ached and that the day's bread ration had been made from mouldy flour and cottonseed. He'd heard that she'd survived the winter, but the sight of her filled him with relief. It was impossible to hide how glad he was; he grasped her thin hands, and kissed her several times on both cheeks.

'Welcome!' Elias hovered behind him like an uncertain host. 'Welcome, indeed.' For a moment it looked as if he might follow Nikolai's example but, instead, he shook Nina's hand and pulled out a rickety chair. 'Please, have a seat. How are you?'

'Well, I can't dance any more, even if there were a company here to dance with.' She limped forward. 'But at least I'm alive.'

'Perhaps when the siege is over, the Kirov doctors will be able to help you?' said Nikolai. 'They're so experienced, and will surely know what to do.'

'I'm sure with modern medicine,' ventured Elias, 'and proper nutrition, and a long rest —'

'I'm afraid that for me to dance again will require a miracle.' Nina gave a tired smile. 'But thank you both for trying. Besides, this war has other victims far worse off than me.' As she looked at Nikolai, her eyes grew even darker.

Please don't mention Sonya! thought Nikolai desperately. *I can't speak of her! Not today!*

Nina seemed to understand. She nodded, a tiny coded message of sympathy, and turned to Elias as if wanting to give Nikolai time to recover. 'The reason I'm here is because Comrade Babushkin said you may need a pianist.'

'You can p-p-play the piano?' Elias's face lit up.

'I used to, quite passably, but I'm very rusty now. Still, perhaps even inadequate hands are better than none.'

'Almost all our musicians are inadequate! I wonder why Babushkin didn't contact you earlier. We've been searching for a pianist for weeks.'

'He said the idea had only just struck him. They were talking about the Kirov, and someone mentioned me; he remembered I played because my old teacher was a crony of his — you know how these Leningrad connections are. Anyway, he seemed quite pleased with himself for coming up with a solution.'

'Belatedly! That imbecilic —' Elias stopped short. 'What I mean is, we'd be extremely g-g-grateful for your help. There's only one problem.' He glanced over to the huge stack of paper. 'As yet, we have no part for you to play from. C-c-c —'

Quickly, Nikolai stepped in. 'Is there any conceivable chance you might help us with this as well? As you see, we're up to our eyes in copying.'

Nina smiled. 'My copying is probably better than my piano playing. And I have nowhere to go this afternoon.' She took off her hat. Her once glossy hair was dull and rough, and her skin had the same greenish tinge as all malnourished Leningraders. But she regarded the world around her with her usual self-possession.

For the next hour, the battered studio was filled with an air of studious industry that made Nikolai feel almost normal. Only when a siren wailed did he remember that everything was far from ordinary, and he himself not fine at all. Within a year, his stable world had been shattered and its inhabitants flung about like dice on a gambling table: Shostakovich packed off to a southern city on the Volga, a place too confined for his restless soul, where he fretted about each successive performance of his symphony. 'My nerves are playing up,' he'd written. 'Thankfully we have a bathroom with a lock on the door, so my tears can flow in peace.'

And what about Sollertinsky, banished to Novosibirsk where the Siberian winds wailed day and night? How was he making use of his quicksilver wit, his knowledge of Shakespeare, his mastery of Sanskrit, ancient Persian and Portuguese?

The pen fell from Nikolai's hand. *We were a triumvirate and we worked together. We stood for intellect, instinct and integrity.* His longing for ordinary life, for an end to the siege, was so strong he felt he would choke. He turned to his current companions as they bent over their work. The thin, maimed, still beautiful Nina Bronnikova; the emaciated, stubborn Karl Eliasberg. These people hadn't been his friends before the Germans marched on the city. Where were his real friends?

And then it happened. His defences crumbled, and the small face he'd kept at bay through sheer determination rushed into his mind. As sweet as a mountain stream, as unyielding as a rock-bed. Stern yet infinitely caring; womanly without knowing it, childish without playing on it; dark-eyed, raven-haired, chubby-cheeked, slim-legged Sonya! The loss of his friends was great, but far greater was the loss he'd precipitated on that day last summer. He'd given away the person most precious to him, had handed her to an unknown woman and left before the train had even pulled out of the station. *Sonya, Sonya.* He couldn't imagine where she was, didn't dare to do so, for as soon as he started his body became slick with sweat, his guts churned, and he loathed himself — for sending her off, for letting her go — with such intensity it terrified him.

Pushing aside the stack of paper, he laid his head on the table. His eyes were streaming but he didn't make a sound. He cried so silently that it was several minutes before he heard exclamations and felt an awkward hand on his shoulder.

'Nikolai? What's the matter?' Elias sounded more worried than ever.

He raised his head, his nose running and his hair soaked through. 'My eyes. So weak these days. They water for no reason.'

Elias hesitated for a second. 'Mine, too. Damn inconvenient, isn't it?' He blundered away to open a window, muttering about vitamin deficiency, scurvy, and the effect of malnutrition on one's retinas. 'Fresh air,' he said reassuringly. 'Fresh air will do you good.'

Nina put out her hand and laid it over his. After a while, she passed him a shred of handkerchief.

He'd never been so grateful for reticence. Wiping his nose and eyes, he picked up his pen again. But even though he copied like a man possessed, concentrating on Shostakovich's maniacally leaping octaves, his heart continued to cry *Sonya, Sonya!* like a gull wheeling above a barge, not knowing where it was headed nor what might be gained from following.

Elias comes home

The sun had been shining for many days, but Elias was feeling increasingly cold. As he left the apartment he realised that he was trembling all over. His fingers were a waxy yellow, his nails as white as plaster. He banged his hands against his thighs but felt nothing; nor could he feel his feet, wrapped in rags and stuffed into his boots. He hobbled around the corner and stood in the sunshine, waiting to thaw.

Nothing happened. His body remained frozen. He felt as if he were looking down on himself, a stick figure in a rag-bag of coats and scarves, leaning against the same wall where once a much better-dressed, nervously correct man had stood, afraid to approach the kiosk standing (if his hazy memory was correct) on the very spot where a steel pillbox squatted. From a great distance, he marvelled at the naivety of the former Karl Eliasberg. Obsessing over the review of a rival who wouldn't even acknowledge him as such! Being scared to converse with a portly music professor in a rumpled suit!

He willed the sun to thaw him, his heart to pump his blood more effectively and his feet to carry him to the rehearsal room on time. *You've never been late in your life*, he told himself, *and you will not be late today.*

The previous week he had trudged once again down Nevsky Prospect to the Arts Department headquarters and waited another two hours under the ticking clock before speaking as fervently as he could on behalf of his musicians. They were ill and weak; they could barely sit on their chairs. A flautist named Karelsky had already died from severe malnutrition, and if the authorities didn't step in many others would also die. The officials listened impassively as he told them of instruments falling from players' hands, and of undermining silences instead of loud morale-raising music.

Apparently, he'd convinced them. The very next day Zagorsky had announced that Radio Orchestra rations were to be increased, and would stay at that level until the day of the concert. Furthermore, all musicians would receive badges marking them out as members of Eliasberg's orchestra, allowing them medical privileges and faster access through checkpoints. But Elias knew it would take far more than extra wheatgerm and watery bean soup to turn back the clock. There was no quick way of transforming a band of walking skeletons into efficient musicians and soldiers.

Sure enough, as he entered that morning — slowly, clumsily, but on time in spite of his frozen feet — the conversation wasn't about fighting or music but about food. Or, to be precise, the lack of it.

As he limped to the podium, a dutiful silence fell; there was a general tightening of bows and opening of scores. This much, at least, he'd achieved. He signalled for an A and waited for them to tune up — not that pitch was of particular concern to the players in front of him. Any musician trained in an army band placed more emphasis on keeping time than staying in tune. The scraping and dissonance, the ragged sliding chords: not so long ago these would have made Elias wince. Now they scarcely bothered him. If the orchestra managed to play the symphony with nothing more than workmanlike skill, he would have pulled off a miracle.

'We'll start with the adagio,' he said, opening the score.

Today he felt more detached than ever — so much so that it felt like calm. He was nothing more than an observer, surveying the orchestra from afar. The only thing that brought him momentarily closer was the sight of Nikolai helping Nina Bronnikova with the piano stool, cradling his left arm behind her in a movement that was like a caress. Then, for a second, blackness roared up in Elias's head. But once Nina's eyes were fixed on the music and Nikolai had returned to his seat, he could retreat once more into his floating state.

After what might have been a few minutes or an hour — it was impossible to tell today — the musicians were ready. The first woodwind chords fell across the room like shadows; the singing violin lines followed with almost unbearable sweetness. The rehearsal room stretched to accommodate the music, and the music filled the whole city, and the empty fields and desolate woods beyond. It rained down on Russian and German soldiers crouched in their trenches, stripping them of both fear and purpose — and then, surely, everything would be all right again, while much of what had gone before (the grinding winter, the exploding streets, the dragging hunger and the slow deaths) was dissolved by the music. Elias's eyelids dropped, and he allowed himself to rest. He didn't need to see the score; he'd read and copied and conducted it so many times, he knew it better than his own body. He felt nothing but immense gratitude to Shostakovich, for saving them all.

Now the music was thinning, like ice at the edge of a lake. This was as it should be. The melody moved downwards, grinding into the uneasy key of C sharp minor. Low woodwind notes hinted at the watery depths: contrabassoon, bass clarinet pulling on the deepest of C sharps like an anchor, yet also releasing, rising, moving up towards the strings. A pizzicato bridge over the water, slipping into E major, leading to —

Something was missing. Elias jolted back into the present. There was blood in his mouth where he'd bitten his tongue, and panic on the faces of his woodwind players. The shock of the return was too great. His icy core cracked in two, and he rapped on his music stand.

'What has happened to the flute solo?' The effort of speaking made his throat feel raw. 'Where the hell is Vedernikov?'

The strings were straggling to a halt, their bows held at awkward angles. 'Does anyone know where our lead flautist is?' demanded Elias.

Someone dared to mutter that perhaps he'd been killed by Shostakovich's excessive demands, and a few embarrassed titters ran around the room, but mostly the musicians shuffled their feet and said nothing.

The second flute raised a tentative hand. 'Perhaps I can take the solo, until he turns up?'

But as if on cue, Vedernikov appeared at the door. His chest was heaving, his hair trailed on his shoulders. 'I'm sorry I'm late.' He blundered towards his seat, cramming his flute together as he went. 'I'm so sorry.'

Elias was surprised at the level of rage he felt. Had he been holding a gun instead of a baton, he would have put a bullet through the heart of this panting wretch who'd interrupted his reverie and snatched away salvation. 'Don't be sorry,' he said coldly. 'Regret is a wasteful emotion.'

Vedernikov looked up, holding the mouthpiece of his flute to his lips. 'It was unavoidable.'

'You've deprived us of your solo and you, in turn, will be deprived. It has already been established that all latecomers lose their bread rations.'

'Please don't do that. The thing is —' Vedernikov bit his lip so hard that white marks bloomed on the purplish skin. 'I was at the cemetery. I was waiting to bury my wife.'

Nina Bronnikova gasped, and Petrov half-rose on his shaky legs. The other flautists laid their hands on Vedernikov's arms, and even the military men coughed with suppressed emotion. But Elias stood like a stone; he could feel neither his toes in his boots, nor the floor beneath his feet.

'The rules stand,' he said, staring at the far wall. 'They can't be bent for one person. Death is all around us! Who knows which of us will be alive tomorrow? The only certainty is that, by the first week in August, we must be capable of playing the Seventh Symphony. Vedernikov, you lose your rations for today. We'll begin from the top.'

He didn't look at the flautist again, nor at Nina or Nikolai; he wasn't strong enough to see grief or shock, not today. His head was swimming and there was an unfamiliar burning in his lungs. The orchestra dragged on through the adagio, which was no longer beautiful, and into the finale, which lacked all vigour and conviction. He conducted mechanically, feeling as if, at any moment, he might topple to the floor.

At the end of the first hour he sank onto a chair and conducted sitting down — something he'd never have dreamed of doing before this nightmare began. But from his chair he had an unimpeded view of Nina Bronnikova's face. Was there reproach in her curved neck and lowered eyes? He found the possibility unbearable, and stood up again, leaning heavily on the chair and conducting with his right hand only.

After the musicians had left, some for sentry duty and some for the bread queues, he allowed himself to sit once more. With his head between his knees, coughing and gasping, he began to recite progressions from the symphony: 'Variation Four, Figure 25, oboe and bassoon. Dynamic: *piano*. B flat against B natural; C major to C sharp minor. Crescendo to *fortissimo*. Back to C major.'

But instead of steadying him, as he'd hoped, the musical equations tumbled into a sea of horrifying images. His father beating a human face with his cobbler's hammer, Shostakovich throwing manuscript pages from the window of an aeroplane. A row of incendiary bombs scattered down a street, blazing like flowers. *And back to C major*, he repeated in desperation, but his thoughts were drowned out by the blows of the hammer. The human profile disintegrated into a cloud of white skin, Shostakovich's face went up in flames, the engines of the aeroplane roared. He was in hell.

Through the chaos a hand touched his forehead, anchoring him. 'We have to get him to a hospital,' someone said.

He opened his eyes to a world that, somehow, was still intact.

'Can you hear me?' Nikolai's straggling hair and beard did nothing to hide his concern.

Yes, I can hear you perfectly, he answered. *Only at present, due to unforeseen illness, I'm unable to speak.*

Nina's face floated behind Nikolai's like a beautiful pale cloud. 'I think he can hear but not speak.'

Even as his lungs rasped for breath, Elias felt enormous gratitude. She could understand him. She knew what he was thinking.

'Try to drink this,' said Nikolai, putting the rim of a glass to his lips.

The tepid water made him gag but it was laced with sugar, which seeped a grainy strength into his limbs. He lay where he'd fallen, listening to the voices, succumbing to the loss of power. It was like being a child again — although his parents had never cared so much.

'He's dreadfully thin.' Nina seemed to forget that Elias was capable of hearing. 'And he's had that cough for weeks. I remember him saying that he'd once had tuberculosis. Do you think —?'

'I don't think it's TB. Perhaps a touch of pneumonia? And certainly nervous exhaustion. He's been working himself to death.'

'Poor Elias.' Nina sounded upset.

'If we can get him to the Astoria,' said Nikolai, 'Tanya will find a bed for him. He has to rest.'

Elias opened his eyes and spoke with a leaden tongue. 'Rehearsals. Shostakovich —'

'Less important than your health. Besides, what good will you be to Shostakovich if you've worked yourself to death before the performance?'

Closing his eyes again, Elias listened to Nikolai arranging his future with surprising decisiveness. The door banged, and now only Nina was left beside him, holding the water glass, checking his pulse.

It seemed rude to lie there silently. Wetting his lips, he practised a couple of phrases in his head — *two-tone motif, six repeated Gs* — and then he tried speaking out loud. 'Thank you,' he managed to croak.

'For what?'

'For playing . . . the piano.'

'But I'm still hopeless. Nowhere near as good as you'd like.'

'Not . . . hopeless.' He turned his head to look at her. 'Not yet . . . excellent. But not . . . hopeless.'

Nina laughed. 'Someone once described you as brutal. But I think honest is a better word.'

'The two are . . . easily confused.' He gave a small nod. He was too tired to say any more, although he wanted to tell her a thousand things: things he'd wanted to say for a long time. Out in the street, the army trucks rumbled on, and through the occasional chink in the noise came the sound of a few birds singing.

The door banged again and Nikolai was back. 'Good news!' he said. 'You'll be taken by car to the hospital. They'll have a bed ready for you there. You're a more important person than you think!'

'One night only,' said Elias weakly. 'Tomorrow we must rehearse.'

Nikolai ignored this. 'Now, what about your mother? Is she able to look after herself for a few days, or is she completely bedridden?'

'She is . . . She is completely —' Elias turned his head away, and mumbled the last words into the floor.

'*What* did you say?' asked Nikolai sharply.

'She's dead. My mother is dead.'

Nina grasped his hand. 'When? When did this happen?'

'Two days ago.' He bit his lip to stop himself crying and heard again the scraping of Valery's sled as the runners bumped over the dry mud. He saw Valery's small hands alongside his on the rope, and the half-fearful look on the boy's face as they reached the cemetery gates.

'God, I'm so sorry.' Nikolai sounded shocked. 'Why didn't you say anything? You worked yesterday, and all day today, without telling us?'

'I . . . couldn't. I don't know why.' It was no explanation, but it was the truth. He licked the metallic taint of blood off his lip: it tasted of death. He had wrapped his mother's body in the old crocheted blanket and carried it down the first flight of stairs. As emaciated as she'd been, the weight had almost proved too much for him. Only the fear that Mr Shapran would find him collapsed on the landing, with his dead mother beside him, had forced him on, one stair at a time, his arms burning and his eyes leaking tears.

'No wonder you're near collapse,' said Nikolai. 'Have you been giving all your rations to her?'

'I was trying to stop her disappearing.' How had her life slipped through his fingers? She was alive when he went to the bathroom to scrape at his face with the blunt blade, yet by the time he'd emerged, raw-chinned, hurrying, she had gone. He knew it instantly. The room was ringing with absence. After checking that her eyes were closed, and pulling the sheet over her face, he'd closed the door and left for rehearsal. All day yesterday, he had said nothing, spoken of nothing but work. Returning to the apartment in the evening had been the hardest and loneliest thing he'd ever done in the whole of his hard, lonely life.

Nina was still holding his hand. 'You did everything anyone could.' She had no way of knowing this, but the characteristic ring of truth in her voice was somehow comforting.

———✦———

After coping so long on his own, being in the hospital was curiously soothing. White-clad staff passed by quietly; the ill and the wounded lay still under their covers. Unlit chandeliers hung over the makeshift wards like the canopies of oak trees. Elias was fed, sometimes he was washed; he was treated with no more and no less respect than anyone else. It was only when he stepped shakily back into the real world a few days later and returned to the Radio Hall that he remembered what he'd been through, and what lay ahead.

Nikolai looked at him in an assessing way. 'Why don't you shorten rehearsal time? At least for a couple of days, until you get some strength back.'

Elias shook his head. 'We need every minute we can get.'

'You're a stubborn bastard. You and Shostakovich have a lot in common. In a word, pig-headedness.'

'Speaking of Shostakovich,' said Elias, 'do you know how he is?'

'He's worried. Worried about the war, worried about catching typhus, worried how long Leningrad can survive under siege. Essentially, he's the same Dmitri we've always known and loved.'

'But has he mentioned —' Elias fiddled with his music stand. 'The symphony? You told me he was concerned that Toscanini may botch it in America — but what about this performance, *our* performance?'

'Nothing yet,' admitted Nikolai. 'But the last letter from him was some time ago. A good deal of post isn't getting through.'

'Of course.' Elias tried to sound matter-of-fact. It was unlikely that Shostakovich would expend much thought on a makeshift orchestra in

Leningrad, when his symphony was gaining the attention of eminent conductors and critics all over the world. Yet he couldn't help hoping for — what, a sign? Something to show that Shostakovich believed in what they were doing, and that it mattered. Stifling a sigh, he lowered his music stand. 'Not very dignified to conduct from a chair, I know, but collapsing mid-rehearsal would be less so.'

There turned out to be one other advantage to his new, lowly position. Viewed from a chair, the orchestra seemed less of a solid mass and more a collection of individuals. He was able to see veins standing out on necks, and nervous twitching in the bars before a solo. He was less audible and less visible — but at last he was on the right level.

After the rehearsal was over, several of the musicians came up to enquire about his health, and to commiserate over the loss of his mother.

'They seem to like me better,' he said to Nina, in slight surprise.

'Of course. Now they see you as a human being, instead of a conductor.'

'Because my mother died?' He was confused. 'Or because I've been in hospital?'

'Because you're vulnerable.' Nina closed the lid of the piano. Her knack of summarising things made him see life didn't need to be as complicated as he'd always found it.

'Are you ready to go?' Nikolai was stationed by the door. Over the winter he'd developed a strange stillness about him — a static, waiting quality. With his long beard and eyebrows he reminded Elias of a moss-covered statue. Arrested in time, as they'd all been, by an ill twist of fate and by the siege. When would they be released?

Very slowly, they made their way through the ruined city, Nikolai carrying Elias's small bag and Elias carrying the huge score. He'd boiled down his leather briefcase many months earlier; it had yielded a peculiar-tasting chunk of protein, which he'd told his mother was pork aspic, and it had lasted them some weeks.

The streets were no longer muddy but were still marked by the deep ruts from army vehicles and tanks. Young people moved in the same way as the elderly, slowly and stiffly. Only the rustling green trees seemed alive. Summer was here again, but it had returned to a suspended city: smashed, ruined, still surrounded by the enemy.

At the thought of a stalemate, of entrapment stretching ahead with no end, Elias felt the familiar stirrings of panic. How could he inspire exhausted Leningraders and their Party leaders if he had no belief in a future? His fear grew, as it always did, at the prospect of Shostakovich sitting by his radio in Kuibyshev, listening to him conduct the Seventh Symphony. But today the thing that frightened him most of all was the thought of walking back into his empty apartment.

The closer they got, the more nervous he became. Nikolai had stopped trying to make conversation, and they turned the corner in silence. Elias kept his head down and his eyes fixed on the broken cobblestones.

'Look!' Nikolai nudged him. 'You have a welcoming committee.'

There on the front steps sat Valery, tracing patterns in the dust with his stubby fingers. As soon as he caught sight of them, he jumped up. 'Mr Elias! Hooray, you're home!'

'Nice to see you, too.' Elias coughed — it was the dust, surely, that made his eyes prickle and his voice come out slightly clogged.

Valery looked earnestly at Nikolai. 'Mr Elias has been giving me some of his rations. He says I need to get plump and strong, the way I used to be.' He stood back, flexing imaginary muscles on his stick-thin arms.

'That's kind of him,' said Nikolai. 'Though he might consider looking after himself as well as other people.'

'I'm fine,' mumbled Elias. 'Just doing what anyone else would.'

Valery took the score out of his hands and held it as if it were made of glass. 'This is Mr Shostakovich's work,' he informed Nikolai. 'He's very famous. Soon there'll be a big concert, with Mr Elias in charge.'

'So I've heard,' said Nikolai. 'Shall we go inside now?'

And so Elias came home again, flanked by an eager knock-kneed boy and a generous, grief-stricken man. As he pushed open the door of the apartment and caught sight of the empty bed, he'd never been so glad of the company.

The letterbox

It seemed strange that no one had ever touched the trees. When Nikolai looked out his window, peering through the criss-crossed tape and scratched glass, he still saw tree-tops, now a deep dark green, in the park. Throughout the dark icy months of winter, every shelled house had been stripped and every bombed factory picked over for fuel. Anything not chained down or locked up had been removed: pulled apart by bare hands, chopped up with hatchets, tugged away on sleds to feed small smoky stoves, staving off a cold so extreme it slowed the blood to a crawl. Furniture, wallpaper, books; dung scavenged from the city stables before the horses were shot and used for meat. Anything with combustible potential had been scavenged — so why had the trees survived?

He gazed at the green clouds rising like smoke signals. Was it sheer romanticism? Perhaps — as well as a nationalistic pride. In Berlin, Hitler had ordered the lime trees felled for aesthetic reasons, while Leningraders had frozen to death rather than desecrate their trees.

The notion made Nikolai profoundly irritated. Considering the state of Leningrad, the mountains of rubble, the smashed churches and broken fountains, pitted streets and gaping holes where gracious apartment blocks had once stood —! He no longer had any patience for Russian romanticism, particularly given the mutilated bodies he'd seen that spring.

Tanya was getting ready to go to work. 'I'm leaving now. There's some rice on the bench for later.' Her coat hung loosely off her shoulders and her scalp glinted through her thin hair, but she seemed more concerned about Nikolai's health than her own. She'd developed a remarkable talent for acquiring black-market supplies (fifty grams of lard here, a small pack of lentils there) for the sole purpose of feeding him.

'Rice.' He nodded vaguely.

'Don't forget to eat it.' She folded her arms. 'You've got to keep your strength up.'

'Keep my strength up? For what?' He was at a loss, in these drifting, monotonous days, to grasp the point of anything.

'For the concert, of course!'

'Ah, the concert,' said Nikolai. 'Yes, it's most important for me to eat cold rice for the sole purpose of playing the violin well enough to distract Leningraders from the truth — that their Party has failed to prevent them from starvation and death.'

Tanya looked reproving, though only a year ago she'd considered concerts a waste of time and money. 'The posters are already up. People are buying tickets. The whole city's looking forward to it.'

'The city would be better off saving its money and going to church to pray that this bloody stand-off will end. What good is seventy minutes of music if we're to be shelled and starved for the next ten years?'

'Don't talk like that. One of the doctors said that, according to Mr Eliasberg, this will be the most important concert ever played in Leningrad! The most important since *time immemorial*.'

There was no trace of Elias in the phrase; Tanya had always embellished stories, particularly when they concerned things she knew nothing about. But the fervour and the belief were recognisable as Elias's own. Nikolai had seen the glitter in his eyes as he drove the orchestra onwards, disregarding the musicians' fatigue and despair. At those times it was hard to believe the rumours that had circulated before the war — the lack of discipline in the Radio Orchestra, the public mutinies and practical jokes, and one musician in particular (was his name Alexander?) who regularly ridiculed not only his colleagues but also his conductor.

Tanya was almost misty-eyed. 'After the concert, morale in the city will soar. That's what the doctor and Mr Eliasberg say. Through the strength of the music, our army will gain strength — and then I expect we'll win the war.'

'Mr Eliasberg has his own axe to grind. The Astoria Hospital may be convinced by his mission, but it's unlikely he's risking his life for this concert for purely altruistic reasons.' Nikolai had become disconcertingly aware of an anger growing inside him. Anger with Tanya for unexpectedly championing a musical cause, and with Elias for growing so bold he made others look cowardly in comparison. With Shostakovich for writing a symphony that had already become symbolic, and with the people of Leningrad who were so desperate they would throng to the concert house to listen to an orchestra of walking cadavers. He was angry with the politicians for setting in motion such a musical farce, and with the pilot who'd risked his life flying the score in over enemy lines, and with the Red Army for not having the strength to push back the Germans. There was only one person in the world with whom he didn't feel angry, and she had become the stuff of fairy tales and fables: the needle in the haystack, the pea under the mattress, irritating his memory, preventing sleep, never forgotten yet never appearing. Day by day, he was drained. He'd survived the winter, only to be fatally weakened by the sight of green trees and the scent of emptiness. *Sonya, you are killing me. Your absence will be my death.*

He watched Tanya tie a scarf over her patchy scalp and bustle out the door. Filled with relief, he ran his fingers through his long beard; at least she'd forgotten to nag him about his hair.

'One more thing.' Her head reappeared around the door. 'You should trim your beard. You look like a sailor, without the legitimate excuse of weeks at sea. When Mr Eliasberg was in hospital, he shaved every day.'

There was nothing to throw at her; most of their possessions had been sold, exchanged, or chopped up for firewood. He waved his hand in a peremptory gesture that might have meant 'All right' or might have meant 'Go away'. It seemed to satisfy her; she retreated again and her footsteps faded down the stairwell.

At last he was alone.

Over the past few months, he'd been trying to exist in the moment. But his desperation for escape was growing. He felt suffocated in this city where resignation coated the streets like the sticky juice from the lime leaves. Officially it had been suggested that the siege would be over by the end of summer — but he could hear the hollowness behind the assurances. Nothing but propaganda, and a large measure of hope.

In the quietness that descended after Tanya's departure, he came to a decision. It wasn't as hard as he'd anticipated, for with the closing of the door he'd finally realised that Sonya was never coming back. He hadn't talked about her for weeks. Tanya no longer spoke her name; their few surviving neighbours passed him quickly in the crumbling stairwell.

With every lost opportunity, every time she might have been mentioned and wasn't, Sonya disappeared a little further. Daily, the images in Nikolai's head were fading — her eyes, her smile, the tilt of her nose. Soon there would be nothing left of her.

He would wait until the night of the concert — this much he owed to Shostakovich, and to Eliasberg. Then he would make his escape. He would invite Tanya to the victory party, which would happen whether or not the performance was a triumph: commissars glowing with unearned pride, musicians seated at a table laden with rich food that might, earlier, have saved other lives. He would slip away and come back here where he belonged, and, finally, he would do it.

He felt for the small tin taped under the windowsill, a strange but not entirely unwelcome gift from a pathologist who'd lived in the apartment below with his wheelchair-bound, music-loving wife. 'She's listened to you practise for years,' he'd said to Nikolai. 'Your playing has been her escape. The least I can do is offer you an escape in return.'

Dr Ostrovsky had died on the coldest day in January, two days after his wife. The ostensible cause of his death was pleurisy, but Nikolai believed otherwise, knowing how much the doctor had loved his wife. After hearing the news, he'd opened the tin and stared at the capsule — cyanide, mixed with acetic acid for what Ostrovsky had called 'more certain results'. How odd that such a small object could smash open a claustrophobic world and let the air in!

He'd believed, for a time, that Nina Bronnikova might be his saviour. In the long vicious grip of winter (searching, always, for Sonya's small figure), he'd glimpsed Nina and his heart had lifted. The occasional sightings had kept him going — as, later, had the certain prospect of seeing her at rehearsals. Her frailty, her rare smile, her battle to accept her ruined career: these had amazed and impressed him. But before long it became clear to him. He'd already loved not once but twice, such fierce and loyal loves they could never be surpassed. What he'd received from his lost wife and his lost daughter was more than anyone could expect in a lifetime. And so he'd retreated from the flame that was Nina, abandoning the possibility of warmth, and he neither missed nor regretted it.

Although the room was full of sunshine, his fingers were numb. The effects of malnutrition had proved far worse than he'd believed possible; he felt cold all the time. He opened his violin case with difficulty, blew on his hands, tried some exercises. But even simple arpeggios were beyond him.

He swore, and threw down his violin with a discordant clash of strings. It was intolerable! To make it so far, and now be unable to play! He looked around for something, anything at all, to burn in the stove. 'But not that,' he said aloud. 'But not you.'

Above his head, behind the ceiling panels, lay the cello, wrapped in threadbare blankets like a sleeping child. He thought back to the first rehearsal, when musicians had unpacked violins with smashed scrolls, and cracked double basses. 'Does anyone know of any spare instruments?' Elias had asked despairingly. Nikolai had shaken his head. The cello would stay hidden, perhaps forever.

The sight of the apartment — the cracks caused by the bomb-blast next door, the dark squares where pictures had once hung — filled him with such rage he could barely contain it. A year ago, this had been his home. A year ago, he could play melodies to make the eyes of his audience glitter with tears. 'And now?' He spat on the bare floor. 'Now I live in an empty shell and play no better than a child.'

Pulling on his gloves, he seized up the hatchet from behind the stove. He slammed the front door behind him and clattered down the stairs two at a time, swinging the axe over the stair rail so recklessly that steel clanged on steel.

By the time he reached the entrance hall, Mrs Gessen had emerged from her door in alarm. 'I thought I heard something. Mercifully, it's only you.' Since the night of the near-miss she'd become uncontrollably nervous; her eyes flickered like a lizard's and her head jerked.

'Yes, it's only me,' repeated Nikolai, but his voice echoed through the damaged hallway, sounding nothing like his.

'What's that you're carrying?' Mrs Gessen's relief visibly faded at the sight of the hatchet. 'Where are you going with that?'

'I need firewood. My hands are numb and I can't practise.'

'But where are you . . . what are you —? Surely not the *trees*?' Mrs Gessen seemed to have absorbed his earlier thoughts; it was as if his anger had run through his cracked floorboards, through ceilings and floors, and finally seeped into her living room.

'Well, there are plenty out there for the taking.' He shrugged. 'If the city wishes to hear the musical evocation of angels, then it must make sacrifices. Don't you agree?'

'Angels?' stammered Mrs Gessen.

'Shostakovich's Seventh.' He spoke impatiently. 'I've been starved for eleven months, my circulation is so wrecked from malnourishment that

I can neither get warm nor play a note, yet in five days I'm expected to perform a symphony for the city. Do you think that's fair?'

'But the trees! If every Leningrader cut down a tree, where would we be?'

'Leningraders do not cut down trees.' He thrust his face close to hers. 'Most, it seems, would rather sit and look at the trees while waiting to die. I refuse to be one of them.' He was so angry that the hallway began spinning around him and he clutched at the stair-rail. As he leaned there, breathing hard, surveying the familiar surroundings — the chipped plaster flowers above the door, the scratched floor, the far wall with its rows of letterboxes — reason reasserted itself. Perhaps he should consider an alternative plan? After all, the trees were in full view of a police patrol, and a madman wielding a hatchet would certainly be arrested. (*Reasonable to the last!* said Shostakovich, in his usual half-admiring, half-mocking way. *How sensible to avoid trouble, so you can go on quietly planning your death!*)

'All right, you win.' Nikolai, wiping his forehead, addressed both Mrs Gessen and the distant Shostakovich. 'The trees can stay.'

Mrs Gessen let out her breath. 'They *are* the property of the city. I would have had to report you if I'd caught you in the act — or even en route to the act. And no one wants to report a neighbour, not after all we've been through together. A whole new collective spirit, that's what these dark times have given us. A brave new —'

'Yes, yes. Excuse me, please.' Nikolai pushed past her new-found idealism and headed towards the letterboxes.

'You won't find any mail today.' She shook her head. 'Not today, and probably not for a long while.' All the same, she moved a little closer; she'd always kept an avid eye on other people's post. 'My cousin works in the postal depot, you know, and she tells me there's been no mail over Lake Ladoga for a week. It's not clear why, but her hunch is —'

'I'm afraid I have no interest in your cousin's job,' interrupted Nikolai. 'Only in mine.' He eyed up the letterboxes in a professional kind of way; his own box sat in the middle of a row, which made his task much trickier. He raised the hatchet high over his shoulder. 'Stand back, please!'

Mrs Gessen let out a shriek. 'Are you crazy? That's public property!'

Ignoring her, Nikolai took a swing and the blade crashed deep into the wood. He wrenched the hatchet free and raised it once more. The second, equally accurate blow splintered the box into dozens of pieces. 'What use is a mailbox if mail is never delivered into it?' he said over his shoulder. 'I'll put it to better use.'

'You're going to burn our mailboxes?' Mrs Gessen sounded aghast.

'No, only mine.' Nikolai began gathering up the shards of wood. 'For today, at least. One box ought to provide sufficient fuel for one hour's practice. Entirely for the benefit of our city, I might add.'

'Enough fuel for today!' gasped Mrs Gessen. 'Do you live only in the present?'

'Not at all.' He clutched the wood to his chest. 'I've already made a plan for tomorrow, and that does involve the trees.'

In his mild-mannered days he'd never have managed to reduce Mrs Gessen to splutters; now, watching her back away and slam the door, he was almost impressed by his achievement. He turned to inspect his handiwork. 'Not bad,' he commended himself. There was a gaping rectangular hole where his mailbox had once been, but the surrounding boxes remained intact. 'Not bad!' he said again.

It was while he was dusting the splinters from the remaining boxes with his sleeve (*Always the considerate neighbour!* commented Shostakovich) that he saw a corner of paper wedged between the back of the lower mailbox and the damp wall behind it. He could just make out a typed last name (his) and the first letters of a street name (also his). He put down his armful of wood, eased the sodden envelope out of the crack and opened it gingerly. A bill for repairs on his violin, dated a whole ten months earlier. He did some rapid calculations. Two weeks after Isaak Erkenov had written this out in his careful handwriting, he'd marched away with a division of the People's Volunteers — and had never come back from the Front.

He folded the note and put it in his pocket. Was Erkenov's widow still alive? He'd have to find out, though how he'd pay the debt was beyond him. How extraordinary that he should find the account after all this time — and only now because of his reckless actions. He looked again at the grimy crevice into which the envelope had fallen. How much more of his mail was lying down there, lost? He fished down the back of the boxes with fingers that, thanks to the wood-chopping, were no longer numb — and felt another corner of paper. As he tried to grasp it, it slipped further down the crack. He cursed and kept trying.

Behind him he heard Mrs Gessen's door creaking open once more. 'You can tell your postal-depot cousin,' he said without turning around, 'that I prefer my mail less than a year old.' Very slowly, very carefully, he slid the envelope up the wall. 'Got you, you bastard!' The Gessens' door slammed shut, sending dust showering off the long-disused light bulb.

For a third time, Nikolai peered down into the crack. Nothing more. He gathered up his wood and set off up the stairs; he'd had enough of Gessen interrogations for one day.

Back in the apartment, the chill was waiting. It seeped into him, a familiar and strangely seductive adversary. How easy it would be to lie down and give in. He went to the stove, threw the wood on the floor, and ripped open the second envelope. It had a Sverdlovsk postmark and had been posted — he peered closely at it — last October. Dull news, then, from his distant relatives in Sverdlovsk who, even in wartime, managed to find the weather the most interesting of topics.

There were two sheets of paper inside but, surprisingly, the top one was typed — unevenly inked and badly aligned. Crouching by the stove, he scanned the page.

> *Our first letter seems not to have reached you . . . We understand the situation in Leningrad is worsening . . . We have attempted several times to contact you by telephone . . . It appears your line is no longer working . . . We wish to reassure you, once again, that your daughter is safe.*

At the bottom of the page was a small smudged stamp: *Miusskaya St. Orphanage, Sverdlovsk.*

Nikolai sank to his knees. He was trembling all over, but not from cold. With fumbling fingers, he pulled the second piece of paper out of the envelope. This was not typed but handwritten, and behind its wobbly lines he heard a small, certain voice:

> *Dearest Papa,*
> *I've had what Aunt T calls a chapter of accidents. The lady in charge is worried you haven't answered her first letter but I told her you're always busy. Please come soon. I miss you so much that I cry every day.*
> *Your loving Sonya.*
> *P.S. Could you bring the cello with you? I am very out of practice.*

He tried to stand up, but his legs were shaking so badly he half-fell against the wall. He leaned there, his heart pounding. *Sonya was alive.* She hadn't been blown into a thousand pieces, had not lain bleeding by a derailed train until her heart gave out, nor mouldered away in a muddy unknown grave.

'My darling Sonya.' His throat was full of tears and he could hardly speak. 'Sonya, hold on, just a bit longer.'

Suddenly he could see her face again, clearly and whole: her velvet-black eyes full of love, her hopeful smile, the dimple at one side of her mouth. She was saying something, though her voice had become so unfamiliar he strained to hear it. 'I knew you would come for me! I knew you would.'

The loneliness that had encased him like a coffin all winter split and fell away from his body. The release felt almost like pain. He crumpled the letter in his hand and held it as hard as he could. *Sonya*. The light in the room seemed to grow in intensity. As he watched, the stripes of sunlight on the floor wavered and ran together, so that he seemed to be standing ankle-deep in bright shimmering water. And still he repeated her name over and over, *Sonya*, *Sonya*, until it rang in his ears like a bell announcing armistice to a relieved and exhausted world.

Priorities

Elias sat on the front steps in the evening sunshine, watching two black beetles parade around a pebbled arena.

'They're useless.' Valery gave the smaller beetle a disappointed prod. 'March, why don't you!'

'Perhaps they need food, like everyone else in Leningrad,' ventured Elias. 'My people don't work very well because they're hungry. I expect beetles are the same.'

'No offence, but your people are musicians. Mr Shapran says musicians are soft. Whereas these beetles are generals, so they should be able to cope with any amount of hardship.' Valery nudged the dawdling larger beetle with his finger. 'That's General Zhukov. If we'd kept him in Leningrad instead of letting Moscow have him, the Germans would have been pushed back in no time.'

'Really?' Elias knew little of the military snarl-ups that had occurred in the early stages of the siege. What he mostly remembered about last summer was the heat, so extreme that it felt almost threatening, and his fear when he first awoke to a skyline bristling with guns.

'And this is General Meretskov.' Valery pushed the other beetle along with a twig. 'He recaptured Tikhvin for us on the ninth of December last year. Then the rail-links to Novaya Ladoga were re-established, and food could be brought across the lake.'

This was something Elias did recall. It had been the one fact to cling to in a month when people had begun stealing ration cards from the dead.

'Exactly! We might all have died if it hadn't been for Meretskov. But look at him now! Bloody useless.' Valery stared at the beetle lying on its back in the dust. 'Do you think he needs some water?'

Elias hesitated. He wasn't sure how to play this game: were they talking about a beetle needing fluids, or the needs of a Red Army general? 'How about some vodka?' he suggested, a little desperately.

'An excellent idea!' Valery shoved a pebble towards the beetle's head. 'Here's a flask, General. To help you on your way.'

Elias watched hopefully but the beetle lay still, and Valery frowned.

'Perhaps he needs sleep?' Averting crises was something Elias did know about. 'Maybe you should put them in their box — I mean, in their barracks — for the night?'

'Zhukov never sleeps. He ran alongside his own convoy all the way to the Moscow front, just so he'd stay awake.' Valery glowered at the motionless beetle. 'That night he was fortified by nothing but a *cup of tea*.'

Elias glanced down the quiet street. Was it too early to go to bed? Tomorrow was the pre-recording of his radio broadcast, a terrifying prospect. The day after that was the dress rehearsal — also terrifying — and then, worst of all, the concert itself. He needed sleep to stave off the thought of what lay ahead as much as to gather strength, but he was reluctant to go up to his empty room. Besides, Valery seemed to like having him around. Not so long ago he'd thought the boy would find him dull, lacking in imagination; even now, when he heard the familiar knocking and opened the door, a muffling shyness descended. But Valery didn't seem to notice, and he included Elias in his games with the seriousness accorded to an equal.

In the distance the guns rumbled on like never-ending thunder. A surveillance plane swooped low over the street, making Elias duck his head away from the roaring shadow. 'What did you say?' He was dimly aware that Valery had asked him something.

'Do you miss her? Your ma, I mean. She nagged a bit, but she was very generous with her cough lozenges and that sort of thing.'

'Miss her?' Elias flushed. He and Valery had talked about air raids and the concert to come, about hunger in general and Valery's specific craving for ice cream — but never once had they spoken of the grey, desolate morning after his mother's death. The pale floating sky, the bumping journey through the streets, the silent procession of people dragging corpses to the cemetery. 'Well, she was old, and very sick. Some would say it was a lucky release.'

'But I guess you get lonely.' Valery balanced a beetle on each thin knee.

His legs were covered all over with the fine downy hair of malnutrition.

Elias's heart lurched at the sight. 'Have you had enough to eat today? I've still got a bit of my bread ration left. We get extra this week because of the concert.'

'I'm all right,' said Valery stoutly. 'I'm mostly hungry for the things I can't have. It's hard getting used to everything being different.'

'I know what you mean.' Elias spoke in a heartfelt voice. He still found it hard to believe that life could change so swiftly and completely: not only was the city shattered, but his own routine existence had been splintered apart. The moment when he unlocked the apartment door each day was the hardest of all. Even now, he listened and looked for his mother, only to be shocked anew by the flat bedcovers and the undisturbed air.

'Look!' Valery was pointing down the street. 'Someone's really in a hurry.'

Elias's eyesight had become so weak that, even with his glasses on, the world was blurred. But, sure enough, someone was sprinting towards them. It was rare these days to see a person running, except when the air-raid sirens started; most walked slowly and unsteadily, as if unsure they had enough energy to make it to the next lamp-post. 'I think it's —' He stood up, alarmed. 'Yes, it's Nikolai.'

'He's your friend, right?' Valery sounded as if he wanted to confirm that it was good news approaching, rather than bad.

'Yes, he's my friend.' With slight surprise, Elias realised it felt all right to say this: not false or forced.

'I'm so glad to find you here!' Panting, Nikolai arrived in front of them and bent double, hands on his knees, recovering his breath.

'Is everything all right?' asked Elias anxiously.

'More than all right!' When Nikolai straightened up, his eyes were shining and his normally sombre expression was infinitely lighter.

Elias stared. 'You've shaved! I've never seen you without a beard.'

'I did it this evening.' Nikolai ran his hand over his chin, still marked with the chafing of an unaccustomed blade. 'The air on my skin feels almost like a kiss!' Tilting his face to the light summer sky, he closed his eyes, looking rapturous.

'Is he drunk?' whispered Valery.

Elias shook his head and waited. At least he knew the news was nothing bad. For a moment, he'd feared that the concert —

But Nikolai had opened his eyes, and they blazed like the sun. He seized Elias by the shoulders. 'It's Sonya. Sonya is alive!'

'She's *alive*? But how . . . where —? That's absolutely wonderful!'

'It's beyond wonderful.' Nikolai sank down on the step as if the elation was too much for him. 'It's a miracle. It's everything I had given up hoping for.'

'Who's Sonya?' asked Valery.

'My daughter. My darling daughter, my Sonya! I found a letter, you see, that had been lost for the last ten months.'

As the familiar wail of the air-raid sirens started up, Nikolai poured out the story: the lost first letter, the long-missing second letter, and the crackling phone call he'd managed to put through from Leningrad's central post office that afternoon.

'I heard her voice!' His own voice was full of wonder and disbelief, as if he'd heard someone speaking from beyond the grave.

'Will you go to Sverdlovsk? How will you get there?' Although the sirens were shrieking, Elias was reluctant to go down to the cellar, out of the sunlight. 'Is someone able to arrange a flight for you?'

'That's the reason I came straight here.' Nikolai paused. 'There's a first-aid plane leaving for Moscow tomorrow evening, and Zagorsky has secured a place on it for me. From Moscow I can take the train to Kuibyshev, where Shostakovich will meet me, and he'll arrange for me to travel on to Sverdlovsk.'

'Moscow? Tomorrow evening? Shostakovich?' Elias was aware that he sounded like a parrot, but he couldn't help himself. 'What about the concert?'

Nikolai bit his lip. 'I'm so sorry. I must go immediately. Please believe me, nothing in the world would make me miss the concert, except this one thing. She's my daughter.'

Elias looked at the lines on Nikolai's forehead, the scratches on his hands, the threads trailing from the hem of his trousers. With one glance he took in Nikolai's exterior, and then he tried, immensely hard, to imagine how it was to be him — what it might be like to love somebody so much that you'd sacrifice anything for them. 'I see,' he said. 'Of course you must go. I do understand.' It was nearly true. Perhaps one day he'd reach that point himself? At that moment, standing in the low sharp sunlight, with the sirens calling, anything seemed possible.

'You do?' Nikolai stood up and gripped Elias's hands. 'To be honest, I thought you'd be angry. I know how much this concert means to you.'

'It's just a concert,' said Elias. 'But if you're meeting Shostakovich, you might let him know that, even with an incomplete orchestra, we'll try to do justice to his symphony.'

'Of course.' Nikolai smiled. 'Now, I suppose we should go down to the shelter.'

'Do we have to?' asked Valery.

Elias hesitated. Since April, most of the shelling attacks had been on the outskirts of the city, and recently there'd been a number of false alarms to remind fatigued Leningraders that, although they were no longer in danger of freezing or starving, they weren't yet safe. 'We probably should,' he said at last.

'Yes, indeed,' said Nikolai. 'Now I have something very much worth staying alive for.'

'How old is Sonya?' asked Valery as he picked up his beetle box.

'Nine. No, ten. She's had a birthday since I last saw her.' The tinge of regret in Nikolai's voice was close to bitterness. He'd found Sonya, but there would be other, smaller losses to come to terms with.

'Is she pretty?' asked Valery casually.

'She's beautiful! But fathers are biased, of course.'

'Do you think a twelve-year-old is too old for a ten-year-old? If that Sonya of yours was on a bombed train and now she's a thousand miles away all by herself, she must be quite a girl.'

'She wasn't very interested in boys when she left. I think she likes cellos better.'

'Oh, she's a musician, too?' Valery stumped up the steps to the front door, his disappointment palpable.

Nikolai laughed. 'What's in the matchbox?'

'Generals Zhukov and Meretskov.' Valery brightened. 'They're having a rest before they go back into battle.'

Elias watched Nikolai and Valery standing at the door, a tall figure in a crumpled jacket and a shorter one in a moth-holed red sweater. At the sight of their heads leaning close over the beetle box, he felt a familiar stab of jealousy. *I could stay in the street and no one would notice. A bomb could drop on my head and no one would —*

'Mr Elias!' Valery turned. 'Come on!'

'I was just telling Valery how grand the Philharmonia Hall is,' said Nikolai. 'And that you'll be rehearsing there in two days' time.'

'Without you, more's the pity.' But Elias was filled with relief and joy; he was included! 'Though now you've cut your beard off,' he added, 'perhaps, like Samson, you've become mediocre? And the Radio

Orchestra already has a plethora of mediocre violinists.'

'Do you know something, Elias?' Nikolai held open the door. 'I think you just made a joke.'

'Yes,' said Elias, stepping into the cool dark hallway. 'I believe I did.'

Dress rehearsal

On the day of the dress rehearsal, purple clouds banked up in the west, massing shoulder to shoulder as if waiting for the command to break ranks and disperse across the city. The low mutter of thunder merged with the distant artillery. Elias had woken with earache so, in spite of the August humidity, he crammed on a furry hat before leaving the apartment. By the time he reached the Philharmonia Hall, the first drops of rain had started to fall.

He was early, but Petrov had arrived even earlier and was pottering about checking the surface of the stage. He'd become so thin that his trousers, winched in with string, would easily have accommodated two of him. 'Has the rain started yet?' He wiped the end of his dripping nose. 'It's not a good day for the run-through.'

'It's never a good day for a run-through. Besides, the worse the dress rehearsal is, the better the performance. You ought to know that.'

'You're absolutely right, Mr Elias. As always.'

Apprehensively, Elias looked about the cavernous concert hall. The only certainty about dress rehearsals was that they forced him to spend a good part of the next day in the lavatory, stricken with nervous diarrhoea. Today's rehearsal would be even more nerve-racking than usual because it was the first time his musicians would play the symphony from beginning to end, all seventy sodding minutes of it. If they collapsed, dropped their instruments, ran out of breath — well, he might as well march to the Neva and hold his head under water until the world dissolved into black.

'Yes,' he muttered. 'Hope for a bad dress rehearsal, Petrov.'

'I certainly will.' Frail as he was, Petrov looked exceedingly determined.

'But don't aim for total disaster!' added Elias, alarmed.

With the storm gathering outside, the light in the hall became increasingly dim, and the cracked white columns towered like tall trees. Two soldiers were setting out chairs on the stage. The clattering and thudding were both familiar and foreign — it seemed like a lifetime since Elias had last heard them.

He watched for a minute, then stepped forward. 'I'd like you to place out some extra chairs.'

'Sir?' The younger soldier looked up. 'But we've been told the exact number required.'

'I want a spare chair there.' Elias walked among the rows, pointing. 'One there, and there, and there.' This would be his private tribute to those unable to play — including Alexander, his long-time adversary, and Nikolai, his new friend. 'The chairs will remain empty,' he said to the soldiers. 'A memorial for the musicians we've lost to the war.'

The orchestra had begun to straggle in, damp-haired, pale-faced. They unpacked in silence, keeping on their coats and their fingerless gloves. The bulky clothes did nothing to hide their emaciation; it was as if the near-unendurable winter they'd been through still lurked in their bones, hampering their movements and slowing their reflexes. As they took their seats, their expressions were half-determined and half-fearful: a Herculean task lay ahead, and they knew they were ill-equipped to meet it.

Elias tried to sound calm. 'Today is an important day for us,' he announced over the rattle of rain on the windows. 'For the first time, we will play the Seventh Symphony in its entirety. If you feel faint during a solo, you may rest only after it's over. Please remember — I'm depending on you. Leningrad is depending on you.'

Thunder groaned above the building, and the musicians shuffled their feet nervously. Elias heard a noise behind him: a few uniformed officials, armed with notebooks and clipboards, were being ushered into the front row. He bowed to each in turn, recognising only the wan Yasha Babushkin and the burlier Boris Zagorsky.

He turned back to the orchestra and gestured to the oboe. 'An A, please.' Thankfully, his voice sounded reasonably steady.

Once the tuning up had flared and died away, he removed his hat and placed it beside him on the floor. 'I considered keeping this on so as not to hear any mistakes. But I'm never at my professional best with a dead animal on my head.'

The musicians laughed, a small ripple that rolled away into the dark wings. They were on his side now, and they were ready to begin.

The light had grown so dim he could barely see the score. Why couldn't they have provided a generator for today? Did things have to be so difficult, right to the end? He raised his music stand a notch, and wiped his baton on his handkerchief; the waft of camphor made him suddenly miss his mother. With a small sigh, he raised his arms.

He was keenly aware of the men behind him, watching attentively, pens poised ready to note his failings. But even more than this he felt the absence of those far more capable of assessment than these tight-lipped political officials. There was no Shostakovich to listen with tilted head, tapping an unlit cigarette on his knee. No Sollertinsky lolling in an aisle seat, affecting nonchalance yet absorbing everything. No Mravinsky poised on the podium, with his distinguished profile set in concentration. But of course, if Mravinsky were here —

There's only me! With slight surprise, Elias brought down his baton, and the first chords sounded full and certain through the dusty hall. Next the trumpets and timpani broke the line of the strings with their repeated, urgent two-note motif. Was it the stormy light that was transforming the sunken-cheeked brass players into powerful men whose insistent notes pulled the orchestra into line and began the ominous game of cat-and-mouse?

Instinctively, he glanced at the string section, searching for Nikolai's half-smile of concentration. Nothing but an empty chair — Nikolai had already been flown out of Leningrad in a flimsy plane, swallowed up by the blood-red sky of evening.

And when he looked for Nina Bronnikova, he saw the piano standing silent and closed like a shuttered window. Some days earlier Nina had strained her wrist, and the doctor had emphasised to Elias several times that she needed rest. 'If she's forced to play the dress rehearsal, she'll never make it through the performance,' he'd warned, as if knowing that, when it came to this concert, Elias's attitude bordered on the fanatical. Nonetheless —

I need her here, he cried silently, his baton slicing through the air, bringing forth a harsh high C from the flutes and the oboes. Panic rose inside him. He was so alone! One man to lead so many — he didn't know if he had the strength for it. And such a long way to go. He felt weak at the thought of the hundreds of pages ahead.

There were ragged entrances and a few botched solos. At one stage Vedernikov turned white and sank back in his chair, and the notes from his flute became patchy and faint. But the music had its own momentum, rolling like a boulder down a gradual slope. All Elias could do was to guide it, hold it back, prevent it from rushing. *Slow down!* he mouthed at Petrov, and miraculously Petrov took in the command and did what he was asked, pulling the whole orchestra back with him, so that the long first movement marched on with inexorable dread to its ending.

Behind Elias the air seemed to stir, but he heard no sound. Had his listeners been moved by the strength of the music? There was no way of knowing, but as he entered the lilting second movement the weight lifted from his shoulders. *The symphony has its own life*, he reminded himself. *You don't have to carry it alone*.

Then, pausing only for a second, the orchestra was treading softly into the adagio, its echoing phrases so plaintive and beautiful that, in spite of their familiarity, the hair on Elias's neck stood on end.

Finally — he signalled to the snare drum — they were rattling into the war-like fourth movement. '*Non troppo!*' he mouthed. '*Allegro non troppo!*' This was the movement that had caused him so many headaches — military fanfares from a depleted brass section, fast precise pizzicato from inexperienced strings — and now, perversely, he didn't want the ordeal to end. But they were almost there, forging into a C major coda that sounded respectably loud. The churning woodwind, the hammering unison strings, the pounding drum duplets — and then an extended moment of silence, and the release.

Where had the strength come from? It seemed as if he'd been infused with the energy of the composers whose music had thundered through this hall. Borodin, Mussorgsky, Rimsky-Korsakov, Scriabin, Stravinsky, Glazunov — not to mention all the conductors who had stood on the podium like lone men before a firing squad. Mravinsky, who'd brought Shostakovich's Fifth to a close amid tumultuous applause; and, nearly fifty years earlier, Tchaikovsky conducting his own Sixth Symphony nine days before his death. All those restless, knowledgeable, egotistical men were there, ranged behind Elias — but they were no longer a threat to him. He let his head hang forward, and sweat poured from his forehead. For the first time in his life he stood shoulder to shoulder with these men, rather than confronting them.

The aftermath was a blur of elated exhaustion. He was aware of

Babushkin clapping him on the shoulder, murmuring 'Quite adequate', and Zagorsky and his assistants departing with slightly smug approval, repeating phrases like 'That should do the trick'. Then he watched the odd process of an orchestra disintegrating, the unified body fragmenting into separate musicians. Sinking into a chair, he announced there would be no rehearsal for the next two days. He would hold a brief meeting the following morning, to talk them through the symphony — not everything had been acceptable, in spite of the official approval — but otherwise the musicians should rest as much as possible.

'Considering the rather extraordinary conditions,' he said, 'you're not expected to perform in tuxedoes or evening dresses — although you may be relieved to hear that I won't be treating the public to this enchanting ensemble.' He glanced down at his holed woollen jacket and trousers. 'Believe it or not, I still have a tuxedo, which on several occasions escaped being used for fuel or foot-rags, mainly because it was fit for neither.' There was a ripple of laughter. 'Two final things,' he added. 'First, I've been assured that we will have electric light for the performance. And secondly, Comrade Zhdanov has announced that there will be a banquet after the concert.' He paused, tightening his belt another notch. 'So make sure you don't eat too much beforehand.' The orchestra laughed at this, too.

Once he was alone, he walked into the auditorium and sat down in the middle of the fifth row. His body ached as if he'd been set upon by a street gang, punched and kicked all over. He stared down at his hands. Ten long years of conducting: had the whole of the last decade led up to this week? Or would he and his patchwork band be forgotten once the Germans were driven back? Would their efforts be remembered if — he clenched his hands and corrected himself — *once* Leningrad was freed? Once the elite swept back into the city, and the Philharmonia stage was filled again with its proper heroes, those elegant professionals plucked from Russia's finest academies, playing perfectly restored eighteenth-century instruments?

As the effects of the adrenaline faded, so too did his euphoric relief. To play the symphony in its entirety was an achievement, but the performance had been far from perfect — the timing was off, for a start. He checked his watch again. *Seventy-three minutes.* Where had the time been lost? Perhaps the third movement, in the final reprise of the main theme: the violas had felt heavy and sluggish. Or possibly the pizzicato section in the fourth movement, which had felt overly articulated and not sufficiently frenzied. *Three minutes slow.* Should he order a section rehearsal tomorrow, after all?

Nikolai, of course, would laugh at this. 'Three minutes? Twenty minutes is gross negligence; three minutes is artistic licence.' But Elias knew exactly how long each movement was intended to be, for Shostakovich had specified timings in a letter to Nikolai. He hadn't written that the first movement lasted 'about' twenty-five minutes, or that the scherzo was 'roughly' eight. When it came to work, Shostakovich used absolutes, a language that Elias fully understood. Having seen the numerals written in Shostakovich's own hand, he'd copied them neatly into his workbook. By the time he'd been ordered to conduct the symphony, the four-part timing was mapped out already in his head.

Frowning, he looked along the empty row. He imagined Shostakovich a few seats away, mouth pursed, eyebrows lowered. What would he have said about today? He never held back when voicing opinions on conductors, even the best and most internationally renowned. Toscanini? A conceited tyrant with the sloppy working habits of the near-sighted! In spite of his hatred of flying, Shostakovich would travel to America himself to prevent Toscanini from butchering another of his symphonies. Leopold Stokowski, on the other hand, was relatively talented, his free-hand technique quite effective, and he'd done a reasonable job on Symphonies One, Three and Six — but he was a little too fond of theatrical stunts to inspire complete trust. Closer to home, it was much the same. 'I admire anyone who can control the Bolshoy Orchestra,' Shostakovich had reportedly said, 'but, to be honest, I don't think Samosud will ever be a great symphonic conductor.' Even the dignified Mravinsky occasionally came under fire for paying too much attention to detail and neglecting the overall plan.

Yes, I know what you think of the others. Elias kept his eyes fixed on Shostakovich's favoured concert-hall seat. *And I'm fully aware of your opinion of conductors: that we're craftsmen rather than artists, interpreters rather than speakers. I'm not asking for your approval — but could you tell me your opinion of today? What did you really think?*

The hall stretched silently around him. The only sound was the faint creaking of his seat. Along the row Shostakovich was staring straight ahead, the unruly lock of hair springing forward over his eyes. He was visible, but not quite solid. The cracked white wall showed through the weave of his suit jacket, the back of his head was blurred like a badly developed photograph. By concentrating very hard, Elias managed to make him less transparent. Then, in a familiar gesture, Shostakovich's hand moved to stroke his chin. His lips were opening, he was about to say something —

'Karl Elias?'

Elias leapt up, banging his knee against the seat in front of him. It was Nina Bronnikova, making her way along the row towards him.

'Am I disturbing you?' she asked. 'Are you still working?'

Had he been talking out loud, or had his conversation with Shostakovich remained safely in his imagination? 'Not working. Not really.' He shook his head. 'I missed . . . That is, *you* missed hearing the dress rehearsal. We finished half an hour ago.'

'No, I heard all of it. I sat right at the back, so as not to distract you.'

In the dim light her face looked paler than ever, and the dark rings under her eyes emphasised her frailty. Her wrist was bandaged, her black jacket was holed, her injured leg was thin. She was lovely. She was perfect.

'What did you think?' he asked casually, though his cheeks were burning.

'It went extraordinarily well.' She sat down beside him. 'Brilliantly, really.'

'I wouldn't say *brilliantly*. In fact, we lost three minutes along the way. But they did well, for a recycled bunch.'

'Zagorsky and the others were impressed. They were talking of positioning speakers towards the front line so everyone can hear the concert — not only our soldiers, but also the Germans. To make them realise that Leningrad will never be defeated.'

'Really? My God, I hope we can live up to the challenge.' He paused, reached out and nearly touched her arm, withdrew his hand again. 'But how's the wrist? I hope you're not in too much pain.'

'It's going to be fine. It must be! I'm determined not to disappoint anyone.'

'You could never disappoint.' He said it instantly, without thinking. 'Least of all me.' He flushed again, yet he didn't regret saying it.

'Thank you.' Nina looked at him. 'You once told me you were no good at paying compliments, do you remember? But the things you say to me —' Quickly, she brushed her hand across her eyes. 'They make me feel as if I'm the luckiest person in the world.'

Elias ducked his head, staring down at his shoes. 'Oh, no, I'm the lucky one. Knowing . . . knowing you.' He wanted desperately to leave this echoing hall, to walk through the streets and talk to her about things other than symphonies and the siege. Would it be inappropriate to ask her back for some tea?

'I stayed behind,' she said, reaching into her bag, 'because I wanted to give you this.'

'Oh! What is it?' He took the small flat parcel. 'A p-p-present? For me?'

'It's just something I thought you should have,' said Nina with a smile.

'M-m-many thanks! I can't remember the last time I was given a present.' Flustered, Elias fumbled at the layers of newspaper.

Under the dirty wrappings there was a soft grey cloth, and inside the cloth was a little charcoal portrait, with the paper slightly torn round the edges.

Elias gasped. 'It's him! It's Shostakovich!' He scrutinised the face. 'But he's so young here, just a boy. Where did you get this?'

'It was made by Kustodiev. I was a friend of his daughter. After he died, Irina asked me to give it to Shostakovich, but he wouldn't take it. He said he's allergic to portraits of himself.'

'It's by Kustodiev?' Elias looked at the signature. 'One of the most famous artists of his time. Wasn't he crippled?'

'Yes, he worked from a wheelchair. Shostakovich went to school with Irina, and sometimes he stopped by their house after class to play the piano for Kustodiev. That's when the portrait was made.'

'But this is really worth something. If you don't want it any longer, you ought to sell it.'

'If I'd wanted to sell it I would have done so in December, when I thought I might die of hunger. No, I want you to have it.'

'But why — why me?'

'Shostakovich once told Irina he'd learnt a lot from her father. About struggling on under any circumstances — and also that, sometimes, working can save you. I thought you, of all people, would understand that.'

Elias liked the portrait so much he could hardly breathe. 'Look! Even at that age he had that . . . that *resolve*.' It was true: the stubborn perseverance was there in the smudged adolescent face, the truculent eyes suggesting he was driven by something not entirely within his control. 'Thank you so much,' he said, wrapping it up again carefully. 'I'll treasure it.'

'Well, I should go.' Nina stood up. 'You must be exhausted.'

'Don't go!' blurted Elias. 'At least, perhaps we could go —' He took a deep breath. 'Perhaps we could go together? You'd be welcome to come back to my apartment for some tea.'

Nina nodded. 'Thank you! That would be lovely.'

When they emerged onto the street they found the storm clouds had cleared and the sky was a deep turquoise. Sunlight slanted across the broken rooftops, casting strange shadows on the wet pavements. They walked slowly, on account of Nina's injured leg and Elias's exhaustion. 'It's not far now,' said Elias, every now and then.

Later he couldn't remember what they talked about. What he did remember was how, pausing at street corners or crossings, he would glance at her clear profile and the curve of her neck, and feel as if he were already home.

<hr/>

It felt odd opening the door to the apartment and ushering Nina inside. He'd spent so little time here since his mother had died. Soft dust lay on every surface, and the air felt thick with grief and silence. As he looked around, the memories and the exhaustion overcame him and he began to shake all over. Very carefully, he laid the portrait on the table and covered his face with his hands.

'I'm sorry,' he said, in a muffled voice. 'I'm just so extremely tired.'

Even boiling water for tea seemed an impossible task. It was all he could do to crawl over to the narrow divan and lie down. Nina covered him with a blanket and sat beside him. After some time, when he hadn't stopped shaking, she lay down beside him and stroked his hair.

It was a long time before he emerged from the darkness and opened his eyes. He was abashed and amazed to realise that, somehow, he had ended up lying on a bed next to the beautiful Nina Bronnikova. But then the year had been so full of strangeness.

'Are you feeling any better?' Nina spoke quietly, and as calmly as if the situation were nothing out of the ordinary.

'A little,' he said, turning his head to look at her. 'I suppose the stress of today's rehearsal was greater than I thought.' He hesitated. 'Do you think Shostakovich would have any faith in what I'm doing?'

'Shostakovich is just one man,' said Nina, 'doing the job he was born to do, in the same way that you do yours. You must try to believe that.' She told Elias what she'd heard about the Shostakoviches' journey east: their long wait to board the overcrowded train to Kuibyshev, Shostakovich standing on the platform with a sewing machine in one hand and Maxim's teddy bear in the other. Seven days and seven nights in a packed carriage: lost suitcases, borrowed socks and underwear. Shostakovich, wearing his old worn suit, wading into the snow at the side of the tracks to rinse crockery, fetching kettles of water from station houses, too shy to strike up conversations, too proud to ask for help, in a constant state of agitation.

'Apparently they got off at Kuibyshev,' explained Nina, 'because he couldn't stand the lack of privacy any longer. They were supposed to go all the way to Sverdlovsk.'

'Shostakovich — shy? But he's so forthright, even abrasive! And so highly respected. He's already a legend.'

'He's a great composer. He may well end up a legend. But in this case, his share of the task is done and now you must do yours. What he might think of your efforts — well, perhaps that's less relevant than you believe.'

They lay there together and watched the golden evening light stretch over the wall. From the other side of the city came the distant wail of sirens; otherwise, all was quiet. Finally Elias plucked up his courage, hitched himself up on the pillows and put an awkward arm around Nina. Her bones jutted through her woollen clothing; her ribcage was as frail as a bird's. But the strength he remembered from their first meeting was still there at her core.

'Don't you ever worry about anything?' he asked softly. 'You seem to have everything worked out.'

Nina laughed. 'If you knew how I felt today! The last time I was in that hall was to hear a performance of Mahler's Fifth. When I walked in that evening, people noticed me. I was considered beautiful back then.' She closed her eyes, but a tear slid down her face and into the pillow.

'You're still beautiful,' said Elias. 'You're more beautiful than ever. Distractingly so. You distract me.' He leaned closer and kissed her forehead, feeling neither tentative nor nervous, and he left his lips pressed against her temple, feeling the even beat of her blood.

'I could conduct to your heart,' he whispered. 'It's as regular as a metronome.'

Slowly, Nina opened her eyes to look at him. 'And yours? Is it steady?'

'Some people say that I don't have a heart. Many people say so. Surely you've heard that?'

She slipped her hand inside his coat and under his shirt, so that her palm lay flat against his chest. 'How could you possibly do what you do and not have a heart?'

When the sunlight had slid away from the room and the sky was turning grey, she got up off the divan. 'I'll see you tomorrow,' she said, kissing him lightly on the lips, refusing his offer to see her home. Nonetheless, he went to the open door and stood there until he could no longer hear her uneven footsteps in the stairwell, and then he went to the window.

She was already in the street, treading carefully through the rubble, her hair glinting black like the wings of a swallow. She was known, and not yet known. He watched her slight, upright figure reach the corner. As she disappeared from sight, he felt a conviction, stronger than any he'd ever felt, that one day she would be his wife.

Now he was alone but not lonely, and he picked up the neatly folded piece of paper from where it lay on the windowsill. Already he knew it by heart.

> *Dear Karl Eliasberg. Warmest wishes for Leningrad premiere.*
> *Deeply regret my absence. Am convinced performance will be*
> *MAGNIFICENT. I greet you warmly.*
> *D. Shostakovich*

He leaned his head against the cracked window. 'You can do it,' he said, refolding the telegram. The chill from the glass entered his skull and spread through his body. It felt like strength.

Epilogue

When the sun hits the edge of the mattress, he opens his eyes. Sleep-dust clogs his vision, and the room is indistinct. He senses, rather than sees, familiar shapes around him: the high rectangular window, the small stove, the dangling light bulb.

It must be late because the sun's already high. It seems surprising, after all that's happened, that the sun still rises. He's no longer the person he was a year ago, and the city, too, has changed beyond recognition. Yet the summer is familiar in all its blowsy green fullness and, as always, the stone walls and streets — however battered — have absorbed its heat.

He stands up and stretches, making his spine crack and his shoulders loosen. As soon as he puts on his glasses, the room jumps to attention. As if for the first time, with the utmost clarity, he notices the straight-backed chair, the right angles of the window, the layered score on the windowsill.

Below the window, the street is quiet and empty, but he can still see her walking there, threading her way past the broken houses, transforming the world. When he closes his eyes, his fingers feel the smooth coolness of her face. Behind him, the stove has become a small point of warmth, a leaping blue flame, and there's the bubbling roar of water coming to a boil.

Later, after a breakfast of strong unsweetened tea and black bread, he'll read over the stack of paper, listening with his eyes, moving his hands in the air, shaping something invisible to others. If the day stays fine and there are no air raids, he'll walk along the canal, just a few bridges, and then back home. It's important not to meet or talk to people in the hours before.

Later still, he'll walk the long stretch of Nevsky Prospect all the way to the Philharmonia Hall, slip in a back entrance and shut himself away in a small one-windowed room. Shortly before 6 p.m., while putting on his white shirt (not pressed as perfectly as he'd like, but clean), he'll turn on the radio to experience the odd sensation of hearing himself speak.

'Comrades,' announces his voice in crackling tones, 'a great cultural occurrence is about to take place in Leningrad. In a few minutes you will hear live, for the first time, the Seventh Symphony of Dmitri Shostakovich, our outstanding fellow citizen.' And he knots a threadbare black tie around his neck, pulls on his jacket and slips a folded piece of paper into his breast pocket. Because he's clearing his throat, he misses a few sentences of his first pre-recorded public address.

Opening the door, he walks steadily down a narrow corridor, leaving behind his radio-self still addressing the city of Leningrad. Or, at least, addressing those not already waiting for him in the auditorium, row upon row, stretching to the very back of the hall. 'Europe believed that the days of Leningrad were over,' the voice behind him is saying. 'But this performance is witness to our spirit and courage. Listen!'

Pausing in the wings, he listens, too. What does he hear at this moment? The scraping of chairs, the small twang of violin strings, a quick arpeggio from a clarinet; and, beyond these, the rustling of clothing and shifting of bodies, some coughing and murmuring, the sounds of anticipation. When he cranes slightly forward, he can see a row of microphones pointed like guns towards the stage, ready to catch the Leningrad Symphony and broadcast it to the world.

He takes a deep breath and steps into the blaze of electric light, far brighter than any sun. Sweat leaps on his back, the orchestra rises to its feet, and the audience also stands, a dark gleaming mass of military badges and medals, and pearls.

Soon the fluttering will stop and the musicians will become still with concentration, their backs straight, their fingers in position, their bows and mouthpieces raised — and their eyes also raised to him. For one perfect complete moment he stands, poised on the edge of silence. The only sound is the telegram in his pocket, rustling as he breathes, moving as steadily as a beating heart.

Acknowledgements

I have found a number of books and articles about Shostakovich and the Leningrad Symphony extremely useful while working on this novel. They include: 'Orchestral manoeuvres' by Ed Vulliamy published in *The Observer Magazine*, 25 November 2001; *Shostakovich: A Life* by Laurel E. Fay; *Shostakovich and His World*, edited by Laurel E. Fay; *Shostakovich: A Life Remembered* by Elizabeth Wilson; *Story of a Friendship: The Letters of Dmitry Shostakovich to Isaak Glikman 1941–1975*, with commentary by Isaak Glikman, translated by Anthony Phillips; *Testimony: The Memoirs of Dmitri Shostakovich* as related to and edited by Solomon Volkov, translated by Antonina W. Bouis; *The New Shostakovich* by Ian MacDonald.

I would like to acknowledge W.W. Norton & Company for permission to quote from the poem 'As if through a straw, you drink my soul' in *Anna Akhmatova: Poems*, selected and translated by Lyn Coffin, 1983.

I am grateful to the following people for their help in varying ways, including general advice and support, close readings of the manuscript and the invaluable offer of quiet writing space: Jill Foulston, Sarah Lees-Jeffries, Rachel Paine and Rob Wilson, Sebastian Schrade, Dulcie Smart, Jon Stallworthy, John Wilson, and Antoinette Wilson. Many thanks to my agent Simon Trewin, my editor Jane Parkin, and Harriet Allan and the team at Random House New Zealand.

Special thanks to Margaret Quigley, Rachel Quigley, and Gustav Hellberg for their constant support and encouragement.